THE MARRYING KIND

Jim said, 'Are you jealous of her, Alison?'

'Me? Why should I be jealous of Roberta?'

'Because you're engaged to me and can't ...' He fashioned a diffident gesture with his hand.

'Can't what?' said Alison.

'Compete, I suppose.'

'Compete over some Irish bloke? I thought you knew me better than that,' Alison said. 'I've enough to do on Gilmorehill without becoming involved in silly mating games.'

'I'm not so sure they are silly. Mating games, I mean.'

'Jim Abbott! I'm surprised at you.'

Deliberately he stretched out his foot and pushed the door closed. He leaned across the bed, put his arm about her, drew her to him and kissed her. He felt her stiffen. He wondered if he had overdone it, if he had roused her resentment. In fact he had no clear indicator as to what she felt towards him any more ...

He could not pursue her. He could only wait, wait with dreadful and uncertain patience for her to emerge again.

Also by Jessica Stirling

The Spoiled Earth
The Hiring Fair
The Dark Pasture
The Deep Well at Noon
The Blue Evening Gone
The Gates of Midnight
Treasures on Earth
Creature Comforts
Hearts of Gold
The Good Provider
The Asking Price
The Wise Child
The Welcome Light
Lantern for the Dark
Shadows on the Shore
The Penny Wedding

About the author

Jessica Stirling, one of Scotland's foremost writers, was born in Glasgow. Her most recent novels have had settings as diverse as Edwardian Glasgow and eighteenth-century Ayrshire.

The Marrying Kind

Jessica Stirling

CORONET BOOKS
Hodder and Stoughton

First published in Great Britain in 1995
by Hodder and Stoughton
A division of Hodder Headline PLC
First published in paperback in 1996
by Hodder and Stoughton
A Coronet Paperback

10 9 8 7 6 5 4 3 2 1

A CIP catalogue record for this title is available from
the British Library

ISBN 0 340 65762 6

Printed and bound in Great Britain by
Cox & Wyman Ltd, Reading, Berkshire

Hodder and Stoughton
A division of Hodder Headline PLC
338 Euston Road
London NW1 3BH

CONTENTS

AUTHOR'S NOTE

ONE

Storm in a Teacup

Of all the men that Alison Burnside had ever loved none meant quite as much to her as the three with whom she'd once shared a body.

There was nothing remotely mystical about the experience and, after a week or two with a blade in her hand, Alison thought little of it. Anatomy was the one aspect of medical training which the laity seemed to latch on to, however, as if the cutting up of a human cadaver was somehow an end in itself. Nobody ever enquired about chemistry or physics and the eyes of family and friends would positively glaze over at the mere mention of vertebrate morphology. But just a hint that Alison's afternoon had been spent in the dissecting-room, slaving over old Tom's diminishing remains, would lead to a barrage of indelicate questions. Somebody, usually her brother Bertie or sister-in-law Brenda, would ask precisely what portion of the corpse had been carved away that day and would shudder with delicious horror when Alison, with some reluctance, divulged the grisly details.

Admittedly when old Tom had been hale, if not exactly hearty, the first glimpse of him laid out stiff, bronze-tinted and naked on the slab had caused the students a certain temporary revulsion too. Also, on the fourth day of anatomy class, a definite rising of gorges and hasty blinking of the eyelids when Mr Strutt, the demonstrator, had unwrapped his instruments and, without much delicacy or tact, had arranged the blocks and boards to raise old Tom's thorax to a convenient height. For a fleeting second it had seemed to the students that the poor old fellow was being hoisted up to give *them* the once over and when Strutt made the first incision along the middle line of the body there was among the group a universal wincing and an audible in-sucking of breath.

From one of the twenty tables behind them they heard a groan and a thud as some sensitive soul crumpled to the floor and just on the edge of Alison's vision a burly young rugby player doubled over and was wretchedly sick.

1

Ally Burnside's team, however, stood its ground manfully.

Declan Slater, who was almost as emaciated as the corpse, swayed not an inch from the table's edge and glamorous Roberta Logie, daughter of a famous surgeon, even uttered a little 'Huh!' as if this initial reflection of the skin was nothing to write home about. Guy Conroy and Howard McGrath pursed their lips, pressed their tongues against their palates and stoutly ignored the sudden overwhelming stench of formaldehyde that rose about them like a cloud.

Old Tom was long gone, of course. All his bits and pieces had been carefully preserved and had been buried with due reverence and respect. He had been one of that band of down-and-outs who sign away their mortal remains to advance the cause of medical science and to earn a pound or two to spend on drink before departure. He had made an important contribution to Alison's education, though, for under old Tom's influence she'd come to appreciate why there was little or no larking about in the big, glass-roofed anatomy hall and why the odour of formaldehyde conferred a strange kind of privilege upon those to whose clothing it clung.

There *was* something different about medical students, some element in that branch of learning which distinguished its acolytes and separated them from the general ruck. Within limits, medical students were permitted to blow off steam in their social life while at the same time observing the sort of monasticism that went with long hours of study, extended terms, difficult examinations and a volume of practical work which constantly threatened to wipe them into oblivion.

Small wonder then that nobody at home could understand why Alison had changed or why on occasion she seemed impatient with family matters. Why she was irritated by her brothers' squabbles, her father's fussy demands and disinterested in the tittle-tattle that centred around the council house in the Glasgow suburb of Flannery Park. All the things that had seemed so vital to her in 1930 had become almost irrelevant by 1933. It was not that she looked down on her family. It was simply a matter of preoccupation, of being constantly, mentally, elsewhere.

Sometimes she envied Declan Slater his unsanitary basement in a shabby terrace house in Greenfield, envied him his exile, his absolute lack of distraction. She envied Declan more than she envied Roberta her big house by the tennis courts in Dowanhill or Howard his 'digs' in the privately owned Bankside Hotel. There was something noble about Declan's suffering, his refusal to knuckle under to poverty, an edge, a *necessity* to his studies which Alison believed she lacked. Number 162 Wingfield Drive was just too comfortable and convenient to be inspirational, for Alison was looked after there by her eldest brother, Henry, and Trudi, his wife, and was expected to make only a modest contribution to the smooth running of the household.

The four-in-a-block, two-storey council house was not as spacious as Roberta's mansion but since Alison's father had flitted across the drive to live with his new wife, Ruby, and brother Jack had married Ruby's daughter, Brenda, number 162 no longer seemed quite so cramped as it had in the past.

Henry and Trudi occupied the back bedroom upstairs. Davy had taken over the upstairs front and Bertie reposed in solitary state in the small bedroom that opened off the living-room. 'Princess Alison' – Bertie's term for his sister – had been offered a choice of rooms but for harmony's sake she had elected to stick to the narrow bed-study which she'd grown used to over the years. How nice, she'd thought, to be able to look from the window across the little park and see the lights of the house where her father, Alex, and Ruby lived. How consoling it would be, she'd thought, to have Dad so close at hand.

In fact, Dad and Ruby spent most of their time in 162 and by the end of her first year at Glasgow University Alison had shed her sentimental notion of family bonding and could have seen the whole damned lot of them far enough. She no longer owed allegiance to the Burnsides. She belonged – the word was not too strong – to the team, to Declan, Guy, Howard, even to Roberta.

Why this assortment of personalities rubbed along so well was a mystery. They were not alike in breeding or background. Roberta was a snob, an intelligent snob but a snob none the less. Guy was handsome, well mannered and gracious, but he said little about his parents and the manner in which they lived in the rich, rural suburb of Bearsden.

Howard was rich, dashing and flamboyant. Son of a professional soldier, he had been raised in a mansion in the Border town of Hawick and groomed for the army from birth. At eighteen he had demanded the right to choose his own career and had elected to 'do' medicine at Glasgow instead of saluting the flag at Aldershot. 'Good for you, lad,' his father had shouted when Howard's decision had been made known to him. 'Royal Army Medical Corps – what!' Howard's reply had been quite unprintable. It had led to him being booted out of the house and warned never to darken the ancestral doorstep again, an order which he was only too happy to obey – provided his monthly remittance arrived on time.

In, say, the Faculty of Law, Alison's council school education might have been held against her, together with the fact that her father's 'position in the city' was only that of a maintenance man in the *Glasgow Mercury*'s machine-room. Alison, however, had a little money of her own. She was not vulgarly spoken and emanated an unobsequious confidence which was entirely classless.

Tall, with a solemn, oval face and dark brown hair, there were times when Alison seemed so studious that even Roberta was inclined to defer to her. She had an attractive quality which caught the boys off guard. And at the beginning of fourth term blonde, blue-eyed Roberta had her nose thoroughly put out of joint when both Howard and Guy confessed that they were falling for Miss Alison Burnside. Fortunately for community spirit Miss Alison Burnside was already spoken for.

Up to that point Alison had kept the facts of her domestic life dark. Now the time had come to tell the team the truth.

They were gathered in Miss Osmond's Lunch & Tearoom, a favourite haunt of students who could afford something better than standard Union fare. Housemen from the Western Infirmary, senior nurses and an occasional junior doctor could be found there too, slicing away at the Grosvenor pie or delving into a plate of the golden-brown chips for which Miss Osmond's was justifiably famous. Service was brisk enough to suit folk who were pressed for time. Prices were reasonable. Even Declan Slater could afford the Scotch broth and was willing to put his pride far enough to one side to devour the two or three extra breadrolls that somehow found their way on to his plate.

'I think,' Alison began, 'I should tell you lot something you don't know.'

'About what?' said Howard. 'Cervical ganglia?'

'What can Alison possibly have to impart about ganglia that hasn't been dunned into us, *ad nauseam*, by old Prof Collings?' said Roberta.

'Old Colly doesn't know everything,' said Howard.

'He knows a jolly sight more than we do,' said Roberta.

'I don't think Colly knows I'm engaged to be married,' Alison said.

Silence around the table.

Guy slid his hand away from the proximity of Alison's sleeve. Declan rolled his eyes as if Alison's news was merely exasperating. Howard let out a short, sharp sigh.

At length Roberta exclaimed, 'Good Lord!'

Howard was next to find his voice. 'When's the happy day?'

'And who's the lucky fella?' Declan added.

'When will you – um, leave?' Guy asked.

4

'Leave? I'm not leaving,' said Alison. 'I've been engaged for ages. I don't intend to rush into matrimony.'

'Troth, though, *has* been plighted?' Declan enquired.

'Years ago,' said Alison. 'Before I came up. I should have told you before now, I suppose.'

Howard said, 'It would certainly have saved Guy here from moping over his beer of a night.'

'Nothing of the kind,' Guy murmured in embarrassment.

When he tilted his chin and looked out of the window to the patch of wintry sky above the terraces of Ashton Street, he reminded Alison of film-actor Ronald Colman – minus the little moustache. She felt sorry for Guy. They all did. He was too earnest and wholesome for his own good.

'You haven't answered my question yet, Ally,' Declan said. 'Who is the lucky fella? Anyone we know?'

'You don't have to tell us if you don't want to,' Roberta put in.

'It isn't a secret,' Alison said.

'Then why haven't you told us before?' said Guy.

'You don't mean to say you're ashamed of him?' said Howard.

'Certainly not,' Alison retorted.

'He isn't, God help us, a doctor?' said Declan.

'He's a school teacher. His name's Jim Abbott.'

'Where does he teach?'

'Flannery Park.'

'Your old *alma mater*?' Howard said.

'Yes.'

'What's his subject?'

'English and History. Jim encouraged me to apply myself and to pass my Higher grades.' Alison was beginning to regret having raised the subject. It seemed as if she had put herself into the position of having to defend Jim. 'You know that my mother died when I was sixteen. Well, I thought it was all up with me at that point. Jim encouraged me to keep going. He persuaded my father to let me remain at school and convinced my brothers that I had – well – brains.'

'Take the brains as read,' said Declan. 'Go on with you.'

'He tutored me privately in Latin.'

'*Amo, amas, amat* and all that – hm?' said Howard.

'That isn't funny, Howard,' Roberta warned.

'Anyway,' Alison went on, 'when I left school to come into medicine, Jim asked me to marry him. And I said I would – as soon as I graduate.'

'You mean this fella's willin' to wait five years?'

'Yes, Declan,' said Alison. 'Jim refuses to let me sacrifice my career.'

'How old is he?' Roberta asked.

'Older than I am.' Alison paused. 'He lost an arm in the war. Shrapnel.'

'How much arm?' said Howard.

'Everything below the lateral head of the left triceps.'

'He was fortunate to survive,' said Howard.

'It's a fair enough piece of surgery,' Alison said, 'considering it was done at a field hospital in emergency conditions. I hardly notice it now.'

'Are you in love with him?' Guy Conroy asked.

'Of course.'

'It goes without saying that he's madly in love with you,' said Roberta.

'He wouldn't have asked me to marry him otherwise, would he?'

'Why choose now to reveal this fascinatin' fact?' said Declan.

'I don't want any of you to think I'm being stand-offish.'

'Somebody asked her to the Union Palais dance, didn't they?' said Howard. 'Didn't they, Guy?'

'What if they did?' Guy answered.

'Don't you see,' said Howard, 'the lady's letting us down gently.'

'Paws off, you mean?' said Declan.

'Precisely.'

'It's not that . . .' said Alison again, though in fact it *was* just that.

She felt her cheeks redden and, to cover her confusion, reached for the teapot and dispensed tea all round.

They had been friends for the best part of three terms and she did not wish to risk losing their companionship. No more, though, did she wish to have to explain what Jim Abbott meant to her or why he gave her so much freedom. At thirty-eight – almost twice her age – Jim was terribly aware of the gap between them. He hadn't prevented her from taking part in the social life of the university. Indeed, he'd encouraged her to become a member of the Queen Margaret Union and any other club or society which took her fancy. He made few, precious few, demands upon her, though Alison knew that every minute he spent away from her was a minute lost out of his life.

She remembered Declan saying, 'When are we goin' to meet this Socratic genius who snatches babes from the cradle of their youth?'

'Oh, shut it, Decker.' Roberta patted Alison's hand. 'I think it's marvellous, absolutely marvellous.'

'What is?' said Guy.

'Such devotion,' Roberta said. 'Alison's chap strikes me as being like one of those knights who goes off on a kingly quest while the lady waits, chaste and modest, for umpteen years. Only the other way around, if you see what I mean.'

'Oh, come on, Bobs!' said Howard. 'Let's not get carried away.'

'In any case,' Alison said, lamely, 'now you know.'

'All cut and dried,' Declan said.

'What?'

'Your future,' Declan said.

And Alison, as she recalled, had nodded gravely.

Now, in the thirteenth term, when lecture-hall was giving way to ward, cadaver to patient, theory to practice, how ingenuous those second-year upstarts seemed. They were still close friends, though, still a team. And it startled Alison to realise that in thirty months she had managed to split her life into two quite separate and distinct halves, neither of which appeared to have much relevance to the other.

On one hand there was a constant scramble for class tickets, cramming for exams, fear of ploughing anatomy, chemistry or physiology, fear of being faced with autumn re-sits or suspensions. Also rag days, carnival processions, union debates, rugby matches, all the usual carousal of university life which, even if economic depression and slump had taken a toll, remained vivid and vital on Gilmorehill.

On the other hand was Flannery Park. There Daddy, Henry, Bertie, Davy and Jack were the men in her life. Trudi, Ruby, Brenda and the brand-new twins made up a decent, go-get-'em suburban family which rode high on the troubled waters of industrial Clydeside.

There was also, of course, Jim Abbott.

Jim still taught in Flannery Park, cooked bachelor suppers in his council house in Macarthur Drive. Waited patiently for Alison to finish her education and marry him. But, come the cloudy autumn of 1933, Miss Alison Burnside had grown so used to Jim's devotion that she betrayed him by having a fling with a younger man.

Music, Brenda had decided, was okay if you were Harry Roy or Arthur Mountsey and got broadcast over the wireless once or twice a week from the Mayfair Hotel, London, or the Palais de Danse, Aberdeen. But nobody, especially *her* husband, could hope to make a decent living playing the trumpet with fat Kenny Cooper and his bunch of dead-beats at the Cally Hall every other Saturday night while living in hope of a job with a theatre orchestra in the pantomime season or summer gigs down the coast.

Nor, Brenda had made clear, was she all that keen to have him galloping out every night in the week to play with the Partick Burgh brass band which paid nothing at all, except so-called 'perks', which only meant free beer now and then or a pass to see Thistle play at home on Saturdays.

Nothing, as Brenda had put it, to butter the bairns' bread or keep her in the style to which she felt she ought to become accustomed. Besides, Glasgow Corporation's housing allocations department wasn't going to hand out the keys of a brand-new council house in a highly desirable garden suburb like Flannery Park unless you had something more behind you than the ability to busk your way through 'My Little Wooden Hut' or 'Muskrat flamin' Ramble'. What Jack had to do was find himself a job, a decent, respectable, nine-to-five job that would bring in a wage-packet regular every Friday night. And if he couldn't find a job for himself then, damn it, Brenda would do it for him.

And, Brenda went on, if Jack didn't fancy settling to married life and its responsibilities – hard cheese! He should have thought of that before he dragged her along to Kenny Cooper's fiftieth birthday party and got her so drunk she didn't know what she was doing. She didn't expect to be taken advantage of by one of the Burnside boys. The Burnside boys were supposed to be so respectable that butter wouldn't melt in their mouths. How did he think she felt having to tell her mother that it wouldn't be a white wedding after all but that it had better be quick, whatever shade she was married in, because if they waited much longer they'd have to roll her down the aisle in a barrel?

Oddly enough, Ruby, Brenda's mother, hadn't gone up in a blue light when Brenda had imparted news of her pregnancy.

'Are you sure, Brenda?' Ruby had said wearily. 'This time, are you really sure?'

'Look,' Brenda had said, arching her back and thrusting out her tummy. 'An' that's only, you know, three months.'

'Is Jack definitely the father?'

'Of *course* he's the flamin' father. What do you take me for?'

'I'll tell Alex tonight.'

What Ruby had actually said to her spouse – who also happened to be Jack's father – would have wounded Brenda deeply: 'She got him.'

Alex's rejoinder would have wounded Brenda even more.

'Not before bloody time.'

The employment of a down-at-heel lawyer to ensure that some quirk of Scots law didn't see Jack charged with incest and shipped off to Barlinnie prison for twenty years had cost the Burnsides a pretty penny. After a great deal of hemming-and-hawing and raking about in dusty tomes, the lawyer's conclusion was that Mr John Burnside and Miss Brenda McColl were not in default of the marriage laws, morally or legally, since they had not been raised as siblings in the same household and, *a priori*, neither one of them was insane.

This last point was debatable. Highly debatable. And, oh, how the Burnside boys had debated it.

Tirelessly, noisily, night after night, they'd squabbled over How This Could Have Happened, until finally, one evening just a week before his wedding day, Jack had lost the wool, had leaned over the supper table and punched his brother Bertie on the nose.

Trudi had screamed at Henry to put a stop to all this nonsense. Davy, grabbing his cap and a lead, had announced that he was taking Pete the dog for a walk, while Bertie, poor old Bertie, had bled all over the corned-beef hash and tipsy cakes until Trudi had slapped a compress on his neck and told him to stop snivelling and to try to pretend that he was a man.

A week later, in Martha Street Registry Office, Brenda and Jack had been spliced for life in a furtive little ceremony attended only by the immediate family, which did not include Bertie, who claimed he had to attend a Co-op management meeting and couldn't possibly get away, or by Alison who was that afternoon delving into old Tom's cranial cavity.

Looking rather grim and distant, Alison did have the decency to turn up at the City Bakeries' Tearoom in Dumbarton Road, however, where Henry had laid on high tea for twelve, which included bridesmaids Vera and Doris, from Brenda's former place of employment, and Alison's 'intended', Mr Jim Abbott.

'Don't you wish it was us, Ally?' Jim had whispered when groom had kissed bride to the accompaniment of half-hearted applause.

And Alison, who regarded the whole affair as unbearably squalid from beginning to end, had dutifully murmured, 'Yes.'

Squalid though it appeared to Alison, Jack's marriage to Brenda McColl was not without compensations. Brenda might be small and a little on the stout side but she was, none the less, a cuddlesome bundle and had none of the inhibitions which many of her contemporaries lugged to the marriage bed.

Jack did not enquire how Brenda had gained so much expertise in 'private matters'. He reckoned her answer would be the same as it was to so many of his questions – 'Vera told me,' or 'Doris said.' Jack was happy enough to accept what had been given him, to stroke Brenda's whisky-coloured hair and feel her warm flanks against his thighs on a cold winter's night.

As time wore on, he would put his fingers lightly about her swollen

9

stomach and lightly drum out the rhythm of 'Two Little Girls in Blue' or one of Borodin's less strenuous overtures while Brenda, who had been groaning in discomfort a moment before, would relax and grumble quietly, saying, 'For God's sake, Jack, what d'you think you're doin'?'

Jack would laugh and blow lightly in her ear until she told him to cut it out. 'They can't, you know, hear you,' Brenda would say, for the doctor had recently confirmed that she was carrying twins.

Jack would laugh again and say, 'Oh, aye, they can,' for the notion of fathering sons filled him with delight and he felt that the sooner he made contact with the wee rascals the better.

When girls were born instead of boys Jack didn't mind at all.

'They're lovely, dear,' he said. 'Just lovely.'

They *were* lovely too.

Everybody, except Bertie, said so.

They were small but uncommonly shapely for babies. One had a dressing of jet black hair, the other a dusting of silvery blonde. Thus Dad and Mum, Burnsides and McColls, were equally represented and, as it were, had a *very* special favourite allocated to them at birth.

Only Jack resisted the temptation to favour one over the other. He loved them both equally. He loved the little dark one because she reminded him of his sister Alison and he loved the wee blondie because in every way that mattered she was her mother's absolute double.

In due course the twins were christened at the font in the local church, with Davy and Alison as godparents.

The blonde was named Ruby, the brunette Alexis.

But it did not take long for the little girls to find their voices and re-christen themselves. Bee and Lexi they became.

And remained.

If, among the Burnside boys, Henry had always been rated the most handsome, Jack, as he grew older, ran him a close second.

He was not so tall as Henry but had a strong square jaw line, broad shoulders and a direct, head-up way of looking at you that indicated candour. He walked briskly and whistled cheerfully as he did the round of Partick's back streets and the streets of what had once been Greenfield burgh.

The old burgh had recently been absorbed by the city of Glasgow and was tucked away, shabby and neglected, in an elbow of docks and warehouses. Jack didn't mind the Greenfield beat. He wasn't afraid of dark alleys and shadowy close-mouths. Jack was just glad to have a steady job. There were worse companies to work for than

Manchester Crown General Life Assurance and he was a damned sight better off than most of the lads with whom he had served his apprenticeship in Ransome's shipyard, young men who were barely scraping by on the dole now.

The Burnsides had been lucky, very lucky. Ransome's closure had propelled Henry into journalism, Dad into a secure job with the *Mercury* and, indirectly, had promoted Bertie to deputy managership of the local Co-operative store where he seemed to be as happy as Bertie could ever hope to be.

Only Davy had been spared occupational upheaval. He had served his time as a bricklayer and, because of Glasgow Council's ambitious building schemes, had never been out of work a day in his life.

It was Brenda who had found Jack the post with Manchester Crown. Jack could never have imagined himself as a brown-suited, white-collar insurance agent. He had passed the company's simple tests in English and arithmetic with flying colours, however, and after two weeks' instruction on the street he was turned loose with cash books, briefcase and collection bag to introduce himself to the good folk of Greenfield and Partick South.

The district was notoriously poor in commission pickings. Jack didn't mind that either. He earned enough to keep his head above water and the wolf from the door. He was affable, open and sympathetic and consequently extracted weekly payments on threepenny and sixpenny policies without too much effort or commotion. Some clients in Partick remembered him from the days when he'd been Mavis Burnside's 'boy' and lived round the corner in Sutton Street. Others recalled him as a solo cornet player with the Old Burgh band or the trumpeter at Cally Hall dances and would ask him if he still played.

Jack would shake his head, grin and say, 'Nah. I'm a married man now,' as if music was a pastime for uncommitted youth, like kick-the-can or leapfrog.

He had the twins, Brenda, a steady job, a council house of his own. And he could still whistle.

By God, he could whistle. He could whistle anything you cared to name, from the latest hit tune to Haydn's Trumpet Concerto.

At first he whistled only to entertain himself but sometimes he got caught in full flow and some urchin would yell, 'Hey, if ye're gonna do that, mister, geez 'Fonso instead.' Jack would pause, wet his lips and render the Gracie Fields chestnut, 'Fonso My Hot Spanish Night', with all the vibrato he could muster, sliding the tune about to make them laugh.

After several such encounters Jack learned to whistle unabashed.

11

He would let his symphonies and serenades go before him from tenement to tenement so that the wives would know he was in the neighbourhood. The women would smile and say, 'It's Mr Burnside, come to collect the insurance money.' And the men of the house, not unkindly, would shout out, 'Aye, here's Whistlin' Rufus lookin' for his dough. Huv ye got the birdseed ready, Agnes?'

Friday evenings and Saturday forenoons Jack was at his busiest. Like all collection agents he preferred to tap his clients while payday cash was still hot in their hands.On Fridays he would work until nine or ten at night. On other days of the week he would undertake a more leisurely round of thrifty households or deal with death-benefits, fire claims and matured endowments.

On that particular Friday afternoon, however, the promise of new business took him early to Greenfield.

After a long, stifling summer the autumn's cool breezes were welcome. The stench that had hung over Glasgow since June had been all but swept away. That scorched metal smell of cinders and coal smoke, petrol fumes, horse manure, tram-sparks and tar lingered only faintly in the air over Walbrook Street's terrace of once-genteel dwelling houses. Number 27 was no better, no worse than the rest of the houses on the street. It stood behind the maze of tenements which flanked Dumbarton Road and the only building along its length which seemed to have retained any dignity was the little, clean-cut, Presbyterian church of St Anne's.

Jack had only one client in Walbrook Street. Elderly Miss Henderson, who still forked out sixpence a week from her meagre income to keep up an antique burial policy, had recommended Jack to her friend Mrs McCusker who, at some point in the dim and distant past, had inherited one of the terraced houses and now rented out rooms there. According to Miss Henderson, Mrs McCusker was keen to invest in a burial policy too. Though Jack had already learned that elderly ladies were a breed apart when it came to financial matters, he had too much integrity not to pursue the business.

The oblongs of grass which had once adorned the fronts of Walbrook Street had been killed off years ago by palls of smoke from the railway. Most of the windows were veiled with torn net curtains or faded paper blinds, grey and secretive, as if the inhabitants were ashamed of their straitened circumstances.

Jack did not whistle in Walbrook Street. He walked in silence past the grim, bashful houses and, hoisting his briefcase under his arm, turned on to the little path that led to the door of number 27.

It was a quarter past four o'clock.

He had taken barely a step towards the peeling front door when it flew open and a girl dashed out. To Jack's astonishment he recognised his sister's dark brown straight-cut hair, familiar beret, and long coltish legs.

He shouted, 'Alison? What the hell are you doing here?'

Startled, she dropped her scarf, gloves and a textbook, and exclaimed, 'Jack! Oh, God! It's our Jack!'

'Aye, it's me, but what are *you* doin' here?'

'I can explain.' Alison said. 'I really can explain.'

As she stooped to retrieve her belongings Jack glimpsed a young man in the doorway behind her. Dark-haired and saturnine. Pointed features, a tousled, down-at-heel appearance.

When he saw Jack staring at him he closed the door immediately.

'Who's that?' Jack said.

'What?'

'That bloke? Were you inside with that bloke?'

'He's a friend – just a friend. From the university.'

'Aren't you supposed to be at a class at the Royal Infirmary?'

'How did you know?'

Hardly more than guesswork based on some half-remembered remark, Jack had no idea, really, how Alison's days were shaped.

Frowning, he watched her gather her scarf, gloves and textbook. Except for spots of high colour on her cheeks she seemed perfectly composed now.

'I was,' Alison said, 'at a clinic in the Royal. I've a lecture at four thirty in the main building. It's just one of those hectic afternoons. I dropped by my – my friend's house to pick up a book. This book, actually.' She held up a weighty volume and gave it a little shake. 'That's all there is to it.'

'Were you inside the house with him?'

'Oh, just for a moment, that's all.'

'What's his name?'

'Declan.'

'Funny sort of name.'

'He's Irish.'

'What's he doing here?' said Jack.

'Not all my friends are well off,' Alison said. 'This is all he can afford.'

'He didn't seem very eager to meet me.'

'He's a bit shy, is our Declan.' Alison hoisted the odds and ends in her arms and ostentatiously consulted her wristlet watch. 'God, look at the time. Sorry, but I'll have to gallop or I'll miss roll-call.' She glanced round at the door then faced Jack once more. 'I take it you haven't come down to Walbrook Street just to spy on me?'

'Eh?'

'No, of course you haven't. Customer, is it?'

'New business, if I'm lucky.'

'The old woman McCusker?'

'Yeah. Do you know her?'

'Not personally. Declan says she's a miserable old cow.' Alison hesitated. 'Look, Jack, I'd be awfully grateful if you wouldn't mention to anyone at home that you met me this afternoon.'

'Why not?'

'It's not that I've anything to hide,' Alison said, 'but you know what they're like. They won't understand.'

'I'm not sure *I* do,' Jack said.

'It's nothing.' Alison managed a smile. 'Nothing at all. Honest Injun!'

'I won't say anything.'

'Good lad,' Alison told him. 'How's Brenda, by the way?'

'Fine.'

'And my favourite twins?'

'Fine.'

'Good, good,' Alison said, then, giving him a quick peck on the cheek, hurried off down Walbrook Street and turned the corner out of sight.

As a clinician it was generally agreed that the venerable Daddy Dobson was a wash-out. His bedside manner was vague and his attempts at old-world *politesse* did little to reassure either his patients or his students. He was, however, marginally more effective in the lecture-room where detachment from all-too-tangible flesh allowed him to delude himself that the practice of medicine had hardly changed in the fifty years since he had walked the wards of the Royal Infirmary on the heels of the great, the sacred, Sir William Tennant Gairdner.

The problem was that Gairdner's many learned tracts had become muddled in Daddy Dobson's mind and he was liable to interrupt a lecture on nasal diphtheria with a twenty-minute discourse on certain moral aspects of money-getting. This was a wee bit too much for the modern majority, as a result of which Dobson's Friday afternoon lectures were never well attended.

The old man still sported high collars, four-inch cuffs, jackets with black beading on the lapels, and a tiny, white, waterfall moustache which he sucked reflectively when he ran out of steam. That said, he rattled through the calling of the roll like a Gatling gun and would often mark you present when you weren't. He was equally careless in

14

filling in end-of-term certificates of attendance, a habit which endeared him, *in absentia*, to many.

Alison arrived in class a split second before Daddy Dobson called her name: 'Burnside?'

'Sir.'

She scuttled down the steep wooden steps of the old classroom and slid on to a bench beside Roberta.

In late-afternoon sunlight Roberta looked more glamorous than ever. She wore an expensive rose-coloured blouse and dusky pink cardigan which disguised her slight tendency to plumpness. Her hair seemed to have been rinsed in twenty-two-carat gold and her lipstick glistened fresh and moist. Half the males in the class – conservative estimate – were gazing at her in wistful admiration, pondering, perhaps, the eternal question of just how close Conroy – or was it McGrath? – had got to bedding her.

'Conroy?'

'Here.'

Guy had already begun to make notes in his stout, stiff-covered notebook and seemed impervious to the vision of loveliness by his side.

'Donaldson?'

'Uh ...'

'Dougald?'

'I'm here.'

'Who?'

'Donaldson, sir. Donaldson's here.'

'Not Dougald?'

'He's here too. I mean, I am.'

'Oh!' No pause: 'Drummond?'

Roberta leaned slightly to her left and whispered, 'Where's Decker?'

'I've no idea,' said Alison.

'I thought you were with Decker.'

'Not I,' said Alison.

From further along the bench Howard McGrath stage-whispered, 'Isn't he with you?'

'Why are you asking *me* about Declan?' Alison snapped.

'All right. Keep your hair on.'

'Missed you at the Royal, that's all,' Guy said.

'I went to the library instead,' said Alison.

'With Declan?' Roberta said.

'No, *not* with Declan. Not with anybody.'

'McGrath?' old Daddy Dobson yapped.

'I'm here, Professor Dobson, sir.'

A moment later, without looking up: 'Slater?'

'Here.' Howard automatically raised his voice a half octave and added a touch of Irish for effect. He had performed this loyal deception often before.

A similar sort of loyalty had lured Alison to Declan's digs that afternoon. No law, moral or social, prohibited you being alone with a member of the opposite sex. But there *were* laws, tacit and unwritten, that dictated the form of such meetings.

Jim was her tutor in this matter too. When it came to interpreting the outs-and-ins of convention, what was done and what was not, Jim Abbott was, in Alison's view, *the* expert.

In fact, Alison was rather tired of Jim's concern for propriety. She had kissed Jim and had been kissed by him. He had even held her in his arms. But he had never lain with her, stretched out like lovers on the grass or among the dunes by Cullen sands. He had never taken her upon his knee, had never tried to touch her breast or thigh. And if she made any little intimate advance he would gently draw away, saying, 'No, Alison, no.'

'Why not?'

'It isn't right.'

Jim was considerate, tender, even romantic at times.

Alison did not doubt that he loved her yet she couldn't understand how any man could be *that* patient and considerate and had recently begun to question just what was real in their relationship and what, by her definition, was false.

Roberta flipped open her spiral notepad. She entered the date, time and the shortform she had devised for Dobson.

Roberta took all her notes in shorthand.

'Yates?'

'*Sah!*'

'Yuille? No Yuille. Very well. Hypertrophic cirrhosis, or the cirrhosis of Hanot as it was called in my young day.'

The energy generated by roll-call carried Daddy Dobson directly into his afternoon lecture. 'As you saw today in the case of the young male subject, this is not, as many authorities seem to believe, merely a manifestation of common cirrhosis but differs from regular cases of alcoholic cirrhosis in that the liver is massively enlarged and deeply bile-stained.'

Staring straight ahead, writing effortlessly, Roberta whispered from the side of her mouth, 'He gave you tea, didn't he?'

'Pardon?'

Alison had been thinking of things other than the cirrhosis of

Hanot. Thinking of the dreadful fright she'd received when Jack had come marching up to Declan Slater's door and the shameful sense of persecution which had followed the meeting with her brother.

'Our Declan, he gave you tea?' said Roberta.

'Coffee actually,' Alison said.

'That foul black stuff out of a bottle?'

'Yes, I can still taste the chicory.'

'If you don't mind my saying so, you want to be careful.'

'What d'you mean?'

'Giving in to Declan.'

'*Giving in?*'

'*Shhh,*' Roberta advised softly.

'Giving in? If that's what you think of me, Bobs . . .'

'*Shhh,*' Roberta said again. 'We'll talk later. Compare notes.'

'About what?'

'Declan Slater,' Roberta said just as old Daddy Dobson swerved away from cirrhosis and fell instead to discussing nostrums in the works of Montaigne.

Seldom did it dawn on the busy little misses of the day that they were fortunate to have escaped the smothering atmosphere of all-female tuition in the old Queen Margaret College, a grim-ish sort of building on the banks of the Kelvin a mile or so from the university heartland.

Suffocating Victorian attitudes, which decreed that middle-class women were frail creatures liable to jeopardise their health and reproductive functions as soon as they set foot outside a domestic environment, were just a joke to Roberta and Alison.

Although Queen Margaret Hall remained open, most of the institution's female students had been incorporated into general medical courses and worked cheek by jowl – buttock to buttock, as the wags would have it – with their male counterparts. Among the new Georgians, to whom even dancing the charleston seemed *passé,* the demise of the hall was not something to be mourned. Mutterings about its closure caused no alarm in the breasts of girls who had never darkened its sombre old laboratories or its genteel glass-case-lined dissection-room. More to the fore in the minds of all students, male as well as female, were upheavals in the sitings of the common hearths, *id est* the Unions.

Since Glasgow University lacked a central campus the vast majority of students lodged not in communal halls but, like Alison and Roberta, travelled home to sup with Mama and Papa and sleep in their own little beds when the day's work was done. For this reason the Unions became the centre of many young lives, places in which to snooze, smoke, chatter, to rail against life's sore trials and manifold tribulations.

The new Men's Union was situated just where University Avenue lurched into Bank Street. It served reasonable lunches, edible dinners and came equipped with a fully tuned piano and several billiard tables. But it was all too spick and span, too clean and spacious to suit a generation which had cheerfully grubbed up in the cramped confines of the old building.

The old building no longer provided a haven of retreat for displaced males. It had been given over to – yes – *the women*. And, in the way of womankind, the new Q-Emmas had scraped, scrubbed, dusted and polished the place out of all recognition and with pastel colours, pile carpets and chintzy little curtains had chased away for ever the reeking ghosts of masculine occupation.

It was to the new QM that Roberta spirited Alison away as soon as Daddy Dobson's class dwindled to its conclusion.

Waving 'Ta-Ta' to Howard and Guy, the pair were off, arm-in-arm, across the ill-lit quad and through the cloisters, heading for a chintz-covered sofa near the fire and a little light repast of tea and hot buttered toast.

It did not take long for Roberta to come to the point.

'Declan,' she said.

'Yes?'

Alison had already decided that she would come clean with Roberta who had absolutely no connection with anyone in Flannery Park.

'I must say, I'm surprised you went home with him.'

'I felt sorry for him,' said Alison. 'He seems so "down" since he came back from vacation. I thought I might cheer him up.'

'That's what I thought too,' said Roberta.

'You? You went home with him?'

'Three or four times.'

'When?'

'Just after Christmas.'

'I thought you didn't like Greenfield?'

'I don't. It's disgusting.'

'Declan isn't disgusting,' Alison said.

'That,' Roberta said, 'is a matter of opinion.'

'He can't help being poor.'

'What did he do to you?' Roberta said.

Alison did not answer.

'Did he attempt to kiss you?'

'He may have done.'

18

'Alison, for heaven's sake! Did he, or didn't he?'

'He did.'

'And you allowed it?'

'I . . .'

'I certainly did.' Roberta admitted. 'Not the first time but the second.'

'Why did you go with him a second time?'

'Because I wanted to.'

'Are you in love with Declan Slater?' Alison asked.

'Don't be ridiculous.' Roberta paused. 'Are you?'

'I'm not sure.'

'Why fall for Declan Slater when you've a perfectly nice chap at home?'

'Declan's – different.'

At the top of the stairs from the coffee lounge a couple of freshers hovered uncertainly then, with an air of daring, entered the common-room and meandered towards a window seat, praying that someone would talk to them. They looked, Alison thought, like lost children.

'Decker's different all right,' Roberta went on.

'I haven't done anything wrong, you know.'

'Don't suppose you have.'

'I probably won't visit him again, not alone.'

'That means you probably will.'

'Did he tell you he was in love with you?' Alison asked.

'Naturally.'

A pause: 'Me too.'

'Did you believe him?'

'No,' Alison said.

'But you'd like to think otherwise, is that it?'

Alison lifted her shoulders and gave a smile that felt rather a lot like a simper. 'What are you saying, Bobs? That Declan's just after a bit of fluff? If that's the case why has he waited so long? If it is *that* he's after then surely he could find someone more obliging than either of us.'

'It isn't *that* at all,' said Roberta. 'I wish it was.'

'What?' said Alison, shocked.

There was a glitter in Roberta's blue eyes which Alison could not interpret. Suddenly she was concerned, not for Roberta but for herself. If Bobs, pretty enough to snare almost any man in college, had already surrendered to Declan Slater's charm then what chance did she have?

'I didn't,' said Roberta. 'But I wanted to.'

'Then we're both in the same boat.'

'No, I don't think we are,' Roberta said.

'I had no idea that anything like this was going on.'

'Of course not,' said Roberta. 'Declan's incredibly discreet. Sly might be a more accurate word for it. In any event, I got over it very quickly.'

'What happened?'

'He asked me for money.'

'He did *what*?'

'He asked me to lend him money.'

'How much?'

'Rather a lot,' said Roberta. 'Fortunately, I hadn't been *quite* taken in. Not that I would have. Gone the whole way, I mean.'

'Did you give him the money?'

'I gave him something. Not much.'

'And then he dropped you?'

'No, I dropped him.'

'But he's still your friend, isn't he?'

'I pretend that he is. I don't want to make an issue out of a situation which was partly my fault in the first place.'

'I thought Declan had more pride than to ask a girl for money.'

'I tell myself that he must have been desperate.'

'Did he give you a sob story?'

'No, he simply told me he loved me,' Roberta said. 'I'd more or less put the entire episode behind me until I realised he'd taken up with you.'

'If he thinks he can squeeze any cash out of me,' Alison said, 'he's got another think coming. For all I've got.'

'You won the Tuxford Prize at school, didn't you?'

'Who told *you* about the Tuxford?'

'Declan,' Roberta said. 'Now do you see why I had to intervene? I mean to say, I don't want you to think I'm acting out of spite.'

'I wonder if Declan's tried to tap the boys?'

'Howard wouldn't part with a penny. And he certainly hasn't asked Guy.'

'Are you sure?'

'Positive,' Roberta said.

From the dining-room across the landing came the rattle of crockery, from the kitchen the hiss of the huge copper urn in which water was boiled. A gaggle of five Arts students burst into the common room, stared disdainfully at the freshers then, chattering volubly, flung themselves on to sofas and into armchairs close to Alison and Roberta.

The topic which engaged them wasn't boys or clothes or the

beauty of Wordsworth's *Prelude* but the forthcoming municipal elections. Party politics, a subject Alison considered dull to distraction. Perhaps she should discuss politics with Declan. Surely, that would dampen his ardour.

She had no intention of writing Declan Slater off just yet, however. She was not without secrets of her own. Four years ago she had imagined herself in love with Walter Giffard. She had learned a great deal from the experience. She was older now, however, wiser in the ways of the world. Money? That, within limits, would not be a problem. But if dear old Declan Slater thought he was about to receive something else for nothing then he was in for a very rude shock.

Alison got suddenly to her feet.

'I'd love to linga-longa, Bobs,' she said, 'but I really must run.'

'Do you have to?' said Roberta. 'I mean to say, I thought we were just embarking on a jolly interesting talk.'

'I appreciate what you've told me,' Alison said. 'I won't tell a soul, of course. About you and Declan, I mean. But I did promise Jim I'd be home by half past six and it's almost that now.'

'Fly then,' Roberta said, hiding her disappointment. 'And be careful.'

'Oh, I will, I will,' said Alison. 'Here, let me pay for the tea.'

'My treat,' Roberta said. 'See you Monday.'

'See you, Bobs,' said Alison, and left.

As head of the household Henry liked to make sure that everyone was accounted for before he took himself upstairs to bed.

He also turned off taps and lights, unplugged the wireless, secured the fireguard and supplied Pete, the dog, with food and water to see him through the night. His last act was to lock and bolt both doors for there had been a couple of burglaries in Flannery Park of late and Henry wasn't one to take chances.

The fact that the house was secure, however, did not necessarily mean that its occupants were all asleep.

The light in Alison's bedroom would frequently burn until two or three in the morning and Bertie, a born insomniac, could be heard padding about in the wee small hours, making himself tea or searching for aspirins. Only Davy seemed to need his shut-eye and would fill the big front room with his snores long before anyone else considered turning in.

Fortunately, Trudi shared Henry's nocturnal proclivity.

They would often sit up in the broad double bed wrapped in dressing-gowns, cardigans and bed-jackets, and sip tea, nibble biscuits and read snippets of news to each other from magazines and journals.

By the light of the parchment-shaded lamps which flanked the bed Henry looked older than his years, Trudi younger. Henry had begun to put on a little weight but he was still dourly handsome and carried an air of probity which Trudi had always found attractive. In contrast Trudi remained as slender and poised as a willow, her fine white-blonde hair and pale, pale eyes giving her, at times, an almost ethereal quality.

However well she had settled into the role of working-class suburban *hausfrau*, she had not sacrificed her individuality to do so. Clearly she was still cosmopolitan, marked out by her manner as well as her clipped 'Swiss' accent. She ran the house like clockwork, took charge of the wages, settled the domestic accounts and was such a wonderful cook that even Bertie was heard to mutter now and then that he didn't know what they'd do without her.

Changes in Henry's relationship with his out-of-the-ordinary wife were subtle and not apparent to his brothers or sister.

Trudi and he no longer made love with any great frequency. The fierce perverted passions which had first brought them together were, it seemed, things of the past. Their love-making now was discreet, tender and orthodox. An unhurried kiss on cheek or lip, a little sigh, an arm about the waist, toes wrestling for possession of the hot-water bottle had become substitutes for more exacting adventures beneath the sheets for, Henry told himself, their union had become one of like minds and relatively free of physical demands.

In those late hours Trudi and he would discuss the state of the world. Fascist marches in Italy, rioting in Jerusalem, the banning of the Iron Guard in Bucharest. Red Menace in Spain. Chancellor Hitler's withdrawal of Germany from the League of Nations. And, of course, the forthcoming Scottish municipal elections which Henry would cover for the *Mercury*.

Henry found it difficult to take local elections seriously, however. His interests lay further afield now, in those dark and dangerous places into which Trudi's knowledge and experience gave him a window.

Trudi would read aloud to him from obscure foreign newspapers which Henry purchased from a little kiosk near Queen Street railway station. She translated fluently from French and German, more haltingly from Italian and Spanish and, by way of commentary, would tell her husband what she had learned of these alien cultures.

Henry was fascinated.

He had known when he married Trudi Keller Coventry that she was an intelligent, well-informed and widely travelled woman. But he had not expected to find in her a partner quite so ideal. He also valued her judgement in domestic matters and admired the tact with which she handled her in-laws. For this reason he felt entirely justified in telling Trudi what Jack had told him about Alison's fancy-man and the chance meeting in Walbrook Street.

'A man, another man?' Trudi said, surprised.

'That's what Jack seems to think,' Henry said.

For reading, Trudi wore a little pair of crescent-shaped glasses in a gold wire frame. She was supported by a heavy, flock-filled bolster and, though the night was mild, wore a crocheted bed-jacket and a wisp of chiffon, like a scarf, about her throat. She tipped her head back, lowered the German newspaper and squinted at Henry curiously.

'Did Jack catch her in the act?'

'What act?'

'Fornication.'

'Don't be daft.' Henry said.

'He saw only that she came out of a house?'

'In the middle of the afternoon, when she should have been at class?'

'How is it you know that she should have been at class? Perhaps the order of the curriculum has been changed.'

'According to Jack she behaved like she shouldn't have been in Greenfield at all,' Henry explained. '*And* she asked him not to say anything about it to any of us.'

'So the first thing Jack does is to tell you?'

'He felt I should know,' Henry muttered uncomfortably.

He was perched on the room's only chair.

He wore shirt and vest and pyjama trousers and reminded Trudi of an Italian peasant or a Serbian prisoner-of-war, though she could not pin down the points in her history from which such comparisons emerged.

'Why do you tell this to me, Henry?'

'I thought you might have a word with Ally.'

'Where was it you said this encounter took place?'

'Walbrook Street in Greenfield. It's a dump.'

'What if I tell you that Alison is concerned because *she* met *Jack* in the middle of the afternoon in this unfrequented part of the city?'

'Did Alison say something to you about it?'

Trudi answered question with question. 'What was *Jack* up to at that time of day in that place?'

'Hell's bells, Trudi, he was collectin' insurance.'

'That is his story.'

'There's a vast difference between . . . Look, Jack was working.'

'How do you know that Alison was not working also?'

'In a house in Greenfield?' said Henry. 'Anyway, Jack spotted this shady-looking cove—'

'One of her friends. One of – what does she call them – her "team," no?'

Henry rubbed a hand over his jaw and sat forward.

Trudi had successfully confused the issue and, now that he considered it, he was almost willing to admit that he was guilty of jumping to conclusions.

He had been worried about Alison for months, though.

She was no longer his sweet little sister, sober and dependent, clever and pliant. She had become stubborn, at times quite sly. Besides, he'd grown fond of Jim Abbott who, if not quite a brother, had certainly earned the right to be regarded as a close family friend. It had crossed Henry's mind that Alison might meet someone at university whom she preferred to Jim Abbott. He had always considered it courageous of Jim to accept this risk.

'She doesn't talk much about her friends, does she?' Henry said.

'Perhaps it is that you do not listen,' Trudi told him.

'I suppose it could have been perfectly innocent.' Henry unbuttoned his shirt, raised it over his head and, as his face emerged from the folds, added, 'But our Jack doesn't seem to think so.'

'What would Jack know of such matters?' Trudi said. 'He is so besotted with his wife and his new children he cannot see his nose before his face.'

Henry folded the shirt carefully and inserted it into the basket in the corner. Trudi studied him critically over her the rim of her glasses.

'What?' said Henry.

'Alison has done nothing wrong. It is all conjecture,' Trudi said. 'The mountain from the molehill, the storm in the teacup.'

'All right, Trude. You've made your point.'

'I will, however, talk with Alison.'

'Well, it might be useful,' Henry said. 'None of us really seems to know what she's up to these days.'

'And you would not wish for her to get into trouble?'

'Course not.'

'I will talk with her.'

'Thanks, Trudi,' Henry said.

'It is not a problem,' Trudi said and, poking her glasses back on to the bridge of her nose, lifted up her copy of *Der Angriff* and began again to read.

Some Sundays it just wasn't worth while getting out of bed.

And this, Brenda had decided, was one of them.

She had lain as long as possible, snuggled under the quilt with the sheet cowled over her head, listening to her daughters creating havoc in the kitchen below. Her husband's cajoling cries of, 'Bee, put that down. No, I mean it,' or 'Lexi, darlin', I don't think the teddy wants any more porridge,' did not amuse her, for the stamping of little feet was punctuated by wails and yelps of temper, none of them sufficiently prolonged to force Brenda to hoist herself out of bed.

She preferred not to face the rigours of the day until the church bells had summoned the faithful to their prayers. Until Jack had fed and dressed the twins and wheeled them round to the newsagent's shop to pick up the papers and a couple of packets of ciggies. Usually Brenda remained oblivious to the house's atmosphere of burnt toast and frizzled ham, tobacco smoke, dust and pee-pee, but the clammy sounds of a dank, sanctimonious sabbath were a bit too much even for Brenda and she clung to her bed like a sailor to a raft and tried, without success, to go back to sleep.

The house was a two-in-a-block. Living-room, bathroom and kitchenette downstairs and two bedrooms up.

Brenda and Jack had the bigger room to the front and the drone of bus traffic and the occasional snorting of a motorcar seemed more disturbing than Partick's heavy traffic had ever done. Maybe she had just been younger then and had been able to sleep through anything.

In the back bedroom, three steps away from Daddy and Mummy's room, the twins had their lair. One double cot, a frame with a bath on it, two drying racks draped with nappies and more clothes and toys hurled about than you would have imagined possible. Also tiny socks, pretty little shoes, dresses, pantaloons, golliwogs, teddy bears, alphabet bricks and, inevitably, a perpetual guddle of potties, nappies and damp cotton knickers.

Her mother, Ruby, had purple fits every time she came into the house. She went dabbing about like some gaudy seabird, picking up clothes and toys and teacups, crushed biscuits and gnawed rusks, even sweeping up the litter of papers and magazines that Brenda, no neater than her daughters, strewed about in her wake.

Brenda drove Ruby crazy, of course.

And vice versa.

The only good thing Ruby could find to say in Brenda's favour was that she never neglected the children. The house might be as grubby as Paddy's Market but the children were always neat and, indeed, had the scrubbed, pink-cheeked perfection of two little china dolls.

How Brenda managed it was beyond Ruby's comprehension.

Come to think of it, how Brenda managed it was beyond Brenda's comprehension. She took no pride or interest in housework or cooking and only when it came to the twins was she driven to keep them not just clean but shining. She had never gained her mother's approval for anything she'd ever done in her short life but, by God, she'd given Ruby something special by way of grandchildren and she did not intend to let that advantage slip. Consequently she not only put herself out to keep Bee and Lexi smart but also concerned herself with their health and well-being and, whenever Jack was not around, fussed over them obsessively.

When Jack was at home it was a different story. Brenda trusted Jack because he was the only person who never criticised her. He accepted what little she chose to offer him and indulged her laziness without complaint. She also trusted him because she was the mother of the precious twins and, however attentive she might be to their welfare, she had nothing on Jack when it came to doting. He adored his daughters and, by inference, adored Brenda too, a situation which Brenda naturally exploited.

'Jack?' she called out from the bed.

'Yep.'

'What are they doin'?'

'Helpin' me wash up.'

'Have they got on their pink bodices?'

'They have, they have.'

'Don't let them get, you know, wet.'

Gales of childish laughter rose from the kitchen as if Bee and Lexi were mocking her concern. The twins were much more interested in making soap suds and in assaulting the iron frying pan with a bristle brush than in anything Mummy and Daddy might be saying. Even so, Brenda felt a ridiculous prickle of resentment. She rolled on to her side and pawed the sheet from her face.

'Jack?'

'What?'

'Did you get my ciggies?'

'Yep.'

'And the *Post*?'

'Yep.'

'What time is it?'

'Ten past twelve.'

26

'Okay, I'm gettin' up.'

More mirth, as if the girls found this announcement hysterically funny.

Resentment swelled in Brenda's chest like heartburn. She had a good mind to let them fend for themselves. But she would need at least a couple of hours to get them bathed, dried, dressed and combed before half past three o'clock, at which hour the ritual of high tea at the Burnsides took place. She didn't really mind the Sunday visit. It saved her thinking what to cook for tea and also meant that she would be relieved for a while of the clamouring attentions of her daughters, who had of late grown too mobile and too voluble for her liking. She did, however, feel hemmed in by the inflexibility of family obligation, for Brenda could not abide having to be somewhere at a specific time and having to jog herself along to get there.

'I'm gettin' up,' she called out again and, holding the quilt to her breast, managed to elevate herself into a sitting position. 'Okay?'

There was no response from below, only a peculiar silence and that strange hollow feeling you get when the outside door opens and the faint hiss of rain unexpectedly enters the hall.

Frowning, Brenda listened to the voices, low at first then rising.

Who was it? Alison? Yes, Alison had arrived.

The twins' monkey-chatter was drowned out by an angry adult argument, and when Lexi howled, Brenda shot out of bed and, clad only in her rumpled nightgown, headed instantly for the stairs.

Bee's piping wail joined her sister's. Alison's voice was louder still, though, and Brenda was surprised by the vigour of her sister-in-law's language.

'You bastard, Jack, you promised you wouldn't tell.'

'Och, Ally, I only mentioned . . .'

'You told Henry. He told Trudi and she's been at me all morning.'

'I thought Henry should know . . .'

'Know what, Jack?'

Alison ignored Brenda when she appeared on the stairs. Bee was clinging to Daddy's trouser leg and Lexi, on her knees, was holding her sister's hand. The pair of them, frightened by their aunt's temper, were wailing away good style.

In a black overcoat, beret and trailing scarf Alison looked mad enough to scare the wits out of anyone. Brenda had never seen Ally Burnside enraged before. There was something gratifying in the sight of the so-called Princess of Wingfield Drive in a temper. If it hadn't been for the children Brenda would have flung herself into the argument just for the sake of it.

Instead, she bounced downstairs, yelling, 'You leave my bairns alone.'

'I never touched your precious bairns.'

'Easy, Ally, take it easy,' Jack said.

Brenda scooped Lexi into her arms. Jack, taking his cue, stooped and plucked up Bee and held her against his chest. The little girls buried their faces in Mum and Dad's shoulders and peeked out at their aunt, their wails turning to sobs now that they were secure and protected.

'What's Jack supposed to have done then?' Brenda said.

'It's between Jack and me, Brenda, so I'll thank you not to interfere.'

'She's got a fancy-man,' Jack said, sighing.

'*I haven't got a fancy-man.*'

'Stop, you know, that shoutin',' Brenda said.

'I knew this would happen,' Alison cried. 'I knew everybody would jump to the worst possible conclusion. I don't run my life like a railway timetable. I do *what* I like, *when* I like. I *choose* my friends.'

'A fancy-man?' Brenda said. 'You? Don't make me laugh!'

'At least I didn't have to get knocked up to find one,' Alison retorted.

'Bitch!' said Brenda.

'Aye, that's quite enough of that, Ally,' Jack warned.

The twins were watching as if they understood. A full-blown row was novel enough to intrigue them even if they had no clue as to what was going on. They looked from Alison to Jack to Brenda, pert little heads rotating, fists closed tightly on the fabric of shirt and nightgown.

Brenda produced her matronly shuffle, waggling her hips. She hoisted Lexi higher in her arms as if to give her daughter a better view.

Wagging a forefinger in her brother's face, Alison said, 'I told you what I was doing in Greenfield, Jack. I assumed you'd have enough sense to believe me. If not sense, at least respect for my intelligence.'

'What's intelligence got to do with it?' said Brenda. 'Unless this lover o' yours is, you know, another bloody genius?'

'Look,' said Alison, lowering her voice, 'Declan Slater . . .'

'Ooo, is that his name?' Brenda put in.

' . . . is not my fancy-man or anything remotely like it. He's a friend, a platonic friend, that's all.'

'Have you told Jim about him then?' Brenda said.

'That's it!' Alison snapped. 'That is it!'

'She didn't mean it, Ally,' Jack said.

'Oh aye, she did,' said Brenda.

'I didn't think it would be you who drove me out, Jack,' Alison said. 'I just hope you remember to tell Henry *that* when I've gone.'

'Here, you're not goin' to do anythin' daft, are you?' Jack said.

'On the contrary,' Alison said. 'I'm going to do something very sensible, something I should have done years ago, in fact.'

'Eh?' said Jack again.

'I'm leaving.'

'Good,' said Brenda.

'I don't mean here. I mean getting out, getting away from all of you.'

'Alison, you can't.'

'Watch me,' Alison said.

'Goin' to stay with your fancy-man then?' said Brenda.

Alison caught the end of her scarf and with a flick of the wrist flung the loose ends up around her throat. She had on her aloof look again, that assured expression which had always driven Brenda crazy.

'Perhaps I will,' Alison said. 'Perhaps I will at that.'

Jack reached to grab her sleeve but as he did so Bee slipped in his arms and he was obliged to use both hands to steady the child.

He called out, 'Alison, wait,' but by that time his sister had stepped into the open doorway. *'Alison!'*

'Oh, let her go, for God's sake.' Brenda ended her husband's attempts at peace-making by kicking shut the door. 'An' good bloody riddance.'

Jack stared at the metal cage of the letterbox. 'Oh, Jeeze, Brenda, do you reckon she means it?'

'If I had a fancy-man . . .' Brenda began then, glancing at the child in her arms, changed her mind and closed off the sentence with a little grunt. 'Naw, I don't reckon she means it. But I think we'd better get round to 162 as fast as we can.'

'What for?' said Jack.

'Just in case I'm wrong,' Brenda said and, still carrying her daughter, padded into the kitchenette in search of tea, toast and a cigarette before the rush to get ready began.

As a whistler Jim Abbott was not in the same league as his brother-in-law-to-be. None the less he would whistle 'Cheerful Little Earful' whenever he was feeling chirpy which was usually the case on Sunday afternoon when he walked down from Macarthur Drive to the Burnsides' house for high tea and an evening *en famille* with his beloved Alison.

Alison would have been galled to learn that Jim actually thought of her as 'his beloved'. The phrase was not only possessive but had an undertone of Victorian sentimentality which was not something Alison would care to associate with a man she had once admired for his down-to-earth approach to education.

Love had not robbed Jim of his perspicacity, however. He was well aware that Alison regarded him as a bit of an old fogey and that she was less than enchanted by his refusal to sweep her into the shrubbery for something more memorable than a heart-warming cuddle. Resistance to Alison's charms did not become any easier as the months trundled by. He longed to have her long, lithe body lying naked under him and, if only Alison had known it, frequently struggled against sudden urges to take what was due to him now, without benefit of clergy.

On Cullen sands in the blistering heat of an August afternoon, for instance, he had been driven almost to distraction by a glimpse of salt seawater glistening on the fine pale brown hairs of Alison's inner thighs. She had asked him to dry her back. He had done so reluctantly, dabbing the towel on her shoulder-blades and stroking it up into the little beard of wet hair that had escaped her bathing cap. His state of arousal had not escaped her attention and she had kissed him there in the open, in public, had tried to insinuate her tongue into his mouth. He had been forced to pull away before he forgot himself completely and lost control.

Later, at teatime, seated at the boarding-house table, he'd felt quite dizzy as he'd watched her scoffing fish pie, sipping cider from a tall glass and chatting away to Henry and Trudi, their holiday chaperones, as if she was unaware of how desirable she looked in her flimsy summer dress.

Later still, he'd kissed her goodnight. Tucked into the fronds of a withered aspidistra on the first-floor landing, lapped by the persistent odour of kippers and warm old wallpaper, he had allowed her tongue into his mouth, had felt it shiver, glossy wet and inquisitive, against his own until, again, he had separated himself from her and had stepped back, trembling, to light a cigarette. She'd vanished, slamming her bedroom door, before he'd blown out the match.

Henry, in pyjamas, had immediately stuck his head out of an adjacent bedroom door and had said, 'Everything okay, Jim?'

'Fine, fine. Just off now, Henry. Goodnight.'

'Where's Alison?'

'Gone up.'

'Good. Goodnight then, Jim. Another nice day tomorrow?'

'We live in hope,' he'd said.

As a rule hope was enough.

He did not intrude into what went on at university beyond asking a few questions about the professors' teaching methods. In the early days Alison could hardly wait to be with him of an evening, to walk the streets of Flannery Park or, on wet nights, to sit in an upstairs booth in Ferraro's Café drinking endless cups of coffee and blethering on about the content of her day. Jim had listened attentively, and had forgotten nothing.

After the first term or two, however, Alison no longer seemed to feel the need to confide in him. Jim was caution personified. He did not pry. He knew how important it was to give her breathing space. By the end of the third summer term she had given up talking about her university friends entirely. She lived with textbooks on surgery, ophthalmology, human embryology but, Jim noticed, she no longer seemed to need to cram raw facts into her head with the same urgency as before.

'Do you understand all this?' he'd asked, thumbing through a manual on operative surgery.

'Most of it, yes,' Alison had answered. 'Why?'

'How much of this sort of thing have you done?'

'Surgery? A couple of terms. Systematic and clinical.'

'With the knives? On patients?'

'Oh, yes. Under supervision, of course.'

'You didn't tell me.'

'Didn't I? Well, I didn't think you'd be interested. Pretty boring, really.'

Then he'd known for sure that she was leaving him behind and he could only pray that in time she would come back to him.

Sometimes he felt more comfortable with her brothers and in-laws than he did with Alison. Sometimes he felt that all he really wanted was what Henry had, or Jack, or even Alex with his blowsy, big-hearted wife to look after him. None of these feelings and doubts did Jim confess to anyone, certainly not to Alison. He taught school every weekday, saw Alison when she could spare the time, attended church on Sunday mornings and took tea at the Burnsides' house on Sunday evenings. And still he managed to whistle as he walked there, in the hope that things would work out in the long run, that his patience and his virtue would eventually be rewarded.

As soon as he entered number 162 on that drizzling October afternoon, however, Jim sensed that something was wrong.

Everyone was standing about with teacups in hand and mournful expressions on their faces. Only the dog, the twins and Davy were absent which meant that, rain or no rain, Davy had been sent out to

31

trundle his nieces about the streets and keep them out of the way for a while.

Jim said, 'Where's Alison?'

Trudi untied her frilly apron and put it behind her on to a chair. The big table crammed into the window bay had not been set yet. Tea was being served from the old brown pot, in cups without saucers, which was very unusual for a Sunday.

Jim said again, 'Where's Alison? What's happened?'

'No, no, she's okay,' said Henry. 'Not ill, I mean.'

'Tell him, for God's sake,' Bertie said.

'She's – Alison's gone,' said Henry.

'Walked out,' said Bertie. 'Packed her bag an' flounced out.'

'I see,' Jim said. 'Did she give a reason?'

'She seemed to have a lot of reasons, son,' Alex Burnside said. 'She did a fair bit o' shoutin'. I couldn't make much sense of it, m'self.'

'Balderdash!' Bertie plumped himself down in the smoker's chair by the fire. 'You know why she went. You just don't want to admit she's turned out to be the spoiled bitch I always said she was.' He was a small man, excessively prissy and neat, with sharp features and gold-rimmed glasses. 'Somebody'd better tell him. He's supposed to be her fiancé, after all.'

The upper part of Jim's left arm, the stump, had begun to throb, something that hadn't occurred in a good ten years. He reached across his chest, clasped the fold of the empty sleeve and squeezed it tightly.

'It would seem,' Trudi told him, 'that there is involved a man.'

'A lover,' Bertie crowed. 'She's run off with her lover.'

'Bertie, shut your mouth.' Alex thrust a balled fist into his son's face. 'Or I'll shut it for you.'

'Alex, Alex.' Ruby patted him soothingly. 'It's not Bertie's fault.'

'Maybe not. But that wee bugger's snide remarks are beginnin' to get on my wick,' Alex shouted. 'If you can't say anythin' conductive, Bertie, then just keep your lip buttoned.'

'Aye,' Jack added.

'You keep out of it, Jack,' Brenda said. 'It's got nothin' to do with you.'

Alex Burnside had the build of a bantam-weight, with big square hands and a head that seemed just a shade too large for his body. To Jim's knowledge, he had never been a Clydeside hard man, though his features were scarred and, at some point, his nose had been broken. Now, flushed with temper, the pocking stood out vividly and he looked almost savage.

'It's got everythin' to do with Jack,' Alex shouted. 'If Jack hadn't seen her none o' this would've happened an' Ally would still be here.'

Jim sighed, released his throbbing arm, pulled out a dining chair and seated himself upon it.

Trudi said, 'Are you all right, Jim?'

'Yes, I'm fine. I just want somebody to tell me what's going on.'

'That's reasonable,' Alex said. 'Thank God somebody's got some sense.'

'Henry,' Trudi commanded, 'you will tell Jim what has happened.'

'Right,' Henry said and, crouching a little, whispered the tale of his sister's downfall into the ear of her betrothed.

Back in the big house of Kerridge – a building set so far into the Wicklow hills that it was hard to find when sober on a clear summer's morning/let alone drunk in the dark depths of winter – Declan Slater might be considered the wildest young rover who ever walked the sod but even he drew the line at murdering a cat.

Declan had been branded a 'black sheep' at a remarkably early age and had done everything he could to justify the slur as he grew in wisdom and stature. By the time he was fifteen he had been expelled from two Catholic boarding-schools and denounced as an incorrigible case. He was also the terror of his little home town and the defenceless hamlets round it, as well as a thorn in the flesh of the family O'Gilligan of Kerridge and all its cousins and cadets. He had been whipped by priests, belted by his Catholic uncles, thumped by his brothers, shrieked at by his sisters, prayed over by his mother and written off by every last one of them. Except, of course, his dear old Da in whose view Declan was the only true son of Slater and the apple of the old man's Protestant eye.

Mixed marriages were a curse. The O'Gilligans would have as soon handed Kerridge over to a man from the planet Mars as to a Protestant. If the lovely Theresa hadn't been so infatuated with the man they would never have condoned the union. Patrick Slater himself was the son of a marriage which had leapt the great gulf of religious prejudice and nobody knew for sure whether his soul, if he had one, was tinted a nasty orange or proper kelly green.

As the youngest child of the marriage, half the time Declan didn't know who he was either. He had two sisters in the Convent of St Clare and a brother studying for the priesthood, ransom enough to fortune as far as he and his Da were concerned.

Sometimes he, Declan, was all Da, all Protestant. And sometimes the saintly seed of the O'Gilligans infected him with fits of decency. But whether he was acting out the part of Bad Boy Slater or was undergoing one of his rare bouts of Catholic conscience he wasn't wicked enough to kill a cat in cold blood.

The beast was dead when he found it. It lay against the kerbstone of the corner by St Anne's, dusty but otherwise intact and just begging to be salvaged before dogs or urchins got to it and left nothing but a half-chewed tail or a scrag-end of backbone. Within seconds of spotting the corpse, Declan was into the house and out again. After a glance up and down the street, he had slipped the cadaver into an oilskin bag and, carrying it in his arms like a baby, had it on the slab by the kitchen sink in the basement before you could say 'Knife!'

He was relieved to discover that the cat, a male, had been dead for no more than an hour or two. Age perhaps had killed it for there was no wound or swelling to indicate external trauma. He would find out for sure once he'd separated head from body and commenced a preliminary dissection.

From a secondhand bookshop Declan had acquired a volume of coloured diagrams of farm and domestic animals, the parts of which were tabbed in on dainty folds of card so that the veterinary student, or the interested child, might do a little bit of bloodless surgery. He had found the book useful during first year zoology but had hardly opened it since. Now he hastily looked up the appropriate section and propped the book open, side by side with Cunningham's *Practical Anatomy* and Moore's *Medical Ophthalmology.*

Next he cleared the remains of what had passed for supper from the wooden table and lugged from the corner a reading lamp on a long, dusty flex. He placed the lamp carefully on the tabletop and spread beneath it an oblong of waxcloth to which he gently transferred the cat. He fished his dissecting case from under the bed and, with a sigh of anticipation, opened it.

He wasn't thinking of Ally Burnside now or of the run of bad luck Da had had with the Autumn Double at Newmarket. All his cares vanished at the sight of the surgical instruments, so clean and functional. Ebony-handled scalpels, sharp scissors, forceps, needles, a skin-grafting razor which he used for all kinds of work, both coarse and fine.

Dr Flynn, back home in Kerridge, had presented him with the kit. Dr Flynn had told him how much fun it was to be a doctor and how there was a fortune waiting in medicine for a honey-tongued young Irishman. Dr Flynn had also told him how being a doctor put you in the way of meeting a sackful of grand-looking women who were only too eager to take off their clothes for you, out of surgery hours, of course.

But Declan wasn't thinking of Seamus Flynn either that Sunday night in Walbrook Street. His attention was focused on the cat, on the eyes in particular.

Optical anatomy was so delicate, the nomenclature so poetic – the pillars of iris, the spaces of fontana – that Yeats himself couldn't have dreamed up anything more lyrical. Declan intended to rehearse his surgical skills by carefully picking apart the minute network of ligaments which held the eyeballs in place, for the intricacies of ophthalmology intrigued him.

He wouldn't keep the cat long. He didn't want the smell to draw Mrs McCusker's attention to what was going on in her basement. He would work half the night if necessary and, when he was done, he would wrap the remains in brown paper, plop the parcel into the river, cross himself and say a bit of a prayer for the poor beast's soul.

Meanwhile, he had work to do.

He rummaged in the cupboard by the sink, found and put on a pair of medium-weight black rubber postmortem gloves. He fished out a bottle too, uncorked it with his teeth and took a pull of whisky to brace himself. Placing the bottle on the table, he lifted the razor, peered at the veterinary diagram for a moment then systematically began to shave a collar of fur from the cat's gullet.

He had just begun to hum his happy little work-song, 'The Rose of Tralee', when a knock sounded upon the door.

Declan froze.

Grey fur adhered to the razor's edge and tufts floated like thistledown in the lamplight. The cat's yellow eyes stared up at him, dull as lentils, and the line of worn teeth seemed suddenly like a grin.

Soundlessly Declan set down the razor.

Another rap. 'I know you're in there, Declan.'

'Who is it?'

'It's me, of course. Are you or are you not going to let me in?'

'Hold on, hold on.'

A romantic vision of the girl and he bent over the oilcloth in the island of light from the lamp, finding love, like the Curies, in shared experiments, flashed into his mind. Oh, God, no! He might be a bit of a loony, but *that* much of a loony he was not. He knew only too well how a female would react to the sight of a pussy-cat lying dead on the supper table.

'I'm not waiting out here all night, you know.'

'All right, all right.'

Swiftly he folded the edges of the oilcloth over the corpse and stuffed the bundle under the table. He flung the razor into the box, clamped down the lid, shot it across the lino out of sight. He pulled off the gloves, flung them into a corner then, waving his arms to

35

disperse the cat hair, nipped nimbly to the door. Slipping the bolt and fixing a smile, he said, 'Mam'selle, what a pleasant surprise.'

'What have you been up to?'

'Not a thing.'

'Have you been drinking?'

'Just a wee snifter,' he said, 'to stave off the chill of a lonely Sunday evenin'. Talking of which, it's a bit astonishin' to see you here.'

'Do you wish me to go?'

'Now why would I wish that?'

'I thought perhaps you were expecting someone else.'

'The like of who?'

She did not answer him. She sniffed. 'What's that smell?'

'Lord knows,' Declan said. 'It takes an educated nose to separate one smell from another down here. Will you not be takin' your coat off?'

She looked at the books propped open beneath the lamp.

Holding his breath, Declan waited for her to peer under the table. He was vastly relieved when she slipped out of her coat and removed her hat then held them out for him to take away.

He said, 'I thought Sunday night meant dinner with the folks?'

'I've had enough of "the folks" for one weekend,' she said. 'It's cold in here. Poke up the fire. I'll make us tea.'

'That'll be fine,' Declan said. 'But first tell me why you're really here. I thought we'd had a fallin' out.'

'Whatever gave you that idea?'

'A certain coolness in the manner of late.'

'I've been thinking about it,' she said.

'About what?' Declan said.

'Us.'

She was no different from the farm girls behind Mulrooney's tavern or the flirtatious young whores of Dublin town. He had thought her shy but he had been wrong about that. She was merely, and rightly, cautious. Everything she did seemed governed by reason. But some things, apparently, were beyond reason. He would have preferred to spend the evening with the cat. Still, he was never one to look a gift horse in the mouth and it wasn't every night a girl dropped in unannounced.

She wore a pleated skirt that displayed the contour of her hips and thighs, a white blouse with a frilled collar fastened at the neck by a little pearl brooch. He could see the scalloped edge of her underskirt and the straps of her brassière. When she turned towards the sink he wiped his hands on the back of his trousers and stepped against her.

'Isn't it this that you want?' He pressed against her and cupped her breasts gently. 'Is it not this you came for?'

She eased against him and arched her back.

'Yes,' she said. 'Yes, Declan, dearest.'

'Now?' he asked.

'Yes,' she said, 'but kiss me first, if you please.'

'With pleasure,' Declan said and, the cat forgotten, backed her against the edge of the sink and kissed her full on the mouth.

Rain had dwindled with the coming of night. St Anne's faithful few had dispersed homeward after evening service and Walbrook Street was quieter than ever. Even the sounds of footsteps on the pavement seemed muffled by the clothlike air.

'I don't really like this,' Jack said. 'You know, if Ally isn't here we're gonna look a right pair of mugs.'

'It's the logical place to start,' Jim said.

'I suppose so,' Jack said. 'But I'm havin' second thoughts about it.'

'Bit late for that now, old son,' Jim said.

'You're takin' this very calmly.'

'What choice do I have?' said Jim Abbott. 'Which house?'

'That one.'

'Are you sure?'

'Positive.'

'All right, here we go.'

The only light in the communal hall came from an old gas-mantle which burned with a furious hissing noise. The hall was empty. Two doors on floor level. At the rear a black iron railing curved down into darkness. On the left, hidden by an awkward corner, stairs climbed to a landing beyond which the landlady had her billet.

'I don't know which room he's in,' Jack whispered.

'I think I remember Alison saying something about the basement.'

'Down there, you mean?'

'Unless you prefer to ask the landlady?'

'God, no,' Jack said. 'She's a flamin' holy terror. I'm not goin' near her.'

'All right,' Jim said. 'We'll start downstairs.'

Eight steps led down to a narrow corridor. Just sufficient light to grope to the door. Jim struck a match.

Stuck to the frame of the door was a laboratory label with the word *Slater* printed upon it in faded green ink.

'That's him.' Jim leaned against the door and listened.

'What?' Jack said. 'Is she in there?'

Although it had been his suggestion that they search for Alison in Walbrook Street, until that moment Jim Abbott had been convinced that they were here on a wild good chase. He had been irked by the haste with which the Burnsides had leapt to the worst possible conclusion and he had intended to prove them wrong.

Only he knew that Alison had two hundred pounds salted away in a bank account, money inherited from her grandmother and added to what she had won for the Tuxford Prize. He suspected that Alison had enough to live on for a year or eighteen months and might, if she wished, sever all family connections. Now, as he stood by the basement door and picked up soft sounds from within he experienced a sudden fear that he had misjudged Alison completely and might already have lost her to another man.

'I think we've found her,' he said.

'She's in there with him, isn't she?' Jack whispered. 'I was right?'

'Yes, it seems you were.'

'I'm sorry,' Jack said. 'I really am.'

Jim knocked on the student's door.

'Alison, may I have a word with you, please,' he called out.

Scuffles, a little yelp, a grating noise, a long pause.

Jack put his hand on Jim's shoulder and swayed forward.

The door opened an inch.

The face was unmistakably Irish, not so much a stereotype as a distinctive variation on all that one had ever imagined an Irishman to be. Dark curly hair, jet black eyes and a pixilated shape to the features.

'Who the hell are you?' he said.

'I'm Jim Abbott. I'd like a word with Alison, please.'

'Alison isn't here. Sorry.'

He made to close the door again but Jack had gripped the handle and a brief tug-of-war ensued. Declan Slater was the first to give in.

'Look,' he said, 'sure an' I do know who you are. You're the fiancé? But you've gotten the wrong end of the stick. I've seen nothing of Alison since Friday. I'm in here with a friend.'

Jim said, 'May I speak with your friend?'

'No, you may not.'

'Let him in, Decker,' said a voice from within the room. 'I mean to say, we're not doing anything wrong.'

Reluctantly Declan Slater allowed the door to swing open.

The girl was seated at a table with two or three textbooks propped in front of her and a glass of what looked like whisky and water. She was a very pretty girl if, Jim thought, a little on the plump side.

'Look around if you wish,' the girl said. 'Alison positively isn't here.'

Jim said, 'You're Roberta, aren't you?'

'That's neither here nor there,' Roberta Logie told him. 'I'm not your Ally-Pally and that, I presume, is what counts.'

'It is.' Jim bowed graciously. 'Sorry to have disturbed you.'

'It's quite all right,' the girl said and, putting her fingers to her throat, repinned the clasp of the pearl brooch that held her blouse at the collar.

With nothing more friendly than a nod, Declan closed the door.

Jack and Jim climbed out of the half-basement and left the house.

Jack let out his breath, blowing hard.

'Dear God!' he exclaimed. 'What a bloomer! No wonder Ally was mad.'

'No wonder, indeed,' Jim said, wondering just how much madder Alison would be when she discovered that Mr Declan Slater and the young woman she called her friend were studying anatomy together.

'Now what?' Jack said.

'Home,' Jim said.

'But where's Alison?'

'Home,' Jim said again.

When Jim knocked tentatively on the bedroom door Alison paused then said, 'If that's you, Trudi, go away.'

'It's Jim. Are you decent?'

'That seems to be a matter still very much in doubt.'

'May I come in?'

She paused again. 'Yes.'

He opened the door and put his head around it.

She didn't look up, tried not to appear either guilty or contrite. Although she was in bed she had left both the desk lamp and bedhead light on, had a cardigan draped over her shoulders and a book propped against her knees. Somehow she'd expected Jim to find her here and was gratified that he hadn't let her down on that score at least.

'Don't hover, for goodness sake,' she said. 'I'm not going to bite you.'

'Are you still cross?'

'I wasn't cross,' Alison said. 'I was furious. And, no, I'm not. Not with you at any rate.'

'You gave us all a scare.'

'That was the idea,' Alison said. 'No, I take that back. I really did intend to run away.'

'To sea,' Jim said, 'like Walter Giffard?'

'Huh! Fine cabin-boy I'd make.'

'Oh, I don't know.'

39

She saw that he was self-conscious and trying to hide it. He leaned against the wall by the half-open door, hand in his pocket.

It was the first time Jim had set foot in Alison's bedroom. He had glanced into it now and then when he'd been visiting the bathroom across the landing, had glimpsed the dressing-table-cum-desk in the corner, the books and study notes all neatly arranged on shelves to the right of the mirror, the single floor-length curtain on the narrow window. But he had never seen the bed before. Or Alison in it. He felt a stirring again, a strange tumescent echo of the feelings he'd had when he'd glimpsed the blonde-haired girl in Declan Slater's basement.

Alison wore her hornrims and had loosed her hair. The cardigan was draped over her nightdress to cover the exposed flesh across the top of her breasts. It hadn't occurred to Jim before just how cramped the room would be. One chair, the carpentered desk, shelves, the bed. He presumed her clothes were kept in a trunk beneath the bed. Only the warm light made the room bearable.

Alison closed the textbook and tossed it away from her legs. She was aware that Jim was not only curious about her room but about her too, that he was studying her with more than casual interest.

She patted the quilt. 'If you're going to give me a dressing-down, perhaps you should take the weight off.' She sensed his reluctance. 'What do you want, Jim, written permission? I imagine somebody downstairs sent you to placate me, so you can take it that they trust you not to do me wrong.'

'You certainly gave them a turn.' Jim slid on to the edge of the bed and braced himself, one leg crossed over the other. 'As a matter of interest, just where did you go?'

'Ferraro's.' Alison made a sour face. 'Egg and chips and two pots of tea and I was ready to admit I'd made a mistake. Actually, having never left home before, I had no idea where to go.'

'You could have come to my place.'

'Not, I think, in the mood I was in.'

'You'll have heard, of course, that Jack and I were scouring the countryside for you.'

'Dad told me, yes.'

'Guess,' Jim said, 'who we bumped into?'

'If you made a beeline for Walbrook Street, which is just what you would do,' Alison said, 'I imagine you might have met Declan Slater. What did you do to him? Box his ears and warn him to leave me alone?'

'Nothing so crude,' Jim said. 'He seems a decent enough chap.'

'Don't patronise him,' Alison said, 'or me, for that matter.'

40

'Sorry.'

'Did you talk with him?'

'Only a word or two.'

Jim hesitated. If he was going to tell Alison that Slater had had a woman with him then it would be best to do it now. He had warned Jack to say nothing. Jack, once bitten, would probably be too embarrassed to say anything at all to Alison for the next few weeks and would do his best to avoid her. It had been, after all, just a storm in a teacup. But it hadn't blown itself out yet. And Jim had a notion that further squalls might be gathering on the horizon.

'He didn't seem all that pleased to see us,' Jim Abbott said, tactfully.

'Why? Was someone with him?'

She wrapped both arms around her knees and studied him in a way that she knew was uncharacteristically coy and Jim, for a moment, could not bring himself to answer her question. From what did he think he was protecting her? Hurt, disappointment, female treachery perhaps?

'A girl?' she prompted. 'Blonde? On the fat side?'

Jim nodded.

'Huh!' Alison uncoiled her legs and threw herself back against the pillows. She felt no strong emotion, only a trace of self-congratulatory smugness at the fact that she'd guessed right, had not been deceived by Roberta's duplicity. 'I *knew* she was lying. *I knew* Bobs wanted him for herself. I shouldn't have been taken in by her nonsense. It was Roberta, wasn't it?'

Jim nodded once more, then said, 'Are you jealous of her, Alison?'

'Me? Why should I be jealous of Roberta?'

'Because you're engaged to me and can't . . .' He fashioned a diffident gesture with his hand.

'Can't what?' said Alison.

'Compete, I suppose.'

'Compete over some Irish bloke? I thought you knew me better than that.' Alison said. 'I've enough to do on Gilmorehill without becoming involved in silly mating games.'

'I'm not so sure they are silly. Mating games, I mean.'

'Jim Abbott! I'm surprised at you.'

Deliberately he stretched out his foot and pushed the door closed. He leaned across the bed, put his arm about her, drew her to him and kissed her. He felt her stiffen. He wondered if he had overdone it, if he had roused her resentment. In fact he had no clear indicator as to what she felt towards him any more. She had retreated into those labyrinths, those cyprian depths which no man, however

41

sympathetic and understanding, could hope to penetrate. He could not pursue her. He could only wait, wait with dreadful and uncertain patience for her to emerge again.

Alison pulled away and peered at him myopically. She was stirred by the sexual tension in him, relieved that she could, after all, rouse longing in him. Perhaps all her practice with Declan Slater had not been in vain.

'I know what you're thinking,' she whispered.

'It isn't hard to guess.'

'You're thinking what a silly cow I am to make all this fuss over nothing.'

Astonished, Jim opened his mouth to protest and might have blurted out something he would immediately regret if Alison had not flung her arms about his neck and pulled him down on top of her, kissing him with an abandon that he thought just a bit too playful to be entirely sincere.

'Well,' she said, 'I am. A silly cow, I mean.'

From just across the landing came the sound of a flushing lavatory and someone, probably Bertie, breaking wind.

'Oh, God! How romantic!' Alison said and with a rueful sigh rolled away.

Jim too gave a little grunt of laughter, not unmingled with relief. He hoisted himself on to his elbow and slid from the bed. He looked down at her, slender and long-bodied, like an odalisque. He tucked his hand decently behind him, stooped and kissed her once more, on the brow not the lips this time.

'Are you all right now, Alison?'

'Yes,' she said. 'I just wish they'd leave me alone, that's all.'

'Does that include yours truly?' Jim Abbott asked.

'Without you . . .' she began, then turned on her side, framed her face with her hands and fixed him with a seriousness which was almost convincing. 'Why would I want anyone else when I have you?'

Even to Alison her response seemed as facile as dialogue in a novel or from one of those dreary West End plays that wended up to the King's in the summer and autumn season; drawing-room dramas which were supposed to be sophisticated but seemed to her merely silly and remote, full of languorous posturing and brittle responses and lacking in genuine emotion. What was it she'd just asked Jim? Her rhetorical question demanded only one answer. She resented the need for this sly and painful conversational nonsense, this flirting, this lying. Words were too simple to convey what she wanted from Jim Abbott now, actions not simple enough.

Jim took in a breath. 'Why indeed?'

42

She shook her head very, very slightly, as if his reply had somehow confirmed her worst suspicions.

'Goodnight, darling,' she said, a little too curtly.

'Goodnight, dearest,' Jim answered, and slipped away downstairs to report to the heads of the family that all appeared to be well again with their precious Princess Alison.

And Alison, left alone, was just glad that it hadn't been worse.

TWO

Union Debate

Walking into Fitzgerald Street public health clinic in Partick South was like walking into bedlam. Mandatory attendances at the 'Fitz' by fourth-year medical students for the purposes of obtaining certificates of vaccination from the Public Health Authority were regarded if not as a joke certainly as something to be undertaken with tongue placed lightly in cheek.

Smallpox might have diminished as a threat to the community but there were mothers enough concerned for the welfare of their children to fill the waiting room with bawling infants and white-faced seven-year-olds. Public Health officers, nurses and doctors had their hands quite full enough without the arrival every Monday and Thursday of a group of not-quite-competent students.

It did not take long for God's answers to Hippocrates to realise, however, that they would not be standing behind tables as mere protectors of the little vials of glycerinated calf lymph and swabs of antiseptic alcohol but that they, with only a modest amount of instruction, would also be pitched into the fray.

The three members of the team who had drawn the short straw for the Fitz that Monday midday were Declan, Alison and Roberta.

The air between the girls remained frosty and their behaviour towards Declan veered between sarcasm and an obsequiousness which casual observers found puzzling. Declan, of course, loved every minute of it. He swaggered around with a fatuous grin and when pressed by Howard to 'tell all' simply lowered his eyelashes, touched his forefinger tips to his cheeks and murmured, 'Blush, blush,' which, maddeningly, was all the boys could wring from him.

It did not seem to occur to Mr Slater that the rules by which this game was played in the west of Scotland were very different from those he had learned in Wicklow. Nor did it seem to strike Alison and Roberta that they were making fools of themselves.

'Let me help you off with your jacket, Declan.'

'Do you have enough soap, Declan?'

'A piece of chocolate before we start, Declan?'

'Here, Declan, let me take the paper off for you.'

'Don't you have a clean towel there?'

'Take mine.'

'No, take mine.'

The child was dressed in a soiled vest and shorts. He came, barefoot, to the half-open door of the cloakroom in which the students were washing their hands. He was about seven years old, with spindly limbs, large ears and a shaved head. He carried the street with him, pavement dirt engrained into his feet, mud and tar daubing his shins. His presence in the staffroom seemed to indicate an impudence of the sort that went with bare feet and cropped hair.

With two squares of Fry's peppermint chocolate stuck in his cheek, Declan was drying his hands on a towel when the child appeared. He glanced round and enquired sharply, 'Well, what do *you* want?'

'You shouldn't be here, sonny,' Roberta said.

'Yeah, shove off back to Mama,' Declan said.

In the grainy light from the cloakroom window Alison studied the boy curiously. He in turn continued to stare at Declan without greed or curiosity, one hand clutching the crotch of his stained grey shorts.

'He needs the toilet,' Alison said.

'Well, this isn't a toilet,' Roberta said. 'And it certainly isn't a toilet for the likes of him. Go away, boy.'

The child did not seem to recognise their authority over him. Only when Alison crouched down by him did he blink and flinch, very slightly, away.

'It's all right,' she said softly. 'I'll take you to the toilet.'

She offered her hand. The little boy's shoulders retracted and his lip worked against his gums. Alison had a flash of memory: Sutton Street, ragged urchins, herself among them, all unconscious of what they were or what they might become. She saw into the boy's past as clearly as if it was her own and experienced a flicker of shame at what he represented.

'Roberta, the chocolate.'

'What?'

'What's left, give me the chocolate.'

'I'll do nothing of the . . .'

'Give me the damned chocolate, will you?'

Reluctantly Roberta fished in her pocket and produced four squares of dark brown chocolate. She dropped them into Alison's outstretched hand, watched Ally strip off the wrappings and hold the

46

titbit out between finger and thumb. The boy stared at it dumbly.

Alison, saying nothing, brushed the sweetmeat against his lips. Abruptly he opened his mouth and allowed her to place the chocolate on his tongue. The tongue curled inward and the chocolate vanished. Stringy little cheek muscles hollowed as he sucked, and a trickle of brown saliva escaped from the corner of his mouth.

It was, Roberta thought, like watching the feeding of a creature only partly tamed.

'How can you *do* that?' she said.

Alison dabbed away the dribble with her handkerchief and said, 'Because he isn't right in the head.'

'Lice,' Roberta said. 'Of course.'

'I don't think that's what she means,' Declan said.

'Mental abnormality,' said Alison. 'To what degree . . .' She shrugged, got to her feet and held out her hand. 'Come on, son. Never mind them. I'll take you to the toilet. Pee-pee? Okay?'

The boy jerked out his arm and allowed Alison to lead him along the corridor.

Roberta and Declan exchanged glances.

From the waiting-room came the wails of infants and from the hall beyond the cries of young children as little arms were scarified and droplets of lymph rubbed into the skin.

'We'd better report in,' said Declan, at length.

And Roberta, only a little chastened, agreed.

'What happened to the fancy-man, then?' Brenda said.

'Oh, apparently he fancied somebody else.'

'Because you wouldn't give him what he wanted?'

'Something like that,' said Alison.

'Was he, you know, nice?'

'He still is,' said Alison.

'Must be a lot of good-lookin' blokes up at the university,' Brenda said.

'Hundreds of them.'

'I wish it was me,' Brenda said.

'You, what?'

'I wish I had, you know, your opportunities.'

'What's wrong with what you've got?'

'Jack's okay, I suppose.'

'And these?' Alison bent to kiss Lexi on the brow.

'They're okay too,' Brenda admitted.

They were seated on armchairs flanking the coal fire.

The chair's cheap moquette was already threadbare. Alison found

47

its sagging springs comfortable, though, for somehow they seemed shaped to make you part of them. An oilskin groundsheet puddled with water and a zinc bath occupied the rug at her feet. Snug in pink flannel nighties Lexi lay asleep in Alison's arms, Bee in Brenda's.

'What did you come round for?' Brenda said.

'I just dropped in to see how the girls were.'

'I didn't think you'd be, you know, speakin' to us.'

'Do you blame me for being annoyed?' Alison said. 'Nobody likes to be accused of something they didn't do.'

'An' you didn't do it?' Brenda said.

Alison shook her head.

Brenda said, 'What'd you run away for then?'

'I didn't run away,' said Alison. 'I took the huff, that's all. Am I not entitled to take the huff now and then?'

Brenda chuckled. 'Aye, I suppose you are.'

Alison's nieces had forgotten their aunt's tantrum. They had welcomed her with wet, wide-open arms, had duly sprayed and soaked her and had even managed to drop her reading-glasses into the bath while she'd helped Brenda to towel them down and dress them for bed. They were a pampered pair all right, playful and preening. Nevertheless, Alison had stood each in turn upon her knee and, while they'd wriggled and pirouetted and had generally showed off, had peered into their eyes and discreetly examined their joints and the curvature of their spines.

She had no reason to suppose that Bee or Lexi were defective, physically or mentally. They stemmed from sturdy stock and had been born without trauma. Even so, all afternoon she'd been distracted by unwarranted anxiety. Her meeting with the little boy – who shared a name with her brother, Jack – had disturbed her. Also her encounter with his mother, a young, dull-witted woman with a six-week-old infant in her arms.

'Och, there y'are, Jackie,' the young woman had said. 'Have y'done it?'

The baby too had been poorly clad, the woman shawled. The boy had clung to his mother, unperturbed by the steaming kettles, needles and scissors which glinted on the doctor's table. He had been so indrawn that Alison had questioned the woman about him. By way of answer she'd received short shrift.

'Nothin' wrang wi' oor Jackie, sure an' there's no', son?'

'Have you been to see your doctor about him?'

'Them doctors are no fur free, but.'

'Is that why you bring him here?'

'Aye, tae mak' him weel.'

48

'Do you think a smallpox vaccination will make him well?'

'Naw, but it might help him no' tae dee.' Drawing Jackie tight to her side, she had pointedly turned her back on Alison.

Alison had been both touched and angered by the woman's refusal to admit that her son was mentally impaired. She had completed her stint at the clinic with a strange feeling of helplessness.

Only in Brenda's house, cradling Brenda's children, did she find relief from her depression.

Brenda said, 'Do you ever hear from, you know, Walter?'

'Why should I hear from Walter?'

'I thought maybe Jim had said somethin' about him.'

'No,' Alison said. 'Why don't you ask Jack? He works in the same firm as Walter's father, doesn't he?'

'Jack? Don't be daft. I couldn't ask Jack about Walter.'

There was something consoling about Brenda's schoolgirl nostalgia. From the first Alison had found the study of medicine fascinating but it was only recently – today in the Fitz, in fact – that she'd had a glimpse of how heavy its burdens might be. She needed reminders of the old, innocent life to hang on to, and Brenda could always be relied upon to provide them.

'Last I heard,' Alison said, 'Wattie was still at sea.'

'Aye, he was always at sea, that one,' said Brenda, ruefully. 'With you an' with me. Do you ever think about him?'

'I can't say I do.'

'What would you do if he turned up again?'

'I don't think there's much danger,' Alison said. 'Anyhow, I expect he's dropped anchor with dozens of other girls by this time.'

'Dropped anchor,' Brenda said. 'I like that.' She was quiet for half a minute, looking down at Bee whose head had sunk so low against her chest that she resembled a little hedgehog curled up for the winter. 'God, I'm dyin' for a ciggie, so I am.'

'Why don't we put them down in their cot?'

'Jack'll do it when he gets back. He shouldn't be long.'

They were quiet then, the girls, sitting by the fire, the twins on their laps. Brenda was thinking of cigarettes and perhaps of Walter Giffard, her long-lost love, Alison of other things, more solemn and immediate, while the clock on the mantelshelf ticked lazily and the buses hissed past in the rain.

Roberta's father's name was plain, old-fashioned Robert but for a man of his proud standing Robert wasn't distinctive enough.

He'd changed it soon after he'd left the rain-drenched Isle of Clova, where his father had been a crofter. He, Roberta's father, had come down to the city of Edinburgh with not much more than the clothes on his back and the brains in his head to scratch for an education and, in due course, a niche of sorts in polite society. He had taken as a forename that of his mother's family and for fifty years now had been known to all and sundry as Veitch Logie. Correct pronunciation, as he was frequently called upon to explain, being *Veech*, to rhyme – hah, hah – with *leech*.

This, as far as Roberta could make out, was the only joke her father had ever cracked in his life and it was typical of him to repeat it at every opportunity.

She could hardly blame him, really. Mr Veitch Logie's fame and fortune had been built on professional repetition and his sole claim to originality was to have devised a minor surgical procedure for the more or less painless removal of gallstones. The 'Veitch Process', had long ago been superseded by advances in surgery, of course, but her father still rattled on about it as if he had given his name to a mountain in Tibet or a river in Canada and, over dinner, would describe his caseload of cholecystectomies as if he was still breaking new ground.

'Oh, dear!' Roberta's mother would murmur, as Papa rubbed his long, enthusiastic hands over the soup tureen. 'Please God, not *more* bile.'

Bile, however, was more apparent than tolerance in Veitch Logie's character. It was a mystery how he had managed to woo and win such a beauty as Daphne Stalker, youngest child of a family of famous physicians, one of whom had been knighted by Queen Victoria for services to blood-letting. Veitch, alas, was still waiting to be summoned to the palace.

Roberta had inherited her good looks from Mama who was still pretty enough to turn heads at masonic dances and Chirurgical Society picnics. After twenty-three years of marriage to Veitch, however, Mama had grown rather wispy. Perhaps repetition had something to do with it, for Veitch seldom addressed his wife by name but insisted on calling her 'my angel', a habit Mama condoned without complaint. As she grew older, however, Roberta began to suspect that her mother's meekness was not a virtue but a vice and that Mama was not a victim of but a collaborator in the awful, arid marriage.

For fourteen years Papa had more or less ignored Bobs. He was far too occupied with his work and his hobbies to spare her much attention.

Papa fished, Papa played golf, Papa spent hours in his darkroom developing photographs. Papa was a bigwig in the Barns O' Kelvin

Masonic Lodge and, when he was not too busy, Papa made people well again.

After an interval of seven years two boy babies came along in quick succession and Papa's interest in fatherhood had perked up a little. Males, he reckoned, would carry the name of Logie into the future and would extol the importance of the Veitch Process long after he'd gone to meet his maker. Park School as a day-girl was good enough for Roberta. Boarding at Fettes College was not too good for little Veitch and little Stalker. It did not take long for the horrid truth to emerge. The boys had been born with Mama's brains and Papa's cadaverous looks. In consequence hopes for the medical future of the Logies switched to the distaff side.

One evening, when she was fifteen, Papa had invited Roberta to visit him in his study, something he had never done before. The study lay at the top of the house. It was reached by a steep wooden staircase surmounted by a newel post whose shape Roberta vaguely recognised even then as being less gothic than phallic and whose smooth oval protuberance she had never been able to bring herself to touch. At Mama's insistence, she had worn her school uniform.

The room was poorly lighted. The oriel windows that looked down upon Dowanhill's tennis courts and east to the university tower were heavily curtained, bookshelves and display cabinets glazed with reflections from the desk lamp. Papa was seated in a leather-padded chair behind his formidable desk. He wore his morning coat and a dark grey waistcoat draped with the masonic watch-chain which not even the boys were allowed to play with. His domed forehead shone in the lamplight and, with long fingers bridged beneath his chin, he looked, Roberta thought, more like a gigantic insect than a man.

He made her stand before the desk while he studied her, hands still folded beneath his long, smooth, jutting chin. The skin of his throat had begun to wrinkle, Roberta noticed, not in turkey folds but in strange little crisscross lines, like cracks in plaster. He was sixty-three years old.

'Well, Roberta, I see you are quite grown up.'

'Yes, Papa.'

'You do well at school, I believe, very well.'

'Yes, Papa.'

His gaze slipped over her as if she was a patient upon whom he might soon have to operate. Roberta stood perfectly still. Papa lowered his hands to the desktop and then down into his lap.

'I have something I wish to show you, Roberta,' he said. 'I believe you are old enough not to be shocked.'

'No, Papa.'

'Come, stand by me.'

She obeyed.

The smells of iodine, brandy and tobacco created an aura about him that was both dirty and clean at one and the same time. From a hidden drawer he brought out a folder bound in soft red leather. He placed it on the desk and, glancing up at her, opened it. A photographic enlargement filled the page.

'Do you know what this is, Roberta?'

Without hesitation Roberta answered, 'It's a gallstone.'

'Can you guess where the stone is situated?'

'Is it stuck in the gall-bladder?'

'Indeed, it is. How do you know what a gall-bladder looks like, Roberta?'

'I've heard you talk about it often enough.'

He moved his chair an inch. His shoulder brushed the pleats of her skirt. He turned the page.

Roberta felt blood surge into her cheeks. Sternly, she told herself: He's playing doctors with me. He's jolly well *trying* to embarrass me. Don't let him do it, Bobs. *Don't* let him scare you.

'And this?' Papa asked, mildly.

'I believe it's the female part.'

'Girl or woman?'

'Woman.'

'Why?'

'Because it's hai – hirsute.'

'Quite! Below it, however, is the real object of interest.'

'Swollen knee,' Roberta said. 'Housemaid's knee. Is it bursitis?'

'Good. Very good.' He turned the page again. 'And this?'

'That,' Roberta told him, 'is a male member.'

'How do you know?'

'I've seen – I mean to say – statues, paintings.'

'Does it shock you, Roberta?'

'No, but it doesn't look very nice.' Roberta forced herself to peer, steely-eyed, at the photograph. 'Surely there's something wrong with it? Is it suffering from the disease seamen get?'

Her father raised his eyebrows in surprise. 'Certainly not. Actually, this poor fellow was a shale worker. Regular contact with raw paraffin caused him to develop a tumour of the scrotum. Squamous epithelioma is the precise term.' Roberta scowled at the picture, nose only inches from the plate.

'Did you manage to cure him, Papa?'

She felt her father's hand upon the small of her back, steady and gentle.

'Yes,' he said. 'The young man went back to work, quite well again.'

'How did you do it?'

'I resected the wound and scoured out the surrounding glands.'

'Really!' She injected eagerness into her voice. 'Are there more pictures of your patients, Papa? May I look at them?'

'No, I believe that is enough for the time being, Roberta.' He snapped the folder shut and, rising, walked past her out of the circle of lamplight.

Roberta waited, the hard part over, while Papa folded his arms across his chest and, with the bookcases at his back, turned to make his little speech. She already knew what was coming.

'The boys, your brothers, are a disappointment to me, Roberta. You, on the other hand, have certain qualities . . .' He paused.

'Do you want me to become a doctor?' Roberta said.

'After consideration, I have come to the conclusion . . .' Again he paused.

'That you want *me* to study medicine instead of them?'

'Substantially,' he nodded, 'yes.'

'I thought you didn't approve of women in medicine, Papa?'

'I never said that, not in as many words.'

'I thought you regarded them as unstable?'

'They are, they are. But you are a Logie and are therefore – different.' He advanced to the desk and leaned upon it. 'The study of medicine is very demanding, Roberta. It requires character and dedication. It is particularly difficult for a female and involves many unpleasant things from which you have been protected. Do you feel you are up to it?'

'I'm willing to give it a jolly good try.'

'No,' he said. 'Trying is not enough, not for a son – for a child of mine. If you take it on then you must promise me that you will succeed.'

'Absolutely.'

'Do not be frivolous, please.'

'I'm not being frivolous, Papa.'

'You bear the name of Logie, therefore much will be expected of you.'

'Because you're so famous?'

'Yes.'

She took a deep breath. 'Papa, I won't let you down.'

Fortunately Veitch Logie was a consultant at Wellmeadow Hospital in the county of Stirling and Bobs had no professional contact with him during her student years. Even so, it did not take long for her to discover that her father's conceit was legendary and his reputation a joke.

'Logie? Logie? Are you related to Veitch Logie, by any chance?'

'Yes, sir. I'm his daughter.'

'Good Lord! Oh, well, never mind.'

If only Papa had been content to leave well alone Roberta would have sailed on merrily towards graduation and might even have dedicated herself to the noble calling of remedial surgery, in which branch of the trade women were, if not welcomed, at least tolerated.

Veitch Logie, alas, could not let well alone. However much he respected his daughter's intelligence he was still man enough to want to organise her affairs and, when it became apparent that she lacked due regard for him as a surgeon, the heavy paternal hand came down smack upon her private life.

'I hope you don't take me for a tart, Declan?'

'I take you for what you are, my love; a dear, sweet, honest girl.'

'I'll bet you're only saying that because I lend you money.'

'I would be sayin' it even if you weren't the soul of generosity.'

'Has nothing come through from your father yet?'

'Not a bean.'

'Doesn't he realise how strapped you are?'

'Sure an' he does,' said Declan. 'But there's little he can do about it. The market's been so low in Wicklow he's obliged to hold on for better prices.'

'It must be very difficult being a farmer these days.'

'It's all that,' Declan said. 'I can't be pressin' him for much more than he's given me already. I'll just do the best I can. Money's always been scarce in our family.'

'Is that why you entered medicine? For the money?'

'Partly so, partly so,' Declan told her. 'Also to repay my Da for puttin' his faith in me, and for his sacrifices.'

'Why haven't you told us this before?'

'I'm not one to go complainin'.'

'Have you told Roberta?'

'I have.'

'How often does she come here?'

'Not as often as all that.'

'Does *she* lie on the bed with you?'

'Ssshhh, let's not go wastin' our time talkin' about Roberta.'

'I can't believe it embarrasses you to have two girls at your beck and call.'

'Never heed Roberta. It's you I really love.'

Alison stirred beside him, stretching her legs. She could smell the thin haze of coal smoke in the air but, now that November had come in, the basement was bitterly cold. When Declan tried to pull the rough-haired blanket over them for warmth Alison wouldn't have it. She'd made it clear from the first that her version of love-making did not include intercourse and that he must respect her edict of So Far and No Further or she would stop coming to visit him altogether.

Even so, each Wednesday afternoon she found herself yielding a little more, allowing him that extra inch. He'd had her skirt up about her waist. He'd had his hand on her bare stomach. He'd kissed the flesh of her inner thighs and, almost as a matter of course, had stroked her breasts beneath her blouse. And to this she'd responded, robbed, almost but not quite, of will.

And Declan knew it. Knew that if he persisted she might give in to him. But he refused to push too hard. He needed her almost as much as he needed Roberta and he had no intention of knocking up either one of them. He was in desperate need of the loans of cash they made and would not, therefore, lose control, especially with Ally Burnside. Alison Burnside might have a little money of her own but it was just that, a *little* money. Nothing in the way of a fortune. She came from a house less valuable than his own, from a family without class or influence. Not enough to really tempt him. No, Roberta would be the one for him. Eventually. Her father's cash and influence would help him climb the career ladder. Meanwhile, did either of the greedy little girls really and truly love him? He doubted it. They, like he, were in it only for what they could get.

'You don't love me, Declan,' Alison said. 'Why pretend?'

'Does this look like I'm pretendin'?'

'Pure physical reaction, that's all.'

'I'll be careful,' Declan said. 'I know what to do.'

'I'll bet you do.'

He moved against her. Her skirt was still hitched up. He could see the smoothness of her stockings and, as he settled over her, glimpsed the white flesh of her thighs. He knew what he might do, what he might not do. He was as wary with Ally as he was unwary with Bobs.

'No, Declan. N.O.'

They lay on the bed because there was no other furniture sturdy enough to support them. The bed served Declan as both couch and armchair. He sprawled on it to read, knelt by it to write. He slept in it, buried deep in sheets and blankets and, now that it was winter, with his old tweed overcoat thrown over it like a quilt. Once or twice a week he also lay on top of it with Roberta.

Alison was quite aware of the fact that she shared him with Bobs. He had one who knew about the other, one who did not; a very risky situation. Roberta, heavy, scented, warm and soft as some great angora-wool doll. Alison, tall, slender and sallow, smooth-skinned, the secret parts of her scalloped with fine brown hair. When he rolled into bed, he would dream of one and then the other, pairing them in his imagination until, languorously, he fell asleep.

Diligently he placed a hand upon Alison's breast.

It was, Alison thought, as if she was back again in the shadows of the yew hedge in Macarthur Drive with Walter Giffard. Walter had put his hand upon her breast too, touching her while she'd kissed him in wonder and dread. She harboured no such emotional confusion over Declan Slater. He was lean to the point of emaciation, yet there was something so wiry about his body that his pixie face seemed like a mask put there only to hide his strength. She had a teasing desire to see him naked, to invite him to take his clothes off and lie, shivering, on top of her. Not that she ever would, of course.

It was enough to have him kiss and caress her, lie half upon her, rubbing against her stomach through the cloth. Her breasts were not especially sensitive and fondling produced only a small degree of sensual pleasure. When he touched her below, however, strange little pulses would start in her belly, pulses which soon mounted to a spongy throbbing which made her want to groan aloud.

Holding him half off with one splayed hand, while he lay half on and rubbed himself against her, that moment was worth the deceit at the heart of their relationship and all the guilt she carried with her back to Flannery Park.

How she could face Jim without blushing, she didn't know.

But she could. And that, alas, was also part of the thrill.

Miss Peggy Lockhart, QM secretary of the Labour Club, was remembered mainly for her performance as a robin in the pantomime *College Pudding* when, fuddled by nerves, she had contrived to topple over the footlights and had wound up frantically fluttering her tail feathers head first inside the drum in the orchestra pit.

Stability being a principal requisite of her present job, she had been the obvious, not to say only, candidate and had consequently been shooed into the post by a narrow majority.

Political differences notwithstanding, Miss Lockhart's relationship with Dipsy McDonald, her counterpart in the Men's Union, was one of love/hate. She loved him and he hated her.

Peggy loved Dipsy in spite of the fact that he held the record for the highest number of 'dipped' subjects in the Faculty of Law and had become a notorious challenge to the learned professors, most of whom were now dedicated to getting the idiot through the degree course before they, or he, reached retirement age. Dipsy was not an easy man to love. He had consumed so much beer during his terms of office that he bore a distinct resemblance to the R101 airship. Indeed, there were fears that one day Dipsy too might spring a leak and explode and bring down the roof of the Union coffee-room or the bar of the Redfern Miners' Welfare in which locations he chose to conduct much of his business. Karl Marx, Ibrox stadium and McEwan's draught heavy were the mainstays of Dipsy's life. For women he had no time at all.

Even if he had been inclined to court the fair sex it's unlikely that he would have been attracted to Miss Peggy Lockhart who, when not dressed as a robin, gave a pretty decent impression of being both a bully and a frump. Her battle-cry, which rang through the committee-rooms and lecture-halls of socialist circles, was, '*I'll* do it. *I'll* do it. Leave it someone who *knows*;' an endearing enough trait without the addition of lisle stockings, shaggy cardigans and a felt hat which hugged her frizzy ginger hair like the casing of a howitzer shell.

For twenty months Miss Lockhart had been a first-class student of pharmacology. Commitment to Labour politics had not disrupted her march towards the attainment of a Bachelor of Science degree. One spring evening, however, she had found herself seated next to Dipsy McDonald at a Labour Club debate and had felt the sudden, fatal sting of Cupid's dart. Next morning red lead had adorned her cheeks, gentian violet her lips and she'd taken to hanging about the door of the Men's Union like some grotesque streetwalker. She would even trail poor Dips away out to Redfern, lurk behind the beer kegs in the Welfare's yard, leap out and accost him with a cry of mock surprise.

'Why, Jonathan, how nice to see you!'

'What the bloody hell are you doin' here?'

'Just passing, just passing.'

'Well, bugger off.'

And he would flap his monstrous arms, leer and shout, 'Chookie, chookie, chookie, chookie,' to remind her of her brief experience as a small, red-breasted bird and laugh until, with a handkerchief pressed to her nose, the QM's Labour secretary would stumble away, humiliated but more in love with the coarse brute than ever and quite determined, by fair means or foul, to win him round.

Fair means constituted the setting up of a modest little debate between newly elected Labour Councillor Bill Mossman, a moderate meek and mild, and an opponent to be chosen by the committee of the Men's Union.

Peggy Lockhart's intention was to infiltrate Dipsy's all-male enclave in her official capacity and to sit across the board making goo-goo eyes at him for as long as it took the boys to quaff a few pints and reach a decision. Only twenty-four hours after she had posted her initial communiqué into the Union pigeon-hole, however, back came Dipsy's hand-printed reply.

All it said was – *Vladimir Kurtz*.

Miss Peggy Lockhart gasped.

Though she knew even then that she was in deep trouble she could not help but admire Dipsy's bold brass neck in daring to bring to Scotland a famous Russian author who was also *Pravda*'s Paris correspondent and, it was rumoured, one of Joseph Stalin's right-hand men.

If it is that he gets a visa, of course,' said Trudi.

'Oh, he'll get a visa, all right,' Henry said. 'It's all very well for the government to expel Russian diplomats and stick up trade embargoes but when they attack the right of free speech they'll find themselves in real hot water with the International Press Federation. Not even Churchill could shout that lot down. Besides, how can we condemn the loss of the right to unrestricted reporting in Germany if we start doing the same thing here?'

'It is surprising,' said Trudi, 'that the courts of the university have not put a stop to it.'

'Gone too far,' said Henry.

'After what it was that happened at Oxford?' said Trudi.

'What happened at Oxford?' Davy enquired.

'Rioting at the university,' Henry answered.

'Students!' said Bertie, with a grunt. 'All the blasted same. Weans with too much money and not enough sense.'

'The Oxford students voted against fighting another war,' said Henry.

'Well, good for them,' said Bertie.

'What would you fight for, Bert?' Davy asked.

'Me? Nothin',' Bertie replied.

'The Co-operative movement?' Henry suggested.

'Maybe. Aye, maybe that.'

'See,' said Davy, 'that's just how it starts.'

'How what starts? I can't imagine Herr flamin' Hitler bein'

interested in squashin' the Scottish Co-operative movement,' Bertie said.

'I would not be so sure,' Trudi told him. 'Today it is something whispered in the Reichstag in Berlin. Tomorrow, you are crouched behind your fruit counter firing a makeshift of a rifle in defence of what you value in life.'

'Jamaican bananas.' Davy said. 'That's all Bertie values in life.'

'An' Indian tea,' said Jack.

With the twins in bed, Jack had dropped round to Wingfield Drive to borrow five cigarettes to see Brenda through until morning. He was in no particular hurry to go home, though. He was seated with his brothers at the supper table, munching slabs of toasted cheese.

'What's wrong with Indian tea?' Bertie demanded.

'Forget Indian tea,' said Henry.

'It's all right for you to say that, you don't have to sell the flamin'—'

'Bertie!' Trudi warned. 'Enough of tea tonight, please.'

'Whatever happened to free speech?' said Jack.

'It is not allowed to our Bertie,' said Trudi, with the trace of a smile. Bertie bit into a slice of toasted cheese, and sulked.

'I still don't see what all the jumpin' up an' down is about,' Davy said. 'I mean, what's so special about bringin' this Russian over from Paris for to talk to the students? Is our Ally goin' to meet him, or somethin'?'

'Our Henry is.' said Trudi.

Henry said, 'Alison isn't much interested in politics.'

'Aye, we all know what she's interested in.'

'Bertie!' Trudi warned again, sharply this time.

'All right, all right.'

'It's a tremendous *coup* for the university Labour clubs,' Henry explained. 'As well as being a famous international book-author, Kurtz is also a feature writer for the communist press in France. He's got a lot of clout. They say Joe Stalin thinks he's the best "voice" in Europe. Herr Hitler had him arrested and flung in prison not so long ago but there was such an outcry from the European press that Adolf had to let him go again. And here he is, turning up at a public debate in Glasgow of all places.'

'Debatin' what, with who?' said Jack.

'It was originally supposed to be Councillor Mossman but he prudently discovered he had a previous engagement,' Henry said. 'Now it's to be a round-table discussion. Fascism versus communism.'

'Who'll be there?' Davy said. 'Oswald Mosley?'

'No. Since he nearly got hung by a gang of Red Clydesiders at the

59

Shettleston town hall a couple of years ago, Ossie's a bit leery of coming north,' Henry said. 'Taking the side of the moderate right, in fact, is my boss – Marcus Harrison.'

'Very cosy,' Davy said. 'Who else?'

'It has not been so far decided,' said Trudi.

'Yes, it has,' said Henry, before he could check himself.

'Who then?'

He hesitated. 'Margaret Chancellor.'

'Who's she?' said Jack.

'Another old friend of Henry's,' Trudi told her brother-in-law, then, just a little pale about the gills, slipped off into the kitchen to grill more bread and cheese.

In Glasgow intercourse between gown and town was closer and more amiable, perhaps, than elsewhere in the academic universe.

It was hard to ignore the university, which some folk regarded as a hideous building set on a magnificent site and others as an edifice of soaring grandeur and a centre of civic pride. Whichever side you were on you could hardly miss the damned place, for its massive tower was *the* Glasgow landmark, and featured prominently in every panorama.

Toddling Govan slum-dwellers and strutting little Kelvinside toffs would have the tower pointed out to them with equal measures of respect. Even in a society sundered by slump and Means Test there was always the hope that education might be the path to true democracy and that wee Angie or skinny Wullie might have the brains to rub shoulders with Miles, Giles and peachcheeked Dianne and level off the conflict between poverty and privilege once and for all. Or perhaps the average Glaswegian citizen tolerated the average Glaswegian student merely because they were really much the same under the skin: cynical, sentimental, aggressive and, on occasions, quite prepared to kick over the traces and raise a little, or a lot, of extremely merry hell.

Rectorial elections, rag days, torchlight processions, firework displays, marathon runs, the daring but illegal scaling of public monuments, and a certain idealised involvement in politics of every hue frequently brought student and citizen face to face.

So it was to be with the Great Debate which, at first, was a figment less of fact than fantasy.

Dipsy had plucked Kurtz's name at random and had flung it at Peggy Lockhart just to scare the lovey-dovey nonsense out of her and teach her to keep her nose out of his business. He had not expected Miss Robin Redbreast to take him at his word, hop on her bike and secure the use of the Maitland Hall, cancel Councillor Mossman and write invitations instead to Margaret Chancellor, doyenne of the left, and Lord Blackstock, owner of the *Glasgow Mercury*, who was everybody's idea of a demon of the right. Or to open his newspaper one bleary morning and have the headline BANNED BOLSHEVIK TO ADDRESS UNIVERSITY leap out at him.

Two days later, with the infuriated cries of his colleagues still ringing in his ears and his father's bank account thirty pounds lighter, Dipsy was aboard the boat-train bound for Paris to find out if Vladimir Kurtz actually fancied a free weekend in Glasgow and, more importantly, if the infamous 'Banned Bolshevik' could speak even three words of English.

What exactly happened in Gay Paree nobody, not even Dips himself, could rightly remember. He had a vague recollection of lots of smoky bars, a very great deal of vodka being poured over his throat and of three very nice girls from somewhere called Montmartre telling him how wonderful he was as they shoved him up the stairs of his hotel.

He had a slightly stronger impression of Vladimir Kurtz, hero of the masses and secret-sharer of the Paris Comintern, giggling like a schoolgirl and prattling away in what seemed like three million words of heavily accented English. And a last, reassuring recollection of being poured on to the boat-train at the Gare du Nord, with old Vladimir shouting at him, 'Hokay, Buddy, I see you Schottland in two veeks. You haff the vimmin vaiting and the viskey. Hokay? Hokay? Bye-bye. Bye-bye.'

Later that rainy week when Miss Peggy Lockhart darted out of the shelter of the cloisters and accosted Dipsy as he lumbered across the quad, he was still sufficiently elated to spare her a moment of his valuable time.

'But, Jonathan, *I* didn't *know* you *knew* such a *famous* man.'

'Vlad? Him an' me,' said Dipsy, smugly lacing his digits, 'like that.'

'Oh, Lord!' said Miss Lockhart, lost in rapture. 'It's going to be such fun.'

'Who've you got? Blackstock?'

'Marcus Harrison.'

'Confirmed?'

'Confirmed.'

'Who else?'

'Margaret Chancellor.'

'Huh!' said Dipsy McDonald, wrinkling his nose. 'Is that the best you can come up with, dear?'

For once, just once, the erstwhile redbreast bridled and showed her true mettle. Raising her forefinger to her throat, she drew a line across it and made a little *schrikking* sound.

'Mr Kurtz,' she said, 'he dead.'

But Dipsy, who had never read *Heart of Darkness*, did not understand the allusion and, with a snort, bowled away across the quadrangle in search of a pint, leaving Peggy Lockhart, like a shadow, to follow on behind.

The time was fast approaching when little sister would surely be exposed to the theories of the good Dr Freud.

Summer term, fourth year, if Henry's reading of Alison's schedule was correct, and she'd be off to spend her Saturdays at Hawkhead or Gartnavel mental institution and, for a brief period, would be obliged to study the deficiencies of the mind rather than the defects of the body.

Henry was certainly not equipped to follow Alison into the tangled regions of a strangulated hernia or along the alimentary canal but he *was* conceited enough to believe that he had a head start on her when it came to psychology. He had read extensively in the field and was more familiar with terms and definitions than any political hack had a right to be.

Freud was his favourite. Henry turned to the works of the wise old Viennese with the same fondness as other men latched on to the novels of Dickens or Trollope. He kept three volumes of Freud's works hidden in a hatbox in the back of his wardrobe, like an unlicensed revolver or a batch of nudist magazines. He would take one out now and then, read and annotate a page or chapter and ponder on its application to his own situation.

Actually he was rather inclined to accept Alfred Adler's concise theory that all human endeavours stemmed from a desire for money, power and the love of women. But that did not explain why he, Henry Burnside, was drawn to women older than himself or why, for the past couple of years, he had lusted after Margaret Chancellor. The answer lay in Oedipus, of course: a nasty concept and the only one of the good doctor's insights which Henry refused to swallow without a large pinch of salt.

Surely he didn't hate his father or harbour jealous rage towards him for marrying the widow, Ruby McColl? He certainly didn't nurture an unconscious urge to usurp dear old Dad in Ruby's bed.

As to his natural mother, he could never quite accept that they would never meet again, that he would never be able to tell her how successful he had become and how well her children were coping without her.

It was undeniable that Mam's sudden death had changed the fortunes of the Burnsides for the better but the circumstances of it still haunted Henry. It troubled him more than a little that he had married a woman who, if not quite Mam's age, was certainly closer to it than to his own.

Now there was his attraction to Margaret Chancellor to cope with. At least Margaret was a bit younger than Trudi and quite different in temperament. Margaret was subtle where Trudi was direct, frank where Trudi was secretive. She was well fleshed and hearty, whereas Trudi was rake-thin and rather brittle. Unfortunately Margaret Chancellor also reminded him of his Aunt Belle which only served to increase Henry's suspicion that perhaps he *was* a classic study in delinquent sexuality after all.

'What is this that you are reading, Henry?' Trudi had once asked him and, when he had shown her the book, exclaimed, 'Freud! That dirty Jew!'

'Jew he may be, Trude, but he knows what he's talking about.'

'He is a goat, a dirty Jewish goat, leering at the little children.'

'Have you read anything he's written?'

'I do not wish to contaminate my thinking with such ravings.'

'How about Adler, then? Maybe he's more to your taste?'

'In future I do *not* wish you to read such disgusting rubbish, Henry.'

'What's wrong with you? I thought you believed in education,' Henry had said. 'Anyway, I'm reading it whether you like it or not.'

'Then keep it out of my sight.'

'Yeah, all right.'

She had gone whisking out of the bedroom, slamming the door behind her and Henry had put 'Oedipus' carefully back in the hatbox.

Later that same night, however, Trudi had apologised for her outburst and had made deep, passionate and silent love to him; then when it was over and he'd been lying sleepily on his back, she had put her mouth close to his ear and had whispered, 'Why do you read these nasty books? Is it to find out why you fall in love with me?'

'Uh?'

'This Freud, he knows nothing of women.' She had taken his hand, had guided it to the triangle of still wet hair between her thighs. 'It is *this* that makes you love me, Henry. It is *this* that makes us one.'

'Sure,' Henry had said. He had been too lazy to argue but had thought, even as he fell asleep, that clever though Trudi was and well versed in the ways of the big wide world there were some things about which she really knew nothing.

* * *

Henry certainly had no intention of discussing Freud with Margaret Chancellor. He had more important things to chew over with the Scottish People's Party's leading light than trends in psychoanalytic theory.

Margaret was already in Agnew's when Henry arrived. Not for him now the cap and muffler that had been the badge of his apprenticeship years, not even the cheap brown suit that he'd once thought so sophisticated. He had learned a lot in the past four years. He came in the smart navy blue business suit that he wore for all important interviews.

He felt relaxed in Agnew's restaurant, a posh little cellar hidden away beneath Argyle Street, within which the rumble of railway trains and the faint crackle of tramcars could be sensed rather than heard. He had dined here often enough to know the menu backwards and to be given a nod of recognition by the head waiter.

Margaret Chancellor was sipping from a glass of port and lemon, a breach of gastronomic etiquette which signified individuality rather than lack of class. She was clad in a peacock blue dress and sported no ornaments apart from a pair of small gold earrings and her worn old wedding band. She was, however, groomed to perfection and still carried a trace of summer suntan, acquired, no doubt, on the lawns and promenades of the conference circuit.

She was the widow of a railway union official who had been killed in the Great War. Henry had first met her when he had been employed as a part-time hack for the SPP's sad little propaganda rag, *The Banner*. Since then Mrs Chancellor had gone up in the world. She had shed her retinue of pompous mediocrities and had fashioned her own brand of politics, closer to mainline socialism.

She had influential friends in all sorts of places and was frequently courted by the parliamentary wing of the Independent Labour Party. She had also evolved a dynamic platform technique and was much in demand as a speaker which brought her, Henry supposed, a decent enough income since no working-class radical with any awareness of the value of money ever got up on their hind legs for free.

Mrs Chancellor smiled as Henry approached. She gave him a little *salud* with the port glass which, with the light shining through it, matched almost exactly the colour of her lips.

If Henry had been a man of less honourable character and not still in love with his wife, then he might have fallen head-over-tail for Margaret Chancellor who, he knew, had a reputation as a free-thinker and was rumoured to enjoy the companionship of younger men, whether they were married or not.

'Henry,' she said. 'I thought you'd have been upstairs in the railway station, clamouring for a word from our famous Bolshevik.'

'I'd much rather dine with you.'

'So long as you're paying.'

Henry seated himself and signalled to a waiter. 'Oh, yes. I can write you off as expenses, Maggie.'

'Good lad,' said Margaret. 'I'd hate to think I was giving myself away for free or that a hard-working chap like you would be out of pocket.'

'Not a chance.' Henry ordered a whisky and soda, glanced briefly at the menu, then took out a narrow leather-backed tablet and a needle-thin propelling pencil and placed them discreetly on the tablecloth. 'Why aren't *you* at Central station as part of the welcoming committee?'

'What do you think it is – the weigh-in for a title fight? No doubt I'll see and hear enough of Vlad the Invader tomorrow night, if he lets me get a *vord* in edgeways.' She winked at Henry. As usual, there was humour as well as speculation in her hazel eyes. 'Handsome young journalists are much more my cup of tea than fanatical Franco-Soviet propagandists. How are you doing, Henry?'

'Well. Pretty well. You?'

'Can't complain.'

'Quote number one?' he asked.

'Oh, no, I can do better than that,' the woman said. 'Much better.' She hesitated. 'Does Marcus know you're canvassing my opinion on Kurtz?'

'Yes.'

'Did he give you a line or two for the piece?'

'Yes.'

'What did he have to say about Kurtz?'

'This and that.'

'Henry Burnside, you'll never change.'

'What do you mean?'

'All that dark inscrutability. I'm not going to eat you, you know.'

'Sorry.' Henry laughed. 'Old habits die hard. In any case I'm not going to carve you up in the morning edition. I learned my lesson years ago, remember, when I slagged off Lady McCaine and she nearly sued the *Banner.*'

'Well, I'm not Elvira McCaine. You can say what you like about me.'

'May I tell the *Mercury* readers that you're terribly attractive and utterly charming and intelligent?'

'Within limits, old lad, within limits,' Margaret Chancellor said, flattered.

'I can see I'm not going to get anywhere with you,' Henry said.

'Do you want to?'

Ruefully, Henry shook his head.

'You're still Trudi Coventry's man, aren't you?'

'Unfortunately, yes.'

'Well, I'm not one to cross Trudi, I can tell you,' Margaret Chancellor said. 'All might be fair in love but not – in my book at least – in war.'

'What does that mean?'

'Politics, Henry, just politics.' She finished the port and lemon and put down the empty glass. 'Before we get into water too deep for either of us, I have something prime to tell you, something you might care to include in your article.'

'Do you now?' Henry's right hand drifted towards the pencil. 'What?'

'Vladimir Kurtz is a sham.'

'You mean he isn't Vladimir Kurtz at all?' said Henry.

'Oh, he's Vlad Kurtz all right, no doubt about that, but all that stuff about how he stormed the Winter Palace when he was seventeen, how he was a translator in Stalin's so-called secretariat and travelled with him to the Siberian front; how he—'

'I have read the books, Margaret,' Henry interrupted. 'Are you saying that Kurtz invented the whole amazing story?'

'Yes. His father was a well-to-do doctor in Rostov. Vlad didn't even meet Stalin until 1928. And when the October Revolution took place Vlad was in Cardiff visiting friends of the family.'

'And the rest of it? His run-in with Hitler's murder gang, for instance?'

'Fiction. Pure fiction.'

'But that's what he's famous for. I mean, nobody cares a hoot that he's a columnist for *Pravda* and stirs up endless trouble for the French government. He's a hero in Britain because he wrote *Comrade Citizen* and *Cloud Across the Sun*. Half the working-class bolshies in Britain think he's the new Messiah. I know chaps who've read only two books in their lives. Both by Vladimir Kurtz. Are you telling me he's trading on a pack of lies?'

'In a nutshell, yes.'

'Why, then, is he tolerated?'

'Suits the Russian line, I suppose.'

'No, I mean, why hasn't he been exposed as a charlatan before now?'

'Because so few people know the truth about him and those who do are unwilling to acknowledge it.'

'What's your source, Margaret? I mean, who told you about Kurtz?'

'Can't say.'

'In that case,' said Henry, 'can't write.'

'What if I told you that my information came from an impeccable source, somebody close to Lord Blackstock? Would you publish it then?'

'In tomorrow's edition? Not a chance. I'd have to track down all sorts of folk just to substantiate your claims, make up a file of names and dates and then try to persuade Marcus Harrison to run the thing.' Henry paused. 'Are you trying to drop me in the soup, Maggie?'

'No, I wouldn't do that.'

Henry sipped whisky and soda, then said, 'If you want Kurtz's reputation undermined you're going to have to do it yourself. Given more time I might have provided you with a lead, a lever, but as it is . . .' He shrugged.

'It's going to be a rough debate tomorrow night, Henry.'

'I'm well aware of it.'

'The Tory rabble will be out in force. I'm told the miners will have supporters inside the hall as well as out. Plus, of course, mobs of squealing students. I wonder if this fellow—'

'McDonald.'

'Yes, I wonder if he knows what he's let loose.'

'McDonald's a fool, a complete fool.'

'You know him?'

'I talked with him briefly.'

Margaret Chancellor cocked her head. He could see wisps of greying hair just above her ear and little creases of flesh beneath her chin. When she sighed her bosom filled the front of her dress like a sail swelled by the wind.

'So you won't help me, Henry? Won't even hint that Kurtz is a fraud?'

'Not unless you wish to give me a quotation.'

'Something you can deny?'

'Yes.'

She shook her head. 'I can't afford to do that.'

'That's wise,' said Henry. 'I reckon there'll be trouble enough at the Maitland without the *Mercury* casting scandalous aspersions on a hero of the people. Are you nervous?'

'Naturally. I just hope Marcus is up to it.'

'I wouldn't worry about Mr Harrison. Nothing ever fazes him.'

She paused, head still cocked, and sighed again. 'Who's the night editor?'

'Simpson Bond. Why?'

'Will he pass what you write without consulting Marcus?'

'Probably.'

'Just a sentence, Henry, a word or two to get me going tomorrow.'

'In direct quotes, attributed?'

'Is that the only way you'll do it?'

'Yes, Margaret. Sorry.'

She hesitated, fingertips splayed across the top of her breasts in a gesture that reminded Henry rather too forcibly of his amorous, asthmatic Aunt Belle and, by an unfortunate association, of his mother.

'All right, old son,' Margaret said. 'You drive a dashed hard bargain.'

'I shouldn't be doing this at all, you know.'

'I know,' she said. 'Right, take this down.'

Henry reached for his pencil before she could change her mind.

In spite of herself Alison was caught up in the fever that swept the halls of Glasgow University and its attendant teaching hospitals. Politics was one sport that medical students tended to leave to their academic siblings in the departments of English and history, a frivolous lot who had more time at their disposal than hard-working medics and who, whether they labelled themselves Tories, Liberals or socialists, all had one thing in common – a commitment to absolute anarchy. It was only because she did not want to be left out that Alison agreed to accompany the team, minus Declan, to the Central Hotel in Glasgow's city centre in the hope of catching a glimpse of Vladimir Kurtz.

'I didn't know it would be like this,' Alison shouted, twisting to look up at Howard McGrath.

'This,' Howard yelled back, 'is nothing to what it's going to be like tomorrow night.'

'I think I might stay away.'

'Alison, you don't mean that?'

'No.' She giggled as if intoxicated. 'No, of course I don't.'

Howard put his arms about her waist and held her tightly as another wave of honest citizens swept into Gordon Street.

'Is he gonna make a speech, hen?' A tiny woman with a shawl-wrapped infant in her arms plucked at Alison's sleeve.

'I don't know. I expect he might.'

'He's up there,' the woman told the infant and, to Alison's alarm, hoisted the baby aloft like a rugby football. 'See, see the mannie,' then with her offspring still raised up she slithered on towards the hotel's towering prow.

Mounted policemen hovered on the fringes of the crowd, big brown horses bucking as tramcars crawled past and taxi-cab drivers, mad at the choked causeway, hooted and honked their horns and bawled obscenities at everyone and their dear old mother.

Lined up in front of the doors of the Central Hotel were ten or a dozen of Dipsy's stalwarts, all uniformly dressed in dark blue topcoats and homburg hats and looking less like praetorian guardsmen than Chicago gangsters. They were certainly more ominous than the helmeted constables who ambled calmly back and forth, joshing with the crowd and, now and then, putting an armlock on some over-eager bolshie who had broken loose from the ranks.

'Why?' Alison shouted. 'I mean, Kurtz is not *that* famous, is he?'

'Well, he's not Al Jolson, I will admit,' Howard told her. 'But for a writer he's famous enough. It's what they *think* he stands for that counts.'

'What's that?' Alison asked.

'Full employment and a living wage,' Guy Conroy told her before Howard could summon up a flip reply.

'I thought he was a communist?'

'He is,' Guy told her. 'Our comrade.'

'Dear me!' Roberta said. 'Guy, you've got it bad.'

'If you ask me,' Guy said, 'the crowd is its own justification.'

'Oh, very profound,' said Roberta. 'Where did you read that nonsense?'

'The *Glasgow Herald*,' Guy told her.

'Naturally,' said Roberta. 'The *Herald* would only be interested if this chap was Harry Lauder or some other comic Scotsman. You're right about one thing, though: Kurtz is an authentic proletarian hero. I think it's wonderful that he should be given such a warm welcome in our city.'

'If he does make a speech,' Guy said, 'you'd better hold on to your hats. Because I for one am going to go wild.'

'I still don't quite know what they're all doing here,' Alison protested.

'Ask yourself this,' said Howard, stooping to make himself heard, 'what are *we* doing here?'

'Good question.' Alison smiled at her protector and rubbed herself against his heavy tweed overcoat.

'Anyhow, what else is there to do on a cold November Thursday in

69

the middle of Glasgow?' said Roberta. 'This is, I suppose, a little bit of history and we are privileged to share in it.'

'It's also,' Howard said, 'dashed good fun.'

'Yes,' Alison agreed and, as the crowd swayed once more, put her arms behind her and clung to Howard with the same degree of tenacity as he clung to her. 'Yes, it is.' She giggled once more. 'Even if nothing happens, even if we don't see Kurtz, I'm so glad we came. Listen, what's that they're singing?'

'The Red Flag,' Guy told her.

'I don't think I know that one,' said Roberta.

'Just shout, then,' said Guy and, to everyone's surprise, raised his clenched fist towards the lights and, in a deep rich voice quite unlike his own, bellowed out the chorus word for word.

It did not occur to Henry that his sister would be in the crowd in Gordon Street. Personally he had no love for humanity *en masse* and had failed to realise that Kurtz's arrival would cause quite such a commotion. Having put Margaret safely into a taxi, he walked a little way along Union Street towards the Central Hotel, drawn by the singing like a nail towards a magnet. It would not be a huge gathering nor an angry one.

Even so, Henry resented the mob's stupidity in turning out to worship a charlatan like Kurtz.

'C'mon, mister, c'mon. Ye'll miss him, so y'will.'

Three young men in pit boots and cloth caps clattered up behind him, intense and excited as only apprentices can be. They plucked at his sleeve as they came abreast of him as if to drag him along with them, not just into Gordon Street but along the road to Utopia.

Henry snatched his arm away and then, as the apprentices took to their heels, felt a little spurt of rage of a sort that had been absent from his heart for too many months; rage at the shoddiness and deceit that had shaped itself into the likeness of a book-writer from across the Channel, a hero whose whole philosophy was probably based on lies.

'Huh!' Henry said aloud. 'Huh!'

Ten minutes later he was seated at an Underwood typewriter in an office on the fourth floor of the *Mercury* building, hammering out exactly the sort of article that Maggie Chancellor had urged him to write: a piece that would provide her with a weapon against Vlad the Invader and, coincidentally, make Henry Burnside's name a household word.

Whatever white lies Vladimir Kurtz might have concocted to

dramatise his personal history there was no trace of deceit in his statements of belief. He understood completely why the Labour leaders were so alarmed about the swell of anti-fascist feeling that had spread across Europe and how difficult it would be for an honest communist to turn it to good use.

For Vlad Kurtz personal promotion had always gone hand-in-glove with political evangelism and beneath his jocularity was a serious and focused aim. He had come to Glasgow to preach not to pander, which was the only reason he had allowed the fat and foolish student to talk him into the trip in the first place.

Already he had recognised in Britain many of the ingredients which had allowed Adolf Hitler to seize power in Germany, mass unemployment, middle-class disillusionment, Labour's failure to govern effectively among them. The founding of the British Union of Fascists by a former Labour MP was no joke as far as Kurtz was concerned. And the support the fascists received from wealthy and influential press barons like Rothermere and Blackstock could not be lightly dismissed. He was eager to attack the barons through his platform opponent, Marcus Harrison, to try to explain to what would undoubtedly be an antipathetic audience that it was not the communists but certain members of the capitalist establishment who were hell-bent on fomenting social disorder.

The fat student, McDonald, had apparently brought along a girl, a stocky child with a fierce, over-painted face and frizzy red hair. She loitered, simpering, on the pavement by the hotel's main door.

Kurtz was not sure if she had been co-opted to be his 'companion' or if she was merely some tenacious hanger-on.

In either event he had no time to spare for dalliance.

Only minutes before McDonald's borrowed motorcar drew up outside the hotel to whisk him off to address a meeting of pit-workers and to lunch with their leaders, he had been shown an article in the morning edition of the local newspaper and had realised immediately that Blackstock had struck first.

'Who is this who writes these lies about me?' he asked, shaking the paper.

'Are they lies, Mr Kurtz?' the red-haired girl replied.

'Peggy, for Christ's sake!' McDonald, the fat boy, exploded. 'What are you trying to do to me?'

'To you?' Kurtz said. 'To you nothing is done. To me – everything.'

'*Are* they lies?' the girl, smirking, said again.

'Get away from here, you silly bitch. Leave us alone.'

'With pleasure, Jonathan,' the red-haired girl said.

'Wait,' Kurtz said. 'Who is this journalist, you will tell me, no?'

'Search me, Vladimir,' the fat boy blustered. 'Anyhow, nobody reads the *Mercury*. It's just a bloody Tory rag.'

'The reporter's name is Burnside,' the girl said. 'Henry Burnside.'

'Do you personally know of this man?'

'Nope,' the girl said. 'But Margaret Chancellor does.' She grinned evilly. 'And that's all that's gonna count tonight, Mr Communist. Happy landings!'

All this daft political in-fighting didn't matter tuppence to the general student body. Some, like staid Guy Conroy, were moved by the spirit of the occasion but for the most part the lads and lassies on Gilmorehill got on with what they had to do to make the evening memorable.

Chemistry labs reeked of sticky concoctions. In the dispensaries of teaching hospitals little groups of conspirators furtively experimented with rubber tubes and bladders in the eternal search for a perfect bombshell, while their less inspired brethren combed the middens for rotten fruit or purchased from society funds large sacks of flour and boxes of eggs.

Painted slogans were everywhere revealed, great slashing Zs and Ss in black and red and, adorning walls from Hyndland to Charing Cross, the work of one sprinter/decorator whose spelling of *Commie* as *Comy* narrowed the culprit field to Hons Grads, Eng. Here and there about the cloisters there even appeared in transitory blue chalk a selection of Latin quotations which were eventually identified as snatches from Ovid's *Ars Amatoria* and were, in consequence, hastily erased by porters armed with mops.

Along with Guy and Howard, Alison walked the wards of the Western Infirmary in the wake of old T.K. Thomas who was, that morning, unusually sarcastic. He waxed eloquent about 'Red Fever', a condition which he defined as being both epidemic and terminal and whose early signs matched almost exactly those of congenital imbecility.

Class members were glad to escape and did not envy the junior doctors who were stuck with the old buzzard for the rest of the day.

At lunch-time the grassy banks above the River Kelvin were dotted with groups of students wrapped up like Muscovites, all hatching plots, while within the Unions loud inconsequential chat gave way to whispered machination.

Many, Alison among them, looked at the pillared front of the Maitland Hall as if they were seeing it for the first time. Many felt a tingle of excitement at the sight of extra benches being unloaded from vans by workmen in brown overalls. On the roof, high overhead, two nimble-footed nationalists were erecting a Scottish flag while a council foreman barked at them from the pavement and received naught for his pains but cheerful waves.

It was, Alison thought, a strange unsettling sort of day. She would be glad when it was evening and the team would meet for a bite to eat in Miss Osmond's before setting off for the Maitland.

Somehow, today of all days, she needed to be part of the crowd.

She had scanned her brother's article in the newspaper but she could not really see why Howard and Guy were so upset by it. Why Henry's revelations about Kurtz set one young man against the other in snarling argument. She, of course, had never read *Comrade Citizen* and did not see that it mattered very much whether Kurtz's account was truth, half-truth or fiction.

In Flannery Park, on the housing site where Davy was laying bricks, discussion of Henry's article was heated and prolonged. And in the back shop of the Co-operative store Bertie was challenged to defend his brother against a charge of being a rotten fascist sympathiser. Bertie had no inclination to side with Henry, though. He had known for years what Henry was and 'dirty rotten fascist' just about described it.

Down town in the *Mercury* offices Henry too was restless.

He had a study piece to write about proposed changes to the Workman's Compensation Act and tried to immerse himself in White Papers about liability and *Hansard* reports of the latest parliamentary debates. But he was far too unsettled to work and spent the morning fending off cheeky remarks from fellow journalists while nervously awaiting a summons from the editor, Marcus Harrison, a summons that never came. He saw nothing of the editor that day, received not a word of praise or of censure from the office upstairs.

At five o'clock on the dot, armed with pencils and notebooks, Henry left the Magdalen Building to stand himself an early dinner and one stiff double whisky before heading out to the West End to see what, if any, difference his article had made and, of course, to report from the inside the outcome of the Great Debate.

The disadvantage that the Maitland Hall had over the Bute or the Hunter was that meetings held there were, by obligation, open to members of the public.

Division between the factions was not clear-cut, however, and you would have been hard put to separate one sort of mob from another. Gibson Street, Bank Street and the hump-backed reaches of University Avenue were assembly points for various disorderly groups and a few rowdy students, who had been early at the beer, were already hurling water-bombs and rotten eggs at each other across the width of the Radnor.

To avoid the hubbub and with his press card held out before him like a talisman, Henry went in by the back lane.

Margaret had advised him to follow this route to the press gallery and Maitland Lane itself was so crowded with police constables and Al Capone impersonators that Henry suspected the speakers would be brought in this way too. He was tempted to hang around in the hope that he might be able to snatch a word with Margaret or even to wish his boss, Marcus Harrison, good luck but the constables kept the reporters moving along with such efficiency that even Henry did not dare linger.

He was in his seat in the front row of the gallery by ten to seven and found that the hall was already nine-tenths full.

Down by the big double doors the ushers were having trouble controlling the crowd and, fire regulations notwithstanding, Henry had the feeling that by ten past seven every square inch of space within the Maitland would be occupied. He had a certain amount of elbow room, though not much, and a thin, iron-rimmed ledge upon which to rest his notebook.

Fernie Hollinsworth, a photographer from the *Bulletin,* was on his immediate left and the *Bulletin*'s sober reporter, Dunlop, was breathing down his neck. To his right was Eastman from the *Herald,* a wild-haired fellow who dressed like a poet and wrote in the orotund style of Thomas Carlyle. Beyond Eastman was the granite pillar of what had once been the nave and directly below it was the speakers' platform.

'Put the fat in the fire this morning, did you not, Harry, old boy?' said Eastman in his autocratic voice. 'Where did you rake up that stuff about Kurtz's murky past? Did it all come from Madam Chancellor?'

'I do have other sources, you know,' Henry said, curtly. He hated being called 'Harry' and detested the quasi-intellectualism of his *Herald* counterpart. 'I thought you'd have picked it up before I did, since you don't seem to be doing much else of interest these days.'

'I'll bet Harry's wife told him,' Fernie Hollinsworth said.

'My wife? What's my wife got to do with it?' Henry said.

'German, ain't she?' Fernie said.

'Swiss,' Henry told him.

'Aw, I heard she was German.'

'Who ever told you that?'

'He did.' Fernie swung his camera in Eastman's direction. 'Said she was a big pal of Adolf Hitler's.'

'Well,' Henry said, looking at Eastman as he spoke, 'he'd better not say it to me or he'll find himself nursing a black eye.'

'Get your bully-boys on to me, will you?' Eastman said. 'Isn't that the style for people of your persuasion?'

'Rab,' Henry told him, 'bugger off. You're talking rubbish, as usual.'

'I may talk rubbish from time to time,' Eastman said, 'but at least I apply a degree of integrity before I rush into print with fabrications. Nor, Harry, do I perpetrate wild rumours that my wife picks out of the Teutonic press.'

'If you mention my wife again,' Henry said, 'I really will black your eye.'

'He's only jealous,' Fernie said.

'Jealous?' said Henry. 'Of what?'

'Cause he's not married to a German spy,' said Fernie.

Henry reared back and stared at the photographer then, because no other response was possible to such a ludicrous suggestion, he buffed Fernie's nose lightly with his knuckles and laughed.

He might have said more, might even have lost his temper again if at that moment Miss Peggy Lockhart had not hopped on to the platform bearing a big glass water jug and three glasses which she set down carefully upon the centre stage table.

'*Chirrip, Chirrip, Peggy-weggy,*' came a cry from the audience.

It was followed instantly by a loud roar of '*Chookie, Chookie, Chookie,*' and just a split second later, as if moved by telepathy, the entire student body burst into full-throated song:

> On a tree by a river a little tom-tit
> sang, 'Willow, Tit-Willow, Tit-Willow!'
> And I said to him, 'Dickie-bird, why do you sit,
> singing Willow, Tit-Willow, Tit-Willow?'

By the time the ditty had been rendered in toto and Miss Lockhart, blushing like a tomato, had left the platform again, the crowd at the door were turning ugly and Henry, his pique forgotten, had settled down to work.

Over the years Alison had often heard Henry talk of Marcus Harrison and Margaret Chancellor and had tried to imagine what they would look like.

The woman was taller and more elegant than Alison had anticipated and had a confidence and forceful manner of speaking which Alison wished she could emulate. Marcus Harrison, however, was a disappointment. He was small, gentle-seeming and soft and did not at first come across as a man capable of managing an influential newspaper. She found it difficult to link the luminaries on the platform with her brother and would glance up at the gallery from time to time to see if Henry had noticed her. If he had, though, he gave no sign of it.

Roberta's father had turned up unexpectedly.

He was positioned in the reserved section towards the front, seated next to Guy Conroy's father with whom he appeared to be on the best of terms, a situation that both Guy and Roberta found disconcerting. Discussion of its implications was impossible, however, for the noise in the hall had grown thunderous now that the platform party had appeared on stage.

Vladimir Kurtz did not seem like the stuff from which heroes are made. He wore a thick tweed sports jacket, a pair of dark green corduroy trousers and a duck cotton shirt left open at the collar. He was physically no more imposing than Marcus Harrison, although his head, with its mass of tangled grey hair and broad brow, had a certain dignity to it. It would hardly have mattered if Kurtz had turned up dressed as Peter Pan, of course, for the audience was too partisan to care what he looked like. Boos and cheers, hoots, shouts and whistles greeted Kurtz's entry but the atmosphere remained high-spirited and jovial.

The guests were accompanied by officials from the university political societies, Dipsy and Peggy Lockhart among them, a glum and nervous bunch who seemed totally intimidated by the occasion. Even Peggy could hardly make herself heard and it was not until Margaret Chancellor had been introduced that the clamour died down and the audience became quiet.

The SPP leader rose from her chair, planted her hands on her hips like a farmer's wife, and, without reference to notes, plunged directly into her harangue. 'Discontent,' she began, 'is as old as Cain. And what was wrong with Cain? He had a grievance, a justifiable grievance. He lacked status.'

She paused, gave a little smile, then continued. 'He was placed lower in the scheme of things than his brother. And he was not content. How many of us here tonight are content?'

Catcalls answered her question. She ignored them.

'How many of us would wish to rise higher than our brother, to be more than the equal of our neighbour? Many of us. All of us, if we are honest. This sort of discontent is at the root of the strife in our industrialised societies. The answer is to struggle for possession of political power. But how is that power to be attained? By lies.' She swung round. 'By lies, Mr Kurtz? By exempting oneself from the truth? Or, Mr Harrison, by inclining towards the solution of Cain? By murder and assassination, wresting power by brute strength? By overturning the existing social order by means of violence?'

She stretched out a plump left arm and pointed at the Russian. 'By the establishment, Mr Kurtz, of a bureaucracy which is utterly without pity? Or—' she pointed with her right arm '—or, Mr Harrison, by the enthronement of a dictatorship which will destroy every class of person who dares to oppose it? Is that what you want to happen here? Is that your plan?'

Harrison sat back in his chair, arms folded, smiling faintly, his eyes upon his accuser's back.

Kurtz, though, leaned forward, hands between his knees, cigarette wafting smoke across his face. He stared at the floorboards.

'Will we all be equal then?' Margaret Chancellor continued. 'No, we will not. Will there be full order books on the Tyne and on the Clyde? No, there will not. Will every man be the equal of his brother? No, for it will be a parliament of liars, of cheats, deceivers and assassins. It will be government of the people by the most ruthless among us, by the most dishonest.' She paused, then added, 'And this will cure nothing. Nothing. Unless, like the gentlemen behind me, you believe that Cain was *right* to do what he did. Unless you believe that there is *no* better solution than to resort to the law of Cain, the law of the bullet and the knife in the back.'

Alison was seated between Bobs and Howard. Howard had a hand on Alison's shoulder as if he thought she might need to be restrained. Guy was there too, keen and eager, on the bench beyond Roberta. But of Declan there was no sign. To the girls' disappointment, Declan had failed to show up at Miss Osmond's.

Margaret Chancellor went on with her speech. She introduced the subject of socialism and, with a certain wit, broke down its aims and objectives. She gave socialism a patina of consistency, of unity, which it did not possess. Using Henry's article as a base she made a final direct attack on Vladimir Kurtz's integrity then sat down to an ovation that was surprisingly well balanced.

Girls cheered, boys jeered. Pressmen applauded. Miners, dockers and railwaymen who had been lucky enough to gain admission bawled remarks about Maggie Chancellor's sexual habits and her need to find a man to keep her in her place.

In the midst of the hubbub Marcus Harrison was given an introduction and duly rose to say his piece. He seemed diffident and

77

lacklustre, though his soft voice, Alison noticed, had more penetration than one might have imagined and not one word was lost.

He began by remarking casually, 'Eight days ago, at four in the afternoon, I took tea with Chancellor Hitler.' He allowed that to sink in. 'It was very good tea. The pastries were delicious.'

'Get on with it, man. Never mind the menu.'

He looked directly down into the sea of youthful faces and, fleetingly, up at the journalists in the gallery. He took a little step away from the protection of the table and said quietly, 'How odd! That's exactly what Adolf told me to do. "Never mind the menu," he said. "Get on with it." And I asked him, "On with what, Chancellor Hitler?" And, through a mouthful of cake, he answered, "With saving your country from ruin, of course." '

At that moment, without warning, the shelling of the platform began.

Mr Veitch Logie never knew what hit him. He was the first casualty of the attack. The tight rubber bladder filled with a mixture of red paint and molasses was delivered with such venom that it burst on contact with the side of his head. The force of the blow was sufficient to render the surgeon semi-conscious and when the bladder split, as it was intended to do, and paint and treacle spattered his face, his first thought was that the substance was brain matter.

He slumped against George Conroy, moaning.

Conroy, a good man in a crisis, leapt at once to his feet and threw himself to the left just as a hail of eggs rained down on the front benches and, arching high, exploded on the platform.

Marcus Harrison stood his ground. His sole gesture of defence was to raise his left arm to protect his eyes from shell splinters.

He looked out at the battlefield stoically and, rather to his suprise, was joined at the front of the platform by Maggie Chancellor whose pretty dress was already splashed with stinking yolks and sticky trails of albumen.

When the woman groped for his hand and gripped it firmly the editor of the *Mercury* did not resist. And together the pair faced up to the barrage while pressmen in the gallery went frantic trying to find the best angle for their photographers.

UNITED WE STAND. STUDENTS GO TO WAR WITH HITLER. DEMOCRACY AGAINST THE ODDS. MANY INJURED IN STUDENT RIOT.

The morning editions were plastered with such lurid headlines, plus photographs of the political opponents, man and woman, holding hands like a bride and groom while flour bags burst about them.

A great deal of tripe was written, some of it by Henry, about right and left standing together in the face of anarchy, about the madness of Bolshevism, and the need to ban student debates. But the most telling picture never did reach the eyes of the great British public: it was judiciously suppressed by all the editors to whom it was offered.

That picture showed Mr Vladimir Kurtz sneaking away to safety with his jacket drawn up over his head, like a guilty man snapped on the steps of a courthouse. No word was uttered by the Russian, no view put forth, no opinion offered, no interview granted.

As arranged beforehand, he was out of the back door of the Maitland and into Dipsy McDonald's car and tripping up the platform in Glasgow Central station towards the London train before the dust had settled, his reputation as a hero of the people dented but intact.

It was left to Dipsy to pay off the rabble-rouser who had been contracted to save Vlad Kurtz's bacon, to buy the bomber's silence with an extra five shillings slipped into the hand in the cloisters once Senate enquiries and police investigations had been put to rest.

Thirty bob Declan Slater made out of it.

Thirty shiny shillings just for being the first to hurl paint bombs from the shadows of the loft gallery before he slithered down the staircase and left good old human nature to follow its usual barbaric course.

THREE

Daft Friday

Traditionally Daft Friday was the high point of the winter term. In the year of 1933, however, it seemed that Daft Friday might not take place at all. In the wake of the great débâcle it was touch and go whether or not the Senate would ban all student gatherings, including the late-night dance.

What went on in the Senate rooms when the ringleaders of the debate were interrogated was a topic of much speculation. Participants in those long, sweaty sessions remained tight-lipped about the proceedings.

Wild rumours circulated that Dipsy McDonald had been sent down, that Peggy Lockhart had tried to commit suicide by ingesting potassium cyanide but had got the dosage wrong.

The fact that Dipsy was still at large and that Peggy was as brusque and bossy as ever didn't deter the gossipmongers. Nobody really knew the truth of the matter. The true fact was that Dipsy had collapsed in floods of tears and had begged, literally on his knees, to be allowed to complete his course of studies and that the learned gentlemen of the Senate had finally agreed to be merciful just to be rid of the weak-minded fool.

It had been left to Miss Peggy Lockhart to convince the professors that the debate had been deliberately ruined by a group of communist agitators and that the pitched battles which had been fought within the hall and on the avenue outside were not the fault of the student body but were symptomatic of the violent unrest in the world at large.

Whatever her faults Peggy Lockhart could be very persuasive when she put her mind to it.

Journalists' claims that many had been injured were false.

The emergency department of the Western Infirmary had treated a fair number of fat lips, black eyes and staved fingers, of course, and the removal of eggshell fragments from scalps provided some fun for the junior doctors on call.

One elderly toff, who kept claiming to be a surgeon, had been brought in with mild concussion and a severe case of 'paintitis', a complaint which the staff of the emergency room were well used to treating.

Mr Veitch Logie, magnificently bandaged but minus a deal of hair, had been released into the care of his friend, Mr Conroy, shortly before midnight. For the rest, though, student and citizen alike, cleaning-up and repairs were conducted privately and without professional aid.

'You enjoyed it, didn't you?' Jim Abbott asked.

'I suppose I did, in a way,' Alison answered.

'Didn't you feel threatened?'

'Can't say I did. The boys were very protective.'

'Who were you with?'

'Oh, the team. My friends.'

'The Irishman?'

'Decker didn't show up. Not until it was all over. We met him in the avenue later, after we'd struggled out of the hall.'

'Why wasn't he with you inside?'

'Really, I've no idea.'

'Didn't you ask him?'

'He isn't my boyfriend, you know. Never was, never will be.'

'Whose boyfriend is he? The Logie girl's?'

'Well, he is rather sweet on her.'

'Come off it, Alison.'

'All right, all right. He's crazy about her if you must know. And, yes, I suspect that they may be lovers. Is that what you want to hear?'

'I'm sorry. I didn't mean to pry.'

'Oh, you've a perfect right to pry, Jim,' Alison said. 'You've been very patient with me.' Without breaking step, she insinuated an arm about his waist and hugged him. 'It won't be long now, thank God.'

'What won't?'

'Graduation. The end of it.'

'And then?' Jim Abbott asked.

The afternoon was cold and motionless, hazy with a hoar frost that had failed to lift as the day progressed; a depressing Scottish Sunday when even the dog-walkers in the park seemed like phantoms and the laughter of children mucking about the rock-hard reaches of the burn rose muffled and sinister in the still and misty air. Jim had called early, had suggested a walk. Alison had sensed that he'd wanted more than just the pleasure of her company, for he could have that without leaving the warmth of 162. She had put on her thick black stockings, winter coat and knitted hat and, with her scarf wound about her throat, had led him out into the faint grey fog as if she wanted nothing more than to spend an hour alone with him out of doors.

'And then,' Alison answered, 'we'll be lovers too.'

'Married, you mean?'

'Of course.'

'An odd way to put it,' Jim said.

'You mean we *won't* be lovers?'

'You know perfectly what I mean.'

'Husband,' Alison said primly, 'and wife.'

'Is that still what you want?'

'Yes.'

'Are you sure?'

'*Yes.*'

They walked on quickly, step in step. It was too cold to stroll.

They strode briskly about the pond which was scummed with grey ice and mapped with black patches where the boys had hurled stones and twigs on to it. Even with his coat collar turned up and hat brim pulled down Jim shivered a little, his skin as white as the air he breathed.

'Alison,' he said, 'not *quite* so fast, please.'

'Sorry.' She slowed, shortening her long-legged stride. 'Are you all right?'

'Fine, fine,' he said. 'I'm just not as young – as fit as you are.'

'Do you want to go back?'

He shook his head. 'Not yet.'

'To your place?'

He gave her that quick, darting, far-away glance which she had never been able to interpret and which, though she would not admit it, troubled her conscience considerably.

'No,' he said.

'Not even to talk, just talk, the two of us?'

'We're expected for tea.'

'Of course we are,' Alison said.

'Are you disappointed in me?'

'That's a funny word – disappointed.'

'Are you?'

'I love you, Jim. How could I possibly be disappointed?'

'Because I'm not like the boys you know, like your Irishman.'

'I'm not marrying "my Irishman", who, for the millionth time, isn't mine, anyway,' Alison said. 'God, but you're in a queer frame of mind today, Jim. I'm supposed to be the moody one, not you.'

Jim shrugged, coughed, extracted his arm from about her waist to fish for a handkerchief.

'Are you coming down with something?'

'No,' Jim answered, wiping his lips.

'I can have Guy make you up a cough syrup, if you like. Make you up one myself, for that matter, next time I'm in the dispensary.'

'I've no intention of being anyone's first patient, not even yours,' Jim said lightly. 'In any case, I have a bottle which seems to be doing the trick.'

'What's in it?'

'I don't know. Bought it over the counter. Vegetable extracts. Horehound, lobelia, that sort of thing.'

Alison nodded and then, when he'd put his handkerchief away, took his hand again and they walked on, saying nothing for several minutes.

The pond, thorn hedges, the leafless saplings dropped away in favour of the broad road. A bus came looming out of the mist. A crocodile of small, oddly silent children were being led into the grounds of St Cuthbert's church hall to Sunday School. In an hour or so it would be dark and the streetlights would come on and it would seem as if there had been no day at all.

Alison said, 'I think, if you don't mind, I might go to the Union Palais on Friday week. Someone's invited me.'

'The Irishman?'

'No, Howard McGrath. He's just been ditched by his girlfriend and he's stuck with a ticket. They're all going, all my friends. It's apparently quite an entertaining evening. Seven o'clock until midnight. Would you mind?'

She did not allow him to answer. Part of her desperately wanted him to forbid it, to give her an excuse for petulance, and another part desperately wanted him to concede in practice the freedom he had promised her in theory.

'It's my last opportunity, Jim. Next year I might be on call. And I'm told that everyone should experience a Daft Friday ball at least once. It's nothing serious, you know.'

Jim grinned and squeezed her hand. 'I know. I remember Daft Friday hops from my day. Of course you must go to the ball, Cinderella, especially if some mug has a ticket going a-begging.'

'Are you absolutely sure you don't mind?'

'Not in the slightest,' Jim said then, disengaging his hand from hers, covered his mouth with his handkerchief and began to cough again.

* * *

One of the great luxuries of life in the Logie household, which Roberta did not appreciate until it was too late, was having a bathroom separate from the lavatory.

The bathroom was wooden-walled, sombre and warm. The bath itself was enormous, with huge, broad-mouthed taps, a drain-plunger that looked as if it had been salvaged from a U-boat and a full-length mirror on the wall so that the bather might have the company of his or her reflection while reposing in the tub.

Nanny Williams had bathed Bobs in this room when she was small. Nanny Williams had gone off suddenly when Roberta was about three and had not been replaced until the boys arrived. Then it had been Nanny Grosset, a stern and frumpish woman of sixty or so, who had been more mother's friend than father's, or Roberta's for that matter. Mama, Roberta recalled, had wept when Nanny Grosset had left and Papa had told her to pull herself together.

For eight or nine years Roberta attended to her own ablutions. In the privacy of the bathroom she had experimented with scented oils, creamy lathers, bubbles and sponges and had spent many a happy hour in the tub, floating and dreaming. She had also taught herself how to preen before the mirror and in it had watched her body grow and change.

Never at any point in her progress through adolescence had Roberta been ashamed of her appearance. She adored being alone in the hot, moist atmosphere of the bathroom, enjoyed striking immodest poses before the mirror in imitation of paintings she'd seen in the galleries she visited with Mama from time to time. She loved her shape, the satin texture of her skin. In fact, she was so enthralled by her appearance that the confidence it gave her seemed to spill over into everything she did.

In wards, labs and clinics, even during surgical demonstrations Roberta managed to ignore the pathological damage that time and disease inflicted on the human organism. *Her* body, she firmly believed, was different, too fine to fall prey to illness or deterioration. Her body was her most treasured possession. It could do no wrong. And throughout the winter term, Declan's slavish attentions simply confirmed her own opinion of herself and expanded and enhanced the pleasure of being 'just Bobs'.

She had been soaking in the bath for an hour when the doorbell rang and, a moment later, voices echoed in the hall.

Roberta was not particularly perturbed by the faint, unintelligible greeting-sounds that drifted in to her. It was not unusual for Papa or Mama to receive visitors on Sunday afternoons. Aunt Edith came now and then, Uncle Mark and Aunt Minna, Mr Longfellow, a paediatrician from Ottershaw, Bairnsfather, an anaesthetist. Sundry freemasons. Roberta was not expected to honour the guests with her presence unless she wished to do so. Sometimes the visitors were asked to stay to dinner but it made no difference to Roberta. She would offer her best excuse, slip away and head for Greenfield and Declan, with her sober Sunday clothes protecting her pink and eager body against the cold night air.

'Roberta, dear?'

'Yes, Mama?'

'Will you be long?'

'Ten minutes. Why?'

'We have visitors.'

'Who?'

'New friends of Papa's. They'd rather like to meet you, if you don't mind.'

'Would they? All right.'

Roberta pulled herself out of the bath and reached for the big, pink towel.

Fifteen minutes later she entered the drawing-room.

For warmth – she'd been chilly in church that morning – she'd chosen a woollen tweed dress with pleated skirt and hip yoke. Her hair had recently been cut and shadow waved and she'd arranged it to highlight the natural little curls at the nape of her neck. She looked, she believed, both fashionable and demure and in Papa's drawing-room no one would guess that beneath the dress she wore apricot crêpe-de-chine cami-knickers and the latest in crochet brassières.

She opened the door and breezed in. She had no idea who the visitors might be but expected to be greeted by another boring freemason or some junior surgeon new to the Wellmeadow. The man looked faintly familiar but she had never seen the woman before.

She advanced towards the gathering by the hearth.

Then she stopped dead in her tracks, her smile fading.

'Guy?'

'Hello, Bobs.'

'What – what are you . . .'

'A surprise for you,' Papa Logie said. 'Aren't you pleased to see your friend here with us?'

'I – Yes, of course. I must say, it's . . .'

She shook hands first with Guy's mother then Guy's father and finally, as if she was walking not on but through water, she approached Guy himself.

He didn't shake her hand but leaned foward and kissed her

awkwardly on the cheek. Behind her, she could *feel* Papa's gaze upon her, *hear* Mama's sentimental little sigh of satisfaction.

As she pulled back from Guy their eyes managed to meet and he gave the merest flutter of the brows as if to say that he too was mystified.

'What a charming couple,' Mrs Conroy remarked.

She was a squat little woman, all shoulders and bosom, over-dressed in a satin evening gown.

Mr Conroy – 'George, you must call me George' – wore an expensive dinner suit, silk-trimmed. Papa and Guy were similarly attired.

Before she could help herself Bobs blurted out, 'Are you staying for dinner? I mean to say, *are* you?'

'Yes, so you've no need to go out to the university tonight, dear.' Even as her mother spoke the words Roberta remembered the tale she had been spinning to her parents for most of the term. 'I'm sure the Christian study group will be able to manage without you both just this once.'

Features fixed in a rigid smile, Roberta turned to Guy and in a light, bantering tone, accused him of treachery. 'Oh, Guy, you told them?'

'I'm afraid so,' Guy said. 'I think they rather guessed.'

'Two and two together,' George Conroy said, archly.

'Like Noah's Ark,' Mrs Conroy added.

Papa was standing before the fire.

He still wore the head bandage, less to protect his fading scar than to hide the fact that the new hair growing back was pure white. Roberta suspected that he also liked the way he looked in the turban, which he had re-bound every morning by the nurses in the hospital. He wore it half across his ears and looked less, marginally less, like some gigantic insect. Until, that is, he rubbed his long lean hands together and, as if conferring a special favour, poured and served Roberta a glass of pale sherry.

'You young people may sit together, there on the sofa,' he declared. 'No need to be shy now your secret's out.'

'Secret? What secret?'

'Ah, we know who you've been meeting these past months,' Veitch Logie said, 'at the Christian study group. We thought there might be a young gentleman involved, didn't we, my angel?'

Roberta eased herself on to the sofa as far away from Guy as the contour of the furniture would permit.

'How – how did you find out who – who it was?'

Guy glanced at her, paused, then said, 'I'm afraid I told them, Bobs.'

'Told them what?'

'About us,' Guy said. 'And Sundays.'

'But why?'

'I had to, didn't I?' Guy said, with edge.

Roberta looked around the drawing-room, taking in one face after another, the smiling and expectant Logies, the expectant and smiling Conroys.

'After Dad and your father met at the debate,' Guy continued, 'and found out that we not only shared classes but both went out every Sunday evening to chapel worship then . . .' Guy shrugged.

The light clicked on in Roberta's brain.

'Two and two,' said Mrs Conroy again.

'The jig was up,' said Mr Conroy.

'We thought we'd surprise you,' Mama said.

'None of us object, do we, my angel?'

'*Au contraire*,' said Mrs Conroy before Daphne Logie could answer.

'Object to – to what?' said Bobs.

'Courtship,' George Conroy said.

'Even an engagement,' said Mrs Conroy.

'All in good time, of course,' Veitch Logie said. 'After you both graduate.'

'Engagement to whom?' Roberta said.

'Me, I'm afraid,' said Guy.

In the course of the long and dreary evening Roberta and Guy had only a few minutes alone together.

'Why didn't you tell me you were coming here?' Bobs hissed.

'Because I didn't know until the very last minute. It was as much of a shock to me as it was to you.'

'Why did you have to tell them about me at all?' Bobs hissed.

'What else was I to do?' Guy grumbled. 'At first I had no idea what Dad was talking about when he suddenly began making comments about us meeting secretly every Sunday night. I had to put two and two—'

'Please!'

'Yes, sorry. I had to think very quickly. Fortunately it dawned on me that you were using me as cover. I don't think it's fair of you to turn round and accuse me of disloyalty, Bobs.'

'No, you're right, of course. How was I to know you attended the damned CSG? You never mentioned it to any of us.'

'Howard would have laughed me to scorn. You know how he is about religion,' Guy answered. 'Incidentally, where *do* you go on Sunday evenings?'

Roberta had the decency to blush.

Guy sighed and said, 'Declan's?'

'What if I do? I mean to say, it's got nothing to do with you.'

'It has now,' Guy said.

'If we part amicably our parents will soon get over it.'

'I'm not so sure,' Guy said. 'Apparently we're considered to be ideally suited. My mother said as much. Those very words.'

'Ideally suited! Dear God, I don't want to marry you.'

'No, I know.'

'And I don't expect you want to marry me?' Bobs said.

'Not this year,' Guy said, 'or next, for that matter.'

'What?'

'It is,' Guy went on, 'just unfortunate that my father and yours happened to be seated together at the debate. It didn't cross my mind that they would put two and two – I mean that they would hit it off. They're both freemasons, of course. We may assume some sort of signal or secret sign got them swiftly on to confidential terms. And after that . . .'

'I know,' said Roberta. 'I can imagine.'

'Your daughter? My son! That sort of thing.'

'Yes.'

Roberta leaned her elbow on the table and stared gloomily towards the end of the dining-room where the door was.

Daphne had gone to see about coffee. Mrs Conroy was using the facilities. The fathers had gone upstairs, presumably to drink whisky and chat on the q.t. about masonic matters. Jenny, the maid, an untrustworthy chatterbox, had taken away most of the plates but would return shortly.

'What are we going to do now?' Roberta said.

'For a while – pretend.'

'Oh, how tedious!'

'How serious is it between you and Slater?'

'Not very,' Roberta said.

Guy nodded. He might not be a man of towering intellect but he was sufficiently perceptive to know when he was being lied to.

He said, 'Does Slater have tickets for the Daft Friday dance?'

'I doubt it.'

'I have.'

'Meaning?'

'I don't mind taking you.'

'Charming!'

'Do you have other plans?'

It had been Roberta's intention to spend the whole of Friday evening and part of the night with Declan in the basement in Walbrook Street, to use the Union dance as an excuse for her absence. But she was not going to confess as much to Guy Conroy. She sensed, or imagined, a certain proprietorial insistence in his manner and resented the fact that, like it or not, circumstances had placed her under an obligation to him.

She studied him obliquely. He looked so smooth and handsome that you could hardly believe he was real. Compared to Decker, though, he was dull, dull as ditchwater.

'What other plans?' Roberta rasped.

'To spend the night with Slater, perhaps?'

'I don't have to depend on your charity to find a partner,' Roberta said. 'Nor do I have to tell you what—'

'Howard's taking Alison.'

'What? How did *she* manage to get off the leash?'

'Lord knows, but she has.'

'Has she been making eyes at Howard?'

'I doubt it. Shall we make a four, Roberta?'

'If I don't . . .'

'I'll ask Grace.'

'Grace Robertson?'

'Yes.'

'I didn't even know you knew her.'

'I don't. Not very well.'

'You and little "Saving Grace"? Hard to imagine what you see in her apart from the pure and nauseating light of Christian forgiveness. Times must be hard if you're going out with a classics scholar.'

'I'm not going out with her. I'd prefer to go out with you.'

Mrs Conroy and Roberta's mother appeared together in the doorway, chatting. They were followed by Jenny and her large brown tray.

As the servant advanced towards the table, Roberta whispered, 'All right.'

'Pardon?' Guy said.

'Daft Friday. All right.'

'What will you tell you-know-who?'

'The truth, of course,' Bobs said, lying, for once, without conviction.

In the doorway Mrs Conroy put a hand on Mrs Logie's arm and, head on one side, cooed like a pigeon. 'Oh, don't they make a lovely couple?'

To which Mrs Logie, who had detected the frown on her daughter's brow, answered with a somewhat ambiguous, 'Quite!'

According to T.K. Thomas the laying on of hands was the beginning, if by no means the end, of the true study of medicine.

It was no new experience for fourth-year students to be called upon to examine and pronounce upon a patient but under old T.K.'s eagle eye it was never anything less than an ordeal.

He was not a cruel man but his directness could be acerbic, not to say abrasive, and he had a habit of escorting students from ward to corridor, pinning them against the wall with an arm on each side of their heads and dressing them down in a low, rasping tone which had been known to reduce females and even one or two males to tears. The patients, of course, could not hear what was being said nor could the rest of the class, but otherwise the reprimand was a very public affair and doubly humiliating.

What T.K. sought to inculcate was thoroughness. He could not abide slipshod diagnoses. Woe betide the fourth-year student who neglected to check the admission history before approaching a patient. T.K. was also an advocate of confidence in handling, provided it went with courtesy. Not for him an Olympian indifference to the sick and often terrified object in the bed.

He taught well by example.

'Now, Mrs Quinn,' T.K. would say in the softest tone possible, 'I'm going to be turning you over in a wee minute and I'm going to be pressing very hard on your ribs. You're not tickly, are you? No? That's good. I'll tell you the truth, Mrs Quinn, this is going to hurt a bit so you won't be surprised when it does. You just let me know if it gets too much and we'll stop for a breather.' By this time he would have arranged the patient in position for percussion of the posterior chest wall, say, and with pillows placed, would be tapping away with three bunched fingers of his right hand and, even as he spoke, would be listening for tympanitic or resonant response. 'Well, now, that's a very musical rib you have there. I wonder if you would mind if one of these young people had a listen to it too.'

It took a certain amount of courage to emulate a bedside manner which had been cultivated over thirty years of practice.

There were those to whom it came especially hard, those who could not bring themselves to be other than patronising to some ox-like wretch from the steelworks or some withered crone from a Gorbals' tenement. Roberta was among this number and Roberta had already been on the receiving end of one of T.K.'s 'quiet words' in the corridor.

'There are no ladies in my wards, Miss Logie. There are only females. Female patients *and* female doctors; all one breed and species whether you're in the bed or standing beside it. I will not hear a patient of mine addressed in that tone of voice again.'

'What tone of voice, sir?'

'*That* tone of voice, miss.'

Howard, at times too jocular, had once unleashed the full force of T.K.'s fury by deliberately tickling a young female patient to make her relax.

Guy was so handsome, so seemingly calm that he did not have to do very much at all to instil confidence and co-operation in those whom he was called upon to examine. And Alison, in spite of her seriousness, had the knack of soothing fears with just a word or two at the right moment.

In the matter of deportment as well as diagnostic skill, however, Declan Slater was student of the year.

Male or female, old or young, Declan would use his natural Irish charm to put the patient as much at ease as possible and, emulating his boss, was both thorough and confident in the laying on of hands. He pleased T.K. too by never blurting out opinions across the patient's chest but would wait until he had completed his examination then, almost as if he was the chief, would draw the group away from the bed and confidentially discuss his findings.

Although he was not one to play favourites, T.K. had already declared that he thought Mr Declan Slater would make a very fine physician, to which compliment Mr Declan Slater had responded by confessing that his sights were set on a career in surgery. T.K. had merely nodded, not cynically or dismissively, for he had already spotted in the young man the lambent flame of ambition and knew fine that physic couldn't hold a candle to surgery when it came to glamour and romance.

Glamour and romance were missing from Declan's character, however. Amorousness and hard-headed calculation lay behind his Celtic charm and the ambition that T.K. had diagnosed was much more deep-seated than the professor could possibly have imagined.

When Dipsy McDonald had been recruiting hands to start a violent rumpus in the Maitland Hall, Decker had not been slow to answer the call.

'What for?' he'd said, casually.

'Oh, just for the hell of it, you know,' McDonald had said. 'Things are too staid these days. Nobody runs naked through the cloisters any more and there wasn't one pick-axe handle to be seen at the last rectorial election.'

'No,' Declan had said. 'I don't mean why. I mean, how much?'

'God, man, it's a sportin' gesture. It's expected of us political activists.'

'Then do it yourself.'

'How can I when I'm up there on the podium?'

'How much?'

'Have you done this before, old man?'

'I'm Irish, ain't I? How much?'

'Five bob?'

'Come off it! Do you think I'm going to jeopardise my degree for a lousy five bob?'

'How much *do* you want?'

'Twenty-five bob.'

'Daylight robbery!'

'Take it or leave it.'

'I'll take it,' Dipsy had said. 'Provided you do exactly what I tell you to do and make certain you don't get caught.'

'I won't get caught,' Declan had said.

In the middle of the afternoon he had slipped into the Maitland carrying the paint bombs in a carpenter's bag. He had climbed the ladder to the old organ gallery and had lain there smoking cigarettes and humming 'The Rose of Tralee' quietly to himself while, in due course, the hall filled up. There had been an emphatic thrill in picking out posh nobs in the front rows as targets and hurling down the paint bombs as fast as he could snatch them from the bag. As soon as the bag was empty he'd been down the rickety ladder and lost in the crowd before anyone could spot him.

It had been a great night, a wonderful night and when Declan later discovered that his first victim had been his future father-in-law he had blown half his fee on a bottle of whisky to celebrate.

Declan was not one to become involved in the idiocies of Daft Friday. Communal jollity rendered his charm ineffective and, in white tie and tails, he simply couldn't compete with the chaps from the Union.

In the wards of the Royal or the Western, however, Declan felt himself to be not just the equal of his peers but their superior. And when Guy or Howard unwittingly put him in his place he would summon up an image of Roberta panting on his bed or the long body of Ally-Pally half exposed and would remind himself that what Guy and Howard longed for he already had. And that always made him feel a whole lot better.

Admissions day in T.K.'s ward. Winter weather had already begun to take its toll. A long list to troll through and all beds full.

Hatchet-faced Sister Madigan, a thin-blooded Protestant from the dark side of Belfast, had never been deceived by Declan's elfin charm and had remained immune to all the sly little compliments he'd paid her.

Declan felt as if those gimlet eyes could see right through him and when Sister Madigan was about he tended to keep his mouth shut. She was always present in the chief's room, however, when T.K. briefed the class. McIntyre, the assistant, and a harassed medical clerk were there too and with the hospital's big windows all frosted over with fans of ice there was a tense, sterile feeling in the air and tempers were short.

It was the wrong time, a bad time for Declan to vent his spleen.

He had no excuse for it. Except that he had waited for hours on Sunday night for Roberta to show up, had been eager for her and angry when she had not arrived. He had drunk almost a whole bottle of White Horse and had fallen asleep lying fully clothed on top of the bed. He had wakened with the sound of horse carts dragging by outside, frozen to the bone and sick to his stomach. He had been too cold to get back to sleep and had stirred up enough fire to warm a kettle and had sat there sipping chicory and coffee laced with the very last of the whisky, brooding on what might have kept Bobs from his arms.

'Where the divil were you last night?'

'I beg your pardon?'

'I waited for bloody hours for you, so I did.'

'Something happened at home. I just couldn't get away.'

Declan leaned against the bronze-painted iron radiator at the back of the room, notebook in one hand and a case sheet in the other.

He could feel the cold still in him, seeping through the glass, through his coat, shirt and thin, unwashed vest. He felt as if his skin, like the glass, was rimed with ice and only the faint heat from the radiator kept him from shivering.

'Are you listening, Mr Slater?'

'Sir, yes. I am, sir.'

'Your opinion, Mr Slater?'

'On what, sir?'

'The new patient in bed number five. Draper is, I believe, her name.'

Declan glanced at the record, handwritten on the sheet of paper that he had in his fist. Roberta stood just before him. He thought he could smell the warmth off her, like a new-baked loaf. And he resented the fact that she was plump, well clad, well fed. His stomach moiled. He badly wanted a cigarette. He didn't give a tinker's damn about patient number five.

'What, Mr Slater, will we be looking for first?' T. K. prompted.

'Come on now. We don't have all day.'

The old man didn't look too hot himself this morning. Declan wondered vaguely if wintry weather had affected the old man's waterworks which were, so he'd heard, prone to give trouble from time to time.

Declan blinked, focused, found the clue. Answered, 'Lesions of the heart valves. Specifically the mitral valve.'

'Why?'

'Record of rheumatic fever. Age of the patient.' He paused. 'Syncope.'

He thought he heard Sister Madigan snort but he was too distracted to heed to her warning.

The chief said, 'Syncope?'

'Yes, sir, transient loss of consciousness.'

'I know what it *is*, Slater,' the chief said. 'But I'm interested to learn how you reached such a positive conclusion from the evidence so far before us.'

Declan did not know what came over him. It was as if some demon had spoken from within his breast.

For an instant he felt separated from himself, divided into two halves, one of which stood back, aghast, while the other waved the admission file aloft and screamed, 'Because it bloody well says so here, so it does, written right here in black and white.'

Stunned silence.

All heads turned in Declan's direction. Brows were raised, eyes widened. Roberta gaped at him as if he had suddenly grown horns and a tail.

It was Howard who laughed first.

Then Alison.

Declan felt anger mount into fury, a sudden red rush, justified by the fact that he was the chief's blue-eyed boy, the cat's pyjamas. They should know by now that he was never wrong. They should *respect* him.

He hammered at the paper with his forefinger, jabbering, while everyone, including hatchet-faced Madigan, roared with laughter.

All he could do was roar back, '*Syncope, syncope, syncope. Wrote right here, right here, see, see,*' and beat at the sheet until it tore. '*What's wrong wit' all o' youse, can't ye bloody read?*'

Roberta put a hand on his shoulder. 'Declan, Declan,' she said, in her patronising middle-class Scots voice. 'Declan, you've made a mistake.'

'*Mistake!*' he raved. '*I'm not the one who's makin' a mistake. It's youse, all of youse. Stop laughin' at me or, by God, I'll—*'

95

'Mr Slater,' the chief thundered.

Abruptly Declan's separate selves merged, snapped together in his head with a sound like the *twang* of a broad rubber band.

He held the crumpled admission sheet in both fists and stared, blinking, into the sterile white light of the room and at T.K., out of his chair, looming over him. In a grim, bristling voice the chief told him not to be a conceited fool, to pull himself together or he would be dismissed the class for the remainder of the term and would have to carry the ticket until spring.

'But, it does say . . .' Declan, almost in tears, breathed his last protest.

It was Sister Madigan who, at a nod from the chief, brought the young medical clerk forward and stood him directly before the student.

'Do you know who this is, Mr Slater?' T.K. asked.

'S – Senior clerk.'

'His job?'

'A – Admissions.'

'His name, Mr Slater?'

'I – I don't know.'

'Tell him your name,' T.K. instructed the clerk.

'Cope,' the clerk said, wryly. 'Sydney Cope.'

'In other words, Mr Slater, you glanced at the sheet and misread Syd Cope's signature as a *diagnosis*. Never, *never* have I encountered such carelessness before.'

The class was still sniggering.

It would be the joke, the one good joke of the term, perhaps.

And he, Declan Slater, was the butt of it.

T.K. leaned closer, one hand braced on the window pane. He spoke loudly enough, however, for everyone in the little white room to hear.

'Now it is not your error that makes me suspect your fitness to be a doctor, Mr Slater. The error is bad enough, the carelessness of it. What is unforgivable is your adamant assertion that you were right. Arrogance of that sort has no place in medicine. Confidence is indeed a virtue to be cultivated but arrogance – and incivility – will not be tolerated. Do you understand me?'

'Sir,' Declan mumbled.

'Are you unwell, young man?'

'I – I feel – sick.'

'Sister, take him out.'

'Bismuth, Doctor?' Madigan asked as she steered Declan to the door.

'Nux 6c, four tablets,' the chief answered. 'Tea and some toast too, I think, should do the trick. If you're well enough, Slater, perhaps you may care to join us later on the round.'

'Sir,' Declan mumbled again and, with the bitchy sister from Belfast thrusting his arm half up his back, shuffled out of the room in shame.

Henry Burnside had always been on excellent terms with his immediate superior. Jock Harvey, the *Mercury*'s feature editor, was a quiet, undemonstrative man in his mid forties. Heavy-set and almost as tall as Henry, he had a bear-like gait which went well with his wardrobe of old Harris tweed sports jackets and rumpled corduroys and the round, bottle-bottom spectacles that shortsightedness obliged him to wear.

Books and orchestral music were Jock's passion and the *Mercury*'s team of reviewers had to be on their toes in those particular fields. That said, Jock had more than his fair share of knowledge of the world at large and kept personal taste well to the rear when it came to shaping the regular 'back of the paper' features and planning, a full day ahead, his 'on top of the news' articles.

It couldn't be said that Jock had a soft spot for Henry. In Jock's unvoiced opinion the young journalist's past was just a shade too murky to encourage candour. And his, Burnside's, relationship with Marcus Harrison had elements that could not be easily explained. Something to do with Burnside's wife, so Jock gathered, and her former husband Clive Coventry. Coventry's name still cropped up now and then in small print on the financial pages but the chap had no link at all with 'culture' and did not encroach into the vast circle of Jock's professional acquaintances.

Henry Burnside, however, was a fountain of creative ideas when it came to articles and Jock had never found the young man to be anything less than professional in his in-office dealings.

Jock could float the whisper of a notion and Henry would take it, develop it, research it thoroughly and write it out in one, two or three pieces to any length required. Henry also knew how to run a nice line between politics and entertainment and was, Jock had to admit, the best in the business when it came to writing background articles on issues of the day.

Burnside's account of the riot in the Maitland Hall, for instance, had been a small classic of its kind, his follow-up analysis of 'The Reason Why?' an amusing but deadly attack on the pervasive appeal of communism as a counter to European fascism. Jock had deemed it wise, however, to have those two pieces read *in toto* by Marcus

Harrison since both he and Lord Blackstock were mentioned by name.

Harrison had merely smiled his small, wry smile, had tossed the carbons back across the table with a nod of approval.

'I must be going up in the world, Jock,' he'd said, 'if Henry Burnside thinks I'm a hero. Print them as they stand.'

'The photograph?'

'Oh, use the photograph if you must. Everyone else has.'

Henry, however, was not too sure.

He was not too sure about anything these days, in or out of the office. He'd been alarmed by the mail that his piece on Kurtz had brought tumbling into the office. In language too profane to print in a family newspaper, 'That Bastard Burnside' had been accused of everything from treason to devil worship and informed in no uncertain terms what would be done to him if he was ever caught unawares on a dark night in Shettleston or Govan.

Henry could take all that.

He was less than sanguine about some of the threats unveiled against his family, though, and had begun to wonder if 97/6d a week, plus expenses, was payment enough for becoming a newspaper celebrity.

'They don't really mean it,' Jock had told him.

'Aye, but I think they do,' Henry had answered.

'Do you want me to pass any of these letters to the police?'

'What good will that do?' Henry had said. 'Since they're anonymous?'

'Well,' Jock had said, 'if you do wind up with a knife in your back at least the CID will have somewhere to start.'

'Ha-ha-ha!' Henry had said. 'Very funny, Jock – I don't think.'

In Flannery Park he was by now well known. Folk would nod to him in the street as he hurried towards the bus stop or the railway station and when he popped into Mrs Powfoot's shop he would be treated to comments on and criticism of his most recent pieces. He was famous but he was, and would always remain, a prophet without honour in the confines of Flannery Park. And if he was ever tempted to become big-headed his family were always there to bring him back to earth with a bump.

Henry's horizon, however, was broader than its suburban boundary. He fancied himself to be a true Glaswegian now and rode in high quarters of the city where his brothers would never dare tread. He met with men and women whose names were known to everyone and, when the hate letters began to arrive, it galled him all the more to realise that he could still be the victim of the vulgar rabble which he thought he had left behind.

It was almost the end of the month before he was summoned to the upstairs office by a typed memo left on his desk: *Mr Harrison wishes to see you. 10.30 a.m., sharp.*

Henry climbed the staircase from the hot and noisy reporters' room into the carpeted region of the fourth floor, the muscles of his stomach taut and his heart beating just a little faster than usual.

John Marcus Harrison was small in stature but robust in build. He had a reddish-brown moustache and auburn hair worn longer than was quite the style. He had a penchant for casual clothes and sported expensive silk-weave jackets and soft-collared shirts which went well with his air of bonhomie.

'Henry, sit yourself down. Cigarette?'

'Thank you, Mr Harrison.' Henry took a Churchman from the box, lit it and seated himself, unrelaxed, on the chair before the desk.

Marcus Harrison hesitated.

Behind him were eaves and ledges and a patch of icy blue sky. The old Magdalen Building in Maldive Square was not quite so tall as its neighbours and had no views to speak of from any of its many windows. In the back-light the editor's hair seemed like a russet halo and the smoke from his cigarette like something whipped up out of egg white.

Henry was glad when the editor moved to the front of the desk and, sweeping books and papers away with his elbow, hoisted one buttock on to the desk and folded his arms.

'Well, young man,' Marcus Harrison said, 'it seems you've been getting yourself quite a reputation.'

'For what, Mr Harrison?'

'Don't look so anxious, Henry. I meant it as a compliment. You're not on the carpet. Far from it.'

'That's a relief,' Henry said. 'I thought I might have overstepped the mark, if you know what I mean.'

'The articles were fine,' Marcus Harrison said. 'As to the hate mail, that's a bagatelle. I've seen a lot worse than that in my time. Anyone in the public eye is bound to catch that sort of flak. Jock tells me you're worried about it, though.'

'Aye, maybe a little,' Henry admitted.

'Is Trudi – is your wife concerned too?'

'Why should she be?' said Henry, mildly surprised at the question.

He had almost, if not quite, forgotten that Marcus Harrison and Trudi had been acquainted back in the old days when she had still been Clive Coventry's wife. It was through Trudi's connections that he'd got the job with the *Mercury* in the first place.

99

'I see,' Marcus Harrison said. 'You haven't told her about the hate mail?'

'Nope, I haven't.'

'Is she happy living in Flannery Park?'

'Seems to be. She doesn't complain.' Harrison's questions about Trudi made him uncomfortable, though he wasn't quite sure why. 'She's not in any danger, is she?'

'What makes you think that?'

'The letters, this meeting.'

Marcus Harrison laughed. He had taken the cigarette from his mouth and held it between finger and thumb the way an artist might hold a stick of chalk. He pointed it at Henry and said, 'I wish you hadn't asked that question, Henry. It makes what I'm going to say next sound awfully sinister, which it isn't at all.'

Henry waited tensely.

'Is Trudi still in touch with her family in Germany?' Harrison went on.

'She's Swiss,' Henry said, automatically.

'Oh, come on!' Harrison said.

'Well, whatever she is, the answer's the same – no, she's not in touch with any of her relatives, not that I know of.'

'Doesn't she receive *any* letters from Berlin?'

'Hell's teeth!' said Henry. 'Don't tell me *you* think Trudi's a spy?'

'Ah! So that's what they've been saying, is it?'

'I mean, what the hell's she going to spy on in Flannery Park? My brother's a brickie and my father, as you know, works downstairs in our machine-room. What's Trudi supposed to be spying *on?* How much paper you order? How many bricks it takes to build a council house or how many bags of tea the Co-op sells in a week?' Henry said, snappishly. 'Chancellor Hitler's got more to do with his time and his nation's resources than set up a spy ring in Wingfield Drive.'

'Calm down, Henry,' the editor told him. 'Not for one minute do I think your wife's spying for the Nazis, or anyone else for that matter.'

'Then why did you ask me if she was?'

'I didn't say anything of the sort,' Marcus Harrison said. 'A touch of paranoia showing there, Henry? I thought you had more sense than to listen to silly gossip. Anyone with an alien accent is suspect in this city, especially when things are so unsettled. I mean, it might be worse. They might be accusing her of being Jewish or even a Roman Catholic in cahoots with the Vatican. How would that go down in Flannery Park?'

Henry did not have it in him to laugh. He grunted.

'I simply asked if Trudi kept in touch with her old friends in

Germany,' Marcus Harrison continued. 'And, yes, there is a point to my enquiry.'

'What point?' said Henry. 'Sir?'

'Oh, don't start that, Henry, for heaven's sake,' the editor told him. 'As a matter of fact I'm thinking of sending you *and* your dear wife on a trip to the Fatherland, all expenses paid.'

'For how long?'

'Ten days, couple of weeks, that sort of thing.'

'For what?'

'Copy.'

Henry's grim expression faded. 'Life in Germany Today: How the Ordinary German Citizen Lives: What Difference does Hitler Make?'

'That's three for a start.'

'How much ingress will my press card get me?'

'I can personally arrange some interviews and give you some useful introductions, if that's what you mean,' Marcus Harrison said. 'The Berlin press corps are a clannish lot. I think that's the American influence. Naturally Chancellor Hitler wishes to control information about what he's doing, what he *has* to do to bring Germany back from collapse. Some of that sort of discipline, even if it is a bit sharp and ruthless, might do Britain no harm.' Harrison hesitated. 'Don't you think?'

'I think he might do well to root out the troublemakers in his own party.'

'The ruffians, the hooligans, you mean?'

'Yes,' Henry agreed. 'But what you'll want from me is the domestic aspect, isn't it? I mean you're buying reasonably good information from the agencies as it is.'

'I thought,' Harrison said cautiously, 'that's where Trudi might be of use.'

'I'll need a translator anyway,' Henry said. 'Might as well be the wife.'

'I take it you've no objection to going on a field trip?'

'On the contrary,' said Henry. 'When, though?'

'That's rather up to you. Pick your time.'

'Before Christmas?'

'Christmas in Berlin is always jolly,' Harrison said, 'but no, I think it would be all too easy to be sidetracked by the festivities. I'd suggest the early part of the year. February or March, say.'

'Fine.'

'Meanwhile, if Trudi has any friends with whom she can establish contact so much the better,' Harrison said. 'There is just one other point.'

101

'What's that?'

'I'd prefer it if the idea of a field trip to Germany seemed to come from you,' Harrison said. 'I don't want to put Jock's nose out of joint, you see. If he thinks it's all your idea, he'll be more sympathetic.'

'Jock will bring it to you—'

'I'll huff and puff a little then give it the green light.'

'Fine,' said Henry again. 'When can I impart the glad tidings to Trudi?'

'As soon as you like,' Marcus Harrison said. 'But tell only Trudi, nobody else, not even your father or brothers.'

'In case one of the other papers nicks the idea?' said Henry.

'Well, you can't be too careful, can you?'

'That's true,' said Henry and a few minutes later went rattling back downstairs, a whole lot happier than he had been a half hour ago.

Sometimes it was the Tivoli in Partick or even, now and then, the La Scala in Clydebank. But as a rule the girls were happy enough to settle for a night out at the old Astoria picture house which was tucked away in the shadow of the cranes in the no-man's-land between Whiteinch and Scotstoun.

It didn't matter much to Vera and Doris what was showing. They were content to sit through any rubbish, even ancient cowboy pictures that a rowdy crowd at a kiddies' matinee would have jeered as unconvincing.

Brenda, however, fancied herself as a cineaste, a word she had encountered in a review of a Norma Shearer film, and which she pronounced 'sineest' as if it derived from advertising copy for Custom-Fit hosiery or Travis Banton lingerie. Brenda was a true devotee of the silver screen and, if he'd given her half a chance, would have run rings round that other more solitary dreamer, brother-in-law Bertie. Brenda was a dedicated reader of reviews, a devourer of fan magazines. She could tell you when Jean Harlow went from being a platinum blonde siren to a gay, red-headed hoyden, what Ginger Rogers regarded as Her Secret for Slaying a Stag Line, and Why Screen Love-making had Too High a Price for smart girl Bette Davis.

Jack, of course, had no interest in following his spouse into the catacombs of Hollywood glamour and even Vera and Doris, chums from way back, thought their small, blonde, breathless friend was nuts when it came to movies.

Currently Brenda was drawn to any film that promised a brush with a reckless adventurer, preferably involving whips. She was very attracted to the notion of running away to South America or to the South Seas, geographical locations which she assumed lay side by side somewhere just below the bottom edge of the Sunset Boulevard Star Map she'd carefully cut out of *Photoplay*.

In her secret heart of hearts, as Elinor Glyn might have put it, Brenda Burnside knew that her chances of making it much further than the less-than-tropical beaches of Ardrossan were slim to the point of non-existence. But she did not hold that against her husband or her two little girls and made do instead with a regular Tuesday night trip to the cinema accompanied by her unwed pals from the wrong side of the tracks.

The advantage in going to the Astoria, especially on a Tuesday, was that you never had to queue.

Small though the cinema was it accommodated its local audience comfortably and had on permanent patrol a tough-guy manager so intimidating that even the broken-down seats of the front stalls remained free of chirpers, howlers, raspberry-blowers and flingers of those little objects like bottle-tops and cigarette butts that rose and fell distractingly across the beam of the projector. What went on in the deep, dark rows of the balcony, however, the manager managed to ignore. He was a guardian of public order not public morals and, anyway, had been up there himself with a willing usherette or two. Once upon a time he had even been up there with Vera but neither he nor she could remember the episode very clearly and the smile that the gent in the dickie-bow gave to the ladies as they hustled past him in the foyer was the one he reserved for regular patrons, no more.

'What's on?' Vera asked.

She had passed not a minute before under the titled marque and was at that instant facing a poster of John Barrymore strangling his bearded brother in *Rasputin the Mad Monk*, but she did not appear to make the connection.

Brenda, who was well versed in Barrymore biography but hadn't much of a clue about Rasputin, filled in her ginger-haired friend while Doris purchased tickets. Then all three, clutching handbags stuffed with sweets, cigarettes and cosmetics, headed for the door into the dark.

The second feature was running to its inevitable conclusion.

Joel McCrea in a loincloth was stooped over Dolores del Rio who repined horizontally inside a dug-out canoe.

Brenda's mouth opened. Her pupils fastened on the uneven images as the odour of disinfectant and the sound of jungle drums enveloped her.

'What's 'at?' Doris stage-whispered.

Brenda answered automatically, '*Bird of Paradise*.'

'Have we seen it?'

'Aye, last year.'

'Was it good?'

'Aye, great!' said Brenda.

They were seated by torchlight towards the end of a row in the exact centre of the stalls, just at the ideal spot where the line of the floor breaks and sweeps down towards the screen.

Brenda, enraptured, didn't struggle to remove her heavy coat, nor did she take off her hat. She sat motionless, staring at the gigantic faces and wondering, in a very distant sort of way, what Jack would look like in a loincloth and, without being aware of it, pouting her lips in synch with the lovely Miss del Rio's. Here, in the dark with her friends, she could forget for a while that she was a wife and mother.

The twins were safe at home with Jack. He certainly knew how to look after them. He had grown ever more fond of his daughters as they'd evolved from wobbly wee pink rubber dolls into energetic bundles of mischief. He would play with them for hours and, no matter how hard his day had been, he never lost his temper with them. Besides, on those Tuesday evenings when Alex Burnside was on day-shift, Ruby and he would come round from the crescent and Ruby would cook Jack a proper supper, whatever that meant, and tidy up a bit and the twins would get more attention than was good for them.

No, Brenda had no need to worry about the welfare of her family and consequently suffered no guilt at enjoying a night out with the girls.

At length the music surged, the curtains shivered and closed, and Brenda relaxed. The stalls were pretty full for a weeknight and, turning, the girls looked back at the balcony, which was really no more than a raised tier at the rear of the house. Peering through the dim, brownish glow of the ceiling lights they scanned the seats for signs of any faces that might be familiar.

Courtship and mating, if not marriage, were constant obsessions with the clothing factory girls and Brenda, though she could not help but feel excluded on occasions, was pleased enough to share salacious gossip about people she did not know from Adam.

'Who's that? Is that Jimmy?'

'Nah! Is it?'

'Who's he with?'

'Is that her from the office? Miss La-de-da? What's her bleedin' name?'

'Janey McAfee? Aye, it could be.'

'Is it Jimmy right enough? I canny see.'

'It is, it's him. God, I thought he'd got more sense.'

'He'll have his hands full wi' her.'

'Aye, an' spillin' over.'

They sniggered.

Brenda removed her overcoat and hat, bundled them on to her knee, fished in her purse, found a ciggie and lit it. By her side Doris wriggled this way and that to survey the traffic in the aisles.

Music played faintly, an inappropriate English orchestral romp.

'Hey, Bren.' Vera reached across Doris to tap Brenda's arm and attract her attention. 'See him. Him there.'

Brenda glanced towards the aisle on her right.

The man was tall, made taller by a shiny-brimmed cap of the sort that skippers of South Sea island schooners wore. He had on a short black pea-jacket and a snow-white scarf – surely silk – was loosely knotted in the vee of the collar. It was not the features that Brenda recognised but the languid, rolling gait and the angle of the young man's head, held back with a kind of haughty arrogance as if he was looking down his snoot at everyone and everything.

'Is that not,' said Vera, 'thingmy? Him wi' the bad eye an' the brother?'

'God, so it is.' Doris giggled. 'Remember the birthday party?'

'Yon night at his house. Him an' the brother an' the other yin, aye.'

'I thought I would die when his mammy walked in.'

'Aye. Is that him right enough, Brenda?'

The young man in question had gone on down towards the Exit/Gents sign in the front corner of the house. Brenda, cigarette stuck to her lips, watched.

For a moment he was framed against the harsh, wet light of the tiled corridor, profiled in cap and seaman's jacket, and then the door closed with an audible thud and blotted the vision out.

'Well, is it?'

'Walter!' Brenda said. 'My God, it is! It's Walter.'

She felt suddenly as breathless as if a rope had been pulled tight across the top of her stomach just under her breasts.

'I thought it was. I never forget a face,' Vera said.

'What else d'ye not forget?' said Doris.

'Oh, aye. I remember that too all right. I thought he'd gone t' Austria.'

'Australia,' Brenda said. 'On the boats.'

She was staring, staring hard at the narrow door, waiting for it to open again, waiting to see Walter Giffard, her first love, her first lover.

She tried to feign casualness.

'Does he never write t' you?' Vera said.

'Naw,' Brenda said, wistfully.

'Does he no' send ye things? Like kangaroos?'

'Don't be bloody daft. How could he send her kangaroos?' said Doris.

'He could, if he wanted tae.'

'Baloney! Kangaroos is animals.'

'I thought ye ate them.'

'I suppose ye can. But ye canna send them in a parcel t' Scotland.'

The orchestral romp ended, the final few bars melding into the blare of the soundtrack so that Hollywood and rural England vied with each other for several discordant seconds.

The curtain turned silver, quivered, then opened with a jerk. Censor's certificate and studio credits appeared, listing, on screen. Music with an Imperial Russian flavour flooded the cinema.

The lights dimmed.

From the Exit/Gents doorway Walter Giffard emerged.

He glanced up sidelong at the screen and then, hands in pockets, made his way up the aisle again without undue haste. As he passed the row in which the girls were seated, Brenda tilted her shoulders and lifted up her face in the hope that he might recognise her. But with head held back and the brim of the schooner cap tipped over his brow Walter did not.

Cautiously Brenda turned to follow his progress up the little staircase that led to the balcony and, with Doris and Vera bobbing beside her, craned her neck to catch sight of who Walter might be with.

'Sit flamin' still, you lot,' a middle-aged man in the row behind them growled.

'Get knotted,' Vera said.

'Are you gonna let her talk to you like that, Colin,' snapped the middle-aged man's wife. 'Dirty wee trollop.'

'I'll send for the manager, so I wull,' Colin threatened.

Vera said, 'Send for the bloody manager then.'

'Aye,' said Doris, 'see if we care.'

'Colin Dawson, are you gonna . . . ?'

'You bloody shut it tae,' Colin told his wife.

The domestic tiff that broke out behind them smothered the argument with Doris and Vera. The girls, even Brenda, turned their attention to the screen again and let the ripples of domestic disharmony ebb away as husband and wife bickered in angry whispers and neighbours hissed out, '*Wheesht!*'

Three or four minutes later, when tempers had cooled and all eyes were glued to the Barrymores doing their stuff in a droshky, Doris leaned on Brenda's shoulder and murmured, 'Who's he with? Some big chick, is it?'

Morosely Brenda answered, 'Aye.'

'You should've married that one when ye had the chance.'

'I know.'

'Too late now, but,' Doris said.

And Brenda, sighing again, said, 'Aye.'

'My God!' Howard McGrath said. 'Bobs is right. You really do live like a pig, Declan.' He lifted a stringy garment from the kitchen chair and held it up at arm's length. 'What the devil's this?'

'My underwear, if you don't mind.'

'You wear this? You actually wear this?'

'We can't all be livin' on Mummy's money, Howard.'

Howard dropped the woollen combinations into a corner behind the coal bucket and, stooping a little, brushed the seat of the chair fastidiously with the back of his gloved hand. He flicked his coat-tails under him then cautiously sat down. The dank atmosphere of the basement room was marbled by frost and Howard suspected that he would find ice in the sink and certainly in the bowl of the lavatory at the corridor's end.

'If you've come about the money . . .' Declan said.

Howard tutted. 'I haven't come about the money.'

'Sure an' that's just as well,' Declan said.

'I am fast losing faith in your ability *ever* to pay what you owe me,' Howard said. 'When did you last eat?'

'I eat.'

'You could have fooled me on that score,' Howard McGrath said. 'Presumably if you're so well nourished you wouldn't be interested in partaking of a ham sandwich which I just happen to have in my possession.' From the pocket of his long overcoat he produced a bulky packet neatly wrapped in greaseproof paper. 'Two ham sandwiches to be exact.'

Declan was crouched on the bed, knees drawn up to his chin. He wore pyjama trousers, a cardigan and two pairs of thick stockings. He was white with cold yet his eyes glistened bright and hard in his emaciated face. To Howard he looked rat-like and furtive, yet he was pathetic too, a quality, Howard suspected, which the girls found difficult to resist.

Declan didn't grab the sandwich packet and Howard, after a moment, lobbed it on to the blanket by the Irishman's feet. He lit two cigarettes and held one out to Declan. This offering Decker accepted without hesitation. He sucked on the tobacco smoke, coughed, wiped his mouth with his wrist and continued to glower resentfully at his benefactor.

Howard said, 'All right, Decker. What's up? What's hurting?'

'Nothing's hurting.'

'Come now, I'm a doctor – well, almost. Come along, lad, tell Uncle Howard what's ailing you. Is your pride bruised? Is that it?'

'I'm busy, that's all.'

'Too busy to attend classes?'

'That's my business.'

'You'll dip the class exams and have to carry tickets, if you're not careful.'

'My business,' said Declan again.

'No, it's our business too, Decker, like it or not. We've come too far together to just stand idly by and watch you throw it all away.'

'Throw what away?' said Declan.

'Your career.'

The clenched face opened into a grin and Declan laughed. He made a wild, airy gesture with the hand that held the cigarette. 'My career! My wonderful career! I tell you this, Howard, my career's already settled. I've got my tickets for the term and nobody, *no-body* will be doin' the dip on me, not even that bastard T.K.'

'I *thought* your pride was hurt.'

'I was – there were reasons.'

'You shouldn't have answered back.'

'Who the hell does the man think he is, treatin' me like that in front of everyone?'

'I've seen worse treatment meted out for less,' said Howard. 'You have too. Think what it would have been like if you'd sauced old Collings.'

'I never sauced anyone. I made a mistake, that's all. Christ, are you not allowed to make one mistake in this damned medical factory?'

'All right, keep your shirt on,' Howard said. 'If I were you, though, I'd pull myself together mighty quick and trot up to the ward tomorrow and apologise to T.K. with all the humility you can muster, before he writes you off completely.'

'He won't do that.'

'No?'

'He knows how good I am. He won't hold me back.'

'No doubt he is also smitten by your modesty.'

Declan pinched the cigarette close to the tip, sucked smoke slowly into his mouth with a thin, hissing sound then said, 'Did she send you?'

'We're all concerned about—'

'She didn't send you, then?'

'Ah-hah!' Howard said. 'So that's what's really biting you, is it? You were given a big red face in front of the girls and you thought Alison would be down here at the double to comfort and console you.'

'I don't mean Alison. I don't care about Alison.'

'I'm sure she'd be terribly flattered to hear that, Declan.'

'You can have her if you want her.'

'Most gracious,' Howard said.

'Four days, four flamin' days, though, and not a sign of her.'

'We're talking about Bobs now, I assume.'

'Bitch!'

Howard got to his feet. He was so tall that his head almost touched the ceiling and he had to roll his neck to avoid striking the light-bulb.

'Time for me to go, Declan,' he said evenly.

'*Did* she send you?'

'I came by mutual agreement, if you must know.'

Declan slithered off the bed. So slight was he that in pyjama trousers and cardigan he appeared to be little more than a child, a ragged street urchin who would not have been out of place hawking the middens of Partick South. Howard did not think him pathetic now, however. He had glimpsed Mr Slater's darker aspect, that pitted side of the Irishman's nature which was usually hidden by charm and self-control.

'Why hasn't she come?' Declan said. 'Tell her I'm not pleased.'

'Oh, yes, I'll be sure to tell her that.'

'Tell her to come on Friday, like we arranged. Tell her I'll be all right by then an' I'll be waitin' for her.'

Howard hid his astonishment. He'd had no idea that Roberta had put herself into a position of being at Slater's beck and call. Or was this just another symptom of Declan's incredible egotism?

He fiddled with his elegant overcoat to avoid meeting Declan Slater's eye.

Casually he said, 'Guy may have something to say about that.'

'Guy?'

'Guy, who is partnering her to the Daft Friday ball.'

'No, she's not going to that. Not with Guy Conroy, not with anyone,' Declan said. 'Although I should not be tellin' you these things, sure I should not.'

'Perhaps Alison would do instead?' Howard suggested.

'I've no arrangement with her.'

'Just as well, really,' Howard said.

'What are you meanin' by that?'

'I doubt if I'd be too keen on Ally scampering off just to visit you in the middle of a nice slow foxtrot.'

'You?'

'Me, and Alison.'

'She's got a fiancé.'

'I know.'

'And she's going to Daft Friday with *you?*'

'Dreadful, isn't it?' Howard said. 'I don't know what young girls are coming to these days. However, I will pass on your message, your *command* to Roberta, unless you decide to come out of hiding and grace our little circle with your illustrious presence. In which case you can tell her yourself.'

'Just tell her, Howard, will you?'

'Of course, of course I will,' said Howard and, giving no sign of how he really felt towards the Irishman, left a moment later with an apparently amiable nod of farewell.

In Jim Abbott's opinion university education was not what it was in his young day; which was probably just as well.

The age of 'flappers' and disillusioned ex-servicemen had been too hectic to last for long. Alison's generation had no memories of the Great War. Ally had been only five or six when the war had ended. Her first day at school had been a more momentous event to her than a signing of the Armistice. Back then, too many students had been tainted by the profane experiences of trench warfare and were hell-bent on making up for lost time. By comparison Ally's contemporaries were babes-in-arms. They did not understand how bad it had been. And why should they? This, this *now* was the time of their lives. Besides, he had lied to Alison. He had no memories of Daft Friday dances. He had never been to one. He had been too poor to afford the price of tickets.

Perhaps it was to see, in part, what he had missed that he was seated in the Burnsides' living-room that Friday evening waiting for Alison to show off her brand new ballgown.

There was nothing to stop him taking Alison dancing at the Albert ballroom or the New Locarno. But somehow he had never been able to bring himself to suggest it. He was afraid that Alison would be embarrassed to be seen dancing with a one-armed war veteran almost old enough to be her father.

Jim and the Burnsides weren't hanging about just to admire Alison's dress. They were there to give the once-over to the young man who would partner her to the dance and who had sufficient gall – Henry called it 'nous' – to arrive at the house to collect her. Jim's acceptance of the arrangement struck the Burnsides as peculiar and no amount of reassurance from Trudi could allay their fears that Jim was actively encouraging Ally to throw herself at another man.

'When's he supposed to be here?' Bertie said, glancing first at the clock on the mantle then at his wristlet watch.

'Half seven,' said Davy.

'I hope the bugger's on time. I'm due at a management meeting.'

'I imagine he'll survive without shaking your hand, Bertie,' Henry said.

'Well, I've got a minute or two to spare, I suppose.' Bertie poured tea and lit another cigarette. 'No hurry.'

The house had been cleaned from top to bottom. Trudi and Ruby had put on their best clothes in spite of Alex's assertion that the bloke probably wouldn't step over the doorstep, not if he knew what was good for him.

Alison came downstairs at twenty-eight minutes past seven, just as Davy, who had been hovering by the window, called out, 'Taxi. It must be him.'

When Alison entered the living-room in a swirl of soft peach organdie Jim felt his heart rise into his mouth. She looked far too sophisticated ever to want to become the wife of a humble school teacher. His confidence took even more of a knock when the young man was ushered into the room. McGrath was taller than Jim had expected. He had dark brown hair and a strong-boned face and, although he was not particularly handsome, he carried himself well. His overcoat, Jim noted, was hand-cut and then he stopped looking at McGrath and studied Alison's reaction to the young man instead.

It was, Alison knew, an awkward situation. She felt Jim's eyes upon her. She had dreaded this moment and yet, at the same time, had been excited by the prospect of showing off her friend from university. She couldn't help herself. She still suffered from a need to impress them now and then and Howard would certainly do that. She was proud of Howard, of his easy and familiar manner. He had so much self-assurance that the awkwardness of the situation seemed to evaporate at once. Howard knew precisely what was expected of him. He was not afraid to play his part. Howard wouldn't let her down.

'And this is my fiancé, Jim Abbott.'

A strong grip, a nod, a certain confidentiality in the smile: 'I've heard a great deal about you, sir.'

'Sit yourself down for a minute, son,' Alex said. 'Take the weight off.'

'Dad,' said Alison, with just a touch of patronage, 'the taxi is waiting.'

'Oh, let the meter run,' McGrath said. 'It'll be nine before things warm up, anyhow.' He seated himself on the chair that Davy had promptly vacated.

Jim remained on his feet, shoulder against the wall at the window bay, watching, not amused now but fretful.

'How long does this affair last?' Alex asked.

'Alison will be home by one o'clock, sir.'

'By taxi?' said Bertie.

'Oh, yes.'

'You don't live in Flannery Park, do you?' said Ruby.

'I lodge near the university. My family home's in the Borders.'

'What does your old man do then?' said Alex.

'Dad!' said Alison, chidingly.

'He's a soldier.'

'What regiment?' Jim heard himself ask.

'King's Own Scottish.'

'Was he with them on the Marne?'

'Yes, I believe he was.'

'What rank's he got?' Davy asked.

'Colonel.'

'I see, I see,' said Alex. 'A big cheese, then.'

By now Alison had put on her overcoat and hat and wrapped one of Trudi's chiffon scarves about her throat. She wore outdoor shoes and carried her dancing pumps in a cloth bag in her hand, provincial imperfections which, in Jim's eyes at least, made her seem all the more endearing.

'Dad . . .' Alison said and with no more than that little hint to trigger him, Howard got to his feet and went around the circle once more, politely shaking hands with everyone.

Only when that was done did he turn to Alison. 'All set?'

'Ready when you are.'

Howard glanced at Jim, held his gaze.

Nothing was said, nothing that could be construed as challenge or misinterpreted as reassurance; yet it took the sting from the kiss that Alison bestowed upon Jim, a quick little touching of the lips. He smelled her perfume, Trudi's perfume, then Alison and Howard were gone.

Henry closed the front door.

The sound of Alison's laughter drifted back to them from the path outside, back into the peculiar silence that had settled on the family. They listened in rapt silence as the door of the taxi-cab slammed shut and the vehicle growled away up Wingfield Drive.

Alex cleared his throat. 'Well,' he declared, with patent insincerity. 'I don't think much o' him.'

Bertie, already diving into his coat and searching for his hat, was more honest. He said, 'Well, I thought he was nice, *very* nice.'

'I don't think she'll come to any harm,' said Ruby, vaguely.

Davy, haversack on his shoulder, called out, 'G'night all,' and hurried out of the front door, with Bertie hard on his heels.

It was only then that Trudi put her hand on Jim's shoulder, gave him a little pat of sympathy and understanding. 'You will stay with us for supper, no?'

Jim said, 'No, I think I'd better get on home.'

'Suit yourself,' said Alex and, without more ado, urged Henry to show the teacher to the door.

The taxi-cab sped down the Kingsway towards Dumbarton Road. Ally rested her cheek briefly on Howard's shoulder. 'God, wasn't it awful?'

'Oh, I don't know. It wasn't so bad.'

'Oh, it was, it was awful.'

'It did rather seem as if I was on parade. Can't blame them, I suppose.'

'Jim's face . . .'

'I didn't realise that he was quite so much older . . .'

'I *am* engaged to him, Howard. And I *will* marry him.'

'Of course, you will. Of course.'

'I mean it.'

'Of course, you do. Of course,' Howard said. 'But not tonight.'

Alison sighed. She could smell leather, the rich, heavy nappy material of Howard's overcoat and the light perfume of his shaving soap. When she inclined herself towards him her skirt rustled against the seat's edge and she felt the slither of unfamiliar silk underwear against her thighs.

Howard put his arm about her, not possessively. Once more she rested her cheek against his shoulder and in a strange, timid little voice, quite unlike her own, said, 'No, Howard, not tonight.'

Ruby and Alex left 162 about a quarter past eight to walk round to Shackleton Avenue to keep Brenda company until Jack returned from his late Friday night shift. Ruby linked her arm through Alex's and matched her short, choppy step to his longer stride.

They walked a hundred yards under the streetlights in silence and then, out of nowhere, Alex said, 'He'd make her a right good husband, wouldn't he?'

'Who?'

'I don't mean him. I mean one like him, his type.'

'What type are you talkin' about?'

'That officer's boy, whatsisname again?'

'McGrath.'

'Aye, right.'

Ruby had been turning the same thought over in her mind. She didn't rise to the bait, though. She'd learned in the hard school of the Argyll Hotel, where she'd worked until marriage, that it was always better to express no opinion rather than blurt out the first thing that came into your head.

Ten or a dozen yards further on Alex said, 'I'm wonderin' if we weren't a wee bit hasty agreein' to the engagement wi' Jim Abbott.'

'If it hadn't been for Jim Abbott she'd never have been in a position to meet a man like Mr McGrath – or his type – in the first place.'

'Well, maybe. But Jim hasn't done much for her since, has he?' Alex said. 'All he does is hang around like a spare – like a spare tyre.'

'He loves her,' Ruby said. 'Is that not enough?'

'I wouldn't know anythin' about that love stuff.'

'Would you not now? How about me?'

'You? What've you got to do with it?'

'You waited long enough to get your hands on me.'

'That was different.'

'Was it?' Ruby said. 'If I recall rightly you weren't exactly round at the door every night bearin' bouquets o' roses and boxes o' chocolates.'

'I done your garden.'

'Aye, an' a right mess you made of it too.'

Again the couple walked in silence.

They passed the big opaque, plate-glass windows of the Co-op where Bertie worked without glancing at their reflections, at the unity that the glass made of them as they bobbed on by.

At length Alex said, 'I don't know what he's thinkin' of, lettin' her gallivant out wi' other men.'

'It's only a dance, damn it. She's got a right to enjoy herself.'

'Not when she has a fine-nancy already.'

'It's what *he's* doin' to *her* that worries me,' Ruby said.

'What?' said Alex, breaking stride. 'Who's doin' what to Ally?'

'I don't mean that. I mean – rope.'

'Rope?'

'Givin' her rope. Jim's givin' her too much rope. It's wrong to spoil her.'

'That's just what Trudi says,' Alex put in.

Conversations with Trudi had brought certain facets of Alison's relationship with Jim Abbott into perspective. According to Trudi, the school teacher lacked self-confidence. He was astute enough to let Alison go her own way, though, to make few demands upon her, knowing that if the engagement held, then the marriage would too. Trudi had also pointed out that Alison's graduation from Glasgow University would not be the end of the couple's problems but only the beginning. This obvious fact hadn't occurred to Alex.

'If she was to break off with him . . .' Alex hesitated, then went on, 'I mean, if she was to come to me an' say, "Dad, I'm needin' your advice," . . .'

'Hah!' said Ruby.

'Well, she might.'

'Not her. She'd go to Trudi first, or to Henry.'

'What would they tell her that I wouldn't?'

'They'd tell her to stick by her promise to Jim.'

'Would they?' Alex sounded surprised.

'You don't know your own children very well, do you, dear?'

'Trudi's no child o' mine. Far too old for a start,' Alex said. 'An' Henry, naw, none of us have ever been able to fathom what went on in his head. Even his mam could never understand him.'

'He's what they call a conservative.'

'What's his politics got to do wi' it?'

'Not politics. The way he thinks. He's . . .' Ruby sought for the word but was temporarily unable to explain the difference between what Henry believed and how he behaved. She shook her head impatiently. 'It's not goin' to come to that, anyway, Alex. Alison's a decent girl, sensible. She'll stick with Jim.'

'Aye, but should she?'

'That's not for me to say.'

'Son of a colonel, though,' Alex said. 'Rich too by the look o' him. By God, that would be somethin' to write home about, havin' one like him in the family.'

'Maybe he'll marry Bertie instead.'

'What?'

'Nothin',' said Ruby and, pushing open the gate, walked rapidly ahead, filled with happy anticipation at seeing her grandchildren again and, for once, her own daft wee daughter too.

Five bands, in rotation, played the three halls in the Union. In the library those of libidinous disposition snogged in the alcoves and those to whom no social event was complete without alcohol supped gin and whisky from smuggled silver tassies and thought themselves very daring and modern. Somewhere on the premises Dipsy McDonald had managed to conceal a hogshead of beer and, in open defiance of Senate ordinance, he and his cohorts went strutting around the corridors with brimming tankards held aloft and froth all over their dickie-bows.

Peggy Lockhart, on the other hand, had finally overcome her devotion to the fat law student. She arrived in tandem with a weedy wee joker named Freddie Gore whose avowed ambition was to write the great working-class novel. Freddie was strictly TT and had about as much sense of humour as an Ibsen heroine. But he had already informed Peggy that she alone would be his muse from now on and, to show that he had already gone some way to acquiring a working-class turn of phrase, referred to her endearingly as 'Effing Peggy, the love of mah effing life', and refused to dance the tango to illustrate his solidarity with the oppressed peoples of the Argentine.

The oppressed peoples of Glasgow, taking a breather from the heat of the halls, swanked it on the staircase that led up from the foyer. They draped themselves in Maugham-like poses against the balustrades or snuggled knee-to-knee, kissing in full view of all to demonstrate how much in love they were and how that love would triumph over all adversity, except perhaps being trampled on by the roughnecks who came bounding down the staircase to use the ground-floor urinals.

There were two brief scuffles and, in the half-dark under a towering wall of theological textbooks, one even more perfunctory deflowering which so terrified the parties involved that they both burst into tears and scuttled away, sobbing, in opposite directions to curse the day that Daft Friday madness had driven them carelessly together.

No such nastiness for Alison and Howard, Guy and Roberta. They were models of prudence and rectitude. The most daring thing that happened during the course of the evening was that Howard purchased a miniature of gin from a sleazy young coxswain named Dalrymple, topped up the girls' orange juice – over ladylike protests, of course – then led them all, sweating again, into a third set of the Eightsome Reel.

All the *heuching*, stamping, coat-tail-flying exuberance of the reels, hiphugging Conga lines, shimmy and shake of the ever-popular Charleston, all seemed nothing compared to the late-hour renditions of soft, slow, sentimental melodies which both big bands played in unison. Then the whole building seemed to swim with a heady air of romance which drove out the drinkers and roughnecks and caused their abandoned girlfriends to weep alone in neuks and alcoves or rush heartbroken from cloakrooms, hats askew.

The bands played 'Just One More Chance' and 'Love is the Sweetest Thing'.

116

Out on the dance-floor Alison clung to Howard, Guy to Roberta, each one wondering if what they felt for the other now was just affection or if, like love, it would increase and endure. And if so, just what would become of those feelings after the night was through.

FOUR

Target for a Kiss

The twins had outgrown the pram and were rapidly becoming too obstreperous to be accommodated in the double-sided push-chair which Henry and Trudi had purchased for them. They were wriggly as eels and could easily escape the straps which were intended to keep them secure. And between them they weighed a ton.

Brenda, puffing, had to tug and haul to get them over kerbs and up steps and when she reached a hill of any size would have to thrust into the handle like a pit-pony to make any forward progress at all.

The push-chair, however, remained the lesser of two evils. The alternative was to take the twins by the hand, one on each wing, and risk being tripped every couple of yards or dragged this way and that as they toddled in erratic patterns which could make a trip to the shops seem longer and more circuitous than a chapter from Livingstone's travels.

Jack had an answer. Jack usually did. He would hoist one twin on to his shoulders, button the other to his chest and, like some grotesque creature from legend, would shuffle along under the burden until his strength gave out. Then he would carefully lower both girls to the pavement and let them meander until he'd recovered his breath, reverse their positions on his body and take off again for another three or four hundred yards, a process laughably referred to as 'going for a wee walk'.

Jack wasn't with Brenda that Saturday afternoon when, shoving the push-chair, she trekked across Flannery Park into the unfamiliar neighbourhood south of the school, beyond the railway line. She was heading for a row of shops – 'Wattie's shops'. If that location didn't bear fruit, she would descend into Dunsinane Street and pass the house where Walter lived when, as now, he came home from sea.

Soon after she'd spotted her ex-boyfriend in the old Astoria, Brenda had contrived to encounter Mr George Giffard, Wattie's father, on the street. After ten seconds of casual chat, she had asked him directly if Walter was at home.

'Why, yes,' Mr Giffard had said. 'He's on leave for five or six weeks.'

'Over Christmas, like?'

'So he tells me.'

'Is Scott with him?'

'Scott?' Mr Giffard seemed to have trouble recalling his first-born. 'Scott. Ah, no, Scott, is residing in New Zealand. It appears he has undergone a form of marriage with a – with a lady of Polynesian extraction.'

'A darkie?' Brenda had cried in surprise and delight. 'Scott married a darkie? What does his mam – Mrs Giffard have to say about that?'

'Mrs Giffard is, alas, not very well.'

With difficulty Brenda had kept her face straight.

'Sorry, you know, to hear it.' She'd cleared her throat. 'Walter's not married, is he?'

'Not that I know of,' Mr Giffard had said.

'Never can tell with Wattie, eh?' Brenda had said, cheerfully. 'Maybe he's got a darkie lady tucked away someplace too.'

'There is a woman, a Caucasian . . .'

'Eh?'

'White – but she – she's not our sort, Brenda, not our sort.'

'What sort is she then?'

Brenda knew Mr Giffard hardly at all really, yet a peculiar affinity existed between them as if the straitlaced, long-suffering father found in her an image of the daughter he had never had.

Brenda had the feeling that if they hadn't been standing on a street corner Mr Giffard might have taken her into his confidence and blurted out all sorts of interesting things about Wattie and Wattie's unsuitable woman. As it was, all Mr Giffard said was, 'Brash, alas, too brash,' then, tipping his hat politely, had gone striding off down the Kingsway to catch a tram.

Brenda, not noted for sensitivity, felt sorry for the poor henpecked sod. She wished that things might have worked out differently, in respect of Walter, that is, so that handsome, mannerly, long-suffering Mr Giffard might have had the pleasure of being her father-in-law instead of Alex Burnside.

It was simply in the hope that she might encounter Walter, to talk with him, to try to resurrect some of the carefree, guilt-tingling feelings that he'd once engendered in her breast, that Brenda hurled the push-chair across Flannery Park. Past the school, past the railway steps, she nursed the faint, fond, hopeless hope that she might, by chance, meet Wattie in or around the shops.

Which, by chance, she did.

Same old Wattie. Same arrogant cock of the head. Same loose, untidy look to him, except that the clothes he wore now were fashioned from sailor's fustian, augmented by an orange and lemon mock-silk shirt. He had no suntan, which was a disappointment to Brenda who somehow thought that sculling around the South Seas might have transformed Wattie into the likeness of John Loder. He was just as pale and pasty as he had been at school, just as languid, still with that madly attractive 'lazy' eye, hooded and supercilious.

'Wal-ter! What a surprise!'

'No, it isn't,' Walter said, glancing at her from a great height.

'It is t' me.'

'You saw me in the picture-house.'

'Did I?'

''Course you did. You were with that pair from the factory.'

'Doris and Vera.'

'Right.'

'If you saw me,' Brenda said, 'why didn't you, you know, say somethin'?'

'Like what?'

'Like, "Hello, Brenda. How's it goin'." '

'I was with somebody.'

'So what! Does she keep your tongue in her pocket?'

'What's that supposed to mean?'

'You know fine well what it means,' said Brenda. 'Who were you with, anyway? The Caucasian?'

'The what?'

'It wasn't a darkie, was it?'

'For Christ's sake, what are you rabbitin' on about?' He almost laughed, though, and shook his head. 'You haven't changed, have you?'

'That's for you to say.'

He scrutinised her thoroughly enough to make Brenda flush. Then he shifted his attention to the rowdy objects in the push-chair who were working away ham-fistedly on the straps and buckles, girning and yapping and desperate to be let loose to wreak havoc in Snape's Grocery Store by whose lighted window the group had gathered.

'If they're yours,' Walter said, 'then you have changed.'

''Course they're mine,' Brenda said indignantly. 'What difference do they make to how I look?'

'You look like their mother, Brenda.'

'I am their bloody mother.'

'There you are then,' Walter said.

'There I am, what?'

The shops were crowded with women and children. Menfolk, those in work and out of it, had better things to do than haunt the stores. The men were out enjoying themselves, if you could call it that, on the terraces at Ibrox or Firhill, lost in the greeny-grey spaces of the December afternoon.

How weird, Brenda thought, to be standing in the pale yellow half-light from Snape's window, chatting to Walter Giffard as if nothing had happened to either of them in the past four years.

'You have changed,' Walter said. 'You're a mother now.'

Bee yelled, *'Mammy, Mammy, Mam, Mam.'*

Her sister hit out at her with a small, mittened fist, giggling, then they both squirmed sideways and backwards to look up at the height of Walter as if they did not approve of strange men talking to their mother.

'Mama-mama-mama. Maaaaaah.'

'Hold on a minute, dear. Mum's talkin' to this nice gentleman.' Stooping, Brenda tightened a strap, snapped a blanket across small kicking legs. She glanced up at Walter. 'What difference does that make? I'm still the way I was. More, you know, or less.'

The coat was the best she had, a brown thing that did not suit her colouring but was lined and warm. Her hat was held on with a hatpin which she could feel sticking against her scalp like a bone. She had put on earrings, nice little diamanté things which suddenly seemed not just anomalous but cheap.

Walter gave that almost-laugh again, squinting down at her.

'I'll say this for you, Brenda, you've still got a cute wee bum.'

This wasn't her Walter talking any more; Walter the prudish seducer, the cautious lover. This was Walter off the boats, Scott Giffard's brother, coarse as sackcloth. She was disappointed in him and, at the same time, flattered.

'You should know,' she said, flirting for a split-second before Lexi caught at her hair and pulled her head down.

'Out, out, Lexi *waaan' ouuuw-t.'*

'In a *minute.'*

Brenda disentangled herself from her daughter's clutches, pushed the chair arm's length away but did not release her hold on it.

She said, 'Why did you never write to me, Walter?'

'Hadn't anythin' to say.'

'You could've told me where you were.'

'I thought my old man told you. You seem to be very cosy with him.'

'Well, I had to ask to somebody,' Brenda said. 'What did he say about me?'

'Just that you'd called at the house lookin' for me. It was months later, anyway. All over.'

'What was all over?'

'You an' me. Nah, I don't mean that the way it sounds. I mean, everythin' in this neck of the woods. I had to get out, Brenda, before I got smothered.'

He lifted his shoulders and looked past her, without alarm or curiosity, at arms waving from the push-chair, an image that reminded him of a deity he'd seen in Calcutta on his second voyage out. Though stewards for the P & O weren't much into foreign gods. Balinese dancers were more in their line.

'You weren't stifled, Walter. You could've done anythin' you wanted to. You could've gone to the university too. You could've become a doctor, like—'

'How is Ally, by the way?' Walter interrupted.

'We don't see much of her, thank God. She's too busy hob-nobbin' with her posh friends to bother with the likes of us.'

'She's still at home, though?'

'Aye. Which reminds me, how many times have *you* been home?'

'Twice,' Walter answered. 'Briefly.'

'So you'll know she's engaged to old Wingy Abbott?'

'Yes, I heard.'

'God knows what he sees in her.'

'He's nuts about her, always has been,' Walter said.

'I'll bet he's never had her in bed,' said Brenda.

Walter did not pretend to be shocked. 'He isn't that type. Neither's Ally, come to think of it. It'll be marriage or bust for them.'

'Have you seen her?' Brenda asked.

'Nope.'

'Well, she's not your wee angel any more, Wattie. I heard that she's been runnin' around with other men, young blokes, behind Jim Abbott's back.'

Walter's expression was impassive.

He said, 'Does Jack still play the cornet?'

'Naw,' Brenda said. 'He's at the football, watchin' his brother.'

'You stay in Shackleton Avenue now, don't you?' Walter said.

'What of it?'

'I might drop round some night, okay?'

She looked at him but, not unusually, could read nothing of his intentions in his face. This was what she had come for, she supposed, one sign of interest, assurance that she hadn't lost all her attractiveness and that a good-looking devil like Walter Giffard might still want her, married or not. Somehow, though, she wasn't satisfied. She felt stupid, flirting with a sailorman in front of Snape's window with the twins, her twins, yammering for attention and the greeny-grey sky beginning to curdle into dusk.

'What about, you know, your woman, the cocky-asian?'

'She isn't my woman.'

'So you say.'

'She's Frankie's wife. Remember Frankie?'

Brenda would never forget the hawk-featured sailor who had squeezed her breasts at Scott's birthday party. He had frightened her in a way that no other man had ever done.

She swallowed, asked, 'What's Frankie's wife doin' with you?'

'I'm just showin' her the town,' Walter said. 'While Frankie's at sea.'

'What's her name?'

'Beryl.'

'Does Frankie know about it?'

'Don't be daft.'

'Is she stayin' at your house?'

'With her sister, in Renfrew.'

'For how long?'

'She goes back to Hull on Monday.'

'An' you with her?'

'Maybe,' Walter said. 'I doubt it.'

'Why not?'

'I've had enough of Beryl, to tell the truth.'

The push-chair was shaking now, rocking on its big rubber wheels. A scruffy-looking mongrel, attracted by the racket, sniffed at the edge of the twins' blanket.

'*Doggie, doggie, doggie, Maaah.*'

'Get away t' hell.' Brenda kicked at the dog and yanked the push-chair out of harm's way.

'I can see you're busy,' Walter said. 'I'd better shove off.'

She turned her back on her daughters for a moment and, on impulse, put a hand on his sleeve.

'Three ones,' she told him.

'What?'

'A hundred and eleven. Our number, you know, in the avenue.'

'Best time?'

'Friday night, not too late.'

'What about them?' Walter Giffard said, nodding towards the twins.

'Leave them to me,' said Brenda and, suddenly trembling, thrust herself against the push-chair and set off for home at the double.

Broken shirt buttons were the bane of Alison's life. She recalled how her mother had complained about them too and speculated on how all her boys managed to turn their buttons into crushed aspirin faster than she could replace them.

Alison now knew that it was the weight of the paddle in the hand-cranked washing-machine which did the damage and, being scientifically-minded, had proved her theory by leaning over the open lid to watch the garments being smeared against the sides of the tank. Some dedicated housewives would probably remove the buttons before the wash and sew them neatly on again afterwards but she, with Trudi's approval, preferred to take a chance on some being saved and played roulette with the noisy green device which occupied pride-of-place between the sinks in the kitchen.

Currently the green device was winning and, while Trudi ironed peacefully at her elbow, Alison snipped and sewed and bit away needle-threads, garment by garment, and tried to convince herself that it was good practice for stitching human flesh to which, of course, the cloth bore no resemblance.

For once the rest of the house was deserted. There were no stressful sounds, only the restful slither of the iron, snip of scissors and rumbling little snores from the hearthrug where Pete lay, toasting his belly before the fire.

'You are not tired?' Trudi asked.

'I told you,' Alison answered. 'No. Oddly enough, I'm not.'

'When I was a girl of your age all day I would be sleeping after a ball.'

'I expect balls were bigger in those days.'

Trudi gave a little chuckle at Alison's unintentional *double entendre* but the young woman remained oblivious and went on sewing, her eyes large with concentration behind her horn rimmed spectacles.

Trudi did not attempt to explain the joke.

She too was wary of Alison now, fearful of offending her. She appreciated the difficult time her sister-in-law was having and the peculiar, almost perverse, nature of Alison's relationship with the staid school teacher. For the rest, she could only guess at the pressures that Alison was under, in and out of the classroom, and at the confusion that must surely exist behind her air of competence.

Of all the Burnsides only Trudi was qualified to detect evidence of a passionate nature at work in Alison. She too had been regarded as 'clever' in her youth, quick-witted, precociously well informed. None of those qualities had quenched the fire in her blood, a fever which, before she was twenty, had almost destroyed her. What was most remarkable about her state of mind in those days was that she had *known* what she was doing, had deliberately courted disaster to satisfy her cravings for sexual attention and the knowledge that went with it.

She slid the iron smoothly over the fabric of Bertie's white cotton apron, peeled the apron from the board, folded it neatly and put it down upon the bundle of finished garments in a wicker basket by her side.

Alison said, 'It wasn't a real ball, anyway. Just a dance.'

'But you enjoyed it, did you not?'

'Oh, yes.'

'Did he dance well with you?'

'Howard? Yes.'

'He is not handsome but he is – personable. That is the word?'

'That's the word all right,' said Alison.

'If there was not a Jim, would Howard be more attentive to you?'

Alison glanced up from the needle, prodded her glasses on to her nose. She wore an old school cardigan over a blouse and a blue skirt and looked, at that moment, too young to be seriously discussing men.

'Probably,' Alison said.

'You do not mind that I ask you these things?'

'Why should I mind?' Alison bit at a thread. 'At least none of you have accused me of having a secret affair with Howard.' She paused. 'Not yet, anyway.'

'Why do you say such a thing?'

'Hah!' said Alison with a trace of annoyance. 'Now you're going to tell me I've a subconscious desire for it, aren't you?'

'I was going to say nothing of that sort,' Trudi told her. 'I was going to ask if he had kissed you?'

'Well, that's nice,' said Alison.

'I am not disapproving.'

'I know you're not.'

'*Have* you been the target of his kiss?'

'God, Trudi, you make me sound like a pillbox on the Maginot Line.' Alison managed to grin, just. 'Yes, yes. There you are! I haff bin ze target of heez keess. All right? Satisfied now?'

'How good was he?'

'Morally,' Alison said, 'or technically?'

'I do not understand.'

'Morally, he was *almost* a perfect gentleman . . .'

'Almost, you say?'

'In terms of technical ability Howard turned out to be excellent.'

126

Trudi had stopped ironing now. 'The tongues?'

'Yes, the tongues.'

'You did not know this about him before?'

'Nope. Three years of being pals with Howard and it turns out I know nothing about him. Well, nothing really important, like how good he is at kissing.'

'There is cuddling too? In the taxi-cab?'

'Right there in the back seat.'

'How did you struggle?'

'Ineffectually,' Alison said.

It was Trudi's turn to laugh. She leaned on the ironing board and contemplated Alison with renewed interest.

Alison said, 'I hope you're not going to tell anyone about this?'

'I am not a brother to you. I am confidential,' Trudi said. 'Go on.'

'I liked it,' Alison admitted. 'It was very nice to be kissed by somebody you know you can trust. Just for the sake of it. No strings. No obligations.'

'In a taxi-cab, also,' Trudi said, wistfully.

She remembered a time in Paris before the war when she had been very young indeed. The smell of leather, the richness of the smoke of a cigar, rain rivering the windows, Max Dahrendorf's hard lips upon her soft ones, his hand pushed up between her thighs. How she thought that he loved her more than anything in life. How when the cab set her down at the gate of Papa's hotel, she felt as if her body would burst with longing and that her heart would break if he did not come to her again soon. He did come, all too soon. After which there were other taxi-cab rides, less pleasant, to remember.

Glasgow was not Paris, however, and this was 1933 not 1911.

The little tweak of envy that Trudi felt for Alison's experiment with the soldier's son lasted no longer than the flicker of memory itself.

She said, 'It was better than with Jim?'

'Different,' Alison said. 'Jim hardly ever kisses me, not on the mouth.' Once more she paused, cautiously. 'I love Jim, of course, but . . .'

Now that she said it she was no longer sure it was the truth. Why, for instance, had she found it necessary to add 'of course' to the statement? Intimate conversations with Trudi frequently carried the risk of giving away too much, too many secrets. It was her sister-in-law's coolness, her matter-of-factness, her willingness to bring out into the open all manner of things that most other women sought to keep hidden that lured her, Alison, into indiscretion.

She sewed, saying nothing for a moment, thinking instead of the effect that Howard's kisses had had on her, far different from

Declan's. There had been more than a touch of romance in Howard's approach, just that hint of eagerness which had transformed calculation into promise and promise into pleasure. The taxi-cab ride had left her breathless with excitement, had engendered a centred and quite selfish sexual longing which had tinted their whole evening together and, not unpleasantly, had filled it with expectation. It was not furtive, though, not intense as it always was with Declan, for Howard had nothing to gain, no secret objective beyond the sheer physical pleasure of holding her close, so close that she could feel his heart beating against her breast.

'The boy, Howard, would he marry you?'

'Good Lord!' said Alison. 'What kind of a question's that?'

'It is a reasonable one.'

'Even if Howard is serious about me, which I very much doubt, I wouldn't abandon Jim. I mean, how could I?'

'He is rich, this Howard?'

'The money's on his mother's side, I think.'

'Much, much money?'

'I told you, Trudi, I'm not interested in Howard.'

'He will be a doctor?'

'Without the shadow of a doubt. He's good. He'll go far.'

'As you will, also.'

'I'm not sure I want to. Go far, I mean.'

Trudi lifted the iron and tested it, first with her pinkie and then by laying it flat against her cheek. 'The heat has gone. I must wait for it to warm again.'

'For shirts?'

'Pants,' Trudi said. 'Pants next.'

'Trudi?'

'Hmmm?'

'Do you think it's wrong of me?'

'Wrong to do what?'

'Like other men the way I do.'

Trudi did not laugh. She did not even smile at the young woman's question, that question which every girl, intelligent or not, asked herself a thousand times before she was carried safely to the marriage bed.

'No,' Trudi answered, gravely.

'I like what—' Alison bit off the sentence like a tag-end of sewing thread.

'How they make you feel, no?' said Trudi.

Alison nodded.

'It is natural, quite natural,' said Trudi.

'You told me once that the body was not a mechanism.'

'Did I say that to you? I suppose, yes, I suppose I did.'

'Know what?' said Alison.

'What?'

'I'm beginning to think you were right.'

He had been drinking heavily all through Saturday and had eaten nothing but a heel of toast and a piece of cold bacon which he'd found stuck to the frying pan.

Early on Sunday morning, unable to sleep, he had gone out. He had walked for two or three meaningless hours. He had walked all round the West End, past deserted quadrangles, empty cloisters, silent Unions, locked gates. Past Infirmary buildings with haunting white lights glimmering in the cold, cold haze. Past public houses, boarded and barred, Catholic chapels open for business, churches waiting for the sound of bells. Past dogs and newsagents' shops and solitary men in shirtsleeves, hardier than winter weather, a child or two sent out early. Past Dowanhill's tennis courts, stripped for the season and, quickly, past Roberta's house, solemn as a sermon and apparently devoid of life.

He had never been inside Roberta's house. Had never been invited. Had no entrée, like Guy Conroy. No rights.

Couple of miles east, Bankhead Hotel glowed warm with early breakfast. Howard snug inside. Howard with his private income, his coffee and porridge, kippers, toast and *Sunday Post*.

If Declan had been sure of the road to Flannery Park he might have walked there too, strode past Alison's humble abode, like a night-stalker caught out by dawn. But it was too late by then. Church bells depressed him and the new, sprawling, idiosyncratic suburbs seemed as far away as Dublin town or the beautiful Wicklow hills.

He went back to his basement flat, broke out his last bottle of White Horse and, in lieu of lunch, drank himself, glowering, to sleep.

When he wakened it was dark again, the room icy, and he knew it would soon be time for Roberta to arrive.

'Good Lord, Declan, what have you done? I mean to say, I thought the house was on fire when I saw the glow under the door. What's come over you? Money from home?'

'Last of the coal,' Declan said. 'Blaze of glory, you know how it is.'

'That I do not,' said Roberta, looking round. 'Candles too?'

'Christmas come early.'

'What are you celebrating, may I ask?'

'The fact that you came after all.'

129

'What a fool you'd have looked if I hadn't, roasting your haunches by candlelight all on your own.' She sniffed. 'Have you been drinking?'

'Whisky punch. Want some?'

Roberta didn't answer.

When he stood behind her she allowed him to slip off her overcoat.

Declan said, 'Where are you supposed to be?'

'With Guy at a carol service.'

'But you'd rather be here with me, would you not now?'

Again Roberta evaded the question. When he touched her hair with his fingertips she eased away from him, turning on the heel of one pretty shoe. She was primly dressed, except for the lipstick which she would smear upon him like warm, red butter. She looked around again.

'Must say, Declan, you've got the place looking rather jolly. In a Dickensian sort of way.'

'No effort spared for your pleasure an' comfort, my love.'

'I'm not sure . . .'

'Sure of what? Of me? You can always be sure of me.'

'I doubt that,' Roberta said. '*You* wouldn't be *you* if one could be sure.'

'I still love you, Roberta. You can be sure of that.'

She plucked at a loose blonde curl.

If he had been wholly sober Declan might have recognised signs of doubt. Apprehension had been natural in her during those first visits. She'd been right to be uncertain. She knew what he did to her and what she really wanted him to do. It was herself she'd been afraid of back then, not him. And Declan had no reason to suspect that anything much had changed.

He put a hand – soaped and scrubbed for the occasion – upon her upper arm. He could feel the silky material of her blouse slide against the smooth muscle of the deltoid. He moved his finger up to touch the lateral end of the clavicle, to rub it with a gentle circular motion.

She drew away again.

'Did you not hear me, Bobs? I said I still love you.'

'Yes, Declan, I heard.'

She was certainly very serious tonight. He wondered if what was on her mind was the same thing that was on his, if her reticence was a sign that she had made up her mind, as he had made up his.

She put a hand to the waistband of her skirt, lifted the edge of her blouse.

Declan watched intently. 'Yes,' he said. 'Take it off.'

130

'No,' she said. 'I haven't come for that.'

'What have you come for then? Is it to be makin' fun of me?'

'Don't be ridiculous!' Roberta told him. 'I came to give you this.'

From the band of the skirt she extracted a Christmas card in a stiff white envelope, very slightly crushed. She passed it to him. He took it, watching her now as if, like a cat, she might suddenly turn on him and rake him with a claw.

'What is it?'

'What does it look like? It's a card, and a gift. Open it now if you like.'

Declan slit the seal of the envelope with his thumbnail and shook out the card. It showed a radiant cameo of the Virgin and Child, done to resemble stained glass but heavily sentimentalised. Inside was a more authentic-looking Bank of Scotland ten-pound note.

Written on the card in Roberta's hand was the message, *In the Hope that We May still be Friends*.

'Don't you like it? I thought you might like it, being Irish. It has a sort of Irish look to it, don't you think?'

'What the divil is this supposed to mean?' Declan held the tenner in one hand and the card in the other and waved them at her like tiny semaphore flags.

'I thought you'd prefer money to a knitted scarf. It's a gift, Decker. Strictly non-returnable.'

'I mean, the message?'

'Oh, that! Well, it's just to let you know I'm still fond of you.' She took a deep breath. 'But I won't be coming here again. That part of our friendship's over, Declan. I'm sorry.'

He flung the banknote at her. It struck her breast and fluttered to the floor. 'What is this? Do you think I'm a whore that can be bought off with a bit of money? Jesus and Joseph! I've *told* you I love you, what *more* is it you want from me?'

'I'm – I'm sorry. I didn't mean to insult you.'

'It isn't your damned money I'm wantin', Roberta. It's you.'

'No, that's over, Declan.'

'Because I made a fool of myself, is that the reason? I suppose now I'm a laughing-stock an' you can't go bein' seen about with me?'

'That's – that's just . . . silly.'

'Silly!'

He plucked the banknote from the worn linoleum and tossed it behind him on to the table then, before the girl could evade him, he lunged at her and caught her in his arms, pinning her arms to her side. He smashed his mouth against hers and kissed her, rubbing his lips over and over her lips while she struggled against him. When

131

he pressed against her, forcing her to feel the strength of his desire, she gave out a little whimpering cry and arched her back, tilting her belly against him, going slack.

He did not dare release her.

'Declan, no, please . . . no,' she moaned. 'I don't – want to – with you . . . now.'

'Want to what? You never did. You never gave me anythin' that was worth the havin',' Declan said. 'Was it better with him, with Conroy?'

'How can you possibly think that Guy would . . .'

'I haven't had enough of you yet,' Declan told her, his face an inch away from hers. 'You'll not be gettin' away from Decker Slater as easy as that.'

'I think – that's enough.'

'If it's your money you're worried about, you'll get it all back.'

'Declan, you're hurting me.'

The basement was hot. Dampness, drawn from walls and ceiling, made the air seem foetid. She could hear flames roar in the throat of the chimney and see the glow upon the walls. It was as if the room itself was endeavouring to consume her.

When Declan leaned his hips against the table's edge, Roberta followed him with tripping little steps. She felt full, full and swollen. And foolish too. She knew that she would have to stop him soon and that he would be enraged. It was only his anger that frightened her, not his hurt. Declan had always been dispensable.

'Please, let me go now,' she said.

'Not 'till I've done with you,' he told her.

She felt weak with the realisation that she had driven him to this, that she could not be considered blameless. She had manipulated him, had coaxed the violence that was in him outward, had brought all this upon herself.

He had taken power from her, and she was helpless without it.

She felt him fumble and when she glanced down saw that he had opened his trousers and, naked beneath, had displayed himself. When he drove against her she could feel the material of her black skirt yield and under a layer of winter underwear her body's unfathomable response to his assault. The fact that he had been ready for her seemed inconsequential. There was no pride in him, only an assurance that she could not counter, weakened as she was by guilt. The practical lobe of her brain shrilled at her to resist, to get out of the basement and never talk to Declan Slater again. But another part, stronger than fear, urged her to appease him, just once before it ended.

Away at the back of her mind, as he slipped his hands beneath her skirt and hoisted it up about about her hips, was a nebulous curiosity as to whether or not he had ever had Alison Burnside in this position, if Alison had given in to Declan too and if she, at this ugly, awkward moment, was being compared to the girl from Flannery Park. Then she felt his hands on her, pressing her thighs. And she wasn't thinking of Alison, Howard, or Guy any more. Had no thoughts in her head at all.

She could feel, feel but not see what he was doing to her. She winced. She wished she had worn her crêpe-de-chine or the Milanese silk things edged with lace, not rayon and wool beneath a warm Merino vest. Apricot, apricot not cream. What would he think of her? She winced again as he tugged at the legging, tugged it like rubber across fur. He cupped his hand against her. His face was level with hers. He looked clean, clean as oakwood, or yew. His eyes were bright and a faint rime of perspiration clung to the shadow on his upper lip. She kissed him, tasting salt.

She kissed him again, pressing against his hand.

'I'm not goin' to let you stop me,' Declan told her.

'I know. I know.'

She felt soft against his hand, melting into him, as if some part of her that she had not known existed was oozing out of her. She had begun, unconsciously, to groan. Spreading her feet wide, she braced herself on the heels of her pretty shoes. When he jerked against her, she rocked forward on her toes. She felt the probing, the snouting thing and then, more easily than she would ever have imagined, he entered her, and Declan cried out as if he shared her pain.

An hour later he lay naked on the bed and, tender as a bridegroom, made love to Bobs again, made hay before their time was up and she limped home to Daddy's house to bathe and preen, and pine for more of the same.

'Do you love me now, Bobs?' he asked her. 'Do you not love me now?'

And Roberta, lying, said, 'Yes.'

Alison said, 'Have you done this often before, Howard?'

'Oh, yes. Frequently.'

'With girls, I mean?'

'Not much fun doing it with boys.'

'Don't be a clown.'

'Guy's been around now and then. My brother – once.'

'Not Declan?'

'Lord, no.'

Alison looked about the dining-room of the Bankhead Hotel, with its green flock wallpaper and rubber plants and the glass shell-shaped light fittings which gave the room a cosy glow. The napery was linen, the cutlery silver, the plates, even on a midwinter Monday evening, were fine Willow Pattern with gilded rims, the cups fluted.

'I must say, it's all very civilised.'

'I suppose it is, really,' Howard said.

'Are the bedrooms nice too?'

Howard grinned. 'Miss Burnside, is that a hint?'

'No, I didn't mean . . .'

'I know you didn't. Yes, the bedrooms are exceedingly nice. I have my own desk, wardrobe, and a wash-basin with a shaving mirror over it. Young ladies, however, are not allow to set foot in there. On pain of death.'

'So nobody tries to sneak – you know?'

'One fellow – a law student, of course – tried it a year or two back.'

'What happened?'

'Miss Milroy, God bless her, is endowed with a sixth sense. She can hear the rustle of a skirt or the whisper of a stocking through three layers of brick. The lawyer was caught red-handed and despatched immediately into the night.'

'You have had girls to supper before, though?'

'Yes, yes, yes. I confess.'

'Who? Bobs?'

'Couple of times in second year.'

'Who else?'

'You'll only laugh if I tell you.'

'No, I won't. Promise.'

'Saving Grace.'

'The Christian martyr? Hah-hah-hah-hah!'

'I knew you'd laugh.'

'Well, she is rather good-looking,' Alison said, 'but I wouldn't have put her down as your type. More Guy's, perhaps. Do you fancy her?'

'I found her – interesting, shall we say? We had, in fact, the most terrific squabble. You know where I stand on religion.'

'On the side of the devil,' Alison said.

'Miss Milroy was obliged to ask us to keep our voices down.'

'And she hasn't been back? Grace, I mean?'

'No, mere argument didn't put her off. Give her her due, she really did think I would be worth the effort.'

'Of what?'

'Conversion.'

'Really?'

'What a coup that would have been, uh? The dark, satanic Howard

134

McGrath brought into the light. And, probably, to the altar.'

'You weren't tempted?'

'Not by her arguments, no.'

'By her figure?'

'That,' Howard said, 'is a different story.'

'Is that why I'm here?'

'What?'

'Because you admire my figure?'

Howard neatly crossed his knife and fork over the piece of poached haddock that remained uneaten on his plate. He dabbed his lips with his napkin, back straight and a little frown creasing his brows.

'Are you teasing me?' he said.

'Never!'

You aaarrre, you're teasing me, Ally Burnside.'

'Perhaps a little,' Alison admitted.

'Flirting?'

'Oh, no, Howard. You don't flirt with old friends. It ain't the done thing.'

'Is that all we are, Alison, just old – just good friends?'

'Well, aren't we?'

'I was hoping . . .'

'I know, Howard, I know.'

'I wonder if Jim isn't becoming something of an excuse.'

'Pardon?'

'You heard,' Howard said, and began to eat again.

She watched him, her fork poised.

She wondered if Howard had inherited his style of eating from his father or if it had been dinned into him when he was young. He ate so efficiently, chewed so precisely that she was reminded of other military aspects of his character, signs of regimentation and discipline which he could not seem to shake off no matter how flamboyantly he behaved. When she thought of Howard in the abstract, in bed at night, say, the image most often conjured up was not one of Howard in flowing overcoat and soft hat but of a soldier, trim and taut in lieutenant's uniform, hair cut short, a pistol on a lanyard in his hand.

He polished off the fish, mopped up the creamy gravy with brown bread, did his bit with the napkin again, then asked, 'Does Jim know, for instance, that you're here with me tonight?'

'Of course.'

'You told him?'

'Yes, why wouldn't I tell him?'

'He didn't object?'

'Not in the slightest.'

'Did you tell him that we're going to the King's?'

'Yes. We are, aren't we?'

'That's the whole idea,' Howard said. 'You said . . .'

'That I fancied *White Horse Inn* and you very generously bought tickets.'

His hands were working on a fresh piece of bread, buttering it, adding plum jam from the dish. Alison too continued to apply herself to the business of rounding off the meal. A young woman in a black dress and white pinafore came and removed the dirty plates.

'Thank you, Em,' Howard said politely, not taking his eyes from Alison. When the waitress had gone again, he said, 'I've got it. You told Jim that we were going in a crowd. He wouldn't object to that.'

'Jim doesn't object to anything I do.'

'He should. If you were mine I'd object very much.'

'That's the difference between you.'

'What lie did you tell him?' Howard said.

'Tea here. *White Horse Inn.*' Alison paused. 'Six of us.'

'Why didn't you just tell him the truth?'

'I didn't want him to worry.'

'Has he reason to worry?'

'About what?'

'Us.'

'No reason at all,' Alison said.

'I was afraid you were going to say that,' Howard told her.

'Afraid? Why?'

'It means you don't take me very seriously, doesn't it?'

'No. It means I've known you long enough to trust you.'

'Damn it!' Howard said, testily. 'I don't want you to trust me.'

'I can't help it,' Alison said. 'I do.'

'If there wasn't a Jim, if there had never been a Jim, would you still expect me to behave like a gentleman?'

'Certainly not,' said Alison.

'Well, that's always something, I suppose,' Howard said and, shrugging in resignation, offered Alison first choice from the silver cake-stand, before they left for the King's.

There were no silver cake-stands on Jack Burnside's tea table. Sauce bottles and pickle jars did, however, give a certain comfortable sense of richness and variety, an illusion of middle-class substance which the ashet pie did not justify.

The pie had come from the front tray in the window of Pryce's the butcher's, a cheap meat shop in the row near the hind-end of the park where Brenda often bought the materials of the evening meal. The pie had charred black edges and, on top, little flakes of black pastry mingled with eruptions of grey mince which, alas, reminded Jack of the flies that were often to be seen in the corner of Pryce's window even in midwinter months, as if the butcher kept a stock of them for decoration the way other butchers would stock parsley or cress.

He ate the pie anyway.

He ate the pile of wet, lukewarm peas too. There were no potatoes. Brenda had burned the potatoes. It didn't matter. He had dropped into 162 on his way home and had scoffed a bowl of Trudi's soup by way of a starter. He ate all of the pie except the black border, and pushed the ashet away, saying, 'Good. That was good.'

'Thought you'd like it,' Brenda said.

'What's for afters?'

'Rice an' pears.'

'Good.'

He listened to the grating of the tin-opener from the kitchen and the impatient yelling from upstairs where his daughters, theoretically in bed for the night, were bouncing about the bedroom, waiting for Daddy to come and play and, now and then, girning for water, milk, biscuits or anything else they thought they might get away with before they were forced down to sleep.

Brenda reappeared in the living-room with a dish of cold rice pudding centred by two pear halves in a puddle of sticky syrup.

Jack lifted his spoon.

'By the way,' he said, 'guess who I saw today?'

'The Prince of Wales?'

Brenda dumped the plate before him and retreated to a chair by the fire. She lit a cigarette and hunched forward, watching her husband eat.

Jack laughed. 'Naw.'

'Who did you see then?'

'George Giffard's boy. Him that used to be so keen on our Alison. Him that went off to sea.'

Brenda hesitated, then asked, 'Did you, you know, talk to him?'

'Nope. Saw him in the distance,' Jack said. 'I mean, I hardly know the bloke. I heard he was home, though, on whatever it is sailors get.'

'Leave.'

'Aye.'

'How did you hear he was home?'

'George – Mr Giffard – told me.'

'George now, is it?'

'I see him sometimes in an' out the office. Nice bloke. Wouldn't harm a fly. Always asks after you. Pity about his missus.'

'Was Walter on his own?'

'*That's* his name,' Jack said. 'I knew I knew it but I just couldn't get it into my mind. Time there we all thought it would be a match between him an' Alison. You knew him too, didn't you, honey?'

'Kind of,' Brenda said. 'At school.'

'Some peeper,' Jack said. 'Some eye. I wouldn't like to have an eye like that. Havin' to hold your head back all the time to see where you're goin'.'

'I thought you only saw him in the distance?'

'I passed him on the Ferry Road.'

'Did he say anythin' to you?'

'Nah, just gave me a snooty look. He was otherwise occupied.'

'How?' said Brenda, releasing smoke.

'This big vamp was hangin' on his arm.'

'Uh-huh.'

'What a cracker!'

'Uh-huh.'

'What a size!'

'Jack!'

'Sorry. But she was. Blonde. Plate-igi-num blonde, like yon picture star.'

'Harlow.'

'Aye, an' big.'

'God, you're makin' her sound like the bloody Finnieston crane.'

'Older than him, I think.'

'So what? You're older'n me.'

'She looked a bit like your mother, only—'

'I know,' Brenda said, 'big.'

Jack polished off the pudding, lifted the bowl and licked it clean with the tip of his tongue.

Brenda said, 'Why are you tellin' me all this, Jack?'

'I thought you'd be interested.'

'In Walter Giffard?'

'Used to go dancin' with him, didn't you?'

'Once,' Brenda said. 'Maybe, you know, twice.'

'Down at the good old Cally. Some place, the Cally.'

'What is this?' Brenda said, suspiciously.

'What's what?'

'You're up to somethin', Jack Burnside.'

He gave a fluttery laugh. 'Like what?'

'You tell me about, you know, Walter Giffard an' then you start talkin' about the Cally.'

'We could do with the extra money, for Christmas.'

'God, it's fat Kenny. You've been talkin' to fat Kenny?'

'He wants me to sit in for the Christmas gigs.'

'No.'

'Thirty bob. Easy money, Brenda.'

'No.'

Jack reached for the teapot and poured a stream of dark brown tea into his cup. He stretched out his hand for the milk bottle but, to his surprise, Brenda beat him to it. She did it in a funny sort of manner, pouring milk attentively then, with the sugar-bag in one hand and a spoon in the other, leaning on his shoulder and saying, 'How many?'

'You know how many,' Jack said. 'Two.'

'I don't mean sugar. I mean, how many nights would you be out?'

'Oh, three.'

'When?'

'I'd do Friday. I'm in Greenfield, anyway. I'd take my trumpet with me, leave it at the hall, do the rounds, then . . .'

'What about, you know, your tally, your accounts?'

'I'll be home by one o'clock. I'll do them then.'

Brenda continued to lean against the chairback, sugar-bag in one hand, the other lightly touching her husband's fair hair.

'Friday?' she said. 'Are you awful keen?'

'Not if you're set against it, Bren.'

'I'm not sayin' that. I'm sayin' – are you awful keen?'

'It's good money.'

'All right,' Brenda said. 'Three nights, before New Year.'

Jack looked round, eyes sparkling. 'Hey, hey! That's great! You're sure you don't mind?'

'I'll survive,' Brenda said then, easing herself forward on her toes, cocked her bosom over the chairback and pressed her elbow against it to make it swell. 'Tell me somethin', this big chick Walter had, was she bigger than me?'

Jack looked from his wife's flushed face to her bosom and laughed. He put his hand out and touched her breasts.

'Well—' he said.

'Was she?'

'No chance.'

Brenda kissed him brusquely on the ear then, rather to Jack's chagrin, moved back to the armchair by the fire, smirking, the sugar-bag still in her hand.

* * *

139

Punctuality was one of Dr Theodore K. Thomas's undoubted virtues. He was not one of those autocrats who thought that time and tide were obliged to wait for gentlemen with MD, FRCP printed on their visiting cards. He made it a point of honour never to keep patients or students hanging about if he could possibly avoid it.

You could, in fact, set your watch by old T.K. Nursing staff in the Royal often did just that, checking their chronometers against the arrival of the chief's well-preserved, ten-year-old Napier which, no matter the weather, would whizz into the square behind the Lister wing at precisely twenty minutes past eight o'clock each morning and shudder to a halt in a slot between two shabby little evergreens.

T.K. was not entirely surprised when, on that cold, moist, foggy December morning, one of the shabby little shrubs developed arms and legs and, as he stooped to secure the Napier's on-side door, sidled slyly towards him.

'Yes, Slater?' T.K. said, without turning.

'A word with you, sir, if I may?'

'You've come to apologise?'

'I have that, sir, profoundly and with all my heart.'

T.K. fished under his overcoat, flipped out and consulted his watch then, case in hand, headed across the angle of the square towards the iron-studded back door which would admit him to the towers of the medical wards.

'You'd better walk with me, Mr Slater. I'm not going to be late.'

The student fell into step, skipping and sidling.

Slater still looked like a victim of some slow, wasting disease. But T.K. had encountered many like the Irishman over the years and knew perfectly well that clinical examination would find no trace of physical malfunction and that, beneath the pale skin-and-bone exterior lay a granite-hard determination to succeed in medicine and in life.

The chief was not repelled by ambition, though it was a vice he had never suffered from in his young days, thank the Lord. At least Slater had had the savvy to smarten himself up. He had obviously changed the blade in his razor at last, had given his brogues a lick of brown polish and had ironed his rat's-tail necktie. Effort always roused a certain magnanimity in T.K. Thomas. He allowed the student to hold the door open for him, even thanked him and, as they climbed the cold stone stairs together, lent half an ear to Slater's excuses.

Bevelled-glass doors led off from the staff staircase, revealing perspectives of green linoleum, tiled walls, screens, nurses and an occasional ambulatory patient shuffling monk-like to the lavatory, scenes that old T.K. Thomas had seen several thousand times but which never failed to stir in him a degree of satisfaction that was almost proprietorial.

On the third-floor landing, he stopped and faced the lad.

'It's the booze, Slater, isn't it?' he said, voice echoing down the stairwell.

'No, sir, it is not. A glass of stout when at home, sir, is my limit.'

'What is it then?'

'As I was saying, Chief, it was but a touch of fever.'

'Without a temperature?'

'I – I had had no breakfast, that was the fault.'

The poor lip, the Irishman was about to plead the poor lip. T.K. had heard *that* line often enough before.

Sometimes it was palpably obvious that the boy, or girl for that matter, had clambered out of the lower classes, that desperation as well as poverty were mingled in him and that such was the burden that all but the strongest knuckled under to it. But the best, the very best, were far too proud to admit that they existed on burnt porridge, weak tea and an idealistic belief in a better tomorrow. They understood from the word 'Go' that the gelatinous marrow of a leukaemia patient, the shaggy colon of a colitis sufferer, the granular kidneys of some poor devil dying of chronic nephritis were dumb organs which did not care whether treatment was administered by someone rich or someone poor, that disease was truly the greatest leveller known to man.

'Tell me, Slater, what does your father do?'

'Farms. He's a farmer, sir.'

'In Ireland, I assume?'

'In Wicklow. Times are not so easy with him, sir. Bad harvests—'

'Times are not so easy for a great many people,' T.K. intervened.

He detected a flicker of anger in Slater's eye, enough to suggest that young Mr Slater, master of the blarney, wasn't used to having his sob-story cut off before it reached its climax.

T.K. said, 'What is it you want from me?'

'I don't want you to turn against me, sir.'

'I won't withhold your class ticket, if that's what you mean.'

'No, I didn't think – I mean, though, in the future. I have always held you to be the best of all the teachers, sir, and I wouldn't want to put myself out of favour with you, to be losin' your respect.'

'Go away, Slater,' T.K. Thomas heard himself say.

'I'm not goin' to be poor, like, for much longer.'

'Slater, enough. Please just go away.'

'I'm not sacked, am I?'

'What is *wrong* with you, boy?' T.K. said.

'I've no money . . .'

'That's not a problem that concerns me, Slater, nor one that I would wish to concern me. Go to the kitchens, see if you can scrounge a hot cup of tea. Entertain yourself by blatherin' to impressionable young nurses, or to the cooks. But do not – I repeat, do *not* – press your personal problems upon me ever again. I will not be blackmailed.'

The chief leaned closer. If he hadn't been holding a heavy briefcase, he might have propped his hands against the wall in his habitual lecturing pose.

'I have no sympathy for your predicament, Mr Slater,' he went on. 'You are, as you are well aware, a very clever young man. But I do not *like* you, sir. Fortunately I'm not obliged to like you, only to educate you to the best of my ability. I do not like you, not because you are Irish and certainly not because you are poor, but because you are a sly and ingratiating opportunist.'

'Wha . . .'

'Class in thirty-eight minutes. Good morning.'

T.K. hoisted up the briefcase and, using it as a ram, battered through the door into the ward corridor, leaving Slater standing, gawping, on the landing. He let the door clatter loudly behind him, which caused several of the nursing staff, including Sister Madigan, to glance up in alarm.

It took no more than five seconds for anger at the young man's presumption to transform itself into a glow of self-satisfaction as warm as any that old T.K. had experienced in several years.

By the time he reached the sister he was beaming.

'Are you all right, Doctor?' she asked him.

'Never better.'

'What, if I may ask, was that all about?'

'Just put a student properly in his place, that's all.'

'Slater?'

'Indeed – Slater.' T.K. opened his office door then paused. 'And do you know what, Sister?'

'You enjoyed it.'

'Too true,' said T.K. Thomas and, still beaming, stepped blithely inside to prepare for his morning round.

Trudi had known for ages that Henry had something on his mind. It galled her that she could not fathom what it was and that even in the hurly-burly of fraternal arguments over the supper table she could wheedle no clue from Henry as to what bothered him. She had a feeling, a 'hunch' as Americans called it, that whatever Henry was keeping to himself did not concern Alison, Jack or Bert but she herself, Mrs Trudi Keller Burnside, and that her husband would inform her of it only when it suited him.

Given the mores of the suburban clan, however, she was able to console herself with the thought that 'the surprise' might be nothing but a trivial gift or Christmas treat to which she would be expected to react with astonishment and enormous amounts of gratitude.

Nevertheless, she played her hand cautiously.

'Your self you are not these days, Henry?' she would say, over the page of the newspaper she happened to be reading in bed. 'Do you have pain?'

'No, I'm fine.'

'Do you pine for another woman?'

'Trudi!'

'I am not so young for you.'

'For God's sake!'

'If you wish to make love to somebody . . .'

'Will you kindly cut it out.'

Trudi pouted, prissily.

She could confuse him so easily. Could bring him if not to his knees certainly on to his toes, a power she liked to exercise from time to time. She liked it best when Henry responded sharply, cleverly, demonstrating that masculine cast of mind which she had so admired in him when, four years ago now, he had rescued her from Clive Coventry's clutches.

She would rustle the newspaper and proceed.

'Do you not wish to make love to somebody?'

Henry would groan, roll on to his elbow and lower his face until it was only inches from her own. Then he would nudge up her reading glasses and peer into her pale blue eyes.

'Are we on about Maggie Chancellor again, eh?'

'Is she the one you would wish to make love to?'

'Nope.'

'You are not telling me the truth?'

'The truth? You want the truth?' Henry would say in a tone that would raise in Trudi a frisson of apprehension and excitement. 'The truth is that I'd jump into bed with Maggie Chancellor at the drop of a hat.'

'She is attractive to you because she is fat, I knew it.'

'Except that I prefer to jump into bed with you.'

'You say this only because you are in the bed with me.'

'Well, I'm not in bed with Maggie Chancellor, am I?'

'But you wish to be, no?'

'I could be,' Henry would say. 'Oh, yes, I could be.'

Trudi would flick the newspaper downward and, laying her head against the pillow, would stare straight back at him. 'How?'

'How? Come on, Trude. You know how. I'd say something like, "Maggie, you've got the biggest brown eyes I've ever seen and a chest to match, and I am filled vith zee de-zire for you. I vill even be-kom a paid-up member of zee Labour Party if you vill gimme a roll in the hay." '

'You want her so badly you would even join the Labour Party?'

'That badly, yes.'

'I do not believe you.'

'There you are, then. What are you worried about?'

'I am worried about what it is that worries you.'

'Nothing worries me,' Henry would say and if the signs seemed propitious, would kiss her and insinuate his hand under her woolly cardigan or bed-jacket.

Then, one night towards the middle of the month, after just such a teasing conversation, Henry added sombrely, 'Except Germany.'

Trudi stiffened. She had no reason to be afraid. They had often discussed the German situation. But something in Henry's tone alerted her to danger.

'Germany?' she said. 'Why is it that you are worried by Germany?'

'Because of certain things I hear about the place.'

'Hitler? The rearmament programmes? Political policemen? I tell you, Henry, from all that I have read to you, there is no revolutionary person less than Chancellor Hitler. He is, for Germany, the *necessary* one.'

'Who fed you that line, Trude? Your father?'

'My father?'

'Who art in Germany?'

Frowning, Trudi wriggled against the bolsters and, sitting up straight, placed her hands in her lap. 'It is truly *this* that makes you so worried, Henry? What is happening to my Papa?'

'Is he managing to keep out of prison?'

'I do not know if he is or if he is not.'

'Where do you get your letters?'

'Letters? I do not get letters.'

'Do you pick them up at a Post Office box in town?'

'Henry, what are you saying to me?'

Henry's elbow dug deeply into the pillow and created a fleshy swell, pink-tinted in the lamplight. His handsome features were menacingly close. She could not even turn her head away without

144

seeming to confirm his tacit accusation that she was guilty of some sort of duplicity.

Henry said, softly, 'Know what they're saying about you, Trudi? They're saying you're a German spy.'

'You tell them I am Swiss.'

'Sure, I do. But Swiss, Austrian or German, what does the average Glaswegian care about national barriers? To them you're a Jerry.'

'To whom do you mean, Henry? The family?'

'Reporters, journalists. Even my boss, even Marcus Harrison.'

A tiny, tiny jerk of the head, a lifting of the chin. Beneath the jawline Trudi's skin seemed not just fine but so thin as to be almost transparent.

'Marcus?' she said.

'Anyway,' Henry went on, 'I just hope you *have* been in correspondence with some of the folks back in old Bavaria, because if you haven't you'd better dig out notepaper and a pen and get to work.'

Trudi's lack of comprehension increased her fear.

'What is it you talk about?'

Henry grinned. 'We're going to Berlin.'

'What do you say?'

'You an' me, all expenses paid – we're off to visit Der Fadderland.'

'Marcus!' Trudi exclaimed, mouth twisting.

'My idea, dearest,' Henry told her. 'Harrison endorsed it immediately, though. He hasn't put the word out yet so please keep the lid on it.'

'The lid?'

'Don't tell anyone, not even the family.'

'It is you who are to be the spy?' said Trudi.

'For the *Mercury*?' Henry said. 'Nah, nah!' He paused then, grinning again, added, 'Well, maybe, in a way that's what I am, what all we journalists are these days. Spies. Agents in search of truth.'

'You do not have need of me?'

'Yep, I do. Translator.'

'I do not wish to accompany you to Germany, Henry.'

It was Henry's turn to be surprised. 'Why the hell not? I thought you'd jump at the chance. It isn't going to cost us a bean. Harrison will foot the bill. He'll also lay on some useful contacts. But' – Henry put a reassuring hand against her cheek – 'he's hoping, and I'm hoping, you'll be able to dig up some interesting old acquaintances to give me the low-down.'

'Low . . . down?'

'The griff, the inside story. The Real McCoy.'

'Speak in the English to me,' Trudi snapped.

'All right,' Henry said, taking his hand from her cheek. 'I want to meet your family, Trudi.'

'*Um Gottes willen!*' Trudi exploded. 'I have no family but the family downstairs.'

'I thought you had lots of old chums in Berlin,' Henry said. 'God knows, you were there long enough, weren't you? With Coventry, I mean.'

Until this moment she had felt safe in Flannery Park, part of a family whose concerns were far removed from anything she had known in Paris or Berlin, in Frankfurt or Vienna. Yet it was she who had put Henry to work in the *Mercury*, who had begun a process that now seemed like destiny, when past and present would catch up and confront each other, when the hideous secret she had kept to herself for years might once again surface.

She swallowed and clenched her teeth. 'I do not wish to go there, Henry.'

'Then,' he said, without heat, 'I'll just have to go with someone else.'

'Who else would you go with who could do what I can do?'

He shrugged. 'Margaret Chancellor, maybe.'

'Bastard!' Trudi said. '*Arschloch!*'

'What does that mean?'

'Is it that you cannot guess?'

'Well, I reckon it isn't meant to be flattering. Listen,' he said, 'why don't you want to go back there, even with me?'

'It is a place of bad memories.'

'Is that the only reason?'

'A place of too bad memories, yes.'

'All right.' Henry looked at her strangely. 'I'll just have to tell Harrison to make other arrangements.'

'With Maggie Chancellor?'

'No,' Henry said, 'that was a joke. Bad joke.'

'It is not all bad joke, no?'

'Nope, I'm off to Berlin sometime after Christmas. With you, Trudi, or without you. It's too good an opportunity to pass up.'

'Opportunity? For you to find out about me?'

Henry sighed. 'About Germany, Trudi,' he said. 'About what's happening in the big, wide, wicked world. And to write about it.'

'Like Kurtz?'

'No, like the truth.'

Henry watched his wife carefully, saw her muscles slacken. She leaned back against the bolster but did not look at him. She stared at the unlit light bulb that hung from a cord from the ceiling. Resignation, not enthusiasm, relaxed her. He knew now that some grain of truth lay in the rumours that had accumulated about her, some secret that Trudi had deliberately hidden from him and that she was still anxious to protect.

'I will come,' she said.

'I don't want to force you, Trude.'

'You do not force me. I will come of my own willpower.'

'Free will,' Henry corrected.

'Yes,' Trudi said. 'Free will.'

'Who do you know that might be of use to me?' Henry said. 'Old chums, old friends, family acquaintances, that sort of thing?'

'What sort of old acquaintance do you mean, Henry?'

'Anyone who might give me information on what's really happening in the new Nazi state?'

'The President of the Reichstag? The Prime Minister of Prussia?'

Henry laughed. 'Oh, yeah, he would do very nicely for a start.'

'I will write to him a letter.'

'Are you serious?'

'I am never so much serious.'

'You *know* Hermann Goering? Personally?'

'In the old days, I knew him.'

'But will he remember you?'

'He will remember me,' Trudi said. 'It is this that Marcus Harrison was hoping for, do you not see? Marcus knows too many things. What he did not find out for himself my husband, Clive Coventry, he would have told him.'

'But Goering! I mean, how the hell did you ever get to meet him?'

'Through Papa's introduction,' Trudi said.

'Jesus Christ!'

'Now you have your mind changed? You do not wish to meet the second most important man in Germany?' Trudi asked her husband.

'Are you kidding,' said Henry.

'But you do not wish to kiss me, like before?'

An instant after the moment of decision there came into Henry's eyes a gleam that she had not seen before, a sickening flare of sexual hunger as if he suddenly found himself in bed not with his familiar, shopworn middle-aged wife but with someone young, strange and exciting, someone infinitely corrupt.

'Oh, yeah,' said Henry, biting his lip. 'You bet your boots I do.'

FIVE

The Surgeon's Daughter

Whatever the governors of Wellmeadow Hospital thought of it, Veitch Logie held too much sway for his wishes to be peremptorily denied.

Before the board could pluck up courage to tell the old boy that he couldn't invite Tom, Dick or Harry into the theatre, however, the deed was done and the surgeon's daughter and her young man had been and gone.

Veitch was so determined to impress Roberta and Guy that it did not occur to him that the fourth-year students might have a preformed opinion of his skills based on reports from those who had worked with him and that they had agreed to participate only to discover just how ham-fisted he really was. Stimulated by the prospect of having his eldest watch him work, he rambled on about the day's list of cases throughout the motorcar journey to Bearsden where Guy, looking his usual immaculate self, was waiting to be picked up from the gate of his home.

Twenty minutes later, with Veitch still bragging, the big soft-topped Talbot slithered between the leafless oaks and entered the hospital grounds.

Wellmeadow was one of two hospitals situated along the river between the villages of Ottershaw and Smallwood. Ottershaw Hospital occupied the high ground and even on that foggy December morning presented a stern, Victorian face to the farms in the valley but Wellmeadow Cottage Hospital, three miles to the north-west, still lay veiled in mist. Mock Tudor in style, modern in design, its neat brick buildings were low to the ground and unimposing. Nurses and domestic staff were culled from the local villages, daughters of shepherds and farmers who, sturdy lassies, thought nothing of hoofing three or four miles before and after shift or, the lucky ones, riding home behind Dad on the tractor bar.

It was as well that the nurses were country types for even urbane professionals had trouble putting up with Veitch Logie, as a result of which the welcome accorded to Roberta and Guy was less than warm and in some cases decidedly chilly.

The operating theatre was small but up to date. Even allowing for some tardy healing in the wake of Veitch's little errors, the surgical wards were never crowded. Obstetrics, under the excellent Dr Erskine, bounded along briskly enough. Breeding, like most country matters, was taken seriously in the district. And the resident house surgeon and young Mr Emmslie, Veitch's first assistant, were kept busy with surgical emergencies, for farmers and their labourers were a careless lot, for ever inflicting injury upon their persons with barbed-wire and rusty spikes, sickles, pick-axes and rakes or being kicked by four-footed animals even more recalcitrant than they were themselves.

What was left for Mr Logie were the unabashed results of corporeal disorder. Livers shot by excessive alcoholic consumption, kidneys shrivelled by winter mornings in the byre, abdominal cavities swollen by dietary abuse, the intractable disharmonies of bowel, bladder and spleen that life on the land engendered. The patients were all paying customers, of course, and entitled to the best that Wellmeadow had to offer after the fee had been haggled over and the patient, as thrawn and frightened as a bullock in an abattoir, had been stunned into submission by the efficiency of the nursing staff.

'Calm yourself, Mr Pollock, it's nothing but a severe case of Fiddler's Elbow,' Veitch Logie would inform the patient. 'When I have stitched the ligament and repaired the bursal sac the arm will be as good as new and your fingers will open out again. Tell me, are you able to work with your left hand if need be?'

'What?'

'You don't require two hands to shoo in your cows for milking, do you?'

'I thought you said it was a minor operation?'

'In surgery there is no certainty, Mr Pollock. Lord knows what I will find when I have opened up the joint.'

'Are you tellin' me I might never play . . .'

'Fiddling is not an essential part of your livelihood, is it? So, sir, please do not make a fuss or I may have to send for your wife to talk to you.'

'Aye, all right, all right,' the stricken farmer would say and, without a trace of irony, would plead for the surgeon to try to leave him enough of his right arm to thread through the spokes of a tractor wheel.

Any result short of amputation seemed thereafter like a miracle and to many of the less astute who survived his bread-and-butter surgery Mr Veitch Logie appeared as a saviour.

Wellmeadow's anaesthetist was a lively young woman named Susan Ryan. Veitch Logie had done everything in his power to block Miss Ryan's appointment but her father, a respected dental surgeon, had just enough clout with the board to ensure that the post, for which she was eminently qualified, went to his daughter.

Only Miss Ryan seemed willing to converse with Roberta and Guy as they scrubbed up at the brushed-steel trough and fitted themselves into macintoshes, gowns, gauze-lined 'nosebags' and powdered their rubber gloves.

'First time in a theatre?'

'No, not quite,' Roberta answered.

'Have you assisted before?'

'Not assisting today, surely,' said Roberta, startled.

'Oh, I expect the chief, since he's your father, might let you break the odd ligature container or knot a suture or two.'

'What sort of knot does he favour?' asked Guy.

'Reef or surgeon's will do. The simpler the better. Silkworm gut curls, so don't jerk it. Pull it steadily and evenly.'

'We have both stitched, you know,' Roberta said, 'at the Royal.'

'Miss Ryan was only trying to be helpful, Bobs.'

'Yes, I'm sure she was.'

Although Roberta had never seen her father operate she had heard a very great deal about his 'achievements' and had suffered so many cholecystectomy tales that she expected him to do nothing all morning but snip out gall-bladders. To Bobs' surprise, no such operation was scheduled.

Repetition, thirty-odd years of it, had smoothed away Mr Logie's awkwardness in handling the tools of his trade. The fact that Bobs was impressed by such basic skills only highlighted her inexperience. It would be some years before she would learn that the qualities which separated good surgeons from the merely mediocre were much more subtle than an ability to cut, suture and stitch.

Guy and she were given pride of place at the table, close enough to look into the wound site. Just prior to commencement Emmslie, a stocky man in his mid thirties, with tiny, white, dainty hands, took them aside and warned them not to lean forward or cast shadows across the mid-line of the wound, which was the surgeon's province. It was left to a theatre sister to take them through the instruments and outline the morning list while Veitch Logie and Mr Emmslie studied the case notes and diagrams.

They stood to the side of the crowd around the table and watched the first patient being wheeled in, propped, exposed and swabbed.

Miss Ryan stated what preliminary sedation had been administered, what proportion of compounds she intended to use to keep the patient under. Veitch Logie said nothing. He permitted himself one swift, smug glance at his daughter before, with almost painful slowness, he made his first incision of the day.

At that moment Roberta realised why her father had advanced no further than Wellmeadow in pursuit of his career.

He lacked natural confidence.

By Roberta's side Guy gave an almost inaudible grunt. He too had noticed the fault from which Veitch Logie's bad reputation stemmed.

The first case on the list was an epigastric hernia in a fifty-two-year-old male. Initially diagnosed as a peptic ulcer, only a shrewd local GP, Hector Campbell, had come up with a correct assessment of the patient's complaint and had referred him to the Wellmeadow for surgical examination.

The procedure was not a difficult one. Transverse incision. Gauze dissection to clear fat from the hernial orifice. Closing of the opening in the linea alba by sutures. Veitch laboured slowly and cautiously and seemed, Bobs thought, to age before her eyes.

Excision of a cyst from the breast of a farmer's wife was followed by a tricky appendectomy. The swollen appendix, the chief explained, was anchored by adhesions behind the bowel. He paused long enough to allow Roberta and Guy to peer into the wound before he proceeded to make a formidable operation out of the appendix's removal.

An hour behind schedule the last of the morning's list was wheeled in.

And the trouble really began.

The patient was a sixty-four-year-old corn-merchant with a short history of dyspepsia. He had been under a conservative regimen in the medical ward for some days before recurrrent bleeding had compelled a call for surgery. Plain X-ray had revealed a massive translucent area beneath the diaphragm. Perforated duodenal ulcer was confirmed.

As expected, the ulcer was discovered on the anterior wall of the duodenum. It was Veitch Logie's intention to close the perforation with a line of interrupted sutures reinforced with an omental patch, a procedure he had followed a hundred times and one which presented no serious difficulty to a competent surgeon.

What seemed like seconds of time to Roberta was, however, an accumulation of minutes which caused Susan Ryan increasing anxiety.

Aware of the patient's general condition, she had deliberately kept the anaesthetic 'light'. No sooner had the perforation been exposed, however, than Veitch Logie put down his scalpel and, with hands hanging, turned angrily to the top of the table.

'And what, miss, do you think you're doing?'

Susie Ryan was undaunted. 'Keeping him as shallow as possible.'

'Shallow? What sort of a word is that?'

Roberta watched blood coagulate and drip stickily from the forefinger and thumb of her father's glove. A nurse wiped the splashes smoothly away with a swab of cotton waste which she disposed of in a sterile bin in a corner. Mr Emmslie, who had been preparing the sutures, followed the nurse's movements with his eyes, brown and simian above his mask.

'Stand still, girl, can't you,' Veitch Logie said.

'But you'll slip if—' the nurse said.

'Be quiet.'

It became extremely still in the operating room.

By Roberta's side Guy was rigid with embarrassment. She could hear minute sounds from the organs in the corn-merchant's belly, as if the parts of him were frightened too, like a nest of fieldmice exposed and vulnerable.

'I can't work when the muscles are tight,' Veitch Logie said. 'Didn't they teach you that much, Miss Ryan? Even my daughter knows that much.'

'No, I don't,' Roberta blurted out.

Her father paid her no attention.

Reaching behind him he grabbed Guy by the sleeve and yanked him forward. Covering Guy's hand with his own he extended the young man's fingers to the dusky-pink crest of the abdominal opening.

'Feel that.'

Obediently Guy probed, brushing the petals of flesh gently.

Veitch Logie said, 'How can I possibly be expected to suture when the aperture keeps closing on me like a sheep's arse?' It was the first vulgar word Bobs had ever heard her father utter. 'Don't *you* feel the tension in the muscle wall, young man?'

Guy nodded, dumbly.

'It's all her fault,' Veitch Logie went on. 'That ill-trained female at the top of the table is so concerned with her nice little whiffs and puffs – look, if you won't do as I say, hand over to Emmslie. At least he knows how to obey orders.'

Susie Ryan said, 'If Em obeys this order then you'll have a post mortem on your hands, *and* a full enquiry.'

'How dare you threaten me, Miss. Now do as I say.'

'Like heck I will,' said Susan Ryan. 'Your patient's showing a BP of two-twenty over one-one-five and his heart's not worth a toss. If I put him any deeper you'll wind up finishing on a corpse.'

'Don't dare argue . . .'

'I'm not arguing, Mr Logie. You do your job and leave me to get on with mine. Might I respectfully suggest, however, that you get on with it a great deal quicker if you want this man to survive.'

'Quicker! Quicker!'

Little beads of moisture popped out on the surgeon's brow. They did not have the gelatinous quality of sweat but seemed cold, like melted ice. He stared at the anaesthetist for three or four seconds then, muttering something about 'damned pubescent dope merchants', plucked up a pair of forceps and returned his attention to the patient.

Emmslie slipped a hand on to the anterior wall of the stomach and gradually eased it back to give access.

'Don't pull the bloody veins out, man,' Veitch Logie barked.

'Fair warning, Mr Logie,' came the young woman's voice from the top of the table, 'you'd better get a move on if this chap's going back to the ward alive.'

Roberta saw that the corn-merchant's breathing was dangerously shallow and that the slick little ribbons of blood in and under the stomach had become dark and tarry.

She heard Guy murmur, 'Oh, dear! Oh, dear!'

'More oxygen, please, Miss Ryan,' Emmslie said quietly. The young anaesthetist rotated the cylinder disc. 'Good. That's fine.'

Veitch Logie refused to surrender to the nervous exhaustion which had obviously overtaken him. He said nothing until he had drawn the last skin stitch and trimmed it off.

Then, ramrod straight, he called out, 'Kerr? Where's Kerr?'

The houseman answered, 'Here, sir.'

'Give him a transfusion. Lay on oxygen and administer a cc of coramine.'

'Sir.'

'Stay with him in the ward. I'll be with you in half an hour. Any deterioration – Mr Emmslie will know where to find me.'

Before the patient could be covered and removed, Veitch Logie threw down the needle and walked out of the theatre, the door swinging in his wake.

After a pause, Roberta said, 'What – what do we do now, Mr Emmslie?'

'Give him five minutes on his own,' Emmslie said. 'No, make it ten.'

'What for?'

It was Susan Ryan who answered. She had risen behind her apparatus and stretched her arms out like wings, easing tension in her shoulders and neck.

She said, 'To have himself a good stiff drink.'

'Dad *drinks*?'

''Fraid so,' said Susie Ryan. 'Too much, too often. Didn't you know?'

'No, I . . . No.'

To cover Bobs's confusion Guy cleared his throat and asked, 'Will the perforation pull through?'

'Probably,' Mr Emmslie said.

Guy said, 'Is it always as hectic as this in theatre?'

'In this theatre, yes,' said Susan Ryan. 'I'm just glad he's not my father.'

'That's enough, Suze,' Emmslie told her as Kerr reappeared with a bottle of fresh blood upright in both hands and the process of clearing up got properly under way.

A cold crossing he'd had of it. The worst time of year for a journey, even if it had only been the short-seas trip from Stranraer to Larne.

Tossed hither and thither on the mutinous waves of the Irish Sea Declan had been sick for most of the voyage. He'd still been weak and shaky when he'd ridden the trains through Belfast and Dundalk but a half-hour before dusk a blink of sunlight had welcomed him to Dublin by tinting the handsome old buildings like sherry wine, a shade which seemed to augur well for Christmas.

Declan had arranged to meet his Da in the public bar of the Leinster Hotel, down a-ways from St Francis Xavier's Church where his brother had assisted at the Easter mass. Da and he were going on to Kerridge to spend the holiday together, in an atmosphere of stout and sanctimony, no doubt.

Four years since last Declan had been home at Christmas.

In the long summer vacations he'd spent most of his time with Seamus Flynn in the ease and dust of Dublin town or riding over the mountains or wandering about Greystones eyeing the pretty girls on the shingle beach, and sleeping in Flynn's tent in a garden in a house near Delgany. Last summer, though, he'd done the rounds as Flynn's 'assistant' and had met some of the sort of women that Flynn had told him about. When he saw how eagerly they slipped off their dresses and how coyly they flirted about in their underwear, he'd understood

155

the attraction Flynn found in the profession of medicine, as well as the easy fees.

Declan hadn't seen Da face to face since August, then only for a short time since the Flat was in full swing and his Da was strapped for cash.

Somehow, though, as Declan sat in a corner of the Leinster's public bar, nursing a pint and toasting his shanks at the fire, he found he didn't care much whether his Da arrived or did not nor, indeed, if he got to see him at all that Christmastide. All he wanted was respite from the hurt that the Scots women had inflicted upon him, time to let his bruises heal.

He was not entirely surprised, though, when Seamus Flynn showed up.

'So it's yourself, Seamus, is it?' he said.

'It is, it is. What'll you have, Declan? Another of the same or something with a bit more of the teeth to it?'

'Whiskey, if you please.'

'By God, you look worn out.'

'It's been a hard year, Seamus, a hard year.'

'Ach, you're too conscientious by half. For me it was scrape through and be damned with the parchments. What is it you're after?'

'A double to start with,' Declan said. 'How did you know you'd find me here? Did Da tell you I was comin' home?'

'That he did. Just the other day.'

'Where is he?'

Seamus Flynn shook his head. 'God alone could answer that question.'

'Have you seen my mother lately?'

'I have that. Sure I have. Just the other day.'

'How is she?'

'Saintly,' Flynn answered.

Declan gave a little snort, surprisingly free of cynicism.

They settled with their drinks at a corner table.

They were backed by a wall of comfortable tweeds and by hacking jackets, riding breeches and long, mud-spattered coats, for the Leinster was close enough to the hill country for stragglers from the hunt at Meath or Kildare to gather here for a crack and a jar before going home to open their post and eat their dinners. The bar smelled more country than town and was filled with that brand of Irish laughter which was as different in tone from the guffaws of Glasgow men as Brahms is from Beethoven.

Declan stretched out his legs and looked across the table at Dr

Flynn, small and dark-browed, big-shouldered in his cape-like Ulster coat, with the hat, the inevitable soft hat, cocked jauntily over one eye.

Declan, without warning, suddenly began to cry.

'Jasus!' said Flynn, cod-Irish to the core. 'Faith and begorrah, man, is the tipple too strong for youse or what is it ails ye?'

'I – I got ditched, so I did.'

'So that's why you're back for Christmas?'

'It is.'

'Which of them ditched you?'

'Both of them.'

'Nay, me son, they'll just be playin' fast an' loose wit' your afflictions.'

'Oh, stop it, Seamus.' Declan wiped his nose on his cuff like a donkeyman from over the Sally Gap. 'Give the accent a bloody rest.'

'Ja . . . I mean, you fell in love, did you not now?'

'Nah I didn't.'

'I warned you.' Seamus wagged a forefinger. 'Which one was it?'

'Neither. I told you, I'm not that much of an idiot.'

'Which one?'

'The surgeon's daughter.'

'You had her?'

'Yes.'

'And did she not love it?'

'How can I tell? She cut me dead next day.'

Declan drank a mouthful of whiskey to clear his stuffy head. He hadn't intended to lay all of this out for Flynn's examination, not so soon. In fact, he had not intended to impart to Flynn, pal though he was, more than the gist of it, just enough to extract from the doctor a good strong dose of that astringent medicine which was bottled and sold as 'common sense.' Too late now, though. Seamus Flynn had already gotten to the heart of it.

'Was it all the way home?' Flynn asked.

'Yes.'

'Was she hurt by it? Were you rough?'

Squirming a little, unexpectedly modest, Declan shook his head.

'Some like it rough first go out, others take time to come round,' Seamus Flynn told him. 'It's my feeling she'll be back for more. Once they've had it they usually miss it and start to wonder if it'll be better a second time.' He raised his forefinger and tipped his hat. 'They do with me, any roads.'

'I think she's gone off blamin' me for what happened.'

'Tell me, what did happen?'

Declan bit his lip. He sensed a certain prurience in his old friend, as if having all those fancy Dublin ladies and all those saucy country girls at his beck and call was not enough for Seamus Flynn, as if he also needed to share, by proxy, the thrill of innocence lost.

'She was willin',' Declan murmured.

'Keen, was she keen?'

'I suppose she was.'

'How long were you saddled?'

'Long enough.'

'And then again?'

'Yes,' Declan said, uncomfortably.

'Longer?'

'Yes.'

'She'll be back for more,' Flynn predicted, sitting back and lifting his glass to his lips. He sipped, said, 'What about the other one, the poor one?'

'No, she never would. I wouldn't want her to either, come to think of it.'

'I thought she was eager?'

'I don't trust her,' Declan said.

Flynn laughed.

Declan said, 'Funny. Funny peculiar. But it's true. I never did trust her.'

'So you never took her?'

'No, and now she's gone her own way too, I think.'

'But you're still mad in love with the lady? Bobs?' Flynn added a little 'huh!' and repeated, 'Bobs!' as if the very silliness of the name rendered the girl unworthy of sympathy. 'You want more of her, that's all. Jasus, man, it's not as if she was your first. I tell you what you need, Declan me son, you need a night in the arms o' Lucy-Anne.'

'Who?'

'You remember Lucy-Anne. Jake's youngest. She'll drop for you in a flash. She'll knock the love nonsense out o' you, sure an' she will.'

'Does she drop for you?'

'When she's in the mood, yes, but it's always you she asks after, Declan.'

Declan stared unblinking into the little glass. The whiskey was different from the stuff served in Scottish bars; distilled from rye not malted barley. Subtle in hue, scent, taste, a strong flavour. He could not recall Lucy-Anne very well, only the crackle of straw under her buttocks and the odour of tussocks in the barn, thin thighs white and welcoming in the half-dark.

158

There had been too many like Lucy-Anne.

Roberta, though, was vivid in his mind's eye. She came to him when he did not want her, dragging a sense of guilt like a chain to bind him. How could he tell that to Seamus Flynn when Seamus had never suffered one twinge of guilt in his life. Thinking of Bobs made Declan want to weep again.

He downed the double and wiped his nose on his cuff.

'What,' he said, 'if I've given her a babby?'

'Huh! Did you not do it right?'

Declan shook his head.

Flynn said, 'It would indeed be evil luck if you got caught first time.'

'It can happen, though,' said Declan.

'Sure an' it can,' Flynn said. 'You're doctor enough to know how it happens.' He paused. 'Doctor enough to know what to do about it too.'

'I could never do that to her, never,' Declan said.

'I could,' said Seamus Flynn. 'I've done it before, often enough.'

'Yes, I thought you might have.'

'It's not difficult, not if you're careful,' Flynn said. 'Perhaps you want it to take, of course. You'd have her for keeps that way.'

'No, not that way.'

He truly didn't want to trap Roberta into marriage. He could never live with her on those terms. He understood in his heart that she'd be better off with Conroy, her own kind. He hated himself, not Bobs, for the weakness she had exposed in him, the damage she'd done to his stubborn Irish pride.

'God, what's wrong with you? I've never seen you so down before.'

'Even if I lose her, have lost her,' Declan said, 'I don't want her to go thinkin' worse of me than she does already.'

Declan finished his stout while Flynn studied him in silence.

'Another, that's what you need,' said Flynn at length. 'Doctor's orders.'

Declan shook his head once more. 'He's not comin' now, is he?'

'Who?'

'My Da?'

Seamus Flynn's manner was suddenly heavy. He squinted at the young man with no trace of the affection which had so far tempered his jocularity.

'No, he's not coming,' Flynn said. 'Did you expect him to?'

'Not really,' Declan said. 'I just thought – Christmas – he might.'

'You can drink with me instead,' Flynn said. 'Joy to the world, hah?'

159

'No, Seamus, I think I just want to get home.'

'To Kerridge?' Flynn said, scathingly. 'To Mama? To your brother, the priest? To the saints in all their glory?'

And Declan nodded. 'Yes.'

Guy's invitation to join the Logies for dinner had been made beforehand and for some inexplicable reason had not been withdrawn after the Wellmeadow débâcle.

Better for all concerned if it had been.

Veitch Logie was obviously in no mood to play the gracious host. He drove Roberta and Guy back into Glasgow in sepulchral silence. It was late evening, about seven, before the Talbot drew up outside the Logie residence in Dowanhill and Guy and Roberta were set down and sent in ahead to tell 'my angel' to have dinner served immediately.

Mama's first words were, 'Well, Guy, did you find it interesting?'

'Yes, Mrs Logie. Most interesting.'

'Did he let you do anything?'

'No,' said Roberta, flatly. 'We only watched.'

'Where is your father?'

'Putting away the motorcar.'

Martyr though she might be, Daphne Logie had sufficient savvy not to press the point. She had endured umpteen similar occasions when, after something had gone amiss at the Wellmeadow, her husband would eat dinner in stony silence and retreat immediately to his study where, she suspected, he drank quantities of brandy and brooded on what had gone wrong.

Veitch was incapable of changing the habits of a lifetime and the presence of a dinner guest did not seem to matter. The atmosphere in the dining-room was so thick with unuttered questions that you could have cut it with a knife.

'Soup, Guy?'

'Thank you, Mrs Logie.'

'Bread roll?'

'If you please.'

'Roberta, another slice of beef?'

'No, thank you.'

'Then pass your father the cabbage, dear.'

'Father?'

Growl.

For dessert steamed fruit pudding and a jug of pouring custard were brought in. Veitch pushed his pudding plate down the table and nodded to Roberta to serve him. Guy, who was not accustomed to

160

rapid consumption, barely had time to dab his lips with his napkin before the traffic in plates began.

'Guy?' Roberta proffered the heavy crystal jug.

Guy took it by handle and base and prepared to decant the creamy yellow fluid on to the slab of pudding in his plate. Before he could adjust his grip, however, Veitch Logie jerked his head and snapped his fingers impatiently.

Carefully Guy set down the crystal jug. 'Sir,' he said, clearly, 'do not snap your fingers at me, if you please.'

Veitch straightened and sat back in his chair.

Guy said, 'I'm not one of your theatre nurses, Mr Logie.'

Roberta glanced from Guy to the jug to her father. Then she stretched out her hand to do her father's bidding. Guy caught her wrist and held it with a featherlight grip.

'Nor,' Guy went on, 'is Roberta.'

Bobs crumpled, elbow on the tablecloth, blonde curls nodding. She caught at Guy's hand, gripped not lightly but tightly.

'And thank God for it,' she said.

'Did something happen today?' Mrs Logie enquired, ingenuously.

'Did something happen?' said Roberta. 'What on earth do you suppose all this truculence is about?'

Veitch had folded his napkin into a little pyramid of cloth which he held between steepled fingers as if he was about to dab at his nostrils. His face remained expressionless. That, Bobs thought, was the oddest aspect of the row, the fact that both Guy and her father displayed not the slightest sign of genuine emotion.

Guy said, 'I am not an idealist, sir, but I admit I was rather taken aback by what I saw today. In that sense it was an instructive visit.'

In Veitch's fingers the napkin slid up until he was peering over its apex.

Guy said, 'I'd failed to realise how much of a strain a surgeon imposes upon himself or how much he is dependent upon the competence of ancillaries. I thought that surgeons were concerned solely with technique. It hadn't occurred to me that there was so much more to it, so much that involved character.'

Veitch Logie's lids lowered and rose again, slowly.

'Go on,' he said.

'I'm sure I speak for Roberta when I say that our ideas of what is demanded of a surgeon have been radically altered.'

'Yep,' said Roberta, pressing her thumb into Guy's palm.

'We've been given no hint of this in our classes,' Guy continued. 'I am, however, a little disappointed that you somehow seem to think that Roberta and I are critical of you and that you've chosen not to

161

allow us to question you on your decisions.'

'Tired. You're tired, aren't you, Veitch?' said my angel, loyally.

'Angry,' Veitch Logie stated. 'I was angry.'

'At what?' said Roberta.

'At the girl, of course.'

'Miss Ryan, do you mean?'

'Yes, Miss Ryan. A know-it-all.'

'I don't think she is.' It was Bobs's turn to receive a secret hand signal from Guy. 'I mean to say, I think she was just doing her job.'

Guy said, 'You didn't feel the wound, Bobs.'

'True,' Roberta admitted.

'What do you mean, young man?'

'I mean, sir, that I couldn't have got my hand in there either,' Guy said. 'If I'd been the surgeon – and I am, alas, a very long way indeed from presuming to know what it's like to be a surgeon – but *if* I had been responsible for repairing the perforation I couldn't have done so under the circumstances.'

'Oh?' Veitch Logie said.

'I assume that what you needed was space?'

'That's a very shrewd observation, young man.'

Guy paused long enough to slip his hand from Roberta's. He folded his arms and turned square to the man. 'Unless I miss my guess, the anaesthetist's prime concern was with the state of the patient while yours centred on access to the site? Are the two factors often incompatible?'

'Frequently.'

Guy nodded as if he was receiving profound information instead of claptrap. He looked so serious that, for a moment or two, even Roberta was taken in. Guy asked another question which her father, taking the napkin from his mouth at last, answered at considerable length.

Then, reaching for the crystal jug with both hands, Guy said, 'Would you care for some custard now, Mr Logie?'

'What do you want of me, young man?' Veitch Logie asked.

'Instruction, sir. To benefit from your vast experience.'

'Very well,' Veitch Logie said. 'Eat up your pudding, Guy, then we'll go upstairs to my study.'

'For what?' Roberta said. 'Brandy?'

'Coffee and a little private conversation,' her father told her, without ire. 'Guy, do you have time to spare?'

'I do, sir,' Guy Conroy said. 'Indeed, I do. All the time in the world.'

Close to Christmas Glasgow's Queen Street station was crowded with travellers. They were mostly students, teachers and business gentlemen with, here and there, a woman or two trailing a retinue of weary children. Mixed inevitably into the doughty throng were labourers and artisans, the cloth-capped brigade, wrapped in grey mufflers, cigarettes hanging from their lips, whisky bottles protruding from their pockets. One, swaying, sang a slurry ballad strictly for his own amusement while another, no more steady, pressed sweets on frightened children and tried to buttonhole young ladies into hearing his tale of woe.

What this particular late evening rush signified, Alison had no idea. She was seldom in the heart of Glasgow after dark and had made no more than half a dozen out-of-town trips by railway train.

She had, therefore, the impression of a city in flux, of tides of citizens constantly ebbing and flowing through the great glass-domed terminal where comfort was the gleam of a tea urn or the coal fire in a waiting-room or even the gas-lit peep-show bookstall. Tonight she imagined herself one of them, steaming out from under the iron canopy, heading – where? With Howard, perhaps? Off to Border country, to the McGraths' estate near Hawick where there would be stags' heads on the walls, muskets above the doors, holly wreaths and mistletoe.

'How long will the journey take?' she shouted above the hiss of steam and the *whump* of a locomotive.

'I'll be home, eating supper, by half past ten,' Howard told her.

'Is that all?'

'Oh, yes, it isn't far, really.'

Howard wore his familiar heavy-skirted overcoat and black homburg and looked, Alison thought, like a specialist dashing off to a difficult case in some far-flung corner of the kingdom. The scuffed-leather Gladstone bag added to the impression of professionalism. Only the length of his hair and his boyish gestures reminded her that he was no more expert than she was.

'One platform ticket,' Howard told her, handing her the billet. 'Since you insist on seeing me off, you may as well give the whole performance.'

'Anna Karenina?'

'Far too messy,' he said. 'In any case, I'm not worth dying for. Am I?'

'Absolutely not,' said Alison, hanging on to his arm as they walked up the platform by the stationary carriages. 'Where does this train end up?'

'London, King's Cross,' Howard told her.

She liked the feel of him, his height, the way he looked down on

163

her, the way he put his arm about her shoulder, protective not possessive. It seemed odd for an officer's son to be so affectionate towards a shipwright's daughter. Not that there was anything in it, of course. They were friends, not sweethearts, and it was strictly as a friend that she had come to see him off.

Declan, so Howard told her, had also gone home for Christmas. Though Howard didn't say so, Alison suspected that he had lent Declan the fare.

Truth was, she didn't much care what Declan Slater did with himself. Categorised as a youthful escapade, interesting and exciting but essentially folly, she had put her intimacy with Declan behind her.

Bobs too had chosen to cut Declan off. Bobs and she had discussed their changed attitudes towards the Irishman over coffee in the QM, guardedly not gushingly, as if they were both a tiny bit ashamed of what they had shared and how, in a sense, Declan had let them down.

Alison said, 'I've never been to London. Have you?'

'Ten or a dozen times. My mother likes to shop in Bond Street.'

'What's it like?'

'Big, busy, exciting. Lots to see and do,' Howard said. 'I'll take you there sometime, if you like.'

'Howard!'

'Just a thought,' Howard told her. 'And not a suggestion.'

'I'd never be able to get away.'

'From what?'

They'd stopped by an open door. Inside, the plum-coloured plush was lit by small globes encased in scrolled glass shades. First class for Howard, of course. Two gentlemen, and a lady in a marvellous fur hat, were making themselves comfortable. Howard seemed in no hurry to climb aboard, though the big clock above the concourse showed one minute to departure time.

He dropped the Gladstone and wrapped his arms about her.

'From what, Alison?'

'Home. I mean – everything.'

'Pity.'

'Isn't it?' Alison said.

'Put your hand in my pocket.'

'What? Here?'

'Go on. Don't be daft.'

She did as bidden and found in the pocket of his overcoat a small square parcel which fitted neatly into the palm of her hand. She kept one arm about him and her body close to his and drew out the parcel as if she were a thief.

164

'Present,' Howard said. 'Don't open it now. Open it later.'

'Thank you but – but I don't have anything to give you.'

'Yes, you do, Ally-my-Pal.'

Whistles blew, guards shouted, doors slammed. Steam hissed from beneath the engine and seeped up from the damp track.

Alison lifted herself on tiptoe, kissed him on the mouth. His lips were warm. He wrapped both arms about her and lifted her up so that she felt as if his kiss was airy, as if she was floating.

Another whistle shrilled, couplings clanked, a porter, walking fast, approached. Still without urgency, Howard set her down and took his arms from about her waist. He hoisted up the Gladstone.

'Bye,' he said.

'Bye, Howard.'

He stepped aboard, closed the door and leaned through the open window just as the train hauled the coach sluggishly away from the platform.

Alison did not attempt to follow. She watched Howard wave himself out of sight and then, only then, holding the little parcel with both hands pressed close to her breast, did she turn away, bemused.

A series of steep, tenement-lined hills connected Dowanhill to Partick. Guy's technique for descending was that of a mountaineer. He took them at a trot, feet angled outwards, body braced against the gradient, while poor Roberta stumbled and stuttered on her heels and struggled to keep up with him.

'What did he say? What did you talk about? I thought he was never going to let you go. Tell me, Guy. Don't be a pig. Tell me.'

'I've told you. We talked about you.'

'What about me?'

'He's concerned about you.'

'I find it hard to believe he's concerned about anyone except himself.'

'No, he is. Genuinely.'

'Well, damn it, you didn't talk about me for two whole hours.'

'He's worried about growing old.'

'Father?'

'He knows he's losing his touch.'

'He actually admitted it?'

'Not in so many words, no. The implication was clear, though.'

'Did he drink much?' Roberta asked.

'Couple of glasses of brandy.'

'You too?'

'One, just one.'

'The slippery slope?' Roberta felt more sure of herself after the side street flattened out on to Dumbarton Road. 'Next thing you know you'll be gargling in secret during the lunch-hour.'

'Like Declan, you mean?'

Roberta stopped to adjust her skirt and wriggle her heels into her shoes now that the pavements were level and the cobbled cliffs behind them.

The corner was lit by the restrained glow of Mackenzie's Retail Furniture Depository, a furnished room behind plate glass. In it Roberta could see her reflection coupled with Guy's, the pair of them hovering by a dining table and, deeper into the gloom, by a pale and insubstantial bedstead.

Guy seemed anxious to be on his way, though the last train through Partick wasn't due for a quarter of an hour and the station was only minutes away. Roberta took his arm politely.

'He asked about Declan,' Guy said. 'He seemed to know – at least to have an instinct – that you'd been seeing more of Slater than you should have.'

'None of his business,' Roberta said. 'Or yours, for that matter.'

'I think it is,' Guy said.

'Don't tell me he pumped you about Declan?'

'Of course he did. Listen, how are you going to get home again?'

'Cab from the rank at Peel Street.'

'I'll drop you there. I don't like the idea of you wandering the streets at this hour of the night. You didn't need to walk me to the station, you know.'

'Come on, surely you didn't think I was going to let you go without finding out what went on between you and Papa, did you? What did you *actually* tell him? What did he *actually* say to you? About – about Declan, for instance?'

'He doesn't seem to like him.'

'To my knowledge, he's never even met him.'

'He, your father, asked if Declan was an RC.'

'Oh, so that's it,' said Roberta. 'It's Orange Lodge prejudice, is it? I cannot understand how grown men can—'

'Perhaps because you're not a freemason,' Guy interrupted.

'What?' said Roberta, taken aback. 'Are you?'

'Not yet.'

They had walked the best part of two blocks and had reached the corner of Dumbarton Road and Peel Street. Ahead of them the bulky iron railway bridge squatted over the thoroughfare.

Under it, though the night was dry, Partick's platoon of die-hard drunks had already assembled to share bottles and cackle like old cockerels. The lights above the marque of the picture-house had gone out and tramcars were few and far between as the burgh closed down for the night. A dog trotted briskly across the tram-tracks, a handsome mongrel with a high proud curling tail. On reaching the pavement, it veered right and trotted aloofly past the drunkards as if they were beneath contempt.

Roberta said, 'You like him, don't you?'

'Who?' said Guy.

'My father.'

'Not particularly. I don't dislike him, though, not at all.'

'You didn't tell him the truth about Declan and me, did you?'

'I don't know what the truth is about you and Slater.'

'I admit I had a – a thing for him. But it's over now. All done, all gone.'

'Why?' said Guy. 'Because you have better fish to fry?'

Roberta prevaricated. 'How can you possibly like my father? You saw how he behaved today. He could have killed that ulcer case.'

'I don't think so.'

'You were as shocked as I was when he bullied Miss Ryan.'

'Was I?' Guy glanced towards the taxi-cabs which were ranked by the corner near the Burgh Hall. 'Look, I'll have to go. First, though, I'd like to see you safe and sound inside a cab. All right?'

'You sly devil, Guy Conroy!' She pointed at Guy accusingly. 'You're after me, aren't you? And you think you'll be able to get me through my father, by – what's the word – by *ingratiating* yourself with him? That really is low.'

'My intentions are honourable.'

'What a ridiculous thing to say.'

'Perhaps,' Guy said. 'But, as it so happens, I agree with your father on certain very fundamental points.'

'What, for instance?'

'That you and I – for instance – are two of a kind.'

'Good God!'

'We're made for each other,' Guy stated. 'Now go and find yourself a taxi-cab and let me get off for my train.'

'Not until you tell me that you . . .'

'I don't have to tell you anything,' Guy said.

' . . . love me, you're mad about me. That you can't live without me.'

'I can live without you,' Guy said. 'It's just that I'd rather not.'

'Wow!' Roberta said.

'And you?'

'Me – what?'

'Haven't you realised yet that you don't want to live without me?'

'Not yet,' Roberta said. 'Possibly not ever.'

'Give it time, Roberta,' Guy Conroy said and signalled to one of the taxi-cabs to come and take the lady home.

Jack had gone happily off to work early that Friday afternoon, lugging with him his black oblong trumpet case as well as his Manchester Crown briefcase.

Brenda was not displeased to see her hubby so full of beans. She'd even allowed him to 'play his lip in' during the course of the week.

He had practised with a thing like a sugar canister stuck into the bell of the instrument, the bell further muffled by a pillow on the bed in their room. He had spent a couple of hours there, cross-legged like a tailor. Bee and Lexi had climbed up beside him, had sat on him or sprawled against him while he ran through a repertoire of nursery rhymes or made funny noises to keep them entertained. And when they had finally, finally been put to bed, he'd sat by them, playing so softly that Brenda could hardly hear him, little lullabies and love songs, until his daughters fell asleep.

It made Brenda feel better to think that Jack was getting something out of it too. No sooner had Jack departed for his Friday round, however, than Brenda had the twins shod, pantalooned and helmetted and had galloped round to her mother's house, wheeling the pair before her in the push-chair.

'Thanks, Mum. Can't stop.'

'Where's she goin' in such a hurry?' Alex had asked.

'Hairdresser's.'

'What for, a dye-job?'

'God knows!' Ruby had said, peeling Lexi out of her pantaloons. 'Might be a Permanent Wave.'

'How long does that last?'

'Month, maybe.'

'Some permanent,' Alex had said. 'How long does it take?'

'She'll be back by five,' Ruby had said as Bee, bouncing on Grandfather's knee, had reached for one of the bon-bons that Alex had managed to balance behind each ear. 'She'd better be. I'm goin' out.'

'Where?' Alex had said in surprise.

'Pictures.'

'Who with?'

'Trudi.'

'What's on?'

'As You Desire Me.'

'Eh?'

'Greta Garbo.'

'Oh, aye,' Alex had said. 'You'll enjoy that.'

'Alex, Bee's eatin' the paper.'

'What? What? Here, wee lamb, spit, spit for Grandpa then.'

To Brenda's chagrin she was unable to find a place to deposit her children that night of all nights. Ruby and Trudi were out together, her father-in-law at work. Alison had a previous engagement and Davy and Henry had gone out for a drink. That left Bertie. She would die before she'd ask Bertie to look after the twins, mainly because she knew what his answer would be.

Chagrin was perhaps not quite the word to describe Brenda's feelings. Mingled with excitement at the prospect of having Walter all to herself again was a nagging suspicion that what she was doing was stupid. Also lurking within her bosom was a desire to show off her bonnie bairns to the man who'd missed his chance.

By half past seven, her sandy hair newly curled and only slightly frizzy, Brenda had the twins fed, scrubbed and togged in nightgowns, dressing-gowns and slippers. For all of thirty seconds they looked so angelic that Brenda almost felt like crying. By twenty minutes to eight, though, she was ready to strangle the pair of them.

'Wha's 'at?'

'That's, you know, a lipstick, honey.'

'Wha' for?'

'To make Mummy pretty. Lexi, please put it down.'

'Wha's 'isss?'

'No, Bee, not the bloody – not my mascara.'

A moment later: 'Mammy, Lexi's gotta funny face.'

'*Lexi!* Put ma lipstick *down*.'

It was never like this in the *Hollywood Book of Beauty*.

There Miss Twenties hovered in a sunlit boudoir before a half-moon-shaped mirror at a dressing-table the size of a football pitch, jealously guarding her bandbox freshness with the gentlest of creams and oils, *caring* for herself and her man and taking *pains* to ensure that she was ever worth loving.

The pain Brenda could understand as she tugged at her dry hair with hot curling tongs, singeing her scalp and almost incinerating her eyebrows, and simultaneously fought with Bee for possession of the last dab of Pond's White Lily cold cream and with Lexi for what remained of her Coral Island lipstick most of which was now smeared all over Lexi's cheeks and nightgown. Not a dickey-bird in the Hollywood book about how to retain that *April joie d'êsprit* while wrestling with rouge and face powder and two inquisitive brats at the pot table in the kitchenette with the clock ticking away and your lover advancing on your front door with all the inevitability of crow's feet and varicose veins.

By ten past eight o'clock the kitchen looked like a cross between an abattoir and a cement factory.

And Brenda was in despair.

She had foolishly imagined that her children would co-operate in her plan of campaign, would be sound asleep when Walter turned up, propped on clean pillows, thumbs in mouths, cute as buttons; that Walter would peep in at them and that his heart would melt at the sight and he would moan softly and shed a manly tear for the bliss he had missed, the happiness that had fallen to another. Then he would take her into the living-room, make love to her on the couch, vow that wherever he roamed he would never forget their night of bliss together.

'Ma dress! Naw, naw, naw, Bee, don't spill the powder on Mummy's pretty – Aaahh, God! *Look* what you've done *now.*'

Brenda tore the tongs from her hair, ripped the dishtowel from about her throat and, with the twins fleeing before her, chased them, not in jest, through the hall, up the stairs and, shrieking, into the back bedroom.

They reached the cot ahead of her, were cowered down and feigning sleep before Brenda could grab a soft part to smack. She raised her hand but did not bring it down, looked down at fluttering eyelids, at flushed little cheeks garish with make-up and knew, just as the doorbell rang, that she had made a terrible mistake, that adultery, in any shape or form, was not for wee Brenda Burnside and never would be again.

She greeted him with her hair like a hayrick and a twin on each arm. 'Hiya, Walter,' she said, with all the panache she could muster. *'Entre dans.'*

Late night in Dowanhill; late night in Flannery Park; Bobs and Trudi, Alison and Brenda, none of the four asleep. Stillness in the air and a hard, cold rain beginning to fall, dampening the tennis courts, sheening the black slate roofs of council houses, several miles apart. Tramcars, almost empty, rattled the length of Dumbarton Road. A last bus prowled down University Avenue past locked gates, darkened cloisters and the tower lost in midwinter haze.

December. Christmas pending.

New Year only a half-step away.

Roberta lay in the bath, stupefied with heat, glazed by steam. Blonde hair, towel-wrapped, resting on a sponge. Body floating, drifting, bumping the sides, breasts heavy and belly sleek, all curving heavily away from her as, through sticky lids, she watched for the sign that hadn't come.

She squeezed her knees together, let them part, watched the wavelets ripple round her abdomen, lick against her nipples, dark as plums.

'Declan,' she sighed softly. 'Oh, Declan Slater, what have you done?'

In the small back room upstairs in Wingfield Drive, Trudi undressed. Backlit by the bulb of the table-lamp, she posed like Garbo and, deepening her little-girl voice, asked Henry to light her a cigarette.

He had, she knew, been watching her over the top of *The Times*.

When he put down the newspaper she placed one foot upon the bedside chair and, wearing nothing else, unclipped the straps of her black lace garter belt and slowly peeled the stockings from her slender legs.

Henry lit two Gold Flake. He shook out the match and, stretching across the bed, slipped one of the cigarettes into his wife's fingers. He did not withdraw but, leaning on the pillow, blew smoke upward so that it clouded her white body and crawled, clinging, to merge with the cloud that escaped her pale lips.

'Have you heard from Germany yet?' he asked, huskily.

Trudi shook her head then, still with one foot upon the chair, bent and cupped a hand to the back of Henry's neck. 'Do you want me to tell you again what they did to me there?'

Henry admitted, 'Yes.'

'Which time?'

'In Munich,' Henry said. 'Start with Munich.'

'Do you also wish for me to show you how they did it?'

Henry meekly nodded his assent.

Across the landing from her brother's room Alison heard the muffled conversation cease, then the creak of bedsprings.

She sighed impatiently but, in spite of herself, listened for the stifled groans that she'd heard so often that they no longer brought thoughts of Declan Slater to her mind.

Once, long ago, she had cowered in this self-same bed and heard the noise of the Rooneys' passion seep through the wall next door. Kind neighbours had suddenly turned to strangers, doing strange, frightening things. Now she knew almost all there was to know, more than most in some ways, about the form of human reproduction. But she didn't know what the heart meant, why she flickered in and out of love, why, when Jim was far away, she loved him more, or why she wanted Howard to hold her close right here and now.

She was dressed in her nightgown, a cardigan thrown over her shoulders. She was seated in bed, knees drawn up, textbook resting against her thighs. It was not the book which held her attention, however, but the brooch Howard had given her, a beautiful little emerald in an antique setting, pin and clasp expensively restored. The box alone was pretty enough to serve as a present. So far she had kept the gift hidden behind books on the shelf above her desk where not even Trudi would find it. It was her secret, symbol of what might have been or, perhaps, of what might yet be.

On impulse she slid out of bed and seated herself at her desk by the window. She switched on the lamp, took out a square, wood-framed mirror and propped it against some books.

She held the brooch between finger and thumb and set it against her hair then against her throat.

As she did so her thumb caught the pin and she felt a tiny, stabbing pain. Holding up her hand, she saw blood upon the ball, a pinprick, ruby red, which as she stared at it grew into a fat little globule. She watched, fascinated, as blood trickled down her hand and stained her sleeve.

Only then did she put her thumb to her mouth and suck the invisible wound to make it heal.

Outside, unknown to Alison, the rain had turned to sleet.

'Look at you,' Brenda said. 'Like a bloody snowman. When did it begin?'

'I'd to walk up from the Kingsway,' Jack said. 'It's only sleet.'

'Well, give yourself a shake. How did it go at the Cally?'

'Fine,' he said, grinning. 'Great.'

'Big turnout?'

'Packed.' He took the towel she offered him and dried his hair vigorously. 'What are you doin' up, anyway?'

'Waitin' for you.'

'Are the girls all right?'

'Course they are. Dead to the world.'

He folded the towel and put it across a chairback, seated himself in the armchair by the fire and stooped to unlace his shoes.

'I'll do that,' said Brenda, kneeling at his feet.

He looked down at her, said, 'You're all done up.'

'I had a visitor.'

'Who?'

172

'Walter Giffard. He just, you know, dropped in.'

'Did he?' Jack said. 'What did *he* want?'

'To see me, to see the twins.'

'Old times, eh?'

Brenda slid her husband's wet shoes into the hearth, lifted one of his feet into her lap and massaged it with both small, plump hands. 'He only stayed for twenty minutes,' she said. 'Hardly worth gettin' dolled up for, was it?'

'Did you know he was comin'?'

'Nope.'

'Why'd you get your hair done then?'

'For, you know, Christmas,' Brenda said.

'Will he be back?'

'Wattie? Nah, nah.'

'He didn't get what he expected then?'

'I don't know what he expected but he didn't get it here.' She drew Jack's foot deeper into her lap and leaned over so that he could see her breasts. 'I'm lyin',' she said. 'I do know what he wanted. He wanted news about your sister.'

'Ally? Really?'

'He wanted to know all about her, about her an' Jim Abbott. If I thought they would get married soon.'

'What did you tell him?'

'I told him he'd missed his chance.'

'What did he say to that?'

'Not much. Just looked, that way he has, down his snoot.'

'I thought you fancied Walter Giffard?'

'Once, maybe,' Brenda said. 'But I'm a happily married woman now.'

'What did he think of the twins?' Jack said, after a pause.

'They were all over him. He was glad to get out alive.'

Jack laughed and shook his head. 'Our Ally, though. He's got no chance with her, no chance at all.' He paused again. 'Are you really happy, Brenda?'

'I'd be happier if you had a thousand quid in the bank.'

'Seriously?' Jack said.

'I'm never, you know, serious,' Brenda said. 'Listen, are you dry?'

'Aye.'

'Well, I'm not.'

'What?'

'Come on, big boy, what'd you think I've been waitin' up for? Cocoa?'

'Is that why you're all done up? For me?'

'Who'd you think it was for? Wattie Giffard?'

'Well . . .'

'That's over. That's the past.' Brenda hoisted herself on to her husband's knee and wriggled comfortably into his arms. 'Look at your lip, all stiff again.'

'My lip?' Jack said. 'Just my lip?'

'Naughty!'

'You started it.'

'Who's gonna, you know, finish it?'

'I am,' Jack Burnside said. 'Here, or upstairs?'

'Here,' Brenda said, warmly. 'Right here. Right here an' now.'

SIX

None So Blind

At Alex's insistence the Burnsides assembled in 162 on Hogmanay to raise their glasses and greet the New Year together.

Jack and Brenda only just made it. They zoomed round from Shackleton Avenue at the last minute with Bee and Lexi wrapped in shawls and quilts and looking like gigantic caterpillars. With much cooing and crooning, the sleepy pair were tucked into Alison's bed only minutes before hooting, hollering and noisy glad-handing erupted in the streets and a prissy English voice on the wireless declared that 1934 had duly arrived.

Mr Rooney from next door was the Burnsides' 'first foot'. Then pals of Davy spilled into the living-room to carry him off on a bachelor spree. To everyone's surprise, Bertie, clutching a bottle of sherry, skipped out to visit some Co-op friend or other, leaving the remaining members of the family to gather round the fireside to talk about the past and speculate on what perils and pleasures might lie in store in the year ahead.

Jim Abbott had just returned from a week-long stay with his mother and sister in Perthshire.

Alison had been looking forward to seeing him again. He seemed more reserved than usual, however, and Alison wondered if he had somehow learned that her theatre jaunt had been with Howard alone. Throughout the celebrations Jim remained uncharacteristically aloof until, about a quarter to three, he made his excuses and, ignoring Alex's tipsy protests that he was spoiling the party, abruptly left for home.

Alison insisted on walking part of the way with him in the hope that she might discover what was troubling him but he resisted her questions, finally lost his temper and snapped at her to mind her own business.

On the lonely walk back to Wingfield Drive Alison was filled with a strange sense of foreboding. Jim's black mood had unnerved her. It hadn't occurred to her that Jim might lose interest in their relationship, might have met another woman in Perthshire, say, whom he preferred to her and that, weary of their prolonged engagement, he might be preparing to throw her over. In the wee small hours of the first day of January, the prospect of being deprived of Jim's support sent her into near panic and, as soon as the twins were bundled up and carried off home, she took herself to bed.

She rose long before the rest of the household, made herself breakfast and, still agitated, took Pete out for a walk. In the dead, grey light of a New Year's morning she walked as far as the canal and back, by which time her brothers were prowling about the living-room and Trudi was immured in the kitchen, busy with preparations for a special family dinner.

Without a word to anyone about her plans Alison donned her overcoat again and set off for Macarthur Drive, determined to have it out with Jim once and for all.

In response to Alison's insistent ringing, he managed to drag himself to the front door and unlock it. Then he staggered back into the bedroom and collapsed on the side of the bed.

Propped on his elbow, chest heaving, he said, 'Sorry.'

'Jim, what is it? What's wrong with you?'

'I'm not – going – to – make it – for dinner.'

The air in the ground-floor bedroom was like ice. Apparently Jim had not had the strength to plug in the electrical radiator, light the bedside lamp or even to struggle into his dressing-gown.

Clothing lay where he'd stepped out of it and his pyjama jacket was on back to front. An uncharacteristic mustiness pervaded the house. The smells of lavender and beeswax which Alison had once thought of as the very breath of middle-class respectability had vanished along with Jim's sister Winnie. But even the more masculine smells of tobacco, Brasso and shoe polish which had made Jim's living-room seem homely had been replaced by a sickly sweet stench which reminded Alison, jarringly, of anatomy rooms and basement mortuaries.

'Alison,' Jim said. 'I'm sick.'

She sat by him, took his hand and felt for his pulse.

To her relief, she found it strong, not thready. When she put an arm about his shoulders to steady him, though, she discovered that his pyjama jacket was saturated with perspiration.

'How long have you been like this?'

'It came – over me – yesterday.'

'Jim, the truth?'

'Weeks – feeling – not myself.'

176

'You haven't been eating properly, have you?'

'I can't – seem to – face food.'

'Tummy upset?'

'Gassy.'

'Have you any pain?' She blew on her fingers, slipped a hand into the opening of his pyjama jacket. 'Here, for instance?'

'No.'

'Here?'

'A little – bit.'

'Take a deep breath. Can you?'

Holding on to her, he sucked air and coughed, not violently.

'Still no pain?' Alison enquired.

'No. Sorry.'

Pleurisy, she knew, could disguise itself as a digestive problem. Jim had suffered from a stubborn cold throughout November, also a hacking cough which had turned loose and productive before it had apparently cured itself.

Obviously she hadn't been paying enough attention.

'It's just – 'flu.' Jim strove to remain casual. 'Be right – as rain by the – weekend.'

'Have you been losing weight?'

'Perhaps – a pound – or two.'

Alison got up and gestured towards the tallboy which occupied a corner of the bedroom. 'Clean pyjamas?'

'Second – drawer.'

She opened the drawer and took out a pair of flannelette pyjamas. She thought of changing the bed-sheets too but she already had a queasy feeling that Jim was beyond home nursing.

She placed the pyjamas by him on the bed and said, 'I'll help you put them on, if you like.'

'I don't – think that – would be – proper.'

'Oh, shut up. Do you want a warm drink?'

'Tea – please.'

He lifted the pyjamas as if they weighed a ton, put them on his lap, fumbled with the cord at his waist. His chest was thin and almost hairless, scar tissue livid on the stump of his arm.

Cord untied, he looked up at her.

'Give me – a minute – alone – please, Ally.'

Alison nodded. She picked his clothing from the floor and went into the living-room. She folded his trousers, shook out his jacket and draped the garments on a chair. Carrying his underwear, shirt and socks, she moved into the kitchen in search of the laundry basket, to give herself an opportunity to think what to do for the best.

177

Breathlessness and sweating indicated respiratory disorder. But which one, and how serious? She really ought to send for Dr Lawrence. But it was New Year's Day and she would probably be palmed off with some young locum whose knowledge was not much greater than her own. She tried to imagine what an experienced diagnostician like T.K. Thomas would do in similar circumstances.

On impulse she opened the lid of the laundry basket and rummaged through Jim's crumpled shirts and vests. She plucked out his handkerchiefs and spread them open with a fingertip.

Among the sticky sputum stains were several little freckles of blood.

Seconds later Alison was running down Macarthur Drive in search of a public telephone.

'About bloody time too,' said Alex, testily. 'Where the heck have you been? We've nearly finished our steak pie.'

'An' where's Jim?' Ruby added.

They were gathered round the dining table which, extended to full length, jutted into the centre of the living-room. The air was rich with the aroma of cooking meats and sugary puddings, the table laden with plates and dishes, sauce bottles, wine bottles, pickle jars and big brown flagons of beer. The steak pie, the Co-op's finest, occupied pride of place, the ashet raised on four cork mats. The pie's golden-brown crust was half demolished and oozed a tide of thick, brown gravy into the corners of the metal dish. Alison knew only too well how fussy her family were about tribal feasts and that steak pie in particular had a bizarre tendency to 'waste' if it wasn't eaten piping hot.

At the top of the table, hard against the window ledge, Davy was smoking a small cheroot and quaffing beer. Henry wore his best three-piece suit, a napkin tucked into the vee of his waistcoat. He gave Alison a disapproving glare.

'I do think you might have made an effort to get here on . . .' The reprimand tailed off. 'Have you been crying?'

'It's Jim,' Alison said. 'He's been taken away.'

'Away?' said Bertie, sitting up. 'To the jail?'

'To hospital.' Alison burst into tears.

Henry helped her to a chair.

'But Jim was here last night, sweetheart,' Alex said. 'I mean, we all saw him, didn't we, boys?'

'Aye, so we did,' said Davy, nodding.

'He was okay then.' Jack dandled Lexi on his knee, feeding his daughter from the same spoon as he fed himself. 'I mean, he seemed fine to me.'

'Do you think I'm making it up?' Alison cried.

'Naw, naw,' said Alex soothingly. 'We're just wonderin' how it happened.'

Crouched by Alison's chair, Henry fished a handkerchief from his breast pocket and gently wiped his sister's eyes. 'Tell us what happened, Ally?'

At that moment Bee made a sudden lunge for a cider bottle. Brenda's reaction was swift. She checked her daughter's inquisitive fist and murmured, '*Sssh*, now, honey. *Sssh-sssh*. Sit nice an' listen to Auntie Alison.'

Alison said, 'I could see Jim was ill, very ill. I telephoned Dr Lawrence and explained the signs. He came straight away, took one look at Jim, bundled him into his car and drove him straight to the hospital.'

'Heart?' said Trudi.

'Chest,' said Alison.

'Which hospital?' said Henry.

'Ottershaw.'

'I thought Ottershaw was in Stirlingshire?' said Bertie. 'What's Lawrence doin' takin' him away out there?'

'He knows the consultant,' Alison explained. 'Leyman. A specialist.'

'In what is it he specialises?' Trudi asked.

Alison took in a deep breath before answering.

'Tuberculosis.'

'What!' Jack and Davy exclaimed in unison.

Brenda scooped Bee into her arms and swung her away from Alison. 'Isn't that, you know, contagious?'

'TB,' said Henry. 'Jesus! Is Lawrence absolutely certain?'

'No.' Alison shook her head. 'But I am.'

'You!' said Bertie, scathingly. 'What do you know?'

'I know this much,' Alison said. 'If radiological examination exposes tuberculous lesions in his lungs, Jim's going to be in hospital for a very long time.'

'Surely he won't, you know, die?' Brenda blurted out.

'He might.' Alison began to cry again. 'Oh, dear God! I don't know what I'll do if that happens. I really don't know what I'll do.'

Marry the other one, Brenda thought.

She prudently held her tongue, though, while Ally-Pally wept as if this turn-up was entirely tragic and not, as it seemed to Brenda, a wee bit of a blessing in disguise.

On the afternoon of January 3rd, when three-quarters of the

179

population had already returned to work, Mr Veitch Logie threw his annual sherry party.

The word 'party' implied gaiety but the event was staid and duty-bound and occupied part of an afternoon when most of the guests would have preferred to be sprawled by their own firesides. You didn't turn up at Mr Logie's party in sports jacket and flannels. The whole stuffy nonsense of best suit and starched collar was required and, though the sherry was usually drinkable, the little trays of canapés which circulated about the drawing-room were scant enough to make you long for a black pudding supper or a bag of chips.

The afternoon of January 3rd, 1934, didn't seem very different from preceding years but beneath the affected air of bonhomie, subtle tensions indicated that all was not well in the house of Logie.

The boys, Roberta's brothers, were home for the holidays. Many years spent out of range of father's influence did not seem to have harmed them at all. Even Roberta had to admit they were quite pleasant chaps, if rowdy, more adept at standing up to Papa than she had ever been.

She might even have taken pleasure in their company if she hadn't been so obsessed with her own affairs.

They were on best behaviour that afternoon, however, for Papa had promised to let them go to the circus with Guy and Roberta if they displayed just a modicum of decorum for two or three hours.

Guy was completely at ease. He seemed to possess a genetic disposition to shine in stuffy social gatherings.

Immaculately groomed, handsome, restrained, everyone admired Guy and commented upon his virtues until Bobs was fed to the teeth of being told how lucky she was to have such a fine, upstanding young man paying court to her. Paying court to Papa, more like, Bobs thought bitterly as that peculiar spongy fullness in her loins sent her again to the lavatory, again to be disappointed.

It was Guy's future which was discussed, Guy's praises which were sung, not hers. Even so, if Roberta had been left to her own devices, she might well have fallen for Guy Conroy in due course. Might have joined with him in holy wedlock, might have clambered up the monkey-puzzle tree of medical advancement with one fist clutching Guy's coat-tails – if only he hadn't been *so* damned devious, *so* damned self-assured.

And if she, throughout the season of goodwill and joy, hadn't been plagued by the nagging suspicion that she was pregnant to scruffy Declan Slater.

Bobs wandered about the drawing-room on that dismal winter's afternoon dazed by fear. She wondered if it might be possible to persuade Guy Conroy to make love to her and to pass the baby off as his. She tried to imagine the immaculate Guy all hot, eager and insistent but all she could conjure up was Guy's hypocritical chant of, 'I don't understand. I don't understand,' when all the time he understood perfectly well.

'And when's the happy day, dear?' said deaf Aunt Edith.

'What?'

'Wedding bells?'

'I'm not getting married,' Roberta said.

'Oh, I heard you were. To that nice young man in the blue suit.'

'His name's Guy, Aunt Edith, and I'm not marrying him.'

'Who is the lucky chap then?'

'There is no lucky chap.'

'Have to be quick, dear.'

'What? Why?'

'Left on the shelf.'

'Sod off!' Bobs whispered, sounding just like Declan.

'Pardon?'

'I said, It's all off.'

'Oh! What is, dear?'

'My marriage.'

'Really?'

'Really. Stalker, bring your aunt another sherry, if you please.'

Taking her by the arm, Guy said, 'I heard that, Roberta. What's wrong with you today?'

'I don't know what you mean.'

'You're behaving very badly.'

'I can't stand Papa's idiotic parties, if you must know.'

'They're not idiotic. Contacts are made, friendships established mainly by social converse.'

'Social converse? I mean to say – dear God, what do I mean to say?'

'I wish you wouldn't take the name of the Lord in vain, Roberta.'

'No, I'm sorry.'

'What *is* wrong with you?'

'Nothing, I'm just rather depressed.'

'The circus will cheer you up.'

'The circus! No, I really won't be happy until the new term begins.'

'Won't be long until Monday. Meanwhile, why don't you try to put a brave face on it for Papa's sake.'

'Papa?'

'Your papa, I mean.'

She disentangled her arm from his, handed him her sherry glass. 'Excuse me, Guy,' she said.

'Where are you off to now?'

'To the lavatory, if you must know.'

'Again?'

'Yes, damn it, *again*. Do you mind?'

She knew that Guy was watching her as she slipped through the crowd of guests and vanished out of the drawing-room door. She doubted if he was intelligent enough to deduce her condition from such vague early signs.

Behind her in a corner of the drawing-room, though, her brother Stalker raised an adolescent eyebrow and cynically whispered, 'Preggers?'

To which her brother Veitch replied, 'You betcha!'

On January 3rd Alison travelled out to Ottershaw by train. She was no less apprehensive than the eight or ten other visitors who rode along the single-track line under the rain-cloaked heights of the Campsie Fells and who walked, silent and indrawn, the half-mile of country lane which led to the gates of the hospital. The day was still an official 'professional' holiday and the stream of visitors who usually filed into the hall of the big house had been reduced to a trickle.

Alison had come 'on spec', as it were.

Jim's widowed sister, Winnie Craddock, had been informed of the situation by telegram and had replied to the effect that she could not leave her mother, who was also ill, before the weekend. Henry and Davy had volunteered to accompany her but Alison had dissuaded them. She thought it best to go alone, at least until she found out what was really wrong with Jim.

She presented herself at the window of the enquiry desk, showed her matriculation card, explained that she was a fourth year medic and the fiancée of a newly admitted patient and soon found herself being ushered not to Jim's bedside but along a gloomy corridor to the administration wing.

This block, like many of Ottershaw's extensions, had been hastily constructed to cope with gassing cases during the Great War. Although it was only early afternoon, lights had been lit in the wooden-walled office and a curtain of fine green linen drawn across half the window. Alison could just make out the lighted pavilions stretching across the moorland plateau, a site, she thought, high enough to catch the wind from the hills and be safe above the level of river mists. The office, like all the rooms in Ottershaw, was chilly.

At first sight Dr Leyman seemed chilly too but, as Alison was soon to discover, her initial impression was false.

Phillip Leyman was of middle height but slight build. He was sharp-featured with keen dark eyes. He wore a white knee-length cotton coat and a white roll-collar shirt. On his feet were white canvas tennis shoes with rubber soles which squeaked a little when he walked. Casual dress did not detract from his briskness in dealing with all the medical and administrative problems which came before him.

Alison would soon learn that here was a man to whom time was precious, that Ottershaw was his kingdom and that he ran it without regard for timewasting conventions.

'Fourth year medicine?' he said in a quick, clickety voice. 'Have you done your TB?'

'Yes, sir,' Alison said. 'Last term. Ruchill.'

'The factory,' the doctor said. 'Learn much?'

'I thought I had.'

'I'm Leyman, by the way. I take it you passed the ticket?'

'Yes, sir.'

'Know your way around a microscope?'

'Fairly well, yes.'

'Come on then.'

He opened a French door in the back wall of the office and, beckoning Alison to follow, stepped out into the dank afternoon air.

It was Alison's first sight of what lay behind the mansion house.

Flowerbeds and evergreens flanked the network of gravel paths which connected the pavilions. Beyond the buildings tall pines bristled on the ridge that bordered the moorland. To her left, across the valley, she could make out the outlines of the Campsie Fells with little lonely farmhouses floating here and there in the mist. In the long glass-roofed conservatories which adjoined the pavilions she could see the shapes of bedridden patients, all as still and quiet as if they were already dead.

Dr Leyman led her along one of the paths, talking as he went.

'Inoculation? Before you did your bit at Ruchill?' he asked.

'Yes.'

'BCG?'

'Yes,' Alison answered.

'I'm sceptical about its effectiveness,' Dr Leyman told her. 'I presume you were instructed in basic methods of prophylaxis?'

'How effective are they?' Alison asked, by way of answer.

He glanced at her, brows raised and laughed. 'Smart wee puss, aren't you, Miss Burnside?'

'I'm sorry. I didn't mean . . .'

'How effective? I'm still alive and kicking, aren't I?'

Alison said, 'I'm not here as a student, Dr Leyman. I'm here because . . .'

'I know – because your fiancée is ill. But, Miss Burnside, you can't just switch merrily from being a medical student one minute to concerned relative the next. You're duty bound to learn as much as you can, to add to what you already think you know, about the tubercle bacillus.'

'Jim – Mr Abbott . . .'

'Has pulmonary tuberculosis.'

'Oh!' Leyman's briskness cancelled out her tears. 'Early or advanced?'

'Early stages.'

'Can he be cured?'

'Probably.'

'No rash promises, though?'

They had reached a short flight of steps which led up to another wooden building. Hand on the doorhandle, Leyman paused.

'No,' he said. 'No rash promises.'

Alison nodded. 'Where are we? Is this Jim's ward?'

'This is our lab,' Dr Leyman answered, and pulled open the narrow door.

Alison had always enjoyed laboratory work. She was stimulated by the sight of Ottershaw's inner sanctum, concern for Jim allayed by curiosity.

By the glow of a bench lamp she saw the glint of microscopes and electrical centrifuges. She smelled the pungent odour of gas burners and petroleum ether. This being the last day of the holiday the room was almost deserted. Only one technician crouched at the bench. He was sipping coffee from an enamel mug and, now and then, would dip forward to peer into the eyepiece of a Zeiss research microscope almost, Ally thought, as if he hoped to take by surprise the organisms that swarmed across the slide.

'McNair,' Leyman called out. 'Visitors.'

'Hmmm?'

The man, in his forties, had a slightly dazed look to him, as if his mind was elsewhere. His hair was thinning on the crown and that, together with his rather worn features, gave him the appearance of an affable monk.

When he spoke his voice had a droll quality which Alison found appealing. 'Just catching up,' he said. 'Who did you say the girl was?'

'Medical student. Come to take a squint at a sputum sample.'

'Anything in particular?'

'The new case, the teacher.'

'Abbott?'

'That's the one. Do you have something we can look at?'

'Sure.'

McNair unclipped the slide from the Zeiss, removed it with fine-point steel forceps and slotted it into a lined wooden box. He opened another box and extracted a broad glass slide which he fitted neatly into the clips. He fiddled with the illuminating apparatus, peeped into the eyepiece then sat back, long legs spread, and sipped coffee again.

'When are you going home, McNair?'

'Soon.' McNair glanced at his wristlet watch. 'Very soon, in fact.'

'What's on the programme for tonight?' Leyman asked. 'Are you cooking a feast for the family?'

'Repairing a drain in our bathroom, actually.'

'Gastronomy and plumbing. A strange combination of pastimes.' Leyman grinned then said, 'Let the lady have a look, please, before you go.'

Obligingly McNair surrendered the padded stool.

Alison seated herself before the microscope.

McNair leaned over her. He smelled, not unpleasantly, of garlic.

'What year?' he asked.

'Fourth.'

'Then you'll know how to work one of these gadgets?'

'Yes, I think so.'

He leaned back and, arms folded, watched Alison adjust focus. She looked into the eyepiece, closing off the world.

At first she saw nothing except staining medium and, within it, the globular universe of the sputum specimen.

'They're there okay,' McNair told her. 'They're just being coy.'

'When was this sample taken?' Alison asked.

'Early this morning,' Dr Leyman answered.

'Much saliva?'

'No. Ordinary mucoid type. Fairly obvious. See them now?'

'Not . . .' Alison began. 'Yes, I do. I see them.'

She saw them very clearly, long and thin and scattered singly throughout the film. She racked her brains to remember what she'd learned at Ruchill. She could hear Prof Finlayson's voice in her ear and, still staring at the bits of translucent bootlace, said, 'Virulent infection. Rapid and possibly progressive.'

'Textbook stuff,' said McNair, shrugging.

Leyman placed a hand on Alison's shoulder. 'We'll do a blood work-up and take samples of both pleural fluid and faeces. Even although the microscopical examination is obviously positive, we'll probably go the whole hog and have McNair prepare a sputum culture.'

'Chest Roentgen?' said Alison.

'Absolutely essential. As soon as our department is back in full swing we'll have X-rays taken to provide an accurate indication of pathological activity.'

Alison slid back from the microscope and got to her feet. 'Now I see why Dr Lawrence insisted on bringing Jim straight to Ottershaw.'

'Oh, your fellow would have received much the same attention at Ruchill or Bridge of Weir,' said Phillip Leyman.

'Baloney!' McNair put in. 'In this place we do everything twice as fast and twice as efficiently as anywhere else. Then, God help us, we do it all again.'

'May I see Jim now?' Alison said.

'Tomorrow, I think,' Dr Leyman said. 'He's not quite himself today.'

'Oh!'

'I know you're disappointed but it's for Abbott's own good. Now, if you'll come back to the office with me I'd like to ask you some questions.'

'I suppose the Board of Health will have to be notified?'

'Lawrence has done so already. It's rather up to us to provide as full a list of contacts as possible, though. That's where you come in.'

'The school,' said Alison. 'God, I'd forgotten about the school.'

'Lots of work for somebody,' Dr Leyman said. 'Come on back to my office. I'll rustle up some tea before we tackle the paperwork.'

'Do you do *everything* yourself, Dr Leyman?' Alison asked.

'Only what's necessary,' Phillip Leyman answered.

To which McNair, by way of comment, uttered a laconic, 'Huh!'

Jack had finally lost patience and gone out. It was left to Ruby to listen to her daughter's rantings about the culpability of James Abbott and, by association, Ally Burnside.

Brenda's tantrum, born of anxiety, had lasted for three days and showed no sign of burning itself out.

'It's all right for her. She's a bloody doctor. She'll have had, you know, injections an' things. Never a bloody thought about my poor wee mites. I mean, you'd think she'd have had more sense of – what's it?'

Seated on the couch with a twin on each side of her, Ruby said, 'Responsibility?'

'Aye, bloody responsibility.'

'I wish you wouldn't swear, Brenda.'

'I'll do what I bloody well like in my own house.'

'Little pitchers have large ears.'

'Eh?'

'The children.' Ruby rolled her eyes, first at Lexi then at Bee.

The girls seemed totally unconcerned about Brenda's abuse of the sanguinary adjective. Perhaps they had grown so used to her scolding tone that they accepted it as part of what mummies are made of. In any case, the twins weren't terribly enthralled by the argument for each had been given a small, cherry-coloured lollipop, the sucking of which demanded full attention. They sat, feet stuck out, nuzzling against Grandma and humming contentedly.

'It's the children I'm, you know, talkin' about,' Brenda went on.

Teacup in one hand, ciggie in the other, she waved them as furiously as if she was conducting the overture from *William Tell*. She felt flushed and would now and then pause to cough and to administer a big round-eyed stare as if to inform Ruby that this was definitely the beginning of the end and that, like Camille, she would be dead and gone before the end of the picture.

Brenda, Jack and the twins had all been examined by Dr Lawrence and appointments set up for X-ray photographs to be taken at the Partick South clinic. It mattered not to Brenda that a host of Jim's colleagues and pupils had had to undergo similar humiliation, that all the Burnsides had been checked out too. Unlike Brenda, they found the procedure merely tiresome and, with the exception of Bertie, were not at all concerned about the results.

'Jim didn't *try* to get TB, you know,' Ruby said.

'Bloody one-man hypodermic.'

'Epidemic,' said Ruby. 'Everyone's going to be fine.'

'How d'you know?'

'Alison told me all about it.'

'Alison!'

'All right, all right. Don't start on Alison again. It's not her fault either. I mean, she's in love with the poor chap.'

'Is she?'

'Of course she is,' said Ruby, with more conviction than she felt.

'Just because she goes to see him every bloody day doesn't mean to say she's, you know, in love with him.'

'He's a very sick man, Brenda.'

'Aye, so? If *he's* had his chips, where does that leave *us*?' She swung the cigarette in the direction of the twins. 'Where does that leave *them*?'

On cue, Lexi uttered a spluttering wee cough which Bee, ever the mimic, imitated exactly.

'*See?*' Brenda shouted.

'Oh, for God's sake!' Ruby tutted under her breath, spat on to her handkerchief and wiped each small, sticky mouth briskly before either twin knew what had hit them. The cure was instant. 'If you're going to hit the roof every time one of them goes *eck-eck*, Brenda, you'll be spendin' a lot of time gazin' down on the rest of us.'

'TB can kill you.'

'I know what TB can do,' Ruby said.

'Vera's cousin's boyfriend went like *that*.' A snap of Brenda's fingers snuffed out the life of the consumptive stranger. 'From bein' a big strappin' lad he went down to seven stones in six months. Then he died. Never had, you know, an earthly.'

Bee offered Grandma a lick of her lollipop. Grandma dutifully stroked her tongue over the cherry-red candy, murmuring, 'Yum-yum.'

Lexi offered her lollipop in turn but Brenda snatched at her daughter's arm, crying, 'Dirty, dirty! Dirty girl! That's how TB gets spread.'

Taken aback, Lexi began to cry. Bee naturally followed suit.

'Brenda!' Ruby hoisted both wailing children into her arms. 'Will you kindly stop all this TB nonsense at once.'

'TB isn't nonsense. TB can—'

'I *know*. I *know*. Kill. But it isn't going to kill any of us.'

'No? What about Jim Abbott then?'

Ruby had the decency to hesitate. Involuntarily her arms tightened about her granddaughters' waists and she drew the children closer as if, for a moment, she too had felt the presence of the insidious disease which lurked in the very air they breathed.

'Well, what about him?' Brenda demanded.

'That's another story,' Ruby said.

Mimosa was the colour he'd chosen. Two yards of broad silk ribbon bound to a card in a cellophane packet. The sort of thing he could keep hidden in his pocket and, when the time was ripe, slip out and give to her.

It was little enough, God knows, but it meant a lot to him. Seeing it in the window of Mrs Deasy's shop three days after Christmas he had felt as if his heart would break. Had gone in, him, Declan Slater, had put his sixpence on the counter and come out with the packet of ribbon tied up in brown paper.

Roberta never wore ribbon. He knew that fine. This, though, was the stuff the girls had coveted when he'd been young. He'd promised himself then it would be ribbon, silk ribbon, he'd buy for the girl of his dreams.

He'd bought it with a piece of the money Da had given him,

counted out from the wad of well-thumbed banknotes which stuffed the pocket of Da's tweed trousers. The deed was done back of the big house, in the empty stable yard, with a view of hills picked bare by wintry weather. It was the only time he'd been alone with Da in the forty hours the old boy had allocated for seasonal celebration and for visiting his wife.

Declan had spent his time with his mother and aunts. The women were more tolerant of him now he was grown and would soon become a doctor. It was peaceful at Kerridge after Da had gone, so peaceful that even Seamus Flynn had failed to lure Declan away to visit the ladies in Dublin and drown his sorrows in drink. He was happy enough to be resting in Kerridge, to nurse for a little while his yearning for Glasgow, for Roberta.

Dermatology, ophthalmology, clinical medicine, venereal disease were the alluring subjects in the spring curriculum.

Declan came back early from Ireland, carrying the ribbon and the gifts of money that his aunts and uncles had seen fit to make to him. He had enough cash to see him through until July, felt refreshed in body, mind and spirit and ready to take up the challenge again.

The letter lay on the damp mat behind the door of the basement flat in Walbrook Street. Declan lifted it with a leap of the heart. He had the lamp on and the envelope open in a trice. He saw Roberta's even, academic handwriting all of apiece on the page and smelled, he thought, her musky scent. Trembling a little, he read what she'd written and marked the time and place of the rendezvous with joy and dread, as if it was the Second Coming she'd asked him to and forgiveness not judgement was implied.

Bathed, shaved and tidily dressed, Declan turned up at Arroll's Dairy Tearooms in Partick East at half past three o'clock on January 6th.

He had never been in Arroll's before but it was as discreet a hideaway as you could imagine. No self-respecting student would be found dead in a place that catered exclusively to working-class women who fancied themselves ladies and to that breed of elderly gent which could make the consumption of a currant bun seem like a mayoral banquet.

Miniature sausage rolls, hard as quartz, were served on paper napkins and fish-paste sandwiches, *sans* crusts, were arranged in dainty triangles on cracked china plates. The air of faded gentility was something old women could grasp and, lacking imagination as well as knowledge, transform into a brush with the upper classes, an aspiration which cost only a few pence more than pie and beans in Dougie's Caff or a plate of mutton broth at home. Consequently the Arroll Tearooms had a regular clientele, quiet and modest and, for the most part, quite solitary, as if they feared that in company they would be found out and mocked for their harmless pretensions.

It was a grey, gritty sort of afternoon. Leaves rustled across the steps of the art gallery. The River Kelvin was corrugated by a steely little wind that also thrummed in the tenement closes and generated an eerie moaning sound in the Arroll's half-tiled window bays. When Declan arrived, Roberta was already seated at a square table under the tall windows.

She may have watched him cross the angle at the tail of Argyll Street, for he had been walking, walking and thinking, for an hour before the meeting. Sober, fed and flushed with oxygen he looked more wholesome now than he had ever done in the forty-odd months of their acquaintance. If Bobs had seen him arrrive, however, she gave no sign of it and remained motionless and contemplative as Declan emerged from the head of the stairs and, pausing, looked across the echoing spaces of the tearoom.

Three elderly women, small and timid as mice, covered their purses and guarded their plates as if this stranger, this youthful stranger, had come to raid and pillage or, worse, create a scene. The only gent in the place cranked his wrinkled neck to watch Declan stride across the room. In the old man's eyes was a trace of unresentful sadness as if the meeting of boy and girl brought back memories of some incident in the past, something wished-for and unfulfilled.

Declan ordered teas from the counter. He carried the cups to the table and put them down, saying, 'It's grand to be seein' you again, Roberta.'

Roberta looked up.

He was different, changed. Her mind recorded the fact sluggishly. Same pixie face, same brown eyes. But there was in Declan now a guarded quality that, had she been herself, would have troubled her more than it did. It was almost as if he was afraid of her. As if he knew what she was about to say.

Declan seated himself across the table from her.

She stared at the dark brown tea, thick in the cup.

'Why are we meetin' here?' Declan said. 'Why didn't you come to the flat? Never mind. I brought you a present from owd Oireland.'

She didn't raise her head. 'What?'

He placed the packet before her as if it was a diamond ring.

'Ribbon?' she said, surprised.

'Sure that's what it is.'

'I don't wear ribbon.' She touched a hand to her hair. 'I mean to say, nobody wears ribbon these days.'

'No,' Declan said. 'Still . . .'

'What do you expect me to do with it?'

'Keep it. Put it away in your bottom drawer.'

'My bottom drawer?'

'To remind you of me in days to come.'

'I don't need ribbon for that,' Roberta heard herself say.

There was something so idiotic in his choice of gift that for a second or two her sense of superiority was restored. She lifted the cellophane packet as if it was a biological specimen, held it up to the light and studied it critically.

'Declan,' she said, 'I believe I'm pregnant.'

The old man was still watching. He had a scrawny neck and a shirt with a frayed collar. He had sliced the currant bun on his plate into six portions which he ate with a fork, as if they were pieces of cake.

'Did you hear me, Declan? I think I'm pregnant.'

'Is it not just your imagination?' Declan said.

'Don't be damned ridiculous. I've been sick every morning.'

'Have you missed a period?'

'Are you questioning my judgement?'

'I am, of course I am.'

'I'm three weeks late.'

'Have you always been regular in the past?'

'Like the clock,' said Roberta. 'Now what? Are you going to produce a rabbit or four or five mice and ask me for a urine sample?'

'I just want to be certain, Roberta, like you do yourself.'

'I am certain. Well, ninety-nine per cent.'

'It's not an illness then, anaemia?'

'*No.*'

Declan slid the packet of ribbon from the table and put it in his pocket. He stirred his tea with a spoon, put the spoon into the saucer with a little click.

'Is it my child, or Conroy's?'

'I thought you might try that one,' Roberta said.

'It's a fair question.'

'It *can't* be Guy's child, Declan. It can *only* be yours.'

'That's good.'

'No point in trying to wriggle out of responsibility.'

'One of us has to finish, and it can't be you.'

'What do you mean?'

'Graduate.'

'Why can't it be me?'

191

'Because you'll be at home havin' our baby.'

'Is that your solution?' Roberta said. 'Shuffle me off into a back room somewhere, my career wrecked, while you go cheerfully on your way?'

'I'll be lookin' after us, all three of us.'

'*What?*'

'I'm talkin' about marriage, Roberta.'

'*What?*' she cried again.

'If things are as you say,' Declan told her, 'there's no alternative.'

She darted a glance at the nosey old man then reached forward and gripped Declan by the lapel of his overcoat and pulled him forward.

'Oh, yes, there is,' Roberta said.

'What do you mean?'

'Be rid of it,' Roberta said.

'Oh, Christ! I couldn't even think of doin' that.'

'Not you, you fool,' Roberta said.

'Who then?'

'There must be somebody you can trust.' Bobs sat back. 'Somebody in Ireland, perhaps?'

'I don't want this – I want . . .'

'It's not what you want, Declan. It's what I want that counts. I've worked damned hard for a medical degree and I won't see my career jeopardised just for the sake of your finer feelings, for some unborn *thing* that neither of us wants.'

'Roberta . . .'

'Do you know someone or do you not?'

'Yes,' Declan Slater said. 'I think, in fact, I do.'

'What's his name?'

'Flynn,' Declan answered in a monotone. 'His name is Seamus Flynn.'

Nothing in the appearance of Jim's council house in Macarthur Drive indicated that it had been reoccupied. Consequently when Alison unlocked the front door and a voice shrilled from the unlighted living-room, 'Who's that? Is that a burglar?' Alison almost jumped out of her skin.

Stock still in the little hall, she called out, 'It's me. Alison Burnside.'

Unappeased, the voice from the living-room cried, 'Winnie, Winnie, somebody's trying to break in.'

A shadowy figure appeared at the top of the stairs.

Jim's sister, Winnie, shouted, 'It's all right, Mother. It's only the girl.' She descended, lumbering, towards the hall. She carried clothing in her arms, Jim's clothing. She wore a tweed overcoat and a masculine style of hat with a feather in the band.

'What,' she demanded, 'are you doing here?'

It had been almost a year since Alison had last visited Jim's family in Pitlochry. Winnie had grown stouter. There had never been much love lost between the widow and Alison but they had made the best of it for Jim's sake. It was clear that circumstances had changed, that amnesty was a thing of the past.

'I might ask the same question,' Alison replied.

'Who is it, Winnie? Who's come to call?'

'The girl, Mother, just Jim's girl. You mustn't let her frighten you.' Winnie Craddock paused on the bottom step. 'We've travelled down to see Jim, if you must know.'

'Oh! If you'd given me notice I'd have aired the house and had a meal ready for you,' Alison said.

'I think I can still find the kitchen. This used to be my home too, in case you've forgotten.'

'No, I haven't forgotten,' said Alison. 'Why haven't you put on the lights?'

'I haven't had time.'

'The mains box is under the stairs,' Alison said. 'My brother, Henry, switched off the power. He said it was the thing to do since Jim's not going to be here for a while. I'll switch it on again, if you like.'

The woman nodded curtly. 'You haven't drained the cistern, have you?'

'My brother says that will only be necessary if the weather turns cold.'

'You and your family seem to have things very nicely arranged between you,' Winnie said. 'Well, you won't have to bother much longer. We've decided to give up the house.'

'Why?'

'To save on the rent.'

Alison bit her lip. 'Does Jim approve of your decision?'

'I've spoken to a doctor on the telephone.'

They were still in the hallway, the open door at Alison's back.

Alison said, 'Dr Leyman?'

'I believe that's his name, yes.'

'What did he tell you?'

'That it will be a long time before Jim's fit to look after himself.'

'Really?'

Alison had journeyed to Ottershaw every day before spring term began and had become well acquainted with Dr Phillip Leyman and his methods. She had helped McNair prepare slides in the laboratory, had been shown Jim's X-ray plates and had had the meaning of the cloudy patches explained to her. Visits to Jim's bedside had been limited, however. He continued to suffer reaction to Leyman's initial treatment which consisted of intravenous injections of a solution of thiosulphate of gold and calcium gluconate. Leyman did not set much store by drugs as a rule. He resorted to gold therapy only to reduce the quantity of bacilli in the sputum and check the spread of the disease. In spite of his informal manner everything Phillip Leyman did was to benefit the patient.

Alison doubted if Dr Leyman had told Winnie much about Jim's condition and was certain that he hadn't committed himself to a long-term prognosis.

'When Jim's well enough to leave hospital,' Winnie went on, 'he'll come and stay with us in Pitlochry.'

'What about his teaching job?'

'We'll find something for him to do nearer home.'

'But this is Jim's home.'

Alison's objection was interrupted by a plaintive cry from the living-room. 'Winnie, Winnie, I need the toilet. I can't find the toilet.'

Alison said, 'I'll put on the lights.'

Kneeling, she found the big switch in the cupboard beneath the stairs, threw it and lit up the gloomy house.

While Winnie escorted her mother upstairs to the lavatory, Alison looked round in dismay. Two small suitcases stood by the hearth. Empty grate, bare table, clean ashtrays, an absence of newspapers. It was as if the place had already been turned into a mausoleum. She wondered how Winnie and Mrs Abbott would survive in Macarthur Drive without the comforts of their cottage home, how long they would stay in Flannery Park.

She could hear the poor old woman crying and nagging upstairs and feared that there was more to Mrs Abbott's disorientation than Winnie would admit, that senility had already taken a grip on the old woman's brain.

She loitered aimlessly in the living-room until the women returned.

Old Mrs Abbott was dressed entirely in black. Her hat and overcoat collar were trimmed with black fur and her skirt, in the old style, came down to midshin. Below it were a pair of the same sort of button boots that Alison's grandmother had once favoured.

The woman walked stumpily, one hand groping, the other gripped tight to Winnie's sleeve. Her eyes roved frantically about the living-room and she muttered to herself, 'Where's Jim? It's time Jim was here. I want that boy in here for his tea,' followed by a rigmarole of injunctions too mumbled to be comprehensible.

Winnie pushed her mother down into an armchair.

Alison said, 'She shouldn't be here, you know. I mean, she shouldn't be forced out of her environment. It's distressing to a woman in her condition.'

'Condition? What do you mean – condition? There's nothing wrong with my mother. She just tired, that's all. She's not used to travelling. She'll be perfectly all right after supper and a good night's sleep.'

'It's a long journey out to Ottershaw.'

'Are you trying to keep us from seeing Jim?'

'Of course not,' Alison said. 'I'm just concerned about your—'

'You've always been selfish,' Winnie interrupted. 'It wouldn't surprise me if your carry-on hadn't started this dreadful thing.'

Alison said, 'Tuberculosis is caused by a bacillus. There are a hundred and one reasons why the disease becomes active. Falling in love isn't one of them.'

'Love! Phah!'

Alison said. 'You just want to get him away from me, don't you?'

'Well, you can't marry him, that's certain.'

'Why can't I marry him?'

'Because marriage might kill him.'

'If you mean sexual intercourse,' Alison said, 'as far as I'm aware there's no medical evidence to suggest that sexual intercourse is detrimental to TB sufferers.'

'What if you have a child?'

'What if I do?'

'It's a taint, a terrible taint . . .'

'For God's sake!' Alison exclaimed, almost losing her temper. 'Even if there is a hereditary disposition – which is, in fact, very unlikely – that doesn't mean to say Jim can't father healthy children. How many Abbotts have died of consumption in the past fifty years?'

'None,' Winnie snapped defiantly. 'So it must be something you've done.'

'Or something carried over from the war.'

'That's right, blame the war.'

'I'm not blaming anyone or anything,' said Alison. 'I'm not concerned with why Jim has the disease, I'm only concerned with helping him get well again as speedily as possible.'

'Be that as it may, you *can't* marry him.'

'Can I not? Who says I can't?'

'Jim.'

195

'Jim?'

'Ah, see! You don't know my brother at all, do you? You know nothing at all about him, really.'

'What are you talking about?'

'Talking, talking, talking about,' Mrs Abbott parroted, a gleeful note in her voice. 'Talking, talking, talking, talking, talk, talk, talk . . .'

'Mother, be quiet!' Winnie snapped. To Alison, she said, 'Jim won't marry you now, Alison Burnside, because he won't saddle you with a cripple.'

'That's just ridiculous.'

'None so blind,' Winnie interrupted. 'None so blind as those who will not see. Leave Jim to us, Alison. Make your own way from now on.'

'Jim won't let me.'

'There you're wrong,' the woman said, 'very wrong. Jim will.'

With a sudden icy shiver Alison realised that when all was said and done Mrs Winnie Craddock might very well be right.

The last time the team gathered for lunch in Miss Osmond's was close to the commencement of spring term.

Alison had already told Howard about Jim's illness. She had made it clear that the flicker of a romance between them must be allowed to cool.

Howard was too sensible to ask, 'Is it over between us?'

He knew that Alison would deny that there had ever been anything serious between them. He noticed, though, that she wore the brooch he'd given her which he took as a sign that she wished to remain friends. He enquired after Jim Abbott's health whenever he and Alison met but at the back of his mind, buried in a sediment of selfishness, was the question as to what might happen to Alison if Jim Abbott eventually died.

It was strange how little the team had to say to each other, how awkward conversation had become.

Guy and Roberta sat side by side at the oval table, glum as an old married couple while Declan, looking remarkably healthy, scoffed mutton chops and steamed chocolate pudding and rattled on about the prospective joys of Clerking and Dressing.

They left Miss Osmond's at twenty minutes to two o'clock and loitered on the corner of University Avenue, oddly reluctant to disperse.

'Hello, Guy. How are you?'

'Hello, Grace. I'm fine. Yourself.'

'Fine. Howard?'

'Grace.'

The medics paused, silent and defensive, as the classics scholar, the sweet, simpering smile, sauntered past in the company of two female friends. Grace Robertson, Alison thought, might have the face of a kitten but she probably had the heart of a cat.

As soon as Grace had passed, Howard flashed his eyebrows suggestively.

Alison laughed.

Howard said, 'How frequently do you visit Jim?'

'As often as I can. Dr Leyman's been very kind. He's given me *carte blanche* about visiting hours. I can go after classes if I want. There's a five-fifty bus out and a train back from Ottershaw Halt at a quarter past nine.'

'No other visitors?' Guy asked.

'His mother and sister were admitted at the weekend but they've gone back to Perthshire. I doubt if they'll be back here for a while.'

'Look, if there's anything I can do,' Howard said, 'just say the word. You know you can depend on me.'

'I know I can, Howard,' Alison said. 'And thanks.'

'Come along, Roberta,' Guy said, taking Bobs by the arm. 'And do try to perk up. Declan?'

'No. I'll go this way. Eye Infirmary.'

'Very well,' said Guy. 'See you later – somewhere, I suppose.'

The couple went off up University Avenue.

A moment later Howard and Alison followed while Declan, hands in pockets, lingered on the corner as if he had somehow been left behind.

Given the circumstances, Alison was reluctant to admit that the wintry evenings and weekend afternoons spent at Ottershaw were happy ones for her.

She found Ottershaw Hospital soothing after the bustle of classrooms and big city wards. She also had the feeling that, thanks to Dr Leyman, she was at last learning how medical practice really worked.

Dr Leyman was literally 'at home' in Ottershaw. He lived alone in a small cottage on the edge of the estate, ate his meals in the staff dining-room and often joined ambulatory patients for tea in the conservatory. He deliberately represented activity and purposefulness and strove to transfer a sense of life-worth-living by sheer force of personality.

Alison was not immune to Phillip Leyman's energetic charm but McNair tactfully warned her that every nurse in the place fancied the boss and that female patients were prone to falling head-over-tail in love with him, the more so as he was unmarried.

Only on Saturday afternoon and evening was the doctor absent. No secret assignations for Phillip Leyman, though. Rossendale Street Synagogue was his first port of call, followed by a visit to relatives in Glasgow. Alison liked to imagine that what Phil Leyman prayed for was to see Ottershaw's pavilions empty and abandoned, everyone gone home cured.

It seemed natural to have Jim at the centre of this interesting environment. It was almost as if Jim had wished the sickness upon himself to bring her here. A half-hour by Jim's bedside, saying little, brought her happiness, now that she was relieved of guilt over her sexual experiments with Declan Slater and her romantic fling with Howard. She had no time left to make a fool of herself and the hours of travelling back and forth to Ottershaw only seemed to increase her devotion.

In the evenings Jim's bed was wheeled from the isolation ward into a long glass-roofed corridor where Alison was allowed to visit. Through the open windows the odour of damp earth filtered in clean and cold and it would always seem to be later than midevening, some hour deep into the night when everything was still and sleeping.

Alison would sit by the bed, talking quietly, sometimes saying nothing at all. Worry and excitement were to be avoided at all costs. Healing demanded rest, rest so complete that Alison could not imagine it this side of death. Dr Leyman had told her that when Jim had begun to recover from the initial inflammatory reaction and the possibility of spread into the pleural cavity had been averted, she would be able to spend more time with him, to walk in the gardens and even, come summer, to take him out for tea.

Alison did not dare think that far ahead. She would soon be committed to fifth-year internships and would not be able to call her soul her own. How she would juggle her time then was a matter she did not dare contemplate.

'Has Boris been – asking for me?'

'Yes, of course he has. He sends his best wishes.'

'I'd – like to – see him. Get all the school – news.'

'When you're stronger. Next month, perhaps.'

'What about – Mr Pallant? Have you heard from – him?'

'It's all in hand, Jim. You don't have to worry.'

'I do, though. I don't have – much else to – occupy me.'

'You certainly have no need to worry about money. Your insurance benefits will keep you going until you get back to work.'

He lay on his back, a bolster behind his shoulders so that his upper body was comfortably raised. He kept his head on the pillow, and would lift it sharply only when some fretful thought occurred.

'Winnie says I ought to – give up the house.'

'Do you want to?'

'No.'

'Then pay no heed to Winnie.'

'What if she – if she tells the council?'

'Henry's already written to the council. As long as your rent's paid the council don't care where you are.'

'How long will I – be here?'

'As long as it takes to get you on your feet again.'

He would sigh, let his head fall back, so composed, so thin and stoical that he seemed quite willing to let the real world slip away for ever.

'Mother's – sick.'

'Yes, I know. There's nothing you can do about it, though.'

'I should – be there to – help.'

'What could you do that Winnie can't?'

'Jean or Connie could take her – if things get too – bad.'

'Let them settle it, Jim. Right now you have to think only of yourself.'

'I wish I could fathom out – why it – happened to me.'

'I know, I know. *Ssshhh,* now. *Ssshhh.*'

She would stay with him for a quarter of an hour, twenty minutes at most, then one of the nurses would appear at the corridor's end and Alison would kiss Jim on the brow, wish him a good night's sleep and slip quietly away. She was inevitably surprised to discover signs of life in other wards.

Patients primary and post-primary, with haemorrhage and without it, with TB in the bronchial tree and in the bloodstream, with caseous material in the lobes or fibrosis in the lung tissue. Ambulatory patients in beds, on chairs, at tables playing cards. Patients dressed in cardigans, skirts, flannels, some pathetically young, others despairingly old. Then Ally too would wonder why the tubercle bacillus had chosen to infect Jim Abbott, whether there was meaning to it or if such things happened randomly, mere quirks of fate or as unjust punishment for sins that were no sin at all.

Alison walked down the hospital drive and, by the light of a pocket torch, followed the hedgerows to Ottershaw railway halt.

Darkened countryside did not intimidate her and she enjoyed the ride home in the little rattling carriage with nobody for company but strays from Wellmeadow or a farm lass or dour labourer hopping between villages.

It was Thursday, well into January, with rain smirring across the moor and the station's oil-lamps bleary. Dressed in a raincoat, her scarf tied over her head, Alison climbed the steps from lane to platform.

Oil-lamps flickered. The bare, black boughs of oak and elder clashed in the wind. Only the porter, sheltering in his box, and a solitary passenger huddled against the wall were to be seen.

Alison peered up the line towards Balfron.

The engine's lights glimmered in the far distance like will-o'-the-wisps.

'Alison?'

She started and spun round. 'Who's that?'

'Me. Declan.'

'For heaven's sake! What are *you* doing here?'

He left his position by the wall and came forward to join her. He looked uncommonly smart, almost 'county', in a loden topcoat and little porkie-pie hat.

Alison was taken aback by Declan's sudden materialisation and, to cover her confusion, laughed.

'Found yourself a dairymaid, Decker?' she said. 'Isn't it a bit inconvenient having to travel all this way just for a kiss and a cuddle?'

He nodded, as if her sarcasm was both expected and deserved.

'Where *have* you been?' Alison, relenting, asked.

'Wellmeadow Hospital.'

'Oh, I'm sorry. Are you sick too?'

'I came to see Roberta's old man.'

'At this hour of the night?' Alison said.

'Bobs tells me he sometimes works on late. I missed him by half an hour.'

They stood with their backs to the rain that swirled down the line. The porter had come out of his box and was fiddling with a flag, a whistle and a lantern by the platform's edge.

'Didn't it occur to you that you might meet me here?' Alison said.

'Yes, I thought I might.'

'I hope you're not going to start any nonsense, Declan? It's all over between us.'

'Sure an' I know that.'

The din of the approaching engine killed conversation and it was not until they were seated in one of the compartments and the train had chugged away from the halt that Alison said, 'Did you really come all the way out here just on the offchance that you might meet old man Logie?'

'Aye, I did.'

'Why didn't you tackle him at home?'

'Bobs would be furious if she knew what I was up to.'

In the wan light of the compartment Declan no longer resembled a half-starved pixie but his face was still thin, his sleekness an illusion.

Alison said, 'You've fairly smartened yourself up. Did you come into money or have you just seen sense at long last?'

'If I'd come to my senses sooner,' Declan said, 'I might have gotten you.'

'Gotten me? What do you mean by "gotten me"?'

'Into my bed. Properly into my bed, I mean,' Declan said. 'Trouble was you were never in love with me.'

'Of course not. Well, not all the way in love with you,' Alison told him, then said, 'This is a very odd conversation, Declan. What's come over you?'

'I'm wanting to marry her.'

'Bobs?'

'Bobs it is.'

'So you're here to ask me to keep my mouth shut about our murky past?'

'I just want her to marry me.'

'Oh, my God!' Alison exclaimed. 'Did you trail out here just to ask old man Logie if you could have her hand in marriage?'

'I see now it was daft,' Declan admitted. 'It'll have to be a meeting at his house. They'll not be usherin' me into his presence at the hospital. I had a notion he might be more approachable if I could catch him off his guard, do you see?'

'I'm not sure I do,' said Alison.

'Can I trust you to keep something quiet?'

'Of course you can.'

'Roberta's seven weeks pregnant.'

Alison was silent for half a minute, then said, 'I see.'

'I'm the father.'

'That goes without saying.'

'I've *got* to get her to marry me,' Declan said, 'before she sacrifices the baby.'

'Pardon?'

'Has it taken off.'

'Aborted?'

Declan Slater flinched as if he found the very word offensive.

'I'll have to stop her,' he said desperately.

'Of course. Of course, you will.'

'I'm a Roman Catholic, you see.'

'I thought you didn't believe in anything, particularly mortal sin?'

'It's not just a mortal sin, it's a criminal act,' said Declan.

Alison said, 'You've stopped drinking, haven't you?'

He looked up, scowling. 'What's that got to do with it?'

'Does Roberta know how much you love her?'

'She still thinks I'm just after her money.'

'Aren't you?'

'I was before – but not now.'

Alison was more shocked by Declan's news than she let on. It might have been her, not Roberta, who had given in to Declan's seductive charm and the inexplicable need to explore those fierce experiences which their status as medical students had opened up to them. Pregnancy: the word made Alison's stomach cramp. Pregnancy, without money, without plans. The one thing that would definitely stop you graduating.

Declan said, 'She says she won't marry me. She says she'll see the baby off first and go on as if nothin' had happened.'

'I don't believe it,' said Alison. 'Even Roberta isn't that selfish.'

'Maybe she is, maybe she is at that,' said Declan. 'Oh, sure and I know how it is with the women, how they always like to think of themselves as put upon, but it isn't always the case, is it, Ally?' He glanced suspiciously at Alison as if accusing her of being in cahoots not just with Roberta Logie but with a universal network of self-seeking females who used sex as a weapon, weakness as an excuse. 'Her Da will understand. He'll be the one to help.'

'I wouldn't count on it, Decker.'

'He'll make her marry me. It's not how I'd have wanted it but there's another to consider now.'

'Another?'

'The baby,' Declan said. 'Mr Logie's a family man. He'll understand.'

'Declan,' Alison said, 'Veitch Logie's a freemason.'

'My grandfather Slater was a mason.'

'In an Orange Lodge?'

'Yes, I know what the score is,' Declan said. 'I'm clutchin' at straws, I suppose.'

'Why did you trail out to Ottershaw tonight, Declan? It wasn't to see Veitch Logie at all, was it?'

'No, I came lookin' for you.'

'I thought so,' Alison said, softly.

'I had to talk to someone. Had to tell someone my news.'

'Come and sit by me,' Alison said and, when Declan had shifted to the seat by her side, put an arm about his shoulder. 'Bobs won't go through with it, you know.'

'What? Marriage?'

'No, the other thing.'

Declan rubbed his nose with the back of his wrist.

'I wouldn't be too sure of that,' he said, 'I wouldn't be too sure at all.'

Number 162 was strangely quiet when Henry got home from work that evening. He'd had a busy, if boring, afternoon sifting through the latest parliamentary reports on trade sanctions for an article entitled 'Protectionism: Who Does it Protect?'.

He'd lunched with Margaret Chancellor and had found her views on the subject more informed and more forceful than his own. He'd spent the best part of an hour scribbling away at the table while Margaret sounded off on the evils of American capitalism and the power of the dollar in the world's market places.

It had been Henry's intention to retire upstairs soon after supper and, weary though he was, put in an extra hour at the old Underwood, typing up his notes of the Chancellor interview. When he entered the house, however, the unusual silence caused him a moment of panic and he hurried into the living-room still wearing his overcoat and hat.

'What's up? Is Jim worse?'

Trudi was seated by the fire. Dishes were piled upon the table and there was no sound from the kitchen to indicate that one of his brothers had been press-ganged into washing up.

'Jim?' said Trudi.

Henry put down his briefcase. 'It isn't Jim?'

'I do not know what you mean,' Trudi said.

'Where is everybody?'

'All gone out.'

Feeling just a little foolish, Henry removed his coat and hat. He gestured towards the table. 'So, what's this? Why haven't you – I mean, are you okay?'

'I have been thinking of things, that is all.'

'Not like you, Trude,' Henry said, trying to make light of it.

She stirred herself. 'If you are ready I will serve your supper now.'

'I reckon I might have more of an appetite if you told me what's on your mind first. Come on, Trudi, get it off your chest.'

She stood up, brushed invisible crumbs from her skirt then, rather to Henry's surprise, sat down again.

'I have had word from Germany, a letter by the post of the afternoon.'

'Ah!'

'Henry, I told to you a lie.'

'What sort of a lie?'

'About Goering. I do not know him,' Trudi said. 'I told you lies.'

'No, you didn't,' Henry said, calmly. 'You didn't make up all that stuff about Munich. You knew him. And the other one too – Udet.'

'I was one of many girls. They were famous aeroplane flyers . . .'

'Aces. Yes, I know,' said Henry. 'On the spree after the war. You were flattered. You had a fling with each of them. Champagne and silk sheets. Now the great man is embarrassed to be reminded of his wild youth and claims he doesn't remember you. Why don't you just come clean, Trudi?'

'You will be disappointed in me,' Trudi said.

Her pale blue eyes were fluttering and nervous. He had been around her long enough to sense that she was embarrassed, and perhaps a bit angry and humiliated. It was no more than she deserved for making up stories, Henry thought. He had to admit that he was disappointed at the fact that she had no high-level connections in the new Reich, that his chance of glory by proxy had just gone up in smoke.

He put on his famous stone face, however, and seated himself in the smoker. 'So what's the real story, Trudi? What does the letter say?'

'Goering was not fat then. He was a handsome man before he received in the upper leg the bullet. I did not know his wife, the Swedish woman. He took to morphine and it made him fat. He is not the fool he is made out to be.'

'Why are you telling me this, Trudi?'

'I do not wish you to think it was all lies.'

'Did you lie about Marcus Harrison too?'

'Marcus? What is it about Marcus?'

'How he knows about your Nazi connections.'

'It is not Goering or Ernst Udet that Marcus wishes you to meet.'

'Who is it then?'

'My father.'

'Is that who the letter's really from?' said Henry.

'Yes.'

'Is that who you wrote to in the first place?'

She nodded.

'Show it to me.'

Henry resisted the temptation to snap his fingers. Patience had always been his strong suit. He had engaged in all sorts of strange games with Trudi Keller Coventry over the years. She was deep and devious and filled with queer cold passions and, in that sense, was more feminine than any other woman he had ever met and more

204

interesting too. He accepted her assurance that she loved him but he could not figure out why, after four years of marriage, he still felt that she was dangerous.

'Show me the letter, Trudi, please.'

She reached behind her and brought from beneath the cushion a dun-coloured envelope from which she extracted a single sheet of pale brown paper. She opened it and held it so that her husband could see the heading and the typewritten text, all in German. Henry couldn't read a word.

'It is sent from the National Socialist Office of Acquisitions in Berlin,' Trudi explained, 'where my father is a senior official.'

'I thought he was a hotelier?'

'He was a man of business,' Trudi said. 'It was for business that he went to prison, not for hotel-keeping.'

'Black market?'

'The crime was concerned with money, with the flowing money.'

'Currency,' said Henry. 'Right. Go on.'

'He says he will make us welcome to visit at any time.'

'That's nice.'

'He will do what he is able to do to fill our visit with information.'

'Better and better,' said Henry.

'I think it is that he has some authority.'

'Who does he know? High-rankers, I mean?'

'He does not write about that.'

'So it won't be tea and scones with Adolf,' Henry said, 'or din-dins with General Goering?'

'I doubt it will not.'

'Not even cocktails with Herr Goebbels?'

'I do not think it is amusing,' said Trudi. 'I have done what is my best for you, Henry. If you do not wish for me to go you may take who you prefer as a travelling companion. Margaret Chancellor, perhaps?'

'Don't be daft,' Henry said. 'May I see the letter, please?'

'German you cannot read.'

'I just want to look at it, do you mind?'

'I do not wish you to take it away.'

'Why not?' said Henry.

Trudi shrugged.

'I assume,' Henry said, 'that you wouldn't let me take the letter into the office to show to Marcus Harrison?'

'No. It is a letter to myself.'

'Secrets again, Trude, more secrets?'

'You will find your answers,' Trudi answered, 'when we reach Berlin.'

'What sort of answers?'

'Answers which will not make you so happy, perhaps,' Trudi told him.

Henry stretched his arms and feigned a yawn. He nodded casually at the letter in her hand. 'Put it away, Trudi, put it away.'

'You have no more interest in what my Papa promises?'

'Not,' said Henry, evenly, 'until we reach Berlin.'

SEVEN

A Responsible Man

It was difficult for die-hard reprobates like Dipsy McDonald to realise that some folk matriculated to obtain an education and not just to poke fun at professors, enter the Labour Club's egg-eating contests or get boiled on beverages somewhat stronger than the waters of knowledge. Charities Day, like Santa Claus, was one of those things everyone continued to believe in, however, even when they were old enough to know better. Even sober representatives of the SRC were inclined to suspect that the main purpose of becoming a student was to roll out on a Saturday in January wearing nothing but a smile and a bearskin, and to strike terror into the hearts of Glasgow's good citizens by rattling a tin can in their faces and screaming blue murder for baksheesh.

For Howard McGrath Charities Day was even more of an annual high point than Daft Friday. He applied every reasonable argument to persuade Alison to be Robinson Crusoe to his Man Friday or, if she really wanted to create a sensation, to do it the other way about.

Howard, it seemed, was determined to appear in public clad only in a hairy sporran, a pair of gym pumps and a layer of Cherry Blossom boot-polish. He had even invented a bone – *femur rabbitus* – with a spring-clip in the middle which, in spite of what it did to his breathing, he insisted on attaching to his nose. He was now in the market for a sizeable chunk of prime rib to gnaw on while he jabbered the traditional war cry, '*Ygorra, Ygorra, Ygorra,*' and threatened pretty young secretaries with his big broom-handle spear.

In spite of Howard's pleading Alison refused to give up her Saturday visit to Ottershaw. She declared, rather loftily, that the charity fund would never miss her contribution and that she had better things to do than scamp about the streets begging for money, no matter how worthy the cause. This, Howard snarled, was carrying self-denial too far. What did she think she was – a candidate for sainthood?

Alison stood her ground.

Howard was not just disappointed, he was furious and exchanged hardly a civil word with her for the best part of a week.

Alison wasn't the only member of the team to duck her obligations, though. Howard could raise no enthusiasm in Roberta and Declan either and was left to arrange some second-rate romp with Guy to help top the magical ten thousand pounds which the organising committee had set as its target.

Collection capers were only part of it. The medical club's big dance was to be held in the Ca'doro Restaurant in Gordon Street and as far as budding doctors were concerned it was no contest as to which of the city's umpteen student hops would come top of the heap. The ball at the Ca'doro was the star attraction and, at great expense, Howard had obtained two tickets for the event.

'Very last chance, Alison,' he wheedled, holding up the pink cards.

'No, Howard. I'm sorry.'

'All right. All right, that's it.'

'I mean, go by yourself by all means.'

'Oh, thanks.'

'Or take – take someone else.'

'I intend to.'

'Who?' Sharply.

'Grace.'

'Saving Grace?'

'Yes, unless Guy gets there first.'

'Fine time you'll have with her, I'm sure.'

'Well, if you and Roberta won't play ball,' Howard said, 'it's every man for himself. Besides, from what I hear Grace is determined to explore the precise nature of sin before she gets around to studying repentance.'

'I'm sure you'll be only too willing to help her along.'

'Absolutely,' Howard said, waving the cards. 'No changee mindee?'

'I'm sorry. I can't.'

'On your head be it then.'

'What's that supposed to mean?'

'Absolutely not a thing.'

A forlorn group of students were dropped off at Bearsden railway station: three girls and a boy, all four in crinolines and poke bonnets, shaking their tinnies with a lack of fervour which brought no honour to their college. Even so, the sight of them increased Alison's regret at not being part of it.

Perhaps she was being priggish.

Henry and Trudi had given her a lecture on the subject.

'Jim can't expect you to visit him *every* day.'

'Jim doesn't expect anything. He's just glad to see me.'

'Look, I can go instead of you if somebody *has* to be there on Saturday.'

'Thank you, Henry, but I can manage.'

'You're going to miss all the fun.'

'Yes' – a sigh – 'I know.'

'What about the others? What about what'shername – Roberta?'

'Roberta is unwell.'

'What's wrong with her?'

'It's just one of those female things.'

'Oh!'

'What of the boy, the son of the general?'

'If you mean Howard, Trudi, he's found himself another girl.'

'It is perhaps for the best, no?'

'Oh, definitely.'

It was not for the best, not really. Nothing was for the best these days.

Alison tried not to dwell on Roberta's predicament. It contained too many salutary lessons to be entertaining. She had problems enough of her own without worrying about the spoiled blonde who had once been her friend. Anyway, girls as good-looking as Roberta Logie always fell on their feet.

On that grey January afternoon the big house of Ottershaw had regained something of its grandeur.

Dr Leyman had not yet left for his Saturday outing. In a chequered sports jacket and well-pressed blue flannels he was doing the rounds in his usual brisk, informal manner.

He took time off to eat a sandwich in the staff dining-room with Alison. He informed her that he was well pleased with Jim's progress and hinted that, within a week or two, Jim might be allowed out of bed and put on to a programme of walking exercise.

Finally he asked her, apparently offhandedly, why she wasn't doing her bit for the hospital charities and took in her answer with a little nod, as if it was exactly the reponse he'd expected.

It was half past two before Phillip Leyman left her at the French doors that led to the glass-walled conservatory where Jim spent most of the day.

Head propped on pillows, sheets and fleecy red blankets pulled up to his throat, Jim was wrapped in a kind of limbo which, had he been well, Alison might have interpreted as reverie.

'Alison?'

'Yes, dearest. How do you feel today?'

'What time is it?'

'About half past two.'

'Is it – Sunday?'

'Saturday. Saturday afternoon.'

'I thought I – heard a – football crowd.'

'I doubt it.' Alison checked the temperature chart and pulse-graph that hung at the foot of the bed. 'Probably just a railway train.'

He opened his eyes and studied her dully. He did not seem like her Jim at all. She leaned on the bed, kissed him on the brow.

'I don't think you should – do that, Alison.'

'Why? Does it get you all excited?'

A fortnight ago she would not have risked such a remark. She was gratified by his progress, however, and pleased when he took up the game.

'I hope you're not going to take advantage of my – weakened condition?'

She put her hand to the side of his neck. 'Are you cold?'

'No, I'm not – cold.'

'Pity. I could have climbed in beside you and kept you warm.'

'Dr Leyman wouldn't – approve.'

'Oh, I wouldn't be too sure,' Alison said.

He gave a little grunt of laughter which ended in a gagging cough. Alison plucked the sputum cup from the bedside locker and held it out. He shook his head and gave a final *whooo* of relief when the spasm ceased.

'Better – than – it was, don't you – think?' he said. 'Much better.'

At that moment, out of the corner of her eye, Alison saw something move, a reflection, dark as a shadow flitted over the window glass.

She swung round.

Levering himself up on his elbow, Jim said, 'What the – heck was – that?'

'I've no idea. Lie down, Jim, don't excite yourself.'

He remained raised and, for the first time in a month, alert.

'Am I hallucinating? I could've sworn – No, no, it couldn't be.'

'What?' said Alison in alarm.

'In the – rhododenrons, a naked – man, brandishing – a spear.'

Roberta hadn't set foot in the basement flat in Walbrook Street since November. The place had changed little. Declan's housekeeping had done nothing but show up the shabbiness of the room. Even his attempts at adding cheerful touches of colour – flowers in a vase, an *Irish Weekly* calendar tacked to the wall – seemed, in view of the situation, pathetically inadequate.

Roberta had not intended to come at all. At the last moment she had signed on with the district convenor as an official collector and, purely to escape her father's rigorous curiosity, had dolled herself up in an old peacock dress of her mother's, had stuck on a summer straw hat and a pair of gardening gloves and had sallied forth disguised as 'Spring'.

The fact that she was carrying a foetus, ultimate symbol of fecundity, inside her struck even the pragmatic Bobs as ironical. She gave a little grimace at her reflection in the hall mirror before she opened the door and with a cry of 'I'm off,' eased her way down the steep stone steps to the pavement and headed for Highburgh Road.

She knew that she would eventually wind up in Walbrook Street and that she would find Declan waiting. He'd told her that he had important matters to discuss and because of the baby – solely because of the baby – he had claim on her time now.

The quicker she was rid of them both, the better.

Lysol and carbolic soap had replaced the smells of unwashed bedclothes and rancid ham fat. Roberta was not sure that she did not prefer it as it had been before, for disinfectants reminded her of certain hospital departments which the public, most emphatically, never got to see.

Declan had spread a paper cloth upon the table and had set out tea-things. He closed the door behind her and kissed her tentatively.

'What are you supposed to be?' he asked.

'Spring.'

'Sure and that's just what you are,' he said, 'to me.'

'Turn it off, Declan, please,' Roberta said.

Washed, shaved, hair plastered down with pomade, Declan too looked as if he was sporting a disguise.

Roberta said, 'I take it you've heard from your friend?'

'I have.'

From the mantelpiece he took down a stoppered bottle.

Roberta stared in disbelief. 'What's that?'

'Your sample.'

'What? Do you mean to say Flynn actually sent it back?'

'Yes, of course he did.'

'Pee-pee? By post? From Ireland?'

Obviously it hadn't occurred to Declan Slater that the return of a urine sample in a soda-pop bottle was, to say the least of it, eccentric. The notion of her bodily fluids flitting back and forth across the Irish

Sea brought another grim little smile to Roberta's lips.

'*Is* this man a doctor?' she said.

'I told you, Seamus has a practice in Wicklow and another in Dublin.'

She took the bottle, shook it, and with a show of embarrassment which was ridiculous under the circumstances, hid it away in a pocket of her dress.

She scowled. 'Well?'

'Confirmed,' Declan said.

'Oh, no! Oh, my God! Oh, please, God, no.'

For the first time Roberta gave in to despair. Until then she had managed to suppress acceptance of the plain facts of the case, had denied undeniable physical evidence with a stubbornness which would have enraged her professors. Now, with Declan thrusting Flynn's report in her face, she could no longer evade the issue. She collapsed on to a kitchen chair and slumped over the table, head on her forearms, her face hidden by the brim of the broad straw hat.

When Declan put a hand on her shoulder she shook him off, shrieking, '*I don't want your sympathy, you damned Irish pig.*'

'Now, now, Bobs. Now, now.'

She batted away his hand, her eyes wet and blazing and blue as kerosene. 'Can Flynn get rid of it? You told me he could. You told me he knew what to do.'

'No, I did not.'

'You did, you did,' Roberta shouted. 'Fetch him here to do it.'

'He won't come to Scotland. Not for that.'

'Pay him, pay him anything. *I'll* pay him.' She grabbed Declan's unresisting arm and yanked it this way and that. 'Get him here somehow. If he refuses to come here then I'll go to Dublin. I'll make some excuse to get away.'

'You're not twelve weeks in yet,' Declan said.

'Sixty-seven days. It's safe to do it now.' She paused. 'Isn't it?'

It was the first interruption to the flow of accusation. She stared up at him, anxiously awaiting his answer.

'Induced termination's never safe,' Declan told her, 'even if it's done by a trained surgeon.'

'Ask your friend if he'll do it.'

'Roberta, I can't.'

'I thought you said you loved me.'

'Roberta, it's a criminal offence.'

'Damn you, Declan. If you won't help me, I'll do it myself.'

'You don't know how.'

'Yes, I do. I've read it up.'

He pressed his hands to his mouth and said, 'Holy Mother of God, Roberta, will you not just marry me instead?'

'And throw it all away? Throw it all away for what? For *you*?'

'Is that all that concerns you?'

'What else *should* concern me?'

'The child should concern you,' Declan said.

'I don't want it.'

'Is it the baby you don't want,' Declan said, 'or is it me?'

'Neither of you.' She rocked forth and back, her fists tucked into her lap as if to punish whatever it was that inhabited her for being there at all. 'I want to be the way I was before. I don't want to have to *think* about this thing any longer. I want my body back, Declan, that's what I want.'

'It's too late, Roberta. And I daren't implicate Seamus any further.'

'Then I will do it myself,' Roberta said.

Declan leaned against the table's edge. He made no attempt to touch her, to offer sympathy or comfort now. He had that sly, gliding look in his eye again and the whimper had gone out of his voice.

'Is that all you want, Roberta? To be rid of it?'

'Yes. Yes. How many times do I have to say it? God, Declan, how can you be so stupid? You know what they'll do to me if they find out I'm pregnant. Married or not, I'm out on my ear. No quarter, no stay of execution – *out.*'

'Is graduatin' so important to you then?'

'*Yes.*'

'Then I'll do it.'

'You'll do what?'

'Put it right,' Declan Slater said. 'Get rid of it.'

'Can you – *can* you do it?'

'I spoke to Seamus by telephone last night. He told me exactly what procedure to follow. It isn't very complicated or difficult, provided we take care to eliminate the risk of post-operative infection.'

He left her for a moment, opened a cupboard beneath the sink and returned with the dissecting case.

He opened the lid, displayed the contents.

Roberta, white-faced, said, 'Isn't there something I can take instead?'

'Oh, certainly,' Declan said. 'You could try aloes, or colocynth, or oil of nutmeg. Forty grains of quinine won't kill you. Probably won't work, of course, but you could try it, if you like. Or you could soak white lead in vinegar and drink it like the poor factory girls used to do. Usually they died.'

'Stop it.'

'I have everything I need right here except ovum forceps and a dilator, which I can probably "borrow" from the Royal.'

'So you're not going to do it right now, today?'

'Come on, Roberta, use your intelligence. Today?'

She crouched over her forearms, fists buried in the folds of the summer skirt, then shakily asked, 'When?'

'Whenever suits,' Declan answered. 'Wednesday afternoon, maybe?'

'All right,' Roberta told him. 'Wednesday afternoon it is.'

The naked man with the broom-handle spear was no hallucination. Just Howard. The coating of boot-polish had rubbed off in places so that his skin had the piebald appearance of some horrible tropical disease. Moist air had caused his hair dye to run and the cloth sporran which covered his modesty was decidedly bedraggled. Only the bone clipped to his nose added a touch of the primitive to a portrait more ludicrous than barbarous.

Padding through the French doors, he whispered nasally, 'Dim Abdot?'

'Howard, you idiot, how dare you . . .' Alison began.

'Hudsh, wedgesh,' Howard said. 'Cadn't stop. Shouldn't be hered ad ald.'

'Take that thing out of your nose.'

'Od, ald right,' Howard snapped off the tribal ornament. 'It worked, though. You'll have to admit it worked.'

'What the devil do you think you're playing at, Howard?' Alison hissed. 'Ottershaw's strictly off limits to students. There are sick people here.'

Jim struggled up on to his elbow, his languid, self-absorbed expression replaced by a grin. 'If it's money you're – after, you won't find – much loose change round – here.'

'Nod – I mean, not money. Captives.'

'Captives?' said Alison. 'Howard, you won't get away with it.'

'He might – get away with – you, though,' Jim said.

'What a clever little patient,' Howard said. 'You're absolutely spot on, Mr Abbott. We've come for the Burnside girl. You've had her long enough.'

'I'm not paying good money to – keep her,' Jim said. 'She's a – dashed nuisance – anyway. Quid to – take her away with you.'

'How much to take her away for the evening?'

'Two pounds,' said Jim, promptly. 'If you'll – accept my – IOU?'

'How did you get here, Howard?' Alison said. 'Surely, you didn't travel on the train in that outfit?'

'Nope.' Howard glanced over his shoulder. '*Mais voilà!* as Man Friday might put it. See yonder, wench.'

He pointed through the window and across the lawn. From between the rhododendron bushes a raddled, flat-bed lorry with a wooden tail-gate chugged into view. It had huge, rusting wheel-arches and its drooping exhaust pipe puffed out clouds of blue smoke. Hanging over the tail-gate, cheering and waving, were six or eight other savages a little more warmly clad than Man Friday but obviously from the same tribe.

'You laid this lot on just for me?' Alison asked.

'Don't be daft,' Howard told her. 'It's a raid. Against the letter of the law but strictly within the spirit of the occasion. We came for the boss. If he wants to be back here tomorrow then he's going to have to make a contribution to the cannibal fund.'

'Leyman,' said Jim Abbott, sitting upright now. 'Him, you *can* keep.'

Alison glanced from the vigorous young student to the whey-faced man in the bed. They were, she realised, in cahoots. She felt a sudden surge of elation. She wriggled across the bed, whispered, 'Jim, are you all right?' and when he answered with a nod and a wink, cried out, 'Save me, save me, kind sir.'

'Too late,' Howard told her.

Stooping, he lifted Alison into his arms, then, showing off his strength, slung her across his shoulder and headed for the open doors.

He paused, turned, said soberly, 'Thank you, Mr Abbott. Hope you're on the mend soon,' then carried his prize across the lawn to the waiting lorry and set her down behind the tail-gate.

As soon as Phillip Leyman appeared Alison realised that the raid was a put up job. The doctor was escorted by three or four young savages, including Guy and a reckless female whom Alison, to her astonishment, identified as Saving Grace. Dr Leyman was passive and uncomplaining and carried a leather travelling bag. He was hoisted on to the back of the lorry with sufficient respect to indicate that he had co-operated in setting up the whole ridiculous scheme.

By now the game was up and stealth no longer necessary. Nurses and patients had gathered on the walks and at pavilion windows, cheering and shouting unflattering remarks. Lights flickered on in the conservatories and the gloomy grounds of Ottershaw seemed flushed with gaiety. With a roar from its ancient engine and belch of smoke from its exhaust, the lorry completed a circle and, with its cargo swaying and bellowing, toured the grounds before it nosed down the driveway and headed for the city.

Phil Leyman shouted, 'Good evening, Miss Burnside.'

'Good evening, Dr Leyman.'

'Not in league with this hairy bunch, are you?'

'Not I. But I suspect you are. I'm just a hostage.'

'Thought you might be.' To Alison's surprise he put an arm about her. 'Well, I guess us captives will just have to stick together.'

Alison watched the turrets of old Ottershaw dip and vanish behind the prickling pines and when the lorry bucked flung an arm about Phil Leyman's shoulder to steady herself and to show him how she really felt about rapport.

'I guess we just will, Dr Leyman,' she said.

'In which case, perhaps you'd better call me Phil.'

In spite of the fact that Jim had asked him to look after the house, Henry felt more like a burglar than a caretaker. He would dart furtive glances over his shoulder before he stepped into the little hallway.

On that particular Sunday morning he had barely put foot over the doorstep before a woman he had never seen before rushed out of the living-room, shouting, 'How *dare* you, how *dare* you enter my house. Get out this instant.'

She was broad-shouldered and swollen-thighed, clad only in a nightgown, a floral-patterned housecoat and a pair of felt house slippers. Her mane of sandy-coloured hair was streaked with grey and pegged with ugly metal curling-pins. A final bizarre touch was added by the fact that she was wearing a pair of old gloves caked with coal-dust and was brandishing an iron poker.

Henry lifted an arm to defend himself. 'It's all right. I'm Henry Burnside.'

'Don't you have enough manners to knock?'

'I'm sorry. I didn't expect you to be here. You weren't here when I popped in yesterday afternoon. Jim asked me to keep an eye on the place.'

'Have you spoken to my brother recently?'

'Yes, last Wednesday evening. I spent a few minutes with him, at his request.' Henry sighed. 'I'm handling some of his business affairs.'

'Business affairs? What business affairs?'

Henry said, 'If you put the poker down, Mrs . . .' He realised with a start that he could not recall the woman's name. She gave him no help. 'Sorry if I've intruded. Perhaps you'd prefer me to leave?'

Calming down a little, Winnie lowered the poker and, holding her housecoat across her breast, stalked into the living-room. 'You'd better come in. I'm not prepared for guests, you understand, but I do

216

wish to have words with you and we may as well take the opportunity.'

Henry had a spanner in his pocket. He had heard on the wireless that a cold snap, which had already affected the Midlands, was sweeping north and knew enough about plumbing to wish to protect an empty house against the elements. He was more at home typing letters to council clerks on Jim's behalf and sorting out his brother-in-law-to-be's benefit claims. Sooner or later, though, Jim would have to employ the services of a solicitor.

Henry followed the woman into the living-room.

At that hour of a Sunday forenoon the room had an undecided atmosphere, part disreputable, part genteel.

The woman was probably upset at being caught at menial tasks. Winnie Whatever-Her-Name-Was probably felt that life, or the Great War, had cheated her of servants and other appurtenances which divided the bourgeoisie from artisans and labourers. Henry had met her type before.

'I'm not going to offer you tea, but you may sit down if you wish.'

'Most kind,' said Henry.

She had tied the housecoat tightly and arranged its floral lapels to hide the top of her nightgown. She stripped off the coal-blackened gloves and dropped them into the ash-pail which stood by the side of the hearth. The room was cold, colder than 162 was ever allowed to become. The woman's breath hung in a white cloud before her. Henry tucked the skirts of his overcoat about his legs and seated himself at the oval table in the centre of the room.

'Why is *she* permitted to visit Jim, and I'm not?'

'You'll have to ask the doctors that,' Henry said. 'If it's any consolation I had to request permission to make the visit.'

'Did Jim ask for you?'

'Yes.'

'He hasn't asked for me,' the woman said, huffily.

'Somebody has to take care of Jim's affairs. Make sure the house is secure, that sort of thing,' said Henry.

'I can look after his affairs just as well as you can.'

'Bit difficult when you live in Perthshire.'

'That's why I've moved back here. To be near to Jim. I intend to remain in Glasgow until my brother's fit to travel then I'll take him back home to Pitlochry with me, to recuperate.'

'Hang on a minute,' Henry said. 'Aren't you forgetting something?'

'No, I don't believe I am.'

'My sister?'

'Oh, that's off. Jim will *not* be marrying your sister.'

217

'Did he tell you so in as many words?'

'He won't pass on his disease. He's too responsible.'

'Pass on? Oh, you mean children?'

'Jim won't be able to father children.'

'Won't he?' Henry said. 'That nugget of medical misinformation seems to have escaped my attention.'

'Everyone knows that TB renders a man incapable.'

'Incapable of what?'

'Of – of – fulfilling his marital obligations.'

'You mean it makes him impotent?'

She pursed her lips at the indelicacy, nodded. 'Yes.'

'Rubbish!' Henry said. 'Pure wishful thinking on your part.'

'Well, he certainly can't stay here on his own,' Winnie Craddock said. 'And I don't expect your sister will be willing to nurse a convalescent, not when she has so many other things to do.'

'My God!' said Henry. 'You want to make poor old Jim your prisoner.'

'Nothing of the kind.'

'In a year, two at most, Jim'll be as right as rain,' Henry said. 'He'll be more than up to marriage and to fathering children, probably eager to do so.'

'I think you underestimate Jim's sense of responsibility.'

'And I think you underestimate my intelligence,' said Henry. 'You don't want your brother to marry our Alison, do you?'

'No.'

'Why not?'

'Infatuations never last.'

'Then this one must be setting a record for endurance,' Henry said. 'I'd have thought you'd have been pleased to see Jim happy.'

'I don't think he will be happy – not with her. Jim's done all he can for her. She'll take what she wants, then leave him.'

'You don't know Alison very well if you think that of her,' Henry said.

None the less, even as he defended his flighty sister, he felt a little twinge of apprehension. He couldn't quite put out of his mind Ally's moodiness, her mysterious relationship with the Irishman, her friendship with the soldier's son. Were such episodes an unavoidable part of being a college student, a phase that would pass as soon as Alison graduated or were they, as the woman suggested, signs of an intrinsically selfish nature?

Henry said, 'I think you just want Jim for yourself.'

'I want what's best for him.'

'You want someone to look after *you*, Mrs Craddock, that's my guess,' said Henry. 'That's why you're back in Flannery Park. You see poor old Jim's illness as an opportunity to get him back.'

'I think you should leave now,' the woman said stiffly. 'You've taken up enough of my time and I have things to do to make the house habitable again.'

'All right,' said Henry, rising. 'Tell me, though, who's going to pay the rent on this place and who's going to tell Jim about the changed arrangements?'

Henry watched her eyes cloud with uncertainty. In spite of his antipathy towards women like her, he felt for her plight. He couldn't blame her for struggling against a bleak and lonely future.

Thank God, he had Trudi to take the sting out of growing old.

'Might I suggest,' he said politely, 'that the arrangements I've made for the payment of rental are left as they are? A letter from you to the Housing Department informing them of your temporary residence will be all that's required. As to the other matter – well, why don't we leave that until poor old Jim's back on his pins?'

She glowered at him suspiciously. Manipulative people, Henry knew, were always on their guard against anything that seemed above board.

'I refuse to be pushed to one side,' Winnie Craddock said.

'Nobody's pushing you anywhere,' said Henry. 'I just don't think Jim's in any fit state to have a family quarrel going on around him. Do you?'

'No. I agree.'

'And,' said Henry, tapping on his hat, 'if you need anything done about the house, please don't hesitate to call me.'

'I can manage quite well on my own,' Winnie Craddock said and, without so much as a word of thanks, showed Henry the door.

Jim said, 'You look almost – as – bad as I feel, Ally. Wild – night?'

'Absolutely wild.'

'But you did enjoy yourself?'

'Yes. I'm sorry.'

'What have you to be – sorry about?'

'Well, you lying here while I'm painting the town red.'

Jim coughed then said, 'Just because I'm – crocked is no reason for you to – go into purdah.'

'The Ca'doro has a terrific ballroom. You'd love it.'

'I'll bet – I would,' Jim said, without sarcasm. 'Come on, Ally, don't keep it to yourself.'

'The lorry delivered me home. I had sixty seconds to collect my dress and make-up before I was whisked off to the QM where everybody handed in their cans and the girls got changed and did themselves up. The boys did likewise in the Union, then, would you believe, we climbed back on to the lorry, rolled down to the Ca'doro and arrived in style.'

He watched her carefully while she spoke. He was gratified to detect an optimism which had been missing in her. He envied her more than ever now that fatigue gnawed at his bones and his perceptions were clouded by discomfort. He could only share Alison's pleasures, not participate in them. Although the conservatory was bitterly cold and the night air had the silvery sting of hard frost he could imagine the hot, healthy physicality of the Ca'doro ballroom, like another world, a fantasy.

'I assume Leyman knew about – the raid?'

'Oh, yes. Not even Howard would raid a fever hospital without some sort of permission. He was there, you know. Phillip. Dr Leyman, I mean. He was at the dance.'

'Was he – indeed?' said Jim. 'Did he – dance with you?'

'Of course.' Alison shifted position by the bed. 'He played the piano too. The grand piano beside the bandstand. He looked the part, I must say, in his dinner suit and dickie-bow. He played jazzy stuff. It was all very unexpected. Grace – you don't know Grace, do you? – she got up on top of the piano and danced a Charleston and later on she and Phillip did the tango. Very steamy too. Everyone applauded. I admit that by that time most of us were, well, sozzled.'

'You too?'

'Me too. Sorry.'

'Don't keep apologising,' Jim said. 'Who took – you home?'

'Howard put me into a taxi about half past midnight.'

'Did he go with you?'

'No.'

'Why not?'

'He was completely exhausted,' Alison said, glibly. 'Besides, he and Guy had their hands full with the girl I told you about, the one called Grace. They practically had to pour her into a cab.'

Jim sensed that she was distorting the truth. She did it well, but not quite well enough. He had not entirely lost his acuity. He had been in love with her for so long that there was little about her that he didn't know. Love might be blind at first but after a time it led to a disconcerting clear-sightedness.

'You should have seen her,' Alison went on, 'Grace, I mean.'

He didn't want to hear about Grace. He wanted to hear about Alison. He wanted to ask if Howard had kissed her, if Howard meant anything to her. He had no right to question her, though, and tried, unsuccessfully, to remain unperturbed. He could feel his heart racing, his breath becoming short, that mysterious band across his ribcage tightening to the point of pain. He sat up from the pillow, forcing himself to smile in spite of the anger that whispered within him, a sudden unwillingness to forgive Alison her small, protective lies.

Alison said, 'What's wrong? You look flushed.'

'Of course I look flushed,' Jim said. 'I'm supposed to be sick, remember.'

'I'd better go.'

'Why?'

'I mustn't get you excited.'

'Huh!'

'Are you annoyed at me?'

'Nope.'

'You are. You're annoyed that I went dancing last night.'

'Do what you like,' Jim heard himself say.

'Don't you care?'

'Of course I damned-well care.'

For a moment she was at a loss how to deal with his unexpected abruptness. He watched her closely. He felt alert now, more alive than he had been in months. Would Alison react with guilt or with contrition, or match his anger with some of her own?

She leaned across the bed and patted his hand.

'I'll come back later,' Alison said in the sort of voice he hated. 'When you're feeling more yourself.'

'You might wait long enough for that to happen,' he told her.

'What do you mean?'

'Go on,' he said. 'I'm tired. I want to sleep.'

She hesitated then, in a very small voice, asked, 'See you Wednesday?'

'I'll be here,' Jim said, then turned on his side and tugged up the sheet to cover his face.

For Roberta, Wednesday came all too quickly. The last hour of the morning was devoted to a lecture on Otology, defects and disorders in the organ of hearing. She found it dull, so dull as to be almost soothing.

For seconds at a time she was almost able forget her hunger – she had eaten no breakfast – and the fear that welled within her. She had done everything Declan had told her to do to prepare herself for the ordeal. She knew exactly what the surgical procedure entailed, what risks she would run.

In a week's time, she told herself, it would all be behind her and she would put aside all the nonsense of sex and courtship until she had obtained her degree. After that, she *might* marry Guy, if for no other reason than to please her father. She was determined, utterly determined, not to appear a failure in Papa's eyes. So determined that she would even give up her baby before she would give him the satisfaction of dismissing her as just another idiotic female who had proved herself unworthy of trust.

In this frame of mind Roberta arrived in Walbrook Street, carrying nothing but a little bag of towels and underclothing.

Declan had been absent from classes that morning. The others had been peculiarly stand-offish, as if they suspected that she had something on her mind too weighty to share with them. Guy in particular had been miffed at her for cutting out of Charities Day and had tried to rub salt in the wound by telling her just how gay and fun-loving prim Grace Robertson had turned out to be.

As if any of that mattered now.

The threatened cold front had finally arrived.

You could see it across the river above the Govan shore, a lid of cloud sliding across the frosty blue sky. You could feel the wind that preceded it cutting into and numbing your cheeks.

St Anne's Church was pink and pretty in a patch of afternoon sunlight, the big brick chimney of the Yorkhill laundry too, then they faded into the first swirling snowflakes. Within minutes the skirts of the storm had swept over Finnieston and the Kelvinhaugh. Govan's jibs and cranes, tenements and steeples were consumed and the tattered terraces of Walbrook Street cowered in the face of the blast.

Roberta burst into the empty hallway, leaned against the door to close it, shook granules of snow from her hat and overcoat, then scuttled down the staircase to the basement and rapped on Declan's door.

He opened it instantly.

'God, what a day!' she said. 'What a dreadful day.'

'You're early.'

'What's wrong? Aren't you ready?'

'You'd better come in.'

Anger rising, she stepped over the threshold.

A fire burned in the polished grate and Declan had lighted a table-lamp so that the room had a ruddy, almost fleshy warmth that, in other circumstances, Roberta might have found inviting. The table was set with a teapot under a cosy, cups, glasses and a bottle of Old Highlander whisky. There were no signs of the dissection kit, the ether, enamel basins or cotton padding, the ugly instruments which

Declan claimed to have borrowed from the Royal.

She rounded on him, furiously. 'Have you been drink—'

Her father was seated on a wooden chair on the shadowy side of the fireplace. His long legs in the striped trousers of a morning suit were stretched sideways. One arm was bent, hand placed flat against his jaw as if his pain stemmed from something as simple as toothache. His head was turned away from her and she could hear him sobbing, a strange, dry, *sip-sip-sipping* sound, like the noise a cockchafer makes.

'You bastard, Declan!' Roberta said quietly.

Declan shrugged again. 'I couldn't let you do it, not to my child.'

She dropped the bag, took a step towards her father. 'Papa, I'm . . .'

Veitch Logie stood up, unfolding to what seemed an abnormal height, as if grief and wrath had added to his stature. He extended his hand, palm up.

'Get away from me, girl.' Again he uttered that odd little *sip-sip-sipping* sound. 'We're finished, you and I.'

'Papa!' She hurled herself towards him. 'Daddy!'

Declan caught and held her.

'I'll marry him,' Roberta cried. 'I'll marry Guy, if that's what you want me to do. I'll do anything you want. Anything at all.'

'*He* came to me. He had to come to *me*,' Veitch Logie said. 'I'm ashamed that he had to come to me.' He sucked in breath. 'You've ruined my life, Roberta. I hope you're satisfied.'

'I'm sorry, I'm sorry, I'm sorry, Papa. I'm so sorry.'

'If you'd come to me in the first place I might have been able to do something about it,' Veitch Logie said. 'But, no, you went behind my back. You trusted this young man more than you trusted me. Well, you've made your bed, Roberta, now you must lie on it. I want no more to do with you.'

'But what will I do? I mean to say – *what*?'

'I'll look after you,' Declan said. 'I'll take care of you.'

'You'll get no money out of me, young man,' Veitch Logie said.

'I'm not after your money, Mr Logie. If that had been my purpose I'd have gone about it very differently.'

'I don't know what you'd have done. I know nothing about your generation. Your behaviour is entirely beyond my comprehension. Guy?' Veitch Logie interrupted himself. 'Guy Conroy's too good for you, Roberta. I would hate to see a fine upstanding young man like Guy Conroy squander his prospects on the likes of you.' He reached down by the chair, came up with his long black overcoat and hat and put them on. 'You will not enter my house again, Roberta. I'll make sure your mother understands that I mean what I say. As for you, Slater, if I hear you've terminated my daughter's pregnancy by premature induction I'll do everything within my power to ensure that you serve time in jail.'

'I didn't have to tell you,' Declan said. 'I could've allowed Roberta to go through with it. And you'd have been none the wiser.'

'But you couldn't take a life, could you? Your priest wouldn't let you.'

'So that's what you think? You think because my brother's a priest—'

'Damn your brother. I'll see to it,' Veitch Logie said, 'that an adequate amount of clothing is sent to you, Roberta, but you can expect nothing else. You'll have no charity from me, either of you. As far as I am concerned I don't wish to clap eyes on either of you again, ever again.'

'What *will* I do? What about the baby?

'I suggest you marry this – this Pape. Try to live off his income and see how you like it.'

'That's just what she will do, Mr Logie,' said Declan.

'*My degree, my career?*'

'Hah!' Veitch Logie shook his head, stepped to the door and flung it open. 'You should have thought of "your career" before you opened your legs to every Tom, Dick and Harry.'

'*Daddy!*'

'Let him go, Bobs. For God's sake, let him go,' Declan urged and drew the hysterical girl towards the bed, while Veitch Logie, stiff as brass, walked out and slammed the door.

Outside, the wind whirled snow over the rooftops and around the back court and piled it against the little window above the sink. Declan watched it build a little blue-white barricade against the pane and felt the room grow gradually more insular and isolated.

It had taken him half an hour to settle Roberta down. Once she'd stopped crying, he'd given her tea with whisky in it and had wrapped a blanket about her to keep her warm. He'd recognised signs of shock and had been frightened for the safety of the foetus which, at this early stage, was not yet stable or secure.

Now he lay by Roberta's side on top of the bed, rocking her gently in his arms, telling her that everything would be all right, everything would work out. Finally Roberta rebelled and, with something of her old spark, snapped, 'How?'

Declan had anticipated the question. 'This is what we'll do, love,' he told her, softly. 'First I'll have to ask the landlady for permission for you to come and live here. I'll find you a nice ring to wear, a

224

wedding band which you can be puttin' on when you come home nights. So the old woman won't have fits if she happens to meet you upstairs.' He brushed her blonde hair with his fingertip and pressed himself closer, his front spooned to her back. 'The word will be all through the university in no time, though. No avoiding that.'

'I'll be asked to leave, won't I?'

'Oh, with just a marriage you might have made an argument for stayin' on but with a baby – no.' He went on quickly, 'But if we can keep things fairly quiet until Eastertime then you can write to the faculty with a request for recognition of all the professional exams which you've completed up to that time. That'll just leave the Final Division outstanding.'

'They won't let me graduate without it?'

'They can't. Medical Ordinance is specific on that point,' Declan said. 'But there are other colleges who might be prepared to take you on.'

'What other colleges?'

'Dublin, maybe.' He hugged her closer as she squirmed round to stare at him. 'Listen, if you carry summer term and knock on a year, I can see no reason why you can't go back and complete the degree somewhere other than Scotland.'

'But what will I do with the baby?'

'Listen, listen,' Declan went on, 'at the Eastertime we'll go home to Kerridge – that's where I live – and get ourselves married.'

'By a priest, do you mean?'

'Oh, not to make me happy,' Declan assured her. 'I'd marry you in Hindu if that was what it took but gathering you, and the baby, into the church is the only way we'll ever get my mother to help us. She'll regard you – me too – as souls saved for Jesus. It'll not be locusts and honey, Roberta, I can't promise you that. But in twenty months I'll be qualified to put my name on the register and go into practice of some sort. Soon after, you'll be with me. My partner.'

'Did you think this out all by yourself?' the girl asked.

'I love you dearly, Roberta,' Declan said. 'I would not have had it this way but this way is how it is. The least I can do is to try to make it up to you.'

'Papa will take me back.'

'And shut you away,' Declan said, 'like a leper.'

She rolled on to her back and looked at him out of solemn, red-rimmed eyes. 'He would do that, wouldn't he?'

'Sure and he would. If you went back to him it would have to be on his terms. Scant though they are, Roberta, are my terms not better than his?'

225

'It wasn't my fault,' the girl said. 'None of it.'

'I know,' said Declan Slater. 'I take all the blame on myself. I couldn't put the knife to you, though, no matter how much I loved you. But I *will* look after you, Roberta, you and the baby both.'

'I thought you only wanted money.'

'I did,' Declan said ruefully. 'I still do. By the looks of it, though, neither one of us is going to get your dear Da's cash.' He hesitated then said, 'Perhaps that's the way it should be, after all. Will it not be better in the long run to make it on our own, without depending on another's man's charity?'

She lay passively beneath him, thinking.

At length, she said, 'Do you really love me, Decker?'

'Sure and I do.'

'And you won't let me down?'

'I've made my promise and I'll stick by it.'

'*He* refused to stand by me. *He* didn't even pause to consider it. He dismissed me as if I'd never been his responsibility in the first place.' She uttered a tiny cry. 'Do you know something? I'm almost relieved.'

'Are you now, really?'

'I didn't *want* to lose it. I just didn't know what else to do.' She uttered the tiny cry again, closer to laughter than to tears. 'At least I won't have to marry Guy Conroy. That's one good thing to come out of it.' She blinked, a trace of the old dictatorial coyness in her eyes. 'Where will I sleep tonight?'

'Here,' Declan told her.

'With you?'

'With me.'

'Will it be all right, Declan, given my condition?'

'It'll be even better,' Declan said, 'now you're really mine.'

And Roberta, smiling bravely, nodded her assent.

Quite naturally, Daphne Stalker Logie shed tears when she was informed of her daughter's predicament. After the initial shock had worn off, though, it did not take her long to become slightly less perturbed by what had happened to Roberta than by her husband's edict that she have no more to do with her daughter. For someone as conformist as Daphne Stalker Logie to take a stand against her husband's wishes was unthinkable. She had, however, devised adequate methods of getting her own way in small things and could certainly score points off Veitch when it came to deviousness.

It didn't matter to Daphne that Bobs's young man was a Roman Catholic. She had always supposed freemasonry of the Orange variety to be nothing but an excuse for bigotry. Catholicism seemed much more romantic than repressive Presbyterianism. She found she actually liked the idea of Roberta marrying a man from the other side, saw in Catholic marriage a permanence which made it seem complete.

That evening, while her daughter lay in her lover's arms, Daphne did what any sensible woman would do: she called everyone she could think of and told them the news. First she informed the servants. Next she telephoned her sons at school and imparted the tidings about their sister's condition.

'How's Dad taking it?' young Stalker asked.

'He's sulking in his room.'

'Really mad, is he?'

'Oh, yes, dear. Very angry.'

'Glad it ain't me.' Sniggers in the background. 'Old Bobs, preggers! We didn't think old Guy had it in him.'

'Guy isn't the father, dear.'

'Who is it then? Has she told you?'

'Yes, it's some Irish chap she met at the varsity.'

'*Irish* chap? *A Pape,* d'you mean?'

'I'm afraid so, dear.'

'Bloody hell! I mean, my goodness! Ain't that a turn-up? So there won't be any sort of a wedding then?'

'Oh, yes, dear, I expect there will.'

'In the old pineapple? I mean, chapel?'

'Possibly. Probably.'

'Huh!' young Stalker said with a snarl. 'Well, Mother, you can count us out of that one for a start.'

Other members of the family were less direct than little Veitch and his brother Stalker in displaying disgust, but the implication was much the same: marrying a Tim was the ultimate degradation, a sin worse than adultery, worse than fornication, bastardy or embezzlement. However much they might sympathise with poor old Veitch, from now on there was bound to be an end to friendships, a loosening of family ties.

Daphne was not surprised at her relatives' reactions, nor was she unduly upset by them. She didn't much care what the Logies or even the Stalkers thought.

As for the Conroys – a shriek, a whistling shriek of absolute horror greeted her announcement – she was glad to be rid of them. She even considered telephoning Mr Emmslie but, after reflection, decided not to cheat Veitch of his right to convey the news to his professional colleagues.

She ate dinner alone in the dining-room then, with the servants gone, ensconced herself in the drawing-room to sew shirts and listen to a choral symphony on the wireless.

It was snowing outside. She found the muffled silence soothing. She tried to be calm, to accept things as they were, but she was uncomfortably aware of the stillness upstairs in the study and, as the evening ticked away, her anxiety increased to the point where she could no longer focus on the needle, and the sounds from the wireless became meaningless. She switched off the set and stared at the ceiling.

Three or four minutes later she found herself in the hall, then on the stairs, then on the landing outside Veitch's study. She knocked on the door.

'Veitch?'

'What is it, Daphne?'

'It's after eleven o'clock.'

'I know what time it is.'

'Would you like something to eat? A rarebit, perhaps?'

'I'm not hungry.'

She hesitated. 'Veitch, I hope you're not going to do anything hasty?'

'You may enter if you wish. The door is unlocked.'

She peeped cautiously into the room.

No sign of a rope slung from the light fitting or of poison bottles from the cabinet under the bookcase. Her husband still wore his formal grey waistcoat but he had removed his tie and collar and had rolled up his shirtsleeves and this faintly dishevelled air made him seem relaxed. A glass of whisky stood in the pool of lamplight and before him on the desk leather-bound photograph albums were piled up like a drystone wall. He had a fat green fountain pen stuck in his mouth like a pirate's dagger and a box of cream-laid notepaper and envelopes was perched on top of the albums.

He glanced up, removed the pen from his lips, beckoned.

'Come.'

Obviously it hadn't occurred to him that she might also be suffering. At least he hadn't blamed her for Roberta's stupidity, not yet.

'What are you doing, dear?' Daphne enquired, mildly.

He sat back and stretched his arms above his head.

'Putting my house in order,' he said.

It seemed strange to be alone with him in the study at this hour of the night. Daphne experienced a peculiar prickle of excitement at the knowledge that the house was empty and that any sounds of protest she uttered would bring no intervention or reprieve.

'Come,' he said again, quite softly this time.

She approached the desk.

He drew her to him, arm about her waist. He held her firmly. He smelled of whisky, tobacco and vivid blue ink. He put down the pen, lifted the glass and sipped. He glanced up at her with a tight-lipped smile.

'Letters of resignation,' he said. 'To the governors at Wellmeadow, the Grand Master of my lodge, and the secretary of the camera club.'

'Surely there's no need to resign from everything,' Daphne said. 'It's Roberta who's disgraced herself, not you.'

'If I hadn't spoiled her . . .'

'Spoiled her?'

'I wish – I just wish she'd spared a moment to think of all I've done for her before she climbed into bed with that Pape.'

'Catholic he may be, Veitch, but at least he had the decency to tell you what was going on.'

'He confessed,' said the surgeon, 'yes, but only when it was too late to do anything about it. Ironic, isn't it?'

He tugged Daphne down until she was seated on his knee. Perched on his long, lean thigh she felt like a ventriloquist's dummy. He even kept his left hand upon her back while he slid a photographic album from the pile and dabbed the page with a stiff forefinger.

'You won't remember this, my angel,' he said. 'Nineteen seven. My first gall bladder. Poor quality photograph.' He hauled down another album, tapped the page again. 'Nineteen twelve. The day after Roberta was born.'

'What is it?'

'Male organ.' He closed the book quickly.

'Why are you sorting through your old photographs?'

'Memories,' he said. 'Thoughts.'

'You've years of good work ahead of you.'

'No, no. Enough is enough.' He let the album slide to the carpet and put both arms about her waist. He pressed his long chin into the flesh of her shoulder. 'I intend to sell the house and move. Perhaps to the Hebrides. To Clova, where I was born. Look for a cottage to rent.'

'What about me?'

'Oh, you'll come with me, of course.'

She disengaged herself and got to her feet. 'You're running away,' she told him. 'You're running away from Roberta.'

'I'm retiring, that's all.'

'Retire if you like, Veitch, but not, please, to a windswept piece of rock in the Atlantic.'

'I was born there, and I was happy there as a lad.'

'You were nothing of the kind. You couldn't wait to escape to Edinburgh.'

He raised a hand. 'No, Daphne, I'm settled in my mind.'

'What about the boys?'

'The boys? The boys are well able to look after themselves.'

'And Bobs? Are you really going to abandon Bobs?'

'She's made her bed, she must lie on it.'

'Well, Veitch,' Daphne said, 'if you do retreat to the Hebrides you'll sail without me in your luggage.'

'I beg your pardon?'

'This is my house, my home, and here I stay.'

'But I can't possibly stay in Glasgow after what's happened.'

'Go, go if you wish. But I'm staying put, near Roberta.'

'Why?'

Daphne Logie was not a tall woman but when she straightened her spine and squared her shoulders she seemed to take on Amazonian proportions. When she spoke, though, her voice was not strident.

She said, 'Because Roberta needs me now.'

'But, Daphne, how can I possibly show my face . . .'

'That's up to you, Veitch, but whatever *you* do *I'm* not abandoning Roberta,' Daphne said. 'And that's final. Now, do you want a rarebit or not?'

He frowned, as if the decision was difficult. 'Poached eggs.'

'Angels on horseback?'

'Ideal.'

She glided towards the door. 'Here, or in the kitchen?'

'Here. Please.'

She glided out on to the landing, closed the door of the study and waited at the head of the staircase, her hand cupped over the newel post. She was still standing there when the first almighty roar reverberated through the house. It was followed by a tremendous crash and a splintering of glass. Another bellow followed it and more glass shattered.

Daphne Logie nodded and went on downstairs to the kitchen. She made the rarebit and toast, poached eggs, filled the teapot, set a tray and carried the lot carefully upstairs again.

Anger abated, he was seated behind the desk again, breathing heavily, hair wispy-wild, forearms bleeding from shards of glass, his waistcoat sprinkled with dust. All around him lay broken cameras, bent trays, torn photographs, wrecked trophy cabinets and shattered jars. Daphne stepped carefully over the shrivelled remains of an old gall-bladder, the blue-black relic of a pickled heart and placed the supper tray carefully before her husband.

'Have you finished, dear?'

'Yes.'

'Tea?' she said, calmly.

'If you please.'

'Worcester sauce?'

'Just a touch,' Veitch Logie said and, after his wife had sprinkled his eggs and tucked a napkin beneath his chin, lifted his fork in trembling hands and obediently began to eat.

EIGHT

With Trudi in Berlin

What happened to Henry wasn't the fault of the Foreign Press Association. Newspapermen who had fashioned a career out of reporting the reorganisation of Germany could not be expected to share secrets or sources with a stranger from Scotland. In spite of Marcus Harrison's letters of introduction they felt no obligation to welcome a provincial journalist into their tight-knit circle. With waves of Nazi displeasure breaking over the heads of all foreign pressmen, the fact that Henry appeared out of nowhere accompanied by a German wife caused him to be treated with polite, and quite justified, suspicion.

Edgar Ansel Mowrer, correspondent of the Chicago *Daily News*, Pulitzer Prize winner and ex-President of the FPA, had recently been ousted from his post and forced to flee to Paris. This, in the opinion of Mowrer's colleagues, was no great hardship for a front-line pressman. Paris was where the action seemed to be presently centred, with riots and lawlessness, bonfires, barricades and killing in the streets in the wake of February's fascist coup. As Trudi and he had made the twenty-one-hour train journey from London, even Henry had been more interested in the news coming out of France than what lay ahead in the German capital. To ensure that young Henry Burnside kept his nose to the right grindstone Marcus Harrison had put strings on the budget. The first three nights of the trip would be spent in the Hotel Adlon at fifty marks per day, a generous allowance which Henry, eager to be off and running, did not entirely appreciate.

What Henry craved was access to the 'real life' of Berlin, to cafés and nightclubs, hot spots of decadence and protest which had been driven underground since Hitler came to power.

What he found were military parades and processions so large and well organised that they almost took your breath away. Even Trudi couldn't conceive of a reason why streams of brown-shirted youths should carry torches down the Friedrichstrasse on a windy Monday

233

night or why jackbooted soldiers of the Sonderkommando Zossen, toting eagle and swastika banners, goosestepped past the embassies in the Tiergartenstrasse to the cheers of the lunchtime crowds.

Henry's response to such displays was unexpected. He was thrilled by them and, at the same time, jarred to realise that he could be moved by official exhibitions of power which made the ranting of Glaswegian strikers and Means Test protesters seem tame. He felt his chest swell, not with pride, for he could not share that aspect of the German character, but with the excitement of participation in something which he recognised immediately as power ineffable.

Beside him, on tiptoe, Trudi instinctively raised her arm in the Roman salute and, with a barking sound that was totally unfamiliar to her husband, yelled, '*Heil Hitler, Heil Hitler, Heil Hitler.*'

The city seemed like an ideal setting for military exhibitions. Berlin was clean and sharp and spacious. In the blustery March air it had a monumental assurance, an orderly grandeur which left the grey, impoverished cities of Britain far, far behind.

If he had not had work to do Henry would have happily settled for being one of the many cosmopolitan travellers for whom Berlin had become a mecca. But three days and nights swanning it up in the Hotel Adlon was not beneficial to his purpose. He waited patiently for Trudi to do her bit, for Papa Keller to emerge out of the shadows and direct him to his first real port of call.

It was not Papa Keller who put an end to Henry's fleeting love affair with post-republican Berlin, though, but an anonymous American newspaperman whom Henry had never seen before.

Tomorrow, after breakfast, Trudi and he would leave the Adlon and transfer to the smaller, less expensive hotel which lay around the corner from the Wilhelmplatz. That evening, Trudi went to lie down before dinner. Henry's energetic tours of the city had tired her out. She could not keep pace with him. She had a headache, she said, and must rest.

Henry sat with her in the fourth-floor room. He smoked a fifty pfennig cigar and browsed quietly over the magazines he had purchased from the kiosk in the foyer. Even though he could make out little of the text he was impressed by the images of the new Germany planted in the pages. Superior to English jingoism, stirring and straight-shouldered, somehow bold and proud, the photographs left for dead the cosy little essays which adorned the Scottish tabloids. Outside, the streamlined city hissed in light spring rain. Henry could feel the throb of its mechanical pulses even in a back room in the Adlon.

Above the crenellated rooftops daylight faded into cloud already tinged with neon from the thoroughfares.

He felt restless and strangely agitated. Trudi was already asleep on top of the bed, silky and pale in the half-light, her hair near white. She snored slightly, lips parted.

He kissed her softly on the brow, put on his overcoat and hat, scribbled a note on hotel stationery and was out on the pavement, alone in Berlin, almost before he realised what he was doing.

Whether the American followed him from the Adlon or whether the meeting came about by chance Henry was never quite able to decide.

Ducking between automobiles and tramcars, walking past cinemas, restaurants, discreet bars, big department stores, Henry became for a time part of the flow of a city so far removed from Glasgow that he felt as if he had been transported to a different planet and was separated by immeasurable distances from his father and brothers and the securities of Flannery Park. He strolled west towards the Wittenbergplatz but as he had left his pocket map in the hotel he did not know quite where he was. He marked the corners in his memory, reassured by the knowledge that he might hail a taxi-cab at any time and be returned unharmed to the Adlon, to Trudi. Then, above the hiss of traffic, he caught the eerie roar of lions.

The sound ran like a rivulet down a street to his left. Bathed in light from the sodium lamps and the sheen of a bar-joint's half-shuttered window, Henry listened intently. He heard the roars again, joined now by a jackal's whine, the baying of wolves and, scattered like dry seed in the misty twilight, the demanding chatter of monkeys.

In English, a voice behind him said, 'Feeding time at the zoo, I guess.'

Henry turned on his heel.

The man was about fifty, not tall but bulky. He wore a heavy overcoat but no hat. Rain glistened on his cropped silver-white hair. He had friendly features, rounded but not fat, and a broken nose which reminded Henry of his father and tricked him into assuming that the stranger shared the same tough, vulnerable quality which separated the artisan from the professional man. His voice, American, was rather too light for his shape and had no drawl to it. He spoke in neat, clipped sentences as if he was editing in his head as he went.

Intuitively Henry knew that the man was a journalist.

Henry said, 'I hadn't realised I was so close to the zoo.'

'Yeah, well, in this town it's never very far away.' The American held out his hand. 'Harry. They call me Harry. Is that what they call you too?'

'No,' Henry said. 'Nobody ever calls me Harry.'

'You are Henry Burnside, aren't you?'

'Have we met, at the hotel perhaps?'

'Nossir, this is the first time.'

'Then you're one up on me. Harry what?'

'Just Harry,' the man said. 'Got time for a drink?'

Henry glanced at his wristwatch.

It was not yet seven.

He looked past the man at the empty street of narrow-fronted offices and apartments then round at the tempting lights of the thoroughfare. He could still hear the lions roaring and the mournful howling of the wolves.

He hesitated then nodded. 'Sure.'

Brenda had been waiting for months for Clark Gable's latest, *Dancing Lady*, to wend its way to the Astoria picture-house. By the time the film arrived, however, she had rather lost her enthusiasm and moped out into the breezy night to meet Vera and Doris with something bordering reluctance.

The fact that the twins had taken to standing at the living-room window, noses pressed to the glass, tears staining their cheeks, whenever Mummy left for a night out with the girls might have had something to do with it. Jack had assured her that Bee and Lexi were larking about, all jolly and carefree, split seconds after she'd rounded the corner of Shackleton Avenue. Brenda's guilt was not appeased.

All sorts of things had happened in the early spring to unsettle her, though 'unsettle' was not quite the word to describe how she felt. She knew what was wrong with her, though 'wrong' was not quite the right word either. She was perfectly well in body, had never felt healthier, and the changes that were taking place 'down below' were a lot less mysterious than those which affected her head.

'You're growing up, dear, that's all,' Ruby had told her, a diagnostic comment which Brenda had greeted with derision. She might be growing fat, but she certainly wasn't, you know, *growing up*! Even if she was a wife and mother, she had no intention of growing up.

Growing up was for other people. Growing up was for Ally Burnside, who had gone all peculiar lately, a condition which, in Brenda's opinion, had to do with spending half her time out at the TB hospital waiting for her fiancé to die.

Growing up was for Bertie, in his prudish middle-aged raincoat and too-old hat, complaining about everything like some wee old wifie. Growing up was definitely for Henry who had never been young at all as far as Brenda could remember but who had gained a great slice of her respect by sailing off for Germany as calmly as other people set off for Millport.

Growing up was also for Walter Giffard, apparently. Mr Giffard had told Jack to tell Brenda that Wattie had gone off to sea again accompanied on the trip by the well-developed woman – Frankie's wife – from Hull. He intended to settle in Australia or New Zealand and to take something called his Mate's Ticket, which sounded vulgar to Brenda and not what she would have expected of a boy who had always been top of his class.

On Tuesday-night forays to the Astoria she'd prattled on to Vera and Doris about Henry, Bertie and Ally but had neglected to mention Walter's departure for foreign shores which was too close, too intimate a thing to trade as gossip. Never in a month of Tuesday nights could she have explained to Doris and Vera the mixture of relief and disappointment which possessed her whenever she faced up to the realisation that Wattie was not coming back and that she would probably never see him again.

Harder to explain was the fact that in her heart of hearts she didn't really give a damn about Walter Giffard. Or Vera. Or Doris. Or their idiotic chattering about who was doing what to whom in the sticky heat of the clothing factory. It was *weird* how everything you once thought vital just slipped away and sank without trace in that big muddy puddle called the past.

She was even beginning to go off Clark Gable, which was, you know, something *really* serious to worry about.

'What's wrong with your mug, then?' Vera said.

'Nothin',' said Brenda. 'My mug's fine.'

'Did y' not enjoy the picture?'

'I think I've gone off him,' Brenda answered.

'Who?' said Doris.

'Clark Gable. His ears are too big.'

'You never thought that before,' said Vera.

'Well, I'm thinkin' it now,' said Brenda.

They had emerged from the Astoria about a quarter past ten o'clock. The brusque little wind that had seemed so refreshing in the last of the daylight had taken on a chilly edge. The young women shivered, turned up their coat collars and walked towards the corner around which, on Dumbarton Road, was a clean, well-lighted fish-and-chip shop. They would each buy a bag of chips, would stand in the shelter of a doorway to eat supper and await the arrival of the tramcar that would carry Brenda away into Flannery Park.

'I'm also thinkin',' Brenda went on, 'I won't be comin' out to the pictures on Tuesdays any more.'

'We can make it Thursdays instead, if y' like,' Doris suggested.

'Not, you know, any night.'

'What is this, Brenda? The brush-off?' Vera caught her friend's arm. 'If you've got too good for us just come out an' say so.'

'It's not that,' said Brenda.

'What is it then?' Vera persisted.

'I've got too much to do.'

'Like what?'

'Lookin' after Jack and the twins.'

'You had that to do last week an' all,' Doris said.

'Aye, it's never stopped you before,' said Vera.

They had reached the corner. A few yards to their left the fish-and-chip shop shed light upon the pavement and the wafting odour of frying fat lay warm and heavy on the light spring breeze.

Brenda said, 'Well, it's stoppin' me now.'

'Are you not even goin' for chips?' said Doris.

'I don't think I'll bother. I'd better get home.'

'So the old man's got you under his thumb at last?' said Vera.

'Has he heck,' said Brenda. 'It's just – I'm goin' to be busy.'

'Doin' what?' Vera snapped.

'Havin' another baby.'

A pause: Doris said, 'Is two not enough for you, Brenda?'

'Enough or not' – Brenda folded her arms across her bosom – 'I'm havin' another one.'

'You'll no' catch me gettin' knocked up when I don't fancy it,' Doris said.

'Aye, but she fancies it. Don't ye, Brenda?' Vera said.

'Nothin' wrong wi' big families.'

'I never thought you were the type, but,' said Doris.

'What d'y mean?' said Brenda. 'What *type*?'

'The big, fat mammy type.'

'I *am* a mammy, in case you hadn't noticed,' Brenda said.

'Aye, but the first time was an accident,' said Doris.

'Well, this one isn't,' said Brenda indignantly.

'You can still come to the pictures when . . .'

Brenda said. 'Can you not get into your thick skull, Doris, that I've got *better* things to do.'

A pause: Doris said, 'I'm very hurt, Brenda.'

'Here's ma tram.' Brenda scowled into the distance. 'I didn't expect either of you pair to understand, anyway.'

'So you think we're a bad influence, do ye?' said Vera.

'I never said that.'

'Naw, but you were thinkin' it,' said Vera. 'Go on then. Crawl away back to your man. You were never much of a pal, anyway.'

'Can I come an see it?' Doris said, suddenly. 'When, I mean, it's born.'

'What d'*you* want to see it for?' Vera demanded.

'Och, I dunno. Might be nice to see a baby.'

'A baby? Nice?' said Vera, disgustedly.

'Come if you like.' Brenda stepped on to the cobbled roadway and waved to the tram driver. 'It'll be August before it's, you know, born.'

'What does Jack have t' say about havin' another mouth to feed?'

'Jack doesn't know yet,' Brenda called over her shoulder.

'Is it no' his, then?' said Vera.

'It's his all right,' Brenda called back. 'He's my one and only, Jack is.'

'You're a bigger fool than I took you for then.'

'Think so?' Brenda said. 'Do you really bloody think so?'

She stepped on to the platform of the tramcar, grasped the handrail tightly and swung round again. 'An' I'm not, you know, fat.'

'Hah!' Vera shouted, 'You will be, though, you damned well will be before you're much older,' and, fuming, dragged Doris off to the supper shop to fill the aching void with fish and chips.

The American said, 'First time in the Kleine Scala, Henry?'

'First time anywhere,' Henry answered. 'Quiet, isn't it?'

At that early hour of the evening there was nothing in the Kleine Scala except a dozen tables and a bar.

It was run, so the American told Henry, by a couple named Schwanebeck and until eighteen months ago it had been a high spot of Berlin night-life, a haven for every music-hall artiste who ever drifted through Berlin and, late, late at night, had been the scene of many revels. Comedians and acrobats had performed impromptu routines, girls had danced on tables, conjurors had devised new tricks with *Würste* and hard-boiled eggs and the proprietors of performing seals had rushed headlong through the kitchens in search of fish. For half a century Kleine Scala had been home to a horde of good-natured, reluctant nomads killing time between shows in café-bars and hotel lounges.

Only recently had the trade gone elsewhere.

There was no place for clowns and comedians in Adolf Hitler's city, so the American said, no place for gypsies, for Jews, for the happy-go-lucky travellers who, by their very gaiety, seemed to threaten the solemn purpose of the rulers of the new Reich. The

Kleine Scala, like so many other things in Berlin, had abruptly lost its character, the American said, and Henry, looking round at the listless waiter and the empty chairs, had no option but to believe him.

They sat all alone at a corner table. The American drank Pilsener, ate from a plate of dried eels and, Henry noticed, kept a weather eye on the street outside.

Henry made do with coffee and, because he felt that he needed all his wits about him now, turned down the offer of a cognac to go with it. He listened intently and without interruption to all that the American had to say and waited for the man to tell him what he really wanted.

At length, after a pause, the American said, 'Care to tell me what you're doing in Berlin?'

'Commission pieces,' Henry answered. 'Features.'

'On what? The cartels?'

The question was unexpected. It took Henry a moment to focus his thoughts on what he had learned about German economics. He had heard rumours of cartel-trading, of marriages of convenience between the monopolies who controlled the world's supplies of oil and coal, dye-stuffs, chemicals, rubber and every metal ore you could think of. What such high-powered international dealers had to do with him, or with the *Glasgow Mercury*, he couldn't imagine.

'No,' he answered cautiously. 'I'm here to write about the people, the ordinary people.'

'Ordinary people like the Dahrendorfs?'

'Who the hell are they?'

'Come on, Henry. I know how your wife's connected.'

Henry sat back, sipped coffee. He was outwardly relaxed but inside he was coiled tight as a watchspring. He said, 'How long have you been on the Berlin beat, Harry?'

'Twenty-five years, off and on.'

'It seems you know more about Trudi than I do.'

'That's for sure.'

'So,' Henry said, 'who are the Dahrendorfs?'

Harry smiled sardonically. 'You kid me.'

'Nope. No kid,' Henry said. 'Until this moment I've never heard of the Dahrendorfs.'

'The financiers?'

'What makes you think I might be acquainted with a bunch of German bankers?'

'Your wife used to be married to one.'

'Jesus!'

'Really, you didn't know?'

240

'No.'

'What else don't you know?'

'A whole bloody lot, I'm beginning to think.'

'About the boy?'

'What boy?'

'Gruppenführer Otto Dahrendorf.'

'Never heard of him.'

'Deputy head of SS Group North.'

The coldness started in the pit of Henry's stomach. It was as if he had swallowed a block of ice which, as it melted, spread a chill down into his bladder and up into the cavities around his heart.

'How about Keller? Heard of him?'

'Aye, he's Trudi's father.'

'Know what he does?'

'He's a pen-pusher of some sort.'

'Mainly he's a toll-gatherer.'

'Toll-gatherer?'

'Yeah, he picks up loose change and reroutes it into special funds.'

'What sort of funds?'

'Funds in Paris, Rome, Stockholm, even Madrid.'

'Funds for what?'

The American shrugged. 'Buying patents. Or maybe I should say persuading reluctant sellers to deal only with the Reich. He's a marriage-broker between old contracts and new money. He trades off floating currency for stuff too small for Farben and Standard Oil, the Krupps or Zeiss to bother with.'

'He went to jail for illegal currency dealing,' Henry said.

'Under the old regime. Yesterday's jailbird . . .' Harry shrugged again. 'You want to buy a few shares in a cattle feed company in Manchuria, you go see old Papa Keller. Wood sugar plant in the Balkans? Papa Keller's your man. You feed him dollars, he craps Deutschmarks.'

'The lure of foreign capital,' Henry said. 'Aye, I can follow that. I just didn't know that Trudi's father was – whatever the hell he is.'

'You figured out what they're doing in Germany yet?'

'Give me a chance,' said Henry. 'I've only been here three days.'

'I thought maybe your wife had blabbed.'

'Trudi doesn't blab,' Henry said, 'about anything.'

'You *really* don't know about the boy?'

The cold had reached Henry's throat. He felt as if the muscles of his face were paralysed, the way they had been years ago when he'd worked winter night shifts in Ransome's shipyard on the Clyde. He had been part of the great chain of production then, one ant in the heap. Now he was seated in a deserted café in Berlin talking dollars and Deutschmarks with a guy he'd met only a half hour ago, a chap who seemed to know more about Trudi than he did.

Henry did not have to pretend to understand what the American was talking about. All the dry facts he had consumed, news reports, accounts of Parliamentary debates, government audits plus the stuff Trudi had read out to him from the foreign press, rolled and rumbled through his brain like so many ore-wagons. He might lack the American's on-the-ground experience but he did not lack knowledge of what was happening in Europe or its possible implications.

'You can talk about the boy in a minute, if you like,' Henry said. 'First tell me what you think all this means.'

'Figure it out for yourself.'

'They're paying for the cost of the war.'

'Like hell they are. Planned inflation liquidated those war debts.'

'And stabilising the mark brought in foreign investment,' Henry said. 'So the victors, not the vanquished, have shelled out for the cost of German reconstruction.'

'And shooed Chancellor Hitler into power.'

'The cartels, the acquisitions departments,' Henry said, 'are you telling me the Jerries are waging an economic war? When they own enough patents, enough plant, they can squeeze out foreign competition by controlling the sources of essential raw materials. At the same time, they're making themselves self-sufficient. Cattle food from Manchuria, for God's sake!'

'A good investment, sure.'

'What else?' Henry said. 'Rearmament?'

'Right.'

'Weakening military potential elsewhere in the world?'

'Right.'

'So these traders, these financiers and businessmen are being duped.'

'Hell, no. They'll make their profits. They'll be paid. They're peaceful guys, though. They don't know what's going on. Geopolitics ain't their business.'

'And the German financiers?'

'Agents of aggression,' the American said, 'who know exactly what they're doing and the reason for it.'

'I can't write about any of this, you know,' Henry said.

'Why not?'

'I only work for a wee provincial newspaper.'

'Owned by Lord Blackstock.'

'You do know a lot about me.'

The American nodded. 'What I don't know is whether you're in cahoots with Keller and the Dahrendorfs or whether you ain't.'

'Take a guess,' Henry said.

'My hunch is – you ain't.'

'What if I am?'

'Then I'll be out of sight before they can nail me.'

'Who can nail you?' Henry said. 'This SS Gruppenführer?'

'Maybe.'

'Why are you telling me these things?'

'Because you're bound to meet up with Keller and I reckon you should be briefed to ask him the right sort of questions.'

'So that I can report his answers back to you?'

'Maybe,' the American said again.

'Who do you report back to, Harry? The *Tribune*, the *Washington Post*, the US State Department, perhaps?' Henry didn't wait for the American's reply. He steeled himself, then said, 'Tell me about the boy. Who is he?'

'Trudi Keller's son?'

'SS Gruppenführer Otto Dahrendorf is my stepson, is that what you're asking me to swallow?'

'Yeah, that's what I'm askin' you to swallow.' Henry let out his breath slowly.

'Well,' he said, 'well, well, well!'

'Handy, huh?' the American suggested.

Cautiously, Henry answered, 'Sure, very handy.'

'You'll talk to me again, maybe – later?'

And Henry, icy calm, said, 'Sure.'

The atmosphere which surrounded the midweek dinner party at the surgeon's house in Dowanhill was, to say the least of it, awkward.

All sorts of emotions were at play and good manners and a display of the family silver could not disguise them. The tic at the side of Veitch's mouth, the hard, sad set of his lips, Daphne's artificial smile, Roberta's dreadful dead-fish pallor and Declan's scowl were not the elements from which a truce might be easily forged.

At least the food had improved. Jenny had been given her marching orders and the cook had resigned in protest. The new cook would stand no nonsense and had forbidden Veitch to enter the kichen, an edict which Daphne readily endorsed. My angel had turned out to be less angelic than anyone, even her husband, had imagined. She would brook no hint of anti-Catholic sentiment in her house, upstairs or down, and pointedly reminded her husband that, like it or lump it, the pure Protestant strain of Logie blood was already mingled in his grandchild's veins with that of priest-lovers and Papists. She encouraged Veitch to resign his masonic offices but not his post at the Wellmeadow.

Professional colleagues were aware of the chief's domestic situation but feigned ignorance of it, all except Miss Ryan who could not resist an occasional polite enquiry, 'How's your daughter, sir? Is she blooming?' to which Mr Logie would reply with a non-committal snuffle.

Roberta, in fact, was not blooming.

To judge by her appearance Roberta was at death's door.

'Marriage', or what passed for it, did not suit her at all. She had become shabby and had a drooping, lacklustre quality which only a few insensitive wags put down to excessive sexual indulgence. Most fourth-year students saw Bobs Logie's degeneration as evidence of defeat or punishment for moral waywardness and, harbouring vague suspicions that the condition might be contagious, avoided her like the plague.

Even Howard and Alison felt uncomfortable in her company, for Declan fluttered about her like a mother hen, solicitous to the point of irritation. Roberta didn't seem to mind or, more accurately, Roberta didn't seem to care. Obviously she was only playing out her days as a doctor-in-the-making because it was part of Declan's plan for their future and it was rumoured that an arrangement had been made with the Dean of Studies to allow Roberta to 'vanish' during Easter recess.

Guy, the jilted lover, had quickly taken up with Miss Saving Grace and, showing off his resilience, could be seen trotting up and down the avenue with the lady clinging leech-like to his arm.

'You're better off without him, Bobs,' Alison would say.

'Am I?' Bobs would answer vaguely and glance round to see where Declan had strayed to, as if she needed his approval now to express any opinion at all.

Bobs's mother knew the score, though. And Bobs's mother didn't like it.

In fact, Daphne Stalker Logie wasn't going to stand for it.

Mothering Veitch Logie for twenty-odd years had taught Daphne a thing or two about self-discipline. All it took to trigger her into action was the realisation that her grandchild might be wrested from her and lost across the sea of bigotry that separated Scotland from the Irish Free State.

'I'm inviting the children to dinner, Veitch.'

'What: the boys?'

'No, not the boys. The boys are best left out of it.'

'Do you mean . . .'

'Yes.'

'I told you I wanted no more to do with her.'

'On Wednesday evening at half past seven.'

'Did *he* talk you into this?'

'He most certainly did not. Declan knows nothing of it.'

Veitch shook his head. 'I shan't be here. I've a meeting . . .'

'No, you haven't. You'll be here.'

'I'm not sure I can face him.'

'For my sake, and Roberta's, you'll just have to try.'

Declan wore a Donegal tweed sports jacket, a cotton shirt and a frayed necktie. He had a clean handkerchief in his breast pocket, though, was shaved and smelled of one of the lotions which had been despatched to Walbrook Street in Roberta's hamper some seven weeks ago. He appeared not much less civilised than the average medical student that Veitch encountered from time to time.

Roberta's appearance on the other hand made the old man's heart bleed. He could not precisely define the emotions which clamoured within him at the sight of his lost daughter. His beautiful girl-child was no more. In her place was a woman shorn of self-respect. She was clad in an old summer dress which she had let out around the waist and bodice. Her hair, grown longer, was pinned with kirby-grips like that of a common factory hand. Her eyes had lost their arrogance and her gestures were no longer demanding. Veitch could not bring himself to tell her how awful she looked, how he pitied her for what she had become and it took a maximum effort of will not to rush forward and clasp her clumsily in his arms.

Roberta glanced up as her father moved across the drawing-room towards her. She groped for Declan's hand, found it, clasped it.

Veitch travelled on past the sofa to the cabinet. He unlocked it, took out glasses and a bottle, poured sherry. He handed the glasses to Daphne who passed them on to the children. Children? Yes, that's exactly what they were. Children pretending to be adults. He longed to have his *real* daughter back, the polished version, the clever student. He hardly recognised the version that this boy had fashioned, so lustreless and cowed.

Veitch poured himself a whisky and, standing by the cabinet in the corner, drank it, while Daphne, bright and brittle, spurred the conversation on. He could find nothing to say to a young man who knew more about Roberta than he ever would, who had bared parts of her character that he, her father, had never known existed.

He kept silent, sulking and sorrowful, until dinner was announced

245

then meekly followed his wife and the children out of the drawing-room and across the gloomy hall.

He ate cream of mushroom soup, broke bread, passed salt to his daughter and pepper to the boy who was her husband in all but name. He listened to Daphne draw them out on what life was like living in sin in the wasteland beyond Dumbarton Road. He wanted to talk to them, to tell them what *he* had done that day. If it had been the other young man, Guy Conroy, then he would have dominated the conversation. He would have ignored Roberta and ascribed her boredom to the fact that she was a female.

But Guy Conroy was no more.

Instead there was only this alien, this Irishman, whose sly, luminous eyes seemed to see right through him and who was not impressed.

Twice Veitch cleared his throat. Twice desultory conversation ceased. Twice he restrained himself, dabbed with the napkin, broke more bread.

What could he tell them anyway? That he had removed a brace of infected tonsils from a five-year-old, that he had done, with much help from Emmslie, a rather decent splenectomy. They wouldn't be interested. They wouldn't understand. Halfway through the eating of a steak and kidney pudding, however, the thread that held Veitch Logie's ego in place finally snapped.

He had been listening to talk of Wicklow, of suspect Irish degrees and practices set up in quaint rural townships, of priests and pious mothers-in-law. He suddenly sensed that in losing Roberta he might lose my angel too. It was not so clear-cut as all that, of course, but none the less he was frightened into making a decision. He clanged down the lid of the vegetable dish, threw his fork on to his plate to attract their attention.

His tone was one of exasperation, of annoyance not capitulation.

He heard himself say, 'You'd better come here.'

'What?' Roberta said, dully.

'It's what you want, Daphne, isn't it? It's what this entire charade has been about. For your sake, my angel, I'll help them.'

'I don't need your charity, Mr Logie,' the Irish boy said.

'You certainly need something,' Veitch Logie said. 'Look at you.'

'Sure and it's all I can afford.'

'A blasted sight more than I could afford when I was your age.'

'Veitch,' Daphne warned, 'don't start.'

'Don't start what? I didn't *start* anything. But you can't expect me to sit in perfect silence and listen to this twaddle.'

Roberta turned her head. 'What do you mean – come here?'

Veitch said, 'I suppose you *must* marry in a chapel?'

Bobs glanced quickly at Slater who gave a rapid little nod.

Bobs said, 'It's all arranged. I've even begun instruction.'

'When will this event take place?'

'At the Easter time.'

'Where?'

'In the chapel at Kerridge, where my family lives.'

'Well, don't expect me to be there,' Veitch said. 'I will not – repeat not – take part in a Fenian rite.'

'That's your prerogative, Mr Logie,' Declan Slater said.

'Meanwhile, you'd better shift out of that squalid and unhealthy basement and take up residence here.'

'I'm not leaving Declan,' Roberta told him.

'I'm not suggesting you leave Declan, damn it. Bring him with you.'

'When?' said Daphne.

'Tomorrow,' said Veitch.

'I hope you're not going to try to come between us, Mr Logie.'

'All I'm attempting to do, young man, is bring some order to your lives. What I propose is that you go to Wicklow, or wherever it is you live, at Easter and return married in the eyes of the law. Until then the pair of you may lodge here. In separate rooms, of course.'

'And afterwards?' said Declan. 'After our marriage?'

'You may continue to reside in my house until the child's born, until you complete your studies. Then you may do as you please.'

'In separate rooms?' Declan Slater said.

'Together,' Daphne put in.

Veitch sat back. He felt better already. He had shown himself willing to compromise, to be generous, and in so doing he had reasserted his authority.

He tilted his long chin and rubbed his hands. 'Well, what do you say?'

'We'll have to talk it over,' Declan Slater said.

'Talk *what* over?'

'Now, Veitch, keep calm.'

'Roberta and I. In private.'

Veitch sucked in a huge breath and held it. A lump of steak and kidney pressed just below his sternum and the good feeling of a moment ago had been abruptly snuffed out.

He glowered at the boy then, turning, addressed himself to Roberta. 'Don't you want to come back home?'

'It's up to Declan,' Roberta said.

'Haven't you got a mind of your own any more?' Veitch snapped.

'What do you think, darling?' Roberta said, leaning against Slater.

Veitch Logie winced at the word 'darling'. He sucked in another breath. Discomfort had become pain and his head as well as his chest ached. He could hardly bear the waiting, the suspense. The sheer recalcitrance of these, these *children* who thought that they still had a choice maddened him.

He felt Daphne's hand on his arm and, for once, did not pull away.

They put their heads together, literally. Roberta's lank blonde hair brushed the Irishman's cheek, his lips brushed her ear. Veitch could hear them whispering. Calculating. Conspiring. A sweat of impatience dewed his upper lip. He had not expected them to be anything other than eager, eager and grateful. He felt reduced by their hesitation but, for Daphne's sake, said nothing and seethed silently behind a mask of indifference.

When he could bear it no longer, he shouted again. 'Well?'

'What do you want to do, dearest?' Slater whispered.

'I want a bath,' he heard Roberta reply. And thought how it had come down to this, to plumbing in lieu of patronage.

He felt suddenly useless, useless and weary and dispossessed.

'We'll accept your offer then, Mr Logie,' Declan Slater said. 'We'll be movin' in tomorrow, if it suits.' At which precise moment Veitch Logie slumped across the dining table, dead.

The American left him at the corner of the Lutherstrasse. Almost before Henry realised what was happening the man had slipped away.

No jungle sounds impinged on the night air of the city now. Only the mechanical clashing of tramcars and the hum of automobiles filled the spaces above the rooftops. Henry peered back along the pavement, past shuttered shop fronts and the gridded doors of shady offices and, more empty than calm, wondered if the American had ever been there at all or if, like Hamlet's father, he had been a mere figment of the imagination.

Henry turned up his coat collar and walked as far as the Kurfürstendamm before he flagged a taxi-cab to carry him back to the Adlon.

During the cab ride his mind whirred into gear again.

He didn't doubt that what the American had told him was the truth, that Trudi had a grown-up son.

Uniforms, blood oaths, the great red and black banners, torchlight processions, the chanting of marching songs had already affected him at an elemental level. What he'd responded to here in Berlin was not the display of national pride but a kind of organised corruption so provocative that honest citizens could be sucked into it without ever being aware of what it signified. He had never acquired the habit of taking Trudi on trust. Trust was something you could never take for granted.

He debated whether or not Marcus Harrison knew of the existence of SS Gruppenführer Dahrendorf and, for the first time, squared up to the question of just who Trudi had slept with before he came into her life and what these men meant to her now. Marriages and children were one thing, promiscuous affairs another. Now, riding through the neon-lighted streets of Berlin in a taxi-cab, Henry realised that perhaps Trudi had not lied to him after all, that the Gruppenführer, if he really was her son, might well be the product not of a legitimate marriage but of one of her scandalous affairs.

He had no notion of what he would say to Trudi, if he would confront her directly with what he had learned or if he would play along for a while longer and allow her to lead him deep into a netherworld of duplicity within which, if the American was to be believed, Trudi had once been very much at home.

He crossed the Adlon's glittering foyer swiftly. Too impatient to wait for the elevator, he bounded up the carpeted stairs to the fourth-floor room. He had no key with him but when he tried the door he found it unlocked.

Breathing heavily, he checked, composed himself then stepped quietly into the darkened bedroom and moved on tiptoe to the bed.

'Trudi,' he murmured, then, louder, 'Trudi, I'm back.'

He reached out and brushed his hand down the length of the bed. The coverlet was smooth as silk, and flat.

Henry groped for the switch of the bedside lamp.

The bed, the room, were empty.

Henry looked towards the bathroom.

'*Trudi?*' He darted across the room, pushed open the bathroom door then, stepping back, switched on the chandeliers.

What he did next was quite ridiculous. He dropped to his knees and looked under the bed then, rising again, yanked open the doors of the built-in wardrobes and flipped through the coats and dresses. He had a vague notion that Trudi was hiding from him, that by some means beyond the rational, she had learned of his meeting with the American.

Trudi, of course, was not in hiding.

Trudi had gone.

There was no note upon the pillow or the ornate dressing-table, nothing stuck into the corner of the mirror.

She had vanished even more effectively than the American.

Not for an instant did Henry suppose that he would find his wife in the cocktail bar or the ground-floor dining-room. He was so affected by the atmosphere of betrayal and conspiracy that he was ready to believe that she had left him for good, had abandoned the security of Flannery Park for another sort of life in Germany, a life more exciting, more dangerous, more in keeping with her character and her past.

He recalled her impulsive salutes – '*Heil Hitler, Heil Hitler, Heil Hitler*' – and what she had said about Jews; her selfishness, her efficiency, her hunger, her subtlety in getting what she wanted. He had been consumed by Trudi Keller, deceived by her apparent need of protection and yet he was engulfed by an irrational fear that he would never see Trudi again.

He spoke to himself sternly. 'All right, Henry. Take it easy. Take it easy.'

Panic receding, he seated himself on the bed.

He inhaled deeply, and glanced about the room for clues.

Shoes gone, the best pair. Black overcoat with the fur-trimmed collar. The one svelte dress she had brought with her, a black number, starred with scarlet. She had left dressed for an evening on the town and, Henry suspected, she had not left alone.

Which of the men, the old lovers, had lured her away?

Papa? The boy?

Berlin itself?

He had a sudden hunch that he might be able to tell by the hat she'd worn. Pushing himself from the bed, he moved to the wardrobe and groped in the corner for her hatbox.

The drum-shaped object of striped cardboard which she'd carried from Scotland was missing too. He sat back on his heels, his mind racing. Then, almost casually, he got to his feet and checked out shelves, drawers and, once more, the vacant space beneath the bed.

No, the hatbox, like Trudi, had gone.

Most of the clerks in the Adlon spoke some form of English. They did so reluctantly, spitting out the words as if they hated having to communicate in a foreign tongue. Herr Krauss, chief receptionist, was no exception. He had perfected a narrow, patronising smile which switched on and off like a little strip of neon. He was delighted to be of service to Herr Burnside. Regretted that he had not seen Frau Burnside leave the hotel. He consulted his clerks, his boys. They shook their heads. No one had seen Frau Burnside at all that evening.

Henry turned on his heel and headed for the bar.

Laughter greeted him. It rose like smoke from the group of journalists and newspapermen who occupied the rosewood table under the long mirrored wall. The mirror, cut and bevelled into a hundred little squares, greeted you like the eye of a gigantic housefly, each prism filled with separate images which swirled and changed in response to the movement in the room.

Henry loitered by the arch at the doorway and surveyed the clientèle. He did not expect to find Trudi here. He hoped, though, that someone might take him in hand, that Harry, the American, might pop out of the crowd and save him the embarrassment of actually having to ask if anyone had seen his wife.

A hand on his back made him flinch and spin round.

'You're the Scot, aren't you?'

'Yes.'

'Thought I recognised you.'

The Englishman was handsome in an effete sort of way. Pale, aesthetic features topped a thin inquisitive neck. He wore a dinner suit and the bow-tie bobbed when he spoke. He held a cocktail glass daintily between finger and thumb and, oddly, stared at Henry through it as if through a magnifying glass. Still with the glass held aloft, he picked the cocktail stick from the liquid and stripped a pickled onion from it with his teeth. He sucked the onion thoughtfully for a moment then said, 'Looking for your wife, old chap?'

Henry said, 'As a matter of fact, I am.'

'Gone off with a Jerry.'

'Really? How do you know it was a Jerry?'

The Englishman laughed, teasingly. He was apparently enjoying himself. Henry recognised him now: stringer for a London press agency, connected to the aristocracy, seldom sober.

'Spot 'em a mile away, old chap,' the Englishman said. 'Blond gods, and all that. Damned attractive – if you care for that sort of thing.'

'Are you sure it was my wife?' said Henry.

'Absolutely. Bit of a knock-out, but – pardon my candour – no chicken.'

'Was the Jerry in uniform?'

'Alas, no. Look, I thought you knew about this. Wouldn't for worlds want to put you out. Care for a drinkie?'

'How long since she left?'

'Half hour, three-quarters.'

'Was she carrying anything?' Henry said.

The Englishman had tilted to one side and rested the crown of his shoulder on the gilded post. He held the cocktail glass up and Henry saw that it was miraculously empty. The crowd at the rosewood table were looking towards the doorway, grinning.

'Little drinkie might help refresh my memory,' the Englishman suggested.

'Little punch on the nose might have the same effect,' Henry told him.

'Oh!'

'Oh, indeed!' said Henry. 'I'll ask you again, nicely. Was she carrying anything, anything unusual?'

'She wasn't. The Jerry was.'

'What?'

'A hatbox, actually. Big job. Striped.'

Henry smiled. 'You wouldn't happen to know which way they went?'

'Not a clue. Sorry.'

'Thank you, old chap,' said Henry and, turning on his heel, headed straight for the door to the street.

Given that the regime for recuperative patients was practically timed with a stopwatch the toing and froing of medical staff at Ottershaw seemed by contrast not merely random but almost chaotic.

It was something Jim Abbott hadn't appreciated when he lay alone, sick in body, mind and spirit, in darkened rooms. Once he perked up a bit, though, and was transferred to a community ward, he began to understand that what folk liked about Phillip Leyman was not just his no-nonsense approachability but also the fact that his consultations were totally unpredictable.

He would pop up at all odd times, white-coated and brisk. He would breeze into the middle of a card game or disrupt the serving of a meal and, with a nurse trailing on his heels, would whistle and point to one or other of the ambulatory patients and say, 'Time we had a chat, Bill,' or 'My room on the double, Charlie,' and, twirling the chestpiece of his stethoscope, would head off for the examination room which adjoined the dispensary.

Many of the chores that Dr Leyman undertook seemed far too minor and routine for a doctor of his standing. Of course, it was known that Dr Leyman's real job was to administer to first-stage patients and, alas, to those poor devils who existed in the twilit world of the isolation wards.

It was also rumoured that Dr Leyman conducted post-mortems in the brick-built mortuary which was hidden behind the willow trees on low-lying land towards the river. Few patients ever mentioned that building or made comment when lights burned there, very late or very early.

One advantage of long-term residence in Ottershaw was that all your petty ailments, from aching teeth to warts on the nose, received expert attention and, apart from the fact that they harboured potentially lethal bacilli, most patients had never been so well looked after in their lives. Tedium was the bugbear. But, after a time, even tedium began to have its attractions. Absence of thought, of desire, of striving, of all responsibility became, for some, addictive, and laziness, the enemy of adaption, crept in.

This was not the case with James Abbott.

His problem, in fact, was just the reverse.

The wooden chairs, the narrow bed with its spotless cotton sheets, the oak filing cabinet like a presence in the corner of the room, trays of drugs and sample bottles on white enamelled instrument tables, sterilised thermometers and hated hypodermic syringes with their painful steel needles; the examination-room was no comfortable place to chat. That, however, was just what Dr Phillip Leyman liked to do while he checked medical records against signs and symptoms or performed some menial function like paring a corn or mixing a dose of bitters to stimulate a flagging appetite, for through these seemingly unscheduled meetings he discovered what problems troubled his charges.

Alison had never been permitted to observe this aspect of the doctor's technique. Nor, of course, had Jim, which was why, when his headaches had gone, his cough had eased and his appetite had returned, he struggled to shake off a lingering malaise which he equated with apathy and why, whenever Leyman and he were alone, he negotiated for early release, as if Leyman was some kind of jailer or the chairman of a parole board.

'How long do you intend to keep me here?'

'Until you're well again.'

'How long will that be?'

'I can't say.'

'An informed guess?'

'Six months.' Leyman shrugged. 'But that's not a promise.'

'Am I getting well? I mean, am I going out of here on my own two feet?'

'Of course you are.'

'This isn't just a remission.'

'In God's name, what gave you that idea?'

'Something Alison said.'

Leyman sighed. 'I'm sure she didn't say anything of the sort.

You're not dying. Kindly stop this nonsense.'

'It might be nonsense to you, Dr Leyman, but to me – to me it's vital.'

'I'm not in the habit of lying to patients,' Leyman said, without rancour. 'For the umpteenth time, James, you're suffering from acute miliary tuberculosis, with a septic focus limited to a tiny portion of one lung.'

'And?'

'After only nine weeks of treatment and rest you're showing positive signs of improvement.'

'Permanent improvement?'

'There's no evidence of enlargement of the spleen or of a spread through the lymphatic system. You've been very lucky.'

'Lucky? I don't call being locked away for six months . . .'

'At least six months,' Leyman put in.

' . . . lucky. Why can't I go home and continue treatment as an out-patient?'

'Not,' said Leyman, 'yet.'

'Is it because of my sister? Do you think she can't look after me properly?'

'I haven't thought about it at all,' Leyman said. 'You're a long way from well, James. Can't I pound that into your thick head?'

Jim paused. 'Is it because of Alison?'

'What?'

'If you keep me here, you keep her here too.'

'I'm not keeping Alison anywhere. She comes of her own free will.'

'Because of me?'

'Yes, of course. What are you driving at, James?'

'She thinks you're wonderful.'

'Well, I am.'

'No, don't try to laugh it off.'

'Alison's a highly intelligent girl, very bright, very quick . . .'

'Do you think I don't know that?' Jim said. 'You want her, don't you?'

'You're working yourself up over nothing,' Leyman said.

'Answer my question: do you want her?'

'Yes, I want her,' Leyman said.

'I knew it. I'm not a complete idiot, you know.'

'I want her to come to work here as soon as she graduates.'

'And the rest of it?'

'There is no "rest of it",' Phillip Leyman told him. 'Take your shirt off.'

'What for?'

'I want to listen to your chest.'

'Now, I suppose, you're going to scare me off the topic.'

'Rubbish! Take your shirt off.'

Sulkily, Jim obeyed. His trust in Leyman the physician was complete; his trust in Leyman the man much less so. Leyman's explanation, though plausible, was just too glib. The problem was that he, Jim, had too much time on his hands. He could not relax, could not switch off. He fretted about Alison, Alison and Winnie, Winnie and Mother, money, his future as a teacher. But mostly he fretted about Alison and what would become of her if his condition worsened and he became helplessly dependent on her. The prospect filled him with a smouldering fury that made his pulses beat and his chest heave.

He shivered when the chestpiece of the stethoscope touched his back.

'Breathe,' Leyman told him.

Jim said, 'Have you asked her yet?'

'No, not yet,' Phillip Leyman answered. 'Breathe, for God's sake.'

'Why haven't you asked her?'

'Because she's got too much on her mind as it is.'

'Exams.' Jim nodded and inhaled deeply.

He coughed, pursing his lips, twisting his head away. Leyman handed him a handkerchief from a pyramid on the instrument table. Jim coughed again and automatically peeped at the handkerchief for signs of haemorrhage.

Phillip Leyman said, 'Don't you think it would be good for her to work here, under me?'

'It's got nothing to do with me,' Jim said, as the chestpiece moved, cold and hard and positive, across his back.

'Yes, it has,' Leyman said. 'She'll do what you tell her to do.'

Jim laughed, coughed slightly. 'That might have been true in the past but not any more. Look at me. A one-armed cripple, riddled with TB.'

'You're not riddled with anything,' Leyman said, 'except fear and guilt.'

'Guilt?'

'Breathe.'

Jim swung round on the chair and nudged the chestpiece of the stethoscope away. His shirt hung about his waist and his scars were livid. The stump of his arm hung swollen like old meat.

'I'm tired of breathing on demand,' he said. 'It might be better for all concerned if I just stopped breathing altogether.'

'Do you think Alison would like that?' Leyman said.

'Yes,' Jim Abbott said. 'I think she would.'

'You're in a worse state than I thought you were.'

'You mean I'm dying?'

'I mean you're living *as if* you were dying,' Phillip Leyman told him.

'In this place, do you wonder?' Jim said, angrily. 'Send me home.'

'If I did send you home, what would you do then?'

'Go back with my sister to Pitlochry.'

'And Alison?'

'She – she'd be able to get on with her life without . . .'

'The burden?' Leyman suggested.

'She thinks she owes me something.'

'She does,' Leyman said. 'She told me so.'

Jim said, 'I don't want her to care for me out of a sense of obligation.'

'Guilt, in other words,' Phillip Leyman said.

'I want Alison to – to *love* me,' Jim confessed.

'She does.'

'No. She only thinks she does.'

'That's for her to say, surely.'

Jim said, 'She has choices now, opportunities. You know the boy McGrath?'

'Oh, yes, I remember McGrath only too well.'

'He'd marry her tomorrow if he could.'

'Possibly.'

'Now you come along with this tantalising offer of a job.'

'I'm not trying to steal Alison away from you, Jim.'

'I don't believe you,' Jim said.

'What if I did try to steal Alison away from you? What would you do about it, Mr Abbott?'

'What the hell can I do? *I've* nothing to offer her.'

'The engagement, I take it, is off?' Leyman said.

'No, I – not yet.'

'Answer my question then,' the doctor said. 'What would you do if I turned my undoubted charm on Alison, if I tried to take her away from you with the offer of a lot more than a post on my staff?'

Jim was silent.

'Come on,' Leyman urged him. 'You didn't lose that arm by cowering in a corner of a trench. You've been in worse situations than this and come through.'

'That's banal,' Jim said. 'So banal.'

'I'm a very banal person,' Phillip Leyman said. 'What's more, Mr Abbott, I'm also an orthodox Jew.'

'You mean you'll only marry another Jew?'

'I doubt if I'll marry anyone. I'm not that way inclined. Besides, I've too much to do here to accommodate a wife.' Leyman fiddled with the stethoscope and suddenly planted it on Jim Abbott's chest. 'Breathe.'

The little cold spot of the chestpiece no longer made Jim shiver. He said, 'Do you really want Alison to work here with you?'

'If she's willing.'

'And that's all?'

'That's all,' Phillip Leyman said.

'She could do worse, I suppose.'

'Funny,' Phil Leyman said, 'that's exactly what I was thinking.'

'Hmmm?'

'Breathe, please, Mr Abbott.'

And Jim, inhaling deeply, finally did as he was told.

Once, naïvely, Trudi had imagined that she might provide a place for Papa in Scotland, safe from the corruption that had infected Germany in the wake of the Great War. She had assumed that prison would have transformed Papa into a pathetic old man in need of care and protection. So, in spite of all the bad things he had made her do when she was young, she had flown to Berlin by aeroplane to rescue him from poverty and neglect.

The trip, made almost five years ago, had been a disaster.

Papa was not a broken man, nor friendless. Papa had been taken up by her son, by Otto, a *führer* in the Schutzstaffel who, with breeding, aristocratic connections and striking good looks on his side, had seemed destined even then to rise to the top.

It had hurt her – but it had not broken her heart – to leave them both behind; the child she had rejected twenty years ago and the father who no longer needed her.

She had fled home to Henry and the security of Flannery Park and had assumed that she would never set foot in Germany again. Then her past had caught up with her once more and that twisted strand of fate, woven in her youth, had finally begun to unravel.

The men she had known – slept with – had come back uninvited into her life. Her first husband, Otto Dahrendorf, young Otto's father, was dead but the others were very much alive: Clive Coventry, Marcus Harrison, the lawyer Gerald Dante and a host of spectral lovers to whom, all too willingly, she had given her favours when she was still quite young and pretty. She harboured no guilt over her promiscuity.

Sometimes it seemed as if she had been another person

altogether, that marriage to Henry, her incorporation into the Burnside family, had not merely changed but had obliterated the woman she'd been, that all that remained of Trudi Keller Coventry were debts which must be paid before she could be at peace with Henry and with herself.

In spite of the fears that had plagued her during the journey from Scotland, she'd experienced a subtle thrill at being back in Berlin with Henry at her side. It was as if she had at last managed to put the two halves of herself together and make them match.

It was not to satisfy *her* need for a reckoning that Marcus Harrison had sent Henry to Germany. Trudi was perfectly well aware whose money she carried in the cardboard hatbox and why the German customs officer had refused to open it even when she'd offered it up for inspection. Bribery: a first taste of the grassroots corruption of the new regime, not so very different from the old.

From that moment she had known that somewhere, at some time in the next few days, she was bound to be confronted by her grown-up son.

She had not been asleep upon the bed.

She had been making opportunity.

Four days in Berlin. Last night in the Adlon.

Cash, high-denomination banknotes, still sealed in the hatbox. Henry gone out. She had contrived to be alone, to collude. This, typically, was when Papa would make contact, show off his cunning, exhibit a power as slight and artificial as a conjuring trick.

How they – how Papa – adored the mechanics of duplicity.

He would not send in a man to take her, however. Thank God she was too old and too skinny to be an item of trade and barter. She was worth less to Papa's masters than a boxful of foreign banknotes. When the hatbox had been emptied she would surely be cleared of obligation. They would not use her again. There were other couriers, less adept perhaps, less malleable, but with more conviction than she had ever possessed. They would be the couriers of the future. The game that Papa and she had once played had become too monstrous and too important to be entrusted to an ageing little *hausfrau*.

She had lain like a bride upon the bed in the hotel room. She had heard Henry leave. She had known, with absolute certainty, that they would make contact tonight – simply because they could not bring themselves to be direct, to send up a bellboy or chambermaid to take away the box and furnish her with a printed receipt to fulfil their compulsive need to record even illicit deals and make the small but profitable transaction seem like official business.

So Trudi had lain motionless on the bed, like a bride or a corpse, eyelids closed and had heard the door open and close and had known that someone other than Henry was in the bedroom, looking down on her.

What happened next had astonished her.

The voice, smooth and haughty and hard as cedar-wood, muttered, not in German but in French, '*Mama, c'est vous.*'

She kept her eyes closed, waiting for him to touch her, to kiss her. But he had not changed so much as all that and the gesture, which she had thought she might cherish, was never made.

In German, he said, 'Waken up, Mother.'

Trudi opened her eyes wide.

Her son's pale blue eyes had not lost their luminosity. His white-blond hair still seemed fine as gossamer. Hair and eyes were set off by a deep tan, though how he had maintained it throughout the sunless winter days Trudi could not imagine. His high-collared suit in silky black material had the same threatening formality as an SS uniform and his overcoat, vicuna not leather, was draped over his shoulders like a cloak.

He said, 'Do you have the money?'

'Of course, Otto.' She sat up stiffly.

The sight of him had increased her feeling of age. She could not believe that this grown man was her son, her one and only child. His severity made him seem much older than Henry. He did not smile, did not offer platitudes by way of welcome. She knew, of course, that he despised her. She could not, in honesty, blame him for that. There was no bond between them. Even so, she still recognised in him the toddling child whom she had abandoned into his father's family's care when he was only four years old.

Whatever memory he had of her must be faint, if it existed at all. He was not a Keller but a Dahrendorf, a true German, bred if not born. He had lived in castles, had roamed the countryside around Bad Wiesse, had learned his manners in a Berlin *Gymnasium* and the salons of the well-to-do. How he had fallen in with the Nazis Trudi did not know. She tried to blot from her mind the attraction that flyers and colonels had had for her in Munich just after the war, heroes of the Reich, beaten in war and betrayed by their leaders. But not defeated. She did not dare speculate on what aspects of her own character were hidden away beneath the smooth, tanned skin of the SS Gruppenführer.

She swung her feet to the floor.

He did not assist her, did not touch her. Stood quickly back, heels clicking, as Trudi swayed slightly, a little dizzy with her sudden rising.

'It is in the wardrobe, in the hatbox.'

'How much did you bring?'

'I do not know.'

'Why do you not know?'

'Because it is not my affair, Otto. I am only the courier.'

'Grandfather told me you would also contribute to our cause.'

'I have no money for investments,' Trudi said.

'You should not have married a poor man.'

She opened her mouth to defend Henry or, rather, to explain the circumstances that had led her to marry out of the circle of influence and opportunity which linked the likes of Papa Keller, Marcus Harrison and her ex-husband Clive Coventry. Perhaps that was what Otto despised her for: not her desertion but the fact that she had made nothing of it. How could she possibly explain that it had not been her wish but Papa's, that she had allowed him to be taken from her only because she had not the will to prevent it, because she had been trained from birth to obey.

Trudi said, 'I will fetch the box for you.'

'No,' he said. 'Is it still sealed?'

'As it was given to me.'

'Very well. We will take it together to the office. I will see to it that you reach there safely.'

'And return safely?'

'Naturally. You have nothing to fear from me.'

'Will my papa be there?'

'He will. He must be there to give you a receipt.'

'May I leave a note for my husband, to tell him where I have gone?'

'No. It would not be advisable.'

'But . . .'

'Where is the box?' Otto said.

'There.'

'Good. I will carry it for you. Come.'

Ten minutes later Trudi left the hotel accompanied by her son and, in the back of a black Mercedes, was swept off into the night.

It was neither luck nor coincidence that led Henry to the office in Leipziger Strasse. It was the only address in Berlin that he had in his pocket, the only place he could think of where Trudi might have gone.

He simply did not know where else to begin.

The Office of Acquisitions was housed in a nondescript building above a bookstore, adjacent to the imposing block-long edifice of the Prussian War Ministry. In the ministry lights still burned and the ornate lamp standards, taller than any Henry had ever seen, shed a flickering glow down upon the windy pavements. There were guards by the doors of the ministry. Uniformed men and clerks, female as well as male, came and went from the gates that closed off the interior from the street. It looked threatening and secretive, which the bookstore building did not.

The bookstore building appeared as shabby and harmless as the old tenement warehouses which clustered around Glasgow's Central station. When he looked up at it from the street Henry could see only a couple of lighted windows, green-glazed, close up towards the roof. He had no means of knowing that the office was an annexe of the building in Prinz-Albrecht Strasse, one block behind, where, in the converted Museum of Industrial Art, the Geheime Staatspolizei – the Gestapo – had recently set up shop.

Only one car was parked in front of the bookstore, a sleek black Mercedes with a driver, not in uniform, seated behind the wheel. The glow of a cigar spotlighted his beefy young face. As Henry approached, the driver's eyes rolled towards him, gibbous in the half-light. He took the cigar from his mouth and flicked it through the automobile's side window where it extinguished itself in a splash of sparks almost at Henry's feet. Henry was not deterred. He side-stepped the cigar butt, walked to the car and looked inside.

The driver's expression was arrogant, not suspicious. With more confidence than he felt, Henry thrust the letter he had fished from Trudi's valise towards the car window.

'Do you speak English?' Henry said.

The driver sneered and grabbed the letter before Henry could prevent it.

Henry said, 'There. This building. I have to be here. To meet with my wife and my stepson.'

Apparently the driver did not speak English. Henry had doubts if he was intelligent enough to read his own language. The driver scanned the letter, pointed at the letterhead, jerked his thumb towards the bookstore building, flashed the letter through the window and let it drop, fluttering, to the pavement.

Meekly Henry picked it up. Then he stepped close to the automobile, placed one hand on the roof and the other across the windshield so that his body covered the window space.

He leaned forward until his face was almost inside the car.

Suddenly less sure of himself, the driver squeezed back against the seat.

In good guttural Glaswegian, Henry said, 'Frau Keller, huh?'

The driver was not blond but reddish and had long, almost

effeminate eyelashes which, to Henry's gratification, blinked nervously.

Henry said, 'Gruppenführer Dahrendorf, huh?'

The driver blinked again, then nodded, then scrambled to open the door of the Mercedes and project himself on to the pavement.

He gave a bow, jabbered something which Henry did not understand. He was, Henry realised, hardly more than a boy, a farm boy perhaps, and a head shorter than Henry which certainly aided the cause of intimidation.

Henry tapped himself on the chest. 'Herr Keller.' He sought for the word. '*Sohn. Sohn.* Got it, dimwit? *Sohn. Sohn.* Herr Dahrendorf – *bruder, bruder.*' He pointed up at the bookstore building, held up the letter, tapped his wristlet watch urgently and snapped, 'Now, jump to it, fathead,' which, astonishingly, the driver did.

Seconds later Henry was shown into the building by a doorway in the alley and the driver pressed the lift button for him. The driver was obsequious now; the name Dahrendorf had seemingly done the trick. He smiled at Henry and wagged his head, then pointed up the lift shaft and held up four fingers.

'Fourth floor.' Henry nodded. '*Danke.*'

The driver jabbered something about Gruppenführer Dahrendorf then, with another little bow, backed out of the door and left Henry alone in the hall of the bookstore building.

There were no guards, no signs of activity. The cramped space at the bottom of the staircase was lit by gas, not electricity. The mantles were old, the fittings tarnished. The cage of the elevator was decorated with flat metal fleur-de-lys which, for some reason, made Henry think of Vienna.

The din that the lift made as it ascended was anything but musical, however, and Henry was not surprised when he stepped out of the cage into the dim gas-lit fourth-floor corridor to find someone waiting for him there.

A thin slit of yellow light spilled from an open door and beyond it, in the gloom of the corridor's end, was a tall window, barred with iron.

The man was handsome, white-blond, and wore a tight-fitting black suit.

When he looked into the icy, pale blue eyes, Henry experienced a strange little shock of recognition and knew at once the American had not lied.

'Herr Dahrendorf?' Henry said. 'Gruppenführer Dahrendorf?'

'You are Burnside, are you not?' In English.

'I am,' Henry answered. 'And you, I believe, are my stepson.'

No offer of the hand of friendship, not even one of those clicking little Teutonic bows that represented a stand-offish kind of greeting.

'Why is it that you have come here?' Otto Dahrendorf said.

'To be with my wife.'

'She is quite safe with us.'

'I don't doubt it.' Henry leaned forward and looked pointedly past the young man towards the half-open door. 'Is she in there?'

'She is visiting with us. Did she not inform you of her intention?'

'No, somehow she forgot to do that,' Henry said. 'May I speak with her?'

Otto Dahrendorf hesitated. He appeared to have no curiosity about Henry. His eyes were not inquisitive or troubled. Henry had always prided himself on his ability to hide his feelings but when it came to a stonewall expression Trudi's boy had him beat.

He was surprised, though, at his own lack of reaction to meeting Trudi's son, a relative he hadn't known existed until a few hours ago. Was he still too numb to accept the SS officer for what he was? He didn't feel numb. He felt bright and alert and, oddly, was almost amused by the situation.

If this was Trudi's dark secret, the source of her mystery, then it wasn't so very terrible after all. From what he'd gathered, the kid hadn't even been born out of wedlock but had transformed himself into a bastard by dint of sheer hard work. The really disconcerting thing about Dahrendorf was that he resembled Trudi in so many ways, right down to his stilted rendering of English.

The fact that Dahrendorf was only a year or two younger than he was didn't faze Henry in the least; he *felt* older, much older and wiser than the glorified Boy Scout with his cropped haircut, his martial bearing and stiff, inhibited mannerisms. Dahrendorf also had the disadvantage of being German, of course, saddled with a history of conquest and defeat, with a sense of national pride so intense that it seemed to cancel out all individualism, to make each and every citizen a stubborn conformist and conservative to a fault. Unlike the Scots, the Jerries did not take perverse pleasure in their suppression but had to make an issue out of it.

Henry said, 'Well, Otto, may I speak with her or not?'

'If you will go down below to wait upon the street, she will be with you in a short time.'

'Not good enough,' said Henry. 'I want to see her now.'

'She has business to be attended to.'

'What business?'

'With her papa.'

'Money business,' Henry said. 'The business of what's in the

263

hatbox. Good God, Otto, is this the best you lot can do, to sell shares in a Manchurian cattle-food company to greedy Scotsmen for bucketfuls of hard cash?'

There was no hesitation this time.

Otto Dahrendorf said, 'Perhaps you had better to come in.'

'Really?' said Henry. 'What for, all of a sudden?'

'To meet with Papa,' said Otto and, discarding his manners at last, nudged Henry with his shoulder towards the office's half-open door.

Papa had grown fatter. His belly now was like a huge entity attached to the front of his body by a waistcoat of peacock silk. His dark brown suit had been tailored to contain his monstrous bulk. Even so the jacket bulged across his chest and shoulders and slid up his arms whenever he moved, exposing ruff-like shirt-cuffs and gold links large as pennies. All trace of the suave and graceful man whom Trudi remembered had been consumed by excess flesh and, with his features dragged out of shape by slabby cheeks and jowls, he did not look like her father at all. Only the cap of dark-dyed hair combed into a silly little quiff reminded her that this was the man who had raised her.

In contrast her son was all the things that Papa had never been: lean, hard and disciplined, certainly, but with a mechanical quality to his movements which left no room for gracefulness. She had the impression that Otto hungered not for corporeal pleasure but for pleasures of another kind. And Henry? Henry's height, his dour, dark, handsome features, his essential Scottishness, which she could not even begin to define, seemed, in Trudi's eyes, to give him an advantage over both her father and her son.

She was not particularly surprised by Henry's arrival in the office in the Leipziger Strasse. In fact, she would have been rather disappointed if he had not managed to follow her.

She had made no effort to hide Papa's letter.

She smiled at Henry and, in English, said, 'I see to it you have found me.'

Henry said, 'I wasn't even sure you were lost.'

'I had to come. You understand.'

'I'm beginning to.' Henry jerked his thumb towards Otto. 'Fine boy, Trudi. You should be proud of him.'

'Is it that you know who he is?'

'Sure.'

'I should have told you of him.'

'You should,' Henry said. 'And this is the old man, I reckon.'

'Papa,' Trudi said. 'My husband.'

264

It did not dismay her to be confined in the small, wooden-walled office altogether with her father, her son and her husband. She felt more secure and comfortable now that Henry had arrived.

Otto was as much a stranger to her as she was to him. And Papa behaved as if she was still his little girl, pretty and knowing and malleable. Only Henry really accepted her for what she was and would not hold against her the things she had kept from him about her past.

The desk was too small for Papa. The chair creaked as he hoisted himself up and, stretching, offered Henry his hand.

Henry shook it without much warmth.

Papa Keller said, 'Does she make an interesting wife for you?'

'Oh, aye.' Henry had a cocky little grin upon his mouth, an expression more arrogant than Otto's cold stare. 'I can't imagine a wife more interesting.' He paused, while Papa Keller sank back and enclosed the chair with his buttocks, then he added, 'She's done all kinds of interesting things and knows such interesting people. She fair keeps me on my toes.'

Papa laughed. His jowls wobbled.

'Did you not know about Otto?' he asked.

'Not until tonight.'

'It is peculiar that he recognised me without delay,' Otto said.

There was one vacant chair. Nothing elegant. A plain oak chair with scratched varnish and no cushion. Otto pushed it towards Henry with the sole of his boot and Henry seated himself, side by side with Trudi, both of them before the desk. Otto remained standing, arms folded.

The office was spartan, to say the least of it.

Three telephones upon the desk, together with an untidy pile of banknotes, gave it the impermanent air of a backstreet bookmaker's, through which hard cash flowed like water through a conduit. Light came from a pair of metal-shaded lamps and the window, Henry noticed, was barred like the one in the corridor, only here the bars were new.

'I recognised you only because you look like your mother,' Henry said.

Trudi said, 'Otto will not like you to say that, I do not think.'

Otto said, 'I do not believe you, Herr Burnside.'

'Call me Henry – Otto. We're all family, after all.'

'I am not family to you.'

'You are to her,' Henry said.

'Only by blood.'

'*Only* by blood?' Henry exaggerated his surprise. 'I thought the

265

leader set much store by blood. Hey, you're not going to give me the ultimate big surprise and tell me I'm married to a Jew, are you?'

Otto's mouth opened, his arms swung to his side. He spoke in rapid German to his grandfather who shook his head and jabbered back at the young man. It was the first genuine trace of heat that Henry had detected in either man since he had entered the room. Even Trudi was caught off guard by his remark. She twisted her head and stared at him, eyes round with astonishment.

Henry winked. 'Only kidding, folks,' he said.

'Kidding?' said Otto.

'Joke,' said Henry. 'I make jest, old chap. Smile. Smile.'

'It is not correct to make a joke about the Jews.'

'You're right,' Henry said. 'I apologise.' He placed an elbow lightly on the edge of the desk. 'Blood is not a laughing matter, especially to you Germans. God, it's almost as serious a matter as making money, no?'

'You must not do this, Henry,' Trudi told him.

'Do what, dear? I'm just being conversational.'

'Stop it. You do not understand.'

'Aye, but I do understand. Some of it, anyway,' Henry said. 'I didn't before, Trude, I do now. Now I've lamped your boy, I do.'

'What is it he means?' Otto asked his grandfather.

The fat old man answered in German, quite laconically, Henry thought, given the complexity of the language and the delicacy of the situation.

The Gruppenführer retreated into sulky silence and Papa Keller folded his hands over his enormous belly and leaned back, benign as a Buddha.

He said, 'Is it not the people of Germany you have come to observe and to write into your newspaper stories?'

'It is indeed the people of Germany I have come to report upon,' Henry answered. 'Aren't you the people of Germany?'

'We are not the – what is the word, Trudi?'

'Common people. Ordinary ones.'

'Yes,' said Papa Keller. 'It is the ordinary ones you wish to meet.'

'No,' Henry said. 'I think I really prefer to talk to you and, naturally' – he glanced over his shoulder – 'to Otto.'

'What would it be that we might tell you which would interest the readers of your newspaper in Scotland?' Papa Keller enquired.

'Where that money came from,' said Henry. 'Who sent it. What you're offering in exchange. And, of course, what you intend to buy with it.'

'It is for investment. For the buying of the shares.'

'Shares in bubble companies?' Henry wondered if his father-in-law would understand the expression.

Papa Keller understood perfectly well. He answered, 'They are not bubble companies. We are not cheats.'

'All right,' Henry said. 'I'm just curious as to why the servants of the Third Reich require to smuggle foreign currency into the country in a hatbox if they aren't cheating somebody.'

'Do not ask these questions, Henry,' Trudi warned.

She struggled to hide her anxiety but she had become fearful in the last few minutes. Henry was aware of it but, clearly, had no intention of backing down. How had he learned so much about Papa's 'business'? How had he found out that she had a son and who that son was? What else did Henry know about her? About Papa, Otto, the origins of the money in the box? Did Henry not realise that he was making it ever more difficult for her to pay off her debts and clear her obligations once and for all?

Papa Keller said, 'I have nothing to hide. It is honest work I do here.'

'Except when it flouts the currency restrictions?' Henry said.

Papa Keller spread a fat hand, a gesture of indifference learned in the good old days in Paris. 'Restrictions are made to be broken, if the reasons are correct and the cause is just.'

'The cause?' said Henry. 'Yes, now I'm very interested in the cause.'

'He is asking too many questions,' Otto said.

'Perhaps you are right, Otto,' said Papa Keller. 'I will ask our relative some questions of my own, if he does not object to it.'

'Fire ahead,' said Henry.

'Who told you about Otto, about his high rank in the Schutzstaffel?' Papa Keller asked. 'Was it you, my daughter?'

'How could I tell him?' Trudi blurted out. 'I do not know what Otto does.'

'No, no,' Henry said. 'Trudi never said a word. Cross my heart and cut my throat. She's very discreet, our Trudi. But I expect you know that already, Herr Keller.'

'If not from Trudi how did you learn of him?'

'My editor told me,' Henry said. 'Marcus Harrison.'

'You are not telling me the truth,' Papa Keller said.

'Know old Marcus, do you?'

'He was a partner of my former son-in-law. I met him two times, or three.'

'Before or after – or during – the time you spent in jail?' said Henry.

'This is not what it is you wish to write about,' Papa Keller said.

'Oh, yes, I really think it is,' said Henry. 'Chicanery and double-dealing are always of interest to the great British public, particularly if quite well-known people are involved.'

'Harrison will not allow such lies to be published.'

'Who else is feeding you money, Herr Keller? Clive Coventry, of course. Gerald Dante? Blackstock?' Henry shook his head and answered his own question. 'No, not Blackstock. This is small beer for Blackstock. He'll have other means of funding the German industrial revival, of buying his way into Adolf's good books. Or is all this beneath the leader? Is this something that the leader knows nothing about?'

'Our Leader knows everything,' said Otto, sourly.

'Ah, but does he *understand*?' said Henry. 'Does Adolf have the brains to understand that you're skimming state profits to line your own pockets?'

Otto snarled in German and, with a motion so rapid that it seemed no more than a blur, kicked the chair from under Henry and sent him sprawling to the floor.

'No, Otto,' Trudi shouted. *'Nein. Nein.'*

Her protest came too late. She watched helplessly as her son kicked the side of Henry's head to cut off his accusations and silence his lies, for ever.

NINE

Laying the Ghosts

Henry had no idea where he was or how long he had been unconscious. He came to gradually, aware first of pain, a screaming pain, that ate into the bones of his skull and swirled like fire in his eye sockets. For a single terrifying instant he thought he had been blinded. With tentative fingers he explored his face, found that blood had oozed across his cheek from a swelling on the side of his head. With spittle on his forefinger he cleaned coagulated blood from his lids and, thank God, was able to see again.

What he saw was the inside of a cell. There was nothing to indicate where the cell was sited, whether above ground or below, whether he was a prisoner of the military, the police or of some secret organisation over which Otto Dahrendorf had authority.

In spite of pain and dizziness, Henry could clearly recall the events that had led up to Otto Dahrendorf's attack. For that reason, he did not leap to his feet and begin yelling for release. He lay motionless on his side on the cement floor and tried to take stock of his situation.

A wan bulb encased in heavy mesh was set into the ceiling high overhead. A white enamel basin with a blue rim stood on the floor near his feet, beyond it a metal pail. No other furnishing. No bed, table, chair. He rolled on to his elbow, wincing, and looked towards the heavy wooden door. A small mesh grille at eye level admitted a postcard of brilliant light.

For the time being Henry ignored the door which, he reckoned, would be securely locked and barred on the outside.

Except for the throbbing in his head he didn't feel too bad. He was fairly sure he hadn't been worked over by Otto or one of Otto's henchmen. Talk among newspapermen made sound sense now, however. He had found out something he shouldn't have, had challenged a high-ranking officer of the Reich and insulted his integrity. Otto Dahrendorf was making him pay for it. He wondered, still without panic, if they would kill him. It would be a very simple matter to arrange his disappearance.

269

Only Trudi knew what he had been up to and presumably where he had been taken. He wondered if Trudi had enough clout to ensure that he didn't wind up floating in the Spree or buried in a corner of the Tiergarten. A little cloud of doubt about Trudi's loyalties crossed over Henry's thoughts. Then drifted swiftly away. If he couldn't trust his wife who could he trust?

At least the American hadn't lied to him. Berlin *was* a dangerous place to speak your mind. Papa Keller and young Dahrendorf were engaged in a fiddle of some sort, one that involved Harrison and Clive Coventry as either victims or accomplices. Probably accomplices. He had fallen on that information by luck and guesswork and his brush with Otto Dahrendorf had confirmed it. Exactly what the fiddle entailed and how Papa Keller creamed off profit hardly mattered. Currency speculation and shady share dealing had always been Clive Coventry's *forte*. Old Papa Keller had served time for it, had, as the Americans put it, taken the rap for Clive.

Perhaps this latest piece of financial skulduggery, however officially blessed it appeared to be, was nothing but a payback to Keller for all his years in prison. Even if he did discover how the system worked Henry doubted if he would be able to make sense of it. What mattered – and what made him really mad – was that Trudi had been drawn into the scheme against her will and that his 'trip' to Germany had never been anything but a cover for fascist profiteers back home, the editor of the *Mercury* among them.

Groaning aloud, Henry struggled to his knees.

The cell was windowless. He had no means of knowing whether it was night or day. He swayed, steadied himself with a hand on the wall, as clammy and cold as the skin of a flounder. He leaned his shoulder against it, breathing deeply, gathering his strength.

How long would it take Trudi to get him out? How long would they – whoever 'they' might be – dare hold him without a charge? How would they make sure he kept his mouth shut? Or, and this sudden thought made his head ache more ferociously than ever, did they hope to wring information from him? Did they suppose he had a source in Berlin, some contact who might imperil their operation? If they started that . . . No. He put the thought firmly to one side and concentrated on standing upright.

He was thirsty, hungry too, a fact which suggested he had been out cold for some considerable time.

Water in the bottom of the enamel basin was none too clean. Henry swallowed his saliva and ignored it. He relieved himself into the bucket, and was glad to see that he passed no blood. He fretted a little about the headache, wondered if the kick had caused serious injury, if this muzziness, along with the pain, was what concussion felt like.

He would ask Ally as soon as he got back home.

The screaming started again, suddenly. Henry's blood ran cold.

It was the same screaming which had first penetrated his consciousness, screaming which he'd assumed was some sort of head-noise, screaming which stemmed from inflamed nerves, something he'd imagined.

Nothing imaginary about it. All too real. He had never heard screams like it, great shrill whips of sound that echoed along the corridor outside. He crouched in a corner of the cell and, wincing again, clapped his hands over his ears. He could not stifle that sound, could not even muffle it. At first he thought that it must be a boy, a young boy, who uttered those hideous, high-pitched cries. Then the thought occurred to him that it might be a woman.

Henry took his hands from his ears and, shuffling to his feet, forced himself to the door, forced himself to press his cheek against the woodwork and peer through the little grille.

'Trudi?' he shouted. 'Trudi?'

The screaming stopped as suddenly as it had started.

There was no other sound in the corridor.

Sweat stood out on Henry's brow. He clenched his fists over the lip of the little aperture and crushed his face against the door to see as much of the corridor as possible.

The light was not artificial. Sunlight. March sunlight. So the cells were not situated underground. Something about the volume of light suggested that it was morning, that the window to the outside must be large and south-facing. Henry's perspectives were limited but across the corridor he could make out the doors of several other cells, identical to his own.

One cell door stood tantalisingly open. Within the narrow room a naked woman lay twisted upon the floor.

'Trudi? Trudi?' Henry bellowed, before he could help himself.

Then, when the woman did not move, he realised that the figure was not flesh and blood but a plaster cast, a sculpture, and that the racks behind it were not instruments of torture but workmen's ladders.

Henry let his head fall back, tears in his eyes, and muttered, sobbing, 'Jesus! Aw, Jesus!' His relief was short-lived.

The screaming started up once more.

It rang, rang and echoed like an aria from the corridor to his left. He flattened himself against the door and squinted through the grid. He could see nothing. No guards. No uniforms. Only the long half-

271

tiled corridor which seemed more suited to a school than a prison, the blank, bolted doors, the plaster model lying, obscenely still, on the floor across from him.

The screaming seemed to come out of the sunlight, like a voice from the heavens, the membraneous veils of whitish dust which gave the light shape and definition unmoved by it.

Beating his fists in fury upon the door, Henry shouted, '*Stop it. Stop it. For Christ's sake, stop whatever you're doing to her.*'

After two or three seconds, as if in obedience to Henry's command, the screaming ceased abruptly. Sweat and tears slicking his face, Henry rested his brow against the door. He shivered with revulsion and selfish fear.

A voice said, in English, 'They cannot hear you, my friend.'

Henry peered through the grille again.

He couldn't make out where the voice had come from until the man spoke again. 'And if they could hear you, they would not listen. It is not a woman they have taken downstairs today, however. It is a boy, a young boy. He screams for his mama.'

'What are they doing to him?'

'They make fun of him. You are a Schottlander, yes?'

'Yes.'

He could just discern the shape of a head, the outline of features, in the grille of the door diagonally across the corridor from him. The shape was shaggy, blurred by the slanting of light. There was something vaguely familiar about it though, or, more accurately, about the heavily accented speech.

Henry said, 'Who are you?'

The man said, 'I was in Schottland in the recent time. Before this began in Europe. I talk to students at the university.'

'Listen,' Henry said, cautiously. 'Where are we? I mean, what sort of place is this?' He lowered his voice to a stage whisper. 'Where are the guards?'

'Watching the fun which is down below,' the Russian answered. 'They have taken away the guards of the majority. What need is there for them to be here? There is only one stairs up from the south wing, one locked door to it. You cannot get out. Your friends will not be strong enough to get in.'

'Where exactly are we?'

'Number 8, Prinz-Albrecht Strasse.'

'What is that? I mean,' Henry whispered, 'is it a police station, or what?'

The Russian said something inaudible and in a cell directly to Henry's right somebody laughed scornfully.

'Who's that?'

'Karl. He speaks so little of the English.'

'Why's he laughing then?'

'Only a Schottlander would not know what this place is,' the Russian said. 'It is the old Industrial School, now for the Staatspolizei.'

'Police?'

'The State Police. Gestapo.'

Henry said, 'You're Kurtz, aren't you? Vladimir Kurtz.'

The unseen man in the next cell growled something that sounded like a warning and, for almost half a minute, there was no sound from either cell.

Henry said, 'I was in the university, in the Maitland Hall in Scotland. I know you didn't get to speak. You said nothing to the students for a riot broke out and the debate broke up in confusion.'

'How you were there?' said Kurtz.

'I'm a journalist.'

'The newspaper?'

It was Henry's turn to hesitate.

At length he said, 'The *Mercury.*'

'You write bad things, wrong things,' Kurtz said. 'I hear your name from a girl but it has gone from me.'

'Burnside,' Henry told him. 'I didn't report anything that wasn't true.'

'See, see where your writing of the truth has got to you.'

'I haven't even written it yet,' Henry said. 'Listen, how did they catch you? I thought you were in Paris. I mean, working for *Pravda*, safe in Paris.'

'Not safe in Paris,' Kurtz told him.

'You were arrested in Paris? On what charge?'

'Charge? I am *Kommunist*. I am, in France too, *Rind-Lammfleisch*. Red meat. I am taken from there and brought here to Berlin. Because I am wanted here. I am just trade goods for the French. There are none more selfish even here in Germany, than are the French. Also, none more afraid.'

'What will they do to you?'

Another hesitation, then Kurtz said, 'They want me to give them names.'

'What, fellow travellers?'

'Call them what you like,' said Kurtz. 'I will not do this thing.'

'Can't they make you?'

'I am not like the boy. I do not scream aloud.'

Henry said, 'How long have you been here?'

'Fifteen days.'

'How long do you think they'll keep me?'

'It depends what it is you have done to harm them, in their opinion.'

'I think,' Henry said, 'I put the wind up an SS officer.'

'Struck him?'

'No, just . . . Come to think of it,' Henry said, 'I'm not sure what I did.'

'That is the way of it with so many,' Kurtz told him. 'It is the advantage I have which you do not. I know what I have done and why I am here.'

The man in the next cell spoke: French, Henry thought. He listened to the low, grumbling voice, very calm and stoical, but he could pick up no more than the gist of what was being said. Kurtz did not answer the man and Henry, bursting with questions now, did not dare interrupt.

After a pause, Kurtz said, 'Karl thinks that you have been put here to get me to talk. Is that why you are here, Monsieur Burnside?'

'God, no,' said Henry.

'It is Karl's opinion that I would not be wise to answer your questions.'

Henry said, 'I can understand Karl's suspicion. To tell you the truth, I've come around to thinking you can't trust anyone either. Look, how would it be if I asked you when we get fed?'

'You are hungry?'

'Starving.'

'Soup at noon. It is how we make mark of the time. In the evening, about five, half past, we are given potato stew.'

'No coffee,' Karl said in English, and for some reason, laughed.

Henry said, 'Perhaps they'll send you to one of the camps. My wife says that's what happens to communists.'

'How does your wife know what happens to the red meat?'

Henry said, 'She reads the German newspapers. And the French.'

'She is then an educated woman?'

'Yes,' said Henry.

'She is German?'

'Swiss.'

'She is with you here in Berlin?'

'Yes.'

'She will get you out.'

'I certainly hope so,' Henry said. 'Are they really torturing a young boy?'

'That is what they do here, sometimes.'

274

'But why, for God's sake? I mean what can he possibly know?'

'His father was a leader in the Catholic Centre Party. He organised meetings at which the National Socialists had no representation. He has vanished into the hiding. Taken some powder, as you say. They wish to make an example of him, to frighten the other Catholics. They think the boy knows where his father is and that, if they have enough fun with him, he will tell them.'

'Will he?'

'He has been here four days. If he could tell them anything, he would have told it to them by this time now.'

Henry said, 'I didn't know it was like this. I mean – Jesus!'

Kurtz said, 'The boy, if they are clever they will take him from here to the camps. They will bring his mother to see him and she will tell them all that she knows. She will see that her son is dying and she will tell where her husband is. It will not stop the boy from dying but they will get what it is they want. Do you have insight yet into what it is they want?'

'Power?' said Henry.

'Revenge,' said Vladimir Kurtz.

'For what?'

'For losing the war.'

'No,' Henry said. 'There must be more to it than that.'

'More. Yes, much more,' Kurtz agreed. 'But it is not for you to worry about, Herr Burnside. You will be given your freedom. You will go back to your homeland and publish more lies about the communists and, perhaps, also about the Jews, because it is required by your job.'

Henry wiped his mouth with the back of his hand. He had a salty thirst, quite tormenting, and the swelling on the side of his head was throbbing again. How could he complain about such minor discomforts in the presence of men who, if he understood them correctly, were about to be tortured, possibly killed.

He felt suddenly reduced, almost unmanned by his privileges.

What Kurtz said was true: he did not belong here. This was not his country or his struggle. He had come to Germany out of mild curiosity and to further his career as a journalist. He recalled the riot – the romp – in the Maitland and how important it had made him feel to be embroiled in Maggie Chancellor's little machinations. But all that Glasgow stuff, in retrospect, looked like comic opera.

'At least,' Henry said, at length, 'you won't have to invent this adventure, Kurtz. Think of the book you're going to be able to write about how Hitler really did make you his prisoner. Another bestseller, maybe?'

'Oh, sure, sure,' Vladimir Kurtz said, softly.

And Karl, from the cell next door, called out, '*Pst*, Vlad. Here they come.'

It was one of those magnificent mornings which reminded Trudi of her youth. Spring flowers bloomed on the lawns of the park and in the dark earth of the flowerbeds that lined the broad walks below the terrace of the Spreegarten Café. The sun glittered on the river and on the lake and along the paths that wended between birch trees and pines uniformed officers and their aides rode their horses, black and chestnut and grey, with a vigour that was in itself exhilarating.

The air was still cold, however, and a brisk little breeze from the north snapped at the flags that floated above the café and flapped the scalloped edges of the awnings that gave shade to the rear of the terrace. It was the first week of the new season and most of the women who met there for coffee were dressed in furs. Even the officers who sprawled at the white-painted tables wore greatcoats, though they had flung them open to show off their insignia. They stretched their black-booted legs, smoked, laughed and eyed the women arrogantly while the waiters glided between the tables with silver trays. You could smell strong fresh coffee, hot pork sandwiches and warm Viennese cakes dripping with cream and sprinkled with rich chocolate.

Trudi did not feel out of place among the well-dressed women of the Spreegarten. She had always been at home with the bourgeoisie. The fact that her coat was a little old-fashioned did not matter for she was slender still, and of a certain age, and could carry it off well enough.

The black Mercedes had collected her at the Adlon at half past ten o'clock. Those newspapermen who were still hanging around the foyer had watched her depart with unashamed curiosity. Had watched the boys bring down her luggage and put it into the boot of the black Mercedes. Had watched her sweep across the foyer, lay the room keys down upon the desk and, without a word of farewell or any attempt to pay the bill, go out into the strasse and be carried away.

If she had given the newspapermen an opportunity they might have spoken to her at last. Asked polite questions about the absence of her husband or the owner of the automobile. But she gave them no such opportunity, and, in any case, would have told them nothing for fear of hurting Henry.

She did not know where they had taken Henry. She had watched him being carried out of the office in the Leipziger Strasse by two plain-clothed policemen whom Otto had summoned by telephone and who had arrived within minutes of the summoning. She had been unable to attend to Henry. Had been held in the chair by Otto's fists, pressing down. Papa had held her hands in his across the desk and had assured her that everything would be all right, that Henry would be all right. Because she believed him, she did nothing that she was not told to do, or almost nothing.

She had been driven back, very late, to the Adlon. Had gone to her room. Had bathed. Had fixed her hair. Put on her make-up. Had laid out her best, warm dress and the coat with the fur collar.

Following instructions, she had packed her bags and Henry's. Had placed them by the door. Then she had seated herself on the chair facing the table with the telephone upon it and, wide awake, had waited for morning and the call she knew was bound to come because Papa had told her that she would receive further instructions in the morning and, in this matter at least, she knew he would keep his word.

Now here she was. In the Spreegarten. Papa opposite her at the round, white-painted table. Papa eating a hot pork sandwich. Wiping butter from his lips with his forefinger. Papa, fat as a burgomeister and dressed like a baron. Smiling. As if nothing at all had happened.

Three or four hundred yards away on a spur of metalled road that led into the park from the Brandenburger she could make out the shape of the black Mercedes behind juniper bushes and railings. The driver strolled up and down, appearing and disappearing, the smoke from his cigar like a fleck of cream in the sharp morning air.

Papa was jovial. Pleased to be with her. Dealing.

He said, 'You should eat something, Trudi. You are too skinny.'

'I thought you liked me skinny.'

'It is not fitting for an old married woman.'

'If I am old, what are you?'

'I am in my second flowering, daughter.'

'Like Berlin.'

'Ouff!' he said. 'I wish I could believe that I will be here to see how Berlin – how Germany – will flourish. What a flowering that will be now the leader has taken power at last.'

'How long will the germinating process take?' Trudi asked.

'Ten years.' Papa shrugged.

'Not fifty, not a hundred? Like the Empire of the Romans?'

'We are not Italians, Trudi. When we set our minds to something it will get done well and quickly. We are such a positive people. But why should I tell you that, when you are one of us.'

'In the blood,' Trudi stated.

'Yes, in the blood.' He put the last of the sandwich into his mouth. Chewed. He sipped coffee, put down the cup. 'He is perfectly safe. A headache, that's all. You do not have to see him again, if you do not wish it. He can be sent home without you. He will surely understand how it is.'

'He is not like Clive, Papa.'

'I can see with my eyes how different he is from Coventry,' Papa Keller said. 'What I cannot see is what *you* see in him.'

'I love him.'

'Why do you love him? Is he – a Scotsman – so good a lover?'

'He takes care of me. He will always take care of me.'

'Even now, after what he has found out about you?'

'Yes,' Trudi answered without hesitation. 'Even now.'

But she was not at all sure how Henry would react now that he had been forced to face up to the truth about what she had been and what she had done before he'd met and married her. She knew Henry. Henry would regard her betrayal as a symptom of a much larger betrayal, a betrayal of his family. And it was not just Henry she clung to. She clung to the Burnsides too, to each and every one of them. Small-minded folk, uncertain of their role in life, but so honest, so stubborn in their loyalties that she felt more secure with them than she had ever done with Papa.

She said, 'Where is he? Where have you taken my husband?'

'He is not far away.' Her father paused. Not smiling now. 'Why do you not ask me where Otto is, Trudi? Why do you not ask me about your son?'

'I have no need to ask about Otto. I can see what Otto has become.'

'One does not become elevated to the rank of an SS-Gruppenführer, Trudi, unless one has a very great deal to offer to the Reich. He is destined to become a star in the firmament of the New Order. He is very clever, very industrious. He has laboured hard to attain his present position. Surely you would not take it away from him?'

It hadn't occurred to Trudi before that she might ruin her son's career. She had thought that her father's fears were all for himself, that he was the one who ran the risk of being disgraced, of serving another spell in prison, perhaps.

'These weeks are important to Otto,' Papa Keller went on. 'He is not just an officer for parades, for saluting guardsmen. I will tell you something in very great confidence. On the first day of April General Goering will dismiss Rudolf Diels from his command of the State Secret Police. The Gestapo is not what you imagine it to be. It is a precision instrument and Diels has served Hermann very well. He will be rewarded with some other position, as suits his breeding and his talent. Do these names mean anything to you, Trudi?'

'I have read something of them in the newspapers.'

'The man who will assume command of the Gestapo is Heinrich Himmler and a new epoch in history will begin.'

'What does this have to do with Otto?'

'Otto is General Goering's man. He will observe the fusion and will represent SS interests in the period of transition.'

'And he will work as Himmler's subordinate?'

'For a time, yes,' Papa Keller said.

'But he will still be Hermann Goering's man?'

'He always will be.'

'I understand,' Trudi said. 'And what of your position?'

'I am too old to take much part.'

'And too modest, Papa?' Trudi said.

He did not laugh at her little remark. He slid his fat hand across the iron table and gripped her wrist. 'I am important to Otto. I give him all my support – from the back of the shop, if you understand me.'

Trudi nodded. 'Funding.'

With his left hand Papa fashioned a Parisian gesture, ungainly because of the thickness of his fingers, the width of his wrist. *'Comme ci comme ça.'*

'It is official?' Trudi asked.

'Hermann – General Goering is aware of what we do. He will benefit too.'

Trudi nodded once more. 'You will give Henry back to me? You can make Otto do it. I know you can.'

'Of course I can.'

'What do you want from me in exchange?' Trudi enquired.

'You must persuade your husband to say nothing, to write nothing, to go home and behave as if nothing at all had happened to him here,' Papa said.

'I do not have that much influence over him.'

'Oh, I believe that you do, daughter. If he loves you, he will do it.'

'Why should he do it? Why should I do it?'

'Because Otto is your flesh and blood.'

'As you are?'

'Yes, for Otto – and for me,' her father said. 'So that we will both be safe.'

'If I agree to this, will you send Henry back to me?'

'You may fetch him yourself. Immediately.'

'And then?'

'You will leave Berlin by the afternoon train.'

'What is the alternative?'

'For you to stay here with us.'

'As a hostage?' Trudi said.

'I would not put it in that manner,' her father said. 'Do you not see how I depend upon you, Trudi? I trust you to keep your husband quiet.'

'How will you secure his release?'

'It is already done,' Papa Keller said. 'All I need now is your promise that you will keep your husband silent.'

He lifted her hand and kissed it, as if she was his lover, not his daughter. It was with that same gesture, almost thirty years ago, that he had kissed her mother's dead hand. Trudi had a flash of recollection, not of tenderness, of tears, but of the perfunctory manner in which he had let her mama go, let the hand drop and slither back into the coffin before the coffin was sealed and taken away.

'Your word, Trudi, that is all I require.'

'My solemn word,' Trudi said.

'Yes.'

'You have it, Papa. I will do what you ask of me.'

He took the manila envelope from the pocket of his overcoat and passed it to her across the table.

Out of habit, he glanced this way and that and, Trudi noticed, gave a simpering, apologetic little smile to the grey-clad officers who were watching from a nearby table. She knew what he was saying to them, that this was some kind of payment for favours of another sort, something simple, something sexual. She felt her cheeks redden not with embarrassment but with anger.

'It is an order for your husband's release,' Papa told her. 'Take it to number 8, Prinz-Albrecht Strasse. Give it to the officer in charge of detention, in the south wing. He will bring your husband to you and you will be free to leave. My chauffeur will escort you to the railway station.'

'Whose signature is upon the document?'

'General Goering's.'

'Is that true?' Trudi said.

'It will unlock any door in Berlin, that signature.'

Trudi hesitated, the envelope pressed to her breast.

'Did he – did he remember me, Papa?' Trudi asked. 'Hermann, I mean?'

'Fondly,' Herr Keller said.

Rising, he kissed her hand again then stepped down from the

terrace and waddled quickly off through the sharp spring sunlight, leaving the *chauffeureska* from the black Mercedes to see her safely away.

Osnabrück, Hanover, Rotterdam, the morning ferry from the Hook of Holland; Harwich to Liverpool Street, London to Glasgow; in thirty hours they would be home again. The train had rolled out of the *Stadtbahn* exactly on time and the last image Trudi had had of the great city of Berlin was of Papa's beefy-featured chauffeur, hands in his overcoat pockets and a cigar in his mouth, observing her departure from the platform's edge.

As soon as the train was in motion she'd looked across the compartment at her husband and had said, 'What was it they did to you, Henry?'

He'd answered, 'Nothing.'

The flesh of his cheek was badly swollen. Bruising, blue and purple, had almost closed his left eye, the pupil reduced to a dark little sliver under the lash. The right eye too had been flat and dead and there had been nothing in Henry's expression to indicate what he was thinking or what he felt about her. He'd said hardly a word since she'd collected him from the vast, echoing hallway of Gestapo headquarters.

She'd had to wait a half-hour while the authority of the letter was confirmed and, she'd guessed, while her husband was made to wash and given a razor to shave with. He'd appeared at the south end of the echoing corridor dressed exactly as he'd been the night before. Haggard and bruised but not dishevelled. She'd noticed that the guards had not handled him, that they'd permitted him to walk a little ahead of them. Had even raised their hands to wave him goodbye.

He'd said nothing in the automobile. Had not seemed surprised to see her, to be told that they were leaving Berlin. Hadn't asked a single question and, in response to her questions, had answered in monosyllables, or not at all.

They'd drunk coffee and had eaten rolls in the railway station. The chauffeur had been there all the time, at a separate table, watching them as if he was bored with their company. Henry too had seemed bored. He'd waited with dull, stone-like patience for their train to be announced and had left it to her to find a porter to carry the luggage to their compartment. No sleeping berths had been available at short notice but the chauffeur, just by his presence, had cleared a compartment for them.

They'd been alone when the train had left Berlin. Alone and silent.

At seven o'clock, because she'd insisted on it, they'd spent the last of their spare marks on dinner in the dining-car. She'd had no hunger to begin with but the more she ate the hungrier she'd become. Henry too, though it obviously pained him to chew, had eaten all that was put before him and had drunk more than half the bottle of Hock that Trudi had ordered.

They had sat for a long time in the dining-car, smoking, looking out at the dark landscape, pricked with the lights of towns and villages.

And they had said nothing, had nothing to say. Not yet.

And they had slept in the compartment, Henry's head resting against the mottled plush, Trudi's head upon his shoulder, her hair silvery.

Somewhere, far out, he had put an arm about her and had drawn her close to him. And when she'd wakened at the Dutch border for customs and passport inspection, Henry had already been awake, his eyes fixed upon the daylight that dithered in the window, fixed and expressionless, flat and unrevealing as strips of zinc.

'Henry?'

'What?'

'Is it that you have pain?'

'No,' he said. 'Not now.'

They had waited until they'd boarded the ferry and it had cast off before they'd eaten breakfast. Then, rounding the Hook, they had watched the boat steam out into the brisk, slapping waves of the North Sea.

Now cloud scudded through the sunshine and gulls held clean and white in the long furrow of the wake and the flatlands lay like wisps of brown smoke all along the starboard and Henry, full of bacon and eggs and hot coffee, leaned against the railing with his hat folded into his pocket and his hair blowing about his bruised face. Trudi stood beside him, holding his elbow.

Henry looked back, back at the flatlands, the smoke-brown rim, the edge of Europe. Then he said, 'What did you have to do to get me out, Trudi?'

'I have to make him a promise.'

'Who? Dahrendorf?'

'My father.'

'What sort of promise?'

'That you would say nothing about what happened.'

She clung to his arm, watching him intently while gulls shrieked and the wash spread out, all foam and cream, into the dark currents that surrounded the coast.

At length Henry said, 'Do you know who built this ship?'

'No,' Trudi answered, then added, 'Ransome's?'

'My old man worked on her, long time ago, when he was an apprentice. I never did. She was before my time, this one. He used to tell me about her. They were very proud of her, the biggest ferryboat on the North Sea crossings.' He turned, leaned his back against the rail. 'My dad probably held the hammer that punched in those rivets. They last, don't they? Ships, I mean.'

'Henry, I am sorry.'

'Aye, well, that's the way of it,' Henry said.

'Will you keep silent?' she asked him.

'Is there any reason why I should?'

'What was it they did to you?' Trudi asked suddenly.

'I told you – nothing.'

'Then you will keep silent?' she said again. 'For me?'

'Because of the boy, because of Dahrendorf?'

'He is of my flesh and blood, Henry.'

'Family,' Henry said, nodding.

'No, you are my family.'

'You should have told me about him, Trudi.'

'Yes, that much I should have done. I am sorry, darling. Truly sorry.'

He continued to stare upward at the plume of smoke which billowed away from the hot, blue-painted funnel.

In his eyes, what she could see of them behind the flicker of black hair, was something that had never been there before. She did not know how to interpret it, whether it was hatred or disgust, anger or suspicion. Did not know if it was a positive emotion which is left when something falls away and is lost.

'It's not your fault,' Henry said. 'Not entirely.'

'What will happen, Henry? I am meaning, to us?'

'It's too soon to say,' Henry told her then, taking Trudi's arm, led her below to shelter from the cold sea breeze which in the space of the last few seconds had turned her face quite white.

The funeral was just what you would have expected for someone as important as Robert Veitch Logie. He would have been gratified by the turnout and by the praises heaped upon his memory by the Reverend William Bland. Lodge brethren were out in force. They crowded together on the left of the aisle which split the baronial splendour of Meldrum Old Parish Church, a phalanx of blue and black serge with bowler hats perched in a row along the hymnary shelf like, Alison thought, so many old-fashioned bed-pans. Medical colleagues, not including Miss Ryan, and fellow enthusiasts from

Veitch's photographic club filled the rows before the altar and left the whole of the right side for relatives, close and distant, and a spraddle of unclassifiable mourners, into which latter category Howard and Alison fell.

If Guy was conspicuous by his absence Declan Slater most certainly was not. Nor was Declan's family – inconspicuous, that is. That was the problem, the source of suppressed outrage and of the outbreaks of grousing which marred an otherwise dignified service.

Two or three times the Reverend Bland was obliged to glower at the brethren below him and once he seemed on the point of delivering a reprimand. Indeed, he might have done so if he had not also still been boiling with righteous indignation at the sight of a priest loitering outside the church door and concern that the strangers who were propped up in the gallery might be crossing themselves and surreptitiously tolling their rosaries. As if that wasn't bad enough, what galled the minister and Veitch's relatives even more was that the widow, daughter and son-in-law-to-be didn't seem to give a tinker's curse for convention and shed no tears at all during the oration.

The only person to make public mention of the strangers in the gallery was Sir Hugh Shaw Hutchinson, Bart., Honorary President of Wellmeadow Hospital board and a fellow not well known for tact. In the few minutes allowed him for the professional eulogy Sir Hugh referred to the spread of Veitch Logie's influence and welcomed – welcomed? – those who had travelled from across the seas to pay their last respects. At this, every head turned, every eye squinted up at the hearty old buffer in tweeds and mourning band, and the six very Irish-looking gentlemen who seemed more inclined to *gravitas* than anyone else in the kirk.

It was all Alison could do not to laugh out loud.

Howard, though, was slightly less amused.

Even after four years of medical training Howard had not managed to discover let alone excise the legacy of religious prejudice which had been handed down to him from both sides of his family.

When the service had been concluded and the coffin removed to the hearse to be transported from the sunny heights of Meldrum Street to the old parish kirkyard, around the corner and down the hill, the Orangemen held a series of rapidly convened meetings while the women were separated and penned against the gable wall, Bobs and her mother amongst them.

Declan was here, there and everywhere. He wore a smart black threepiece suit which, Alison learned later, he had filched from young Veitch's home wardrobe and had had professionally altered overnight by a city-centre tailor. He also wore a starched white shirt with a startlingly high collar, and a long black silk tie so effulgently knotted that it lent him the air not of a surgeon in the making but, rather, of a poet whose star was on the rise.

He came sliding through the crowd, moving easily among the freemasons with bows, handshakes and smiles; organising cars, wreaths and flowers and generally behaving as if he, and not Roberta's brothers, were the natural heir to and inheritor of all the responsibility that old Veitch Logie had shed by dying suddenly among the dinner plates.

'Howard. Alison. How decent of you to come. Now, you'll be at the grave for the committal, Howard, but Alison . . .'

'I understand,' Alison said.

Men might bury women, it seemed, but not the other way around. Tradition still prohibited the presence of females at the laying to rest.

Declan, talking low and fast, said, 'Bobs would like you to go back to the house, take a spot o' lunch with us. There'll be quite a crowd.'

'Your folks, Declan?' Howard said.

'Sure, my folks too.'

'Why did you fetch them over?' Howard asked.

Declan glanced round, smiled at someone, shrugged. 'Had to be happenin' sometime. And this was a perfect opportunity, don't you think?' He put his hand on Howard's shoulder and fixed his gaze on his old chum's face. 'They came to pay their respects to Daphne and to be meetin' Bobs. Two birds with one stone.'

'My God!' said Howard, under his breath.

'Come to the burial, Howard, okay?'

'All right, all right,' Howard said testily then, as Declan slipped away again, hand outstretched to greet another guest, he rounded on Alison and said, 'What about you? What are you going to do?'

'I don't know. I should go back for lunch, I suppose.'

'Why?'

'Well, Roberta was our friend.'

'Was?'

'I don't suppose we'll see much of her in future.'

'No, I don't suppose we will,' Howard said, 'not now Declan's got his claws in her. Look at her, though. You'd think she was *enjoying* herself.'

'Perhaps she is,' Alison said.

Black suited Roberta. The trim, bosomy topcoat, sheer black silk stockings, new patent leather shoes. Even the hat with the veil turned back, dramatic and formal in contrast to her curled blonde hair and peach-bloom cheeks. She was not 'showing' yet, at least not much, and her eyes were blue and merry in the airy light that capped the hilltop. She held her mother's hand. My angel seemed less than overcome. She was conversing animatedly with the tweed-clad gent with the crape armband and with the young priest who had loitered outside during the service.

'I wonder if he had to get a special dispensation to attend?' Alison said.

'Who? The priest? Of course he did.'

Noticing her friends Roberta waved and Alison, leaving Howard behind, went over to offer her condolences.

There was activity around the back of the hearse now and the Orangemen had obviously made up their minds to see Logie off, even if it cost them a few principles to do so. Declan was overseeing the arrangement of wreaths and the disposition of the motorcars that would carry those and such as those back from the graveyard to the house in Dowanhill.

Roberta pulled away from her mother and took both Alison's hands in hers. 'Did Declan ask you to lunch with us?'

'Yes. Yes, he did. But . . .'

'Oh, do come, Ally,' Roberta urged. 'I've *so* much to tell you. I just don't know where to begin. *Please* say you'll come.'

Alison glanced over her shoulder at Howard who, with hands in pockets, frowned at her and shook his head.

'All right, Bobs,' Alison said, reluctantly.

'Declan will find you transport,' Roberta said. 'See you later, Ally.'

'See you, Bobs,' said Alison.

Now that spring had come to the moorland plateau the days no longer seemed to pale one into the other and there were diversions to mark out the progress of the week. Flowers had leapt up in the oval beds and the shrubs had taken on a sheen that had not been there a fortnight ago. The tint of the hills had altered too, greening out from dun, though ribbons of snow still lingered in clefts and crannies and the mountains away to the north were capped with white. Rabbits had appeared again upon the lawns behind the rhododendrons. Squirrels were active in and around the huge grey beech trees by the gates and cats, of which Ottershaw had many, lay about on the terraces, licking their paws and sunning their bellies and rolling now and then in lazy animal ecstasy.

Wrapped up warm in his brown-bear cardigan and Ruby-knitted scarf, Jim had taken his hour-long walk, twice around the grounds. He was resting now in the hour before lunch out on a canvas recliner on the flagstones which bounded the lawns.

A couple of blankets covered him and, at Nurse Pringle's insistence, he had taken off his shoes and put on an extra pair of woollen socks. He was warm enough with the sun upon him, but restless somehow, not able to relax away into sleep. He wore a pair of the blue-tinted spectacles that were handed out to all terrace patients and had carried with him, hidden under his cardigan, a copy of a Sydney Horler thriller that his teacher friend Boris had brought him along with a tin of cigarettes, which latter gift had, of course, been confiscated.

Boris had delivered school news with his customary cynical wit. Jim had enjoyed the contact with the outside world. He had been only temporarily engaged, however, and had not been entirely sorry when Boris had left and he could sink down into himself once more, into that state of rather agitated contemplation which passed for restorative rest.

The Horler novel remained unopened under the blankets. He had too much to think about and not enough, not *quite* enough energy to think with. He stretched his arm above his head and half closed his eyes so that sunshine on the blue lenses created a kind of marine twilight, as if he was floating beneath the surface of a tropical sea.

He heard her coming, heard the scrape of her shoes on the flags, the little grunting noises she uttered as she climbed the four shallow stone steps at the terrace's end and navigated between the other beds and recliners that faced the late morning sun.

Jim lay motionless until her shadow fell across him and darkened the spectacle lenses almost to black.

'Hello, Winnie,' he said. 'Long time, no see.'

'I thought you were asleep.'

'Well, I'm not.'

'I've brought you some fruit. Oh, and a pair of mittens from Connie.'

'Mittens,' Jim said, still not stirring. 'That's handy.'

'Is that supposed to be a joke?'

'Not really,' he said. 'Why are you here, Win? Is something up?'

'You don't seem very concerned, even if something was up.'

'Time enough to be concerned when you tell me what it is.'

'It's Mother.'

'I thought it might be,' Jim said. He removed the tinted spectacles and, sighing, said, 'Well?'

'She wants to come and live with me.'

Jim sat up so abruptly that he felt dizzy for a second. He screwed his eyes tight shut and opened them again. If Winnie noticed his distress she chose not to remark upon it. She towered over him, heavy-featured, bristle-haired.

Off to his right he could see the patients who had become his friends propped up in beds or lying in that ordered way they somehow managed to adopt for rest periods: Mr Gollan, Bill Phipps, young Gus Cameron who, Alison had told him, was not making much of a fight of it. They could not help but overhear, for Winnie's voice had developed a strident note this past half-year as if, driven by loneliness, she had abandoned reticence and wanted now to be heard.

Jim swung his feet to the ground. 'Who let you in?'

'Nurse Pringle said it would be all right, provided I didn't stay too long.'

'Why didn't you wait for visiting hour?' Jim said.

'I have other things to do in the afternoon.'

'Don't try to pull the wool over my eyes, Win,' Jim said. 'You came in the morning because you didn't want to run into Alison.'

'She doesn't like me. She never has.'

'You've never given her much opportunity,' Jim said.

Stooping, he found his shoes, stripped off the extra socks, put on the shoes and tied the laces one-handed and with difficulty.

His head was still spinning a little but Winnie, standing, watched without offering to help. Even that simple omission was symptomatic of the change in his sister. Winnie hadn't been particularly happy during their time together in Flannery Park but looking after him had brought her a sort of surrogate contentment, he supposed. For some women having a man to look after was the summit of their ambitions. It had not been his idea to have Winnie move out of Macarthur Drive. *She* had advised *him* to pursue Alison, not to let the girl go.

He did not remind her of it now or point out her inconsistency.

He got up and reached for her arm.

'Come along,' he said. 'We'll take a wee walk and talk about it.'

'Are you allowed to – to walk, I mean?'

'Of course. I'm not crippled, damn it.'

'But you're still sick.'

'No, Winnie. I'm not still sick. I'm getting better.'

He led her from the terrace, down the steps and around the corner of the kitchens on to the woodland path which ran between pines and oaks to the very limit of the old estate then curved back, following the moor's edge, to the wards.

This was the 'measured mile', the circuit around which patients paced their daily exercise. There was also, out there, a stile and a little jungly track by which the more ambitious ambulators could

288

escape for a quick pint of beer at the Ottershaw Keys on the main road below, a breach of the rules that Dr Leyman knew about but prudently elected to ignore.

Jim felt a little shaky but showed no sign of his weakness to his sister who, with face set, seemed oblivious to the prettiness of her surroundings.

He said, 'So Mother wants to come to live in Glasgow, does she?'

'Yes.'

'I thought she was happy on the farm with Connie?'

'Connie's had – I mean, Connie finds it difficult to cope. She has the children to think of.'

'How far gone is Mother?' Jim asked.

'What do you mean?'

'You know what I mean. She's unwell, Winnie. More unwell than I am.'

'She's not. She's perfectly fit.'

'She's senile.'

'How can you say that?'

'Because it's true.'

'She's not seventy yet.'

'She's sixty-six,' Jim said. 'Senility doesn't abide by the clock, though. What does her doctor say? The truth now.'

'She won't recover, not properly. Not all her faculties.'

'Is she difficult?'

'Yes.'

'Delusional?'

'She thinks she's going to die.'

'Well, she is,' Jim said, with a sigh. 'We're all going to die. Unfortunately.'

'She's afraid of it,' Winnie said.

'Aren't you?'

'What?'

'Afraid of dying?'

'I hardly ever think about it.'

'Oh, Winnie, Winnie,' Jim said.

'I've too much to do, too many other things to worry about to give any heed to what might happen to me. It doesn't matter, anyway. I could go tomorrow and nobody would care.'

'You don't really believe that, do you?' Jim said, cautiously.

'It wouldn't matter to you.'

Then he knew she was being manipulative. He'd seen the same technique used by children desperate to have their own way.

Pity me, Winnie was saying. *Help me. Do what I want.*

He was a generous man by nature but he resisted being drawn back into a relationship which offered him only a half-life, by which, in appeasing Winnie, he would surely have to smother his own desires and ambitions.

Winnie darted a glance at him, expectantly.

She was waiting for him to deny her last statement, to assure her that she mattered very much to him, that he would always be there for her, would look after her, would do what she wished.

He still felt a little light-headed. Not dizzy now, though.

He stopped on the path and squared up to his sister.

He said, 'I'm going to marry Alison, Winnie, and that's all about it.'

Winnie's face fell. Her eyes flared and for an instant he detected anger, not just anger plain and simple but a kind of rage that was almost frightening.

'What about Mother?' she snapped.

Jim heard himself say, 'She's not coming to stay in Macarthur Drive, not with you and not with me.'

'We'll give it up then.'

'What? The house? We'll do nothing of the kind.'

'You don't need it. You'll never work again, Jim Abbott. You won't be able to marry anyone. You're – you're finished.'

'Finished?' Jim said. 'I haven't even started.'

'It's that girl . . .'

'Of course it is.'

'You'd give up your health, your family for her?'

'Alison isn't an alternative,' Jim said. 'Alison is it, Winnie. I. T. *It*.'

'I wish – I wish I'd never been born. I mean, she – *she'd* never been born.'

'That's not a very nice thing to say,' Jim told her. 'In any case, Alison was born and we *did* meet and I'm damned if I'm going to let her go.' He waved his hand. 'As for the rest of it, well, I'll take care of that as soon as I'm back on my feet again and Leyman lets me out of here.'

'How long will that be?'

'Three months, six months. I don't know.'

'Doesn't *she* know? Can't *she* tell you?'

'Don't be ridiculous, Winnie.'

'If she told you she was going off with another man, you'd be out of here quick enough.'

'Oh, yes. Oh, yes, yes,' Jim said. 'TB or no TB I'd be out of here like a shot.' He paused, then laughed. 'Hamlet.'

'What?'

'Hamlet. I've just misquoted Hamlet. I must be getting better.'

The rage came flooding out of her. Winnie stamped her foot. He suddenly recalled her as a girl, the older sister, stamping her foot like that, their father laughing at her tantrum and the fury in her. He had thought their father cruel to laugh at Win. He had tried to comfort her later, patting her shoulder as if she was a pony. And he had been hurt when she'd vented the dregs of her anger on him, as if he was irrevocably paired not with her but with the man, with Daddy.

Now she stamped her foot again, and wept.

He felt no pity for her, only a vague dissatisfaction that she'd finally been proved right, that her assessment of him had been so thoroughly accurate.

'Stop it, Winnie,' he said.

She was too far gone. Hysterical, almost.

To Jim's astonishment she let herself fall backwards and, arms outstretched behind her, tumbled into a sitting position on the damp dirt path.

'Winnie,' he said. 'For God's sake, Winnie.'

She sat like some grotesque and ungainly doll, legs stuck out, her body shaken by massive sobs.

In spite of himself he knelt beside her, solicitous and pitying.

'What is it, Win? Tell me what's wrong?'

'Gordon. I want my Gordon,' she wailed.

It took Jim a moment to grasp what she was talking about, to remember his brother-in-law's name, let alone put a face to it. Sergeant Gordon Craddock, his sister's husband, dead in the mud of Passchendaele. Jim had thought that grief was all behind her, that it had burned out long since, but he'd been wrong, so wrong. A great wave of guilt swept through him at his selfishness. He had lost the prime of his youth – yes, an arm too, but Winnie had lost everything.

He saw that now so clearly that it stabbed into his breast like a knife and caused him more pain that any wound, any illness.

Kneeling, he patted her shoulder then, when she wrapped her arms about him and hugged him possessively to her bosom, caved in and comforted her with the false assurance that he would do whatever he could to make her happy and that everything would come right in the end.

'I am,' said Alison, 'very slightly tiddled. Is that the word?'

'It'll do,' said Howard. 'What do you want?'

'High tea, if possible. And a lug to bend.'

He grinned. 'That bad, was it?'

'No, not bad. Not morally reprehensible. Just – unexpected.'

She had been relieved to find Howard at home in the Bankhead

Hotel. She really did need a square meal to sober her up before she went back to Wingfield Drive. She'd drunk too much of the Spanish sherry that had been released from Mr Logie's cellars, too much of the red wine that Declan had dispensed after the menfolk had returned from the burial service.

She should have eaten more at lunch but somehow the sight of the long table weighted with cooked meats and puddings had depressed her appetite. She had picked away at a piece of chicken and kept as quiet as possible while the funeral party, composed largely of members of Declan's family, had demolished the luncheon like so many locusts and, shedding their Christian abstemiousness inch by inch, had got thoroughly wired into the drink.

Alison had expected a cavernous gulf to exist between Declan's bowlegged, tout-like Protestant father and uncles and the pious Catholics on his mother's side but if temperamental differences did exist between members of Declan's tribe they had certainly been put aside that afternoon.

Declan's father's energetic cheerfulness was, she had to admit, infectious. She wondered if Mr Logie's funeral had been intentionally transformed into an Irish-style wake or if, with a prize like Roberta brought to the fold, the gentlemen from Wicklow simply had too much to celebrate to restrain their natural exuberance.

After a time, though, the racket had given Alison a headache and the pungent smells of whisky and beer, as well as the strong red wine, had made her feel slightly nauseous.

She'd no opportunity for a confidential chat with Roberta who was being lionised by her new-found relatives-to-be and who kept as close to Declan as Declan's duties as self-appointed host permitted. By a quarter past four, just as the party was warming up and old uncles and young aunts were being persuaded to serenade the company with maudlin songs, Alison had had enough.

She was by no means the first to leave.

Roberta's brothers, and a Logie cousin from the Isle of Clova, had gone stalking off with faces like thunder about half past two o'clock, and Mr Emmslie, one of Veitch Logie's assistants, had left before that. There had been no lodge brothers, no stick-in-the-mud Stalker relations from Edinburgh, to put a spoke in the Wicklow wheel, however, and, to Alison's surprise, both Roberta and her mother had seemed to be enjoying themselves as much as anyone.

She'd managed only a brief word with Roberta before she'd slipped away.

'Will you come, will you come to Dublin for the wedding?' Bobs had asked her. 'I would so like to have you there. Howard, too.'

Alison had looked over Roberta's shoulder, had glimpsed Declan behind the dining table, glass in one hand, bottle in the other, his high, starched collar undone, his black cravat askew. Remembering how it had been between them, she'd heard herself say, 'Bobs, we'd love to, but – exams coming up – study – you know how it is?'

'Yes, of course. You'll come and visit us afterwards, though, won't you?'

'Where?'

'Here, silly. Right here, when we get back.'

'Aren't you staying on in Ireland?'

'Of course not. Why would I stay in Ireland when I've a perfectly good home here?' Bobs had laughed, shaking her blonde curls. 'I mean to say, someone has to look after Mummy now Daddy's gone.'

'You,' Alison had said, 'and Declan?'

'It's an ideal arrangement,' Bobs had said then, with a strange gleeful shrug of the shoulders, had added, 'Odd how things work out, isn't it?'

The Bankhead seemed like an ideal halfway house, a place in which to balance the wayward happenings in Dowanhill against the humdrum monotony of Wingfield Drive and the unnatural tranquillity of Ottershaw.

Fish, tea and toast sobered her, two scones and a crunchy meringue completed the job. She leaned back in the chair and contemplated Howard with satisfaction. No other word would suit the improvement in her mood.

'Well,' Alison said, 'at least we know what's happening to Roberta. She'll go to Ireland at Easter accompanied by her adoring mother and she'll return as Declan Slater's wife to support him through his final year.'

'And her career?' said Howard.

'No, that's gone for ever. She'll become a doctor's wife instead of a doctor. I doubt if we'll see much of her, even before Decker graduates.'

'He won't want to have anything to do with us,' Howard predicted. 'He has what he wants now and we'll only remind him of how he got it.'

'I wonder where he'll go,' Alison said. 'How far, and in what direction?'

'Upwards,' Howard said. 'To the top.'

'Do you think Bobs will inherit?'

'Something's bound to be left for the sons, her brothers, but most of it, including the house, will be passed on to Mrs Logie,' Howard conjectured. 'And our Declan, to all appearances, has entranced that dear lady just as he entranced the rest of us – well, some of us.'

'I expect you're right,' Alison said. 'Grim prospect, isn't it?'

'Only from our point of view,' Howard said. 'I expect Declan will make a perfectly adequate husband and father, though, and in a year or two Roberta won't have a moment to spare to dwell on what might have been.'

'Declan and I . . .' Alison began. 'You know – almost.'

'I know,' Howard said. 'We all knew.'

'And I thought I was being so discreet,' Alison said, reddening slightly. 'Was it that obvious?'

'It was obvious that you were too intelligent to offer Roberta any serious competition.'

'Is that what I was doing? Competing with Bobs?' Alison said. 'Good Lord! I thought I was just having a fling. What about you, Howard? What will you do when we finally trot out into the big wide world, clutching our degrees?'

Howard grinned. 'RAMC?'

'The army? You can't be serious?'

'No, of course I'm not serious. I thought I might apply for a post in Dumfries Royal under Gunnion. He's the best man in the field of orthopaedics which, at the moment, is a subject which appeals to me.'

'We will see each other won't we? At least keep in touch?'

'I certainly hope so,' Howard said, wistfully. 'You're going to marry him, aren't you? Your teacher, I mean.'

'I think so.'

'You *think* so? I was under the impression it was all signed and sealed.'

'I've been offered a post at Ottershaw. Leyman wants me there.'

'Or does Leyman just want you anywhere?' Howard said.

Alison bristled. 'You wouldn't say that if I were a man, would you?'

'No,' Howard agreed. 'Probably not.'

'Why say it now then?'

'Because you aren't a man,' Howard informed her. 'What does your teacher have to say about Leyman's offer?'

'I haven't discussed it with Jim yet. I haven't discussed it with anyone,' Alison said. 'I thought I'd ask your advice first of all, see what you thought about it, oh great panjandrum.'

'It's not up to me,' Howard said. 'I wish it were.'

'Do you? I thought we were over that?'

'You may be over it, Al, but I'm not.'

'Oh, Howard. I'm sorry.'

'For what?' He shrugged. 'Anyway, we're talking about your future, not mine. Ottershaw? Is it the subject that appeals to you, or the man?'

'Leyman's a fine doctor. I'd have an opportunity to do research.'

'Oh, is that the attraction? Alison Burnside – MD?'

'I'm certainly not going to settle for general practice, if I can avoid it. I want to do something more with what I've got, what I've gained.'

'*And* marriage? *And* children too? What does your teacher have to say about that?'

'He'll do what I want.'

Howard was silent for a moment then said, very softly, 'I see.'

Everyone at 162 Wingfield Drive was mightily surprised when Henry and Trudi returned early from the trip to Berlin.

Though not noted for their sensitivity the boys had a feeling that they hadn't been told the whole truth about what had happened in the German capital, that Henry's tale of a fight in a bar and a hasty departure was really a trifle far-fetched. The fact that Trudi was willing to confirm the story, however, appeased the Burnsides' curiosity, though Bertie could not resist the odd dig about the bruises on Henry's face and got shouted at by Trudi for his sarcasm.

If Alison had been less preoccupied with her own problems she might have wheedled something out of Trudi or have confronted her oldest brother and asked for honest answers. As it was, however, Trudi and Henry had put up barriers and said little about what had happened abroad. She, Alison, sensed that they were unhappy, so subdued in each other's company as to be almost morose. She had sufficient tact not to interfere.

Besides, routine soon took over and, within a few days of the prodigals' return, Henry was back at work and Trudi had assumed command of the household once more.

At night, though, late at night, Alison would hear the couple whispering across the landing, as if they shared a secret so audacious, or so unpleasant, that it could not be discussed anywhere else but in the bedroom.

The first of Henry's articles appeared ten days after his return. It was disappointingly uninformative and did not – as Davy and Bert had hoped it might – contain a blow-by-blow account of Henry's bar-room scrap.

To Alison the article seemed weak, hardly more than a few uncritical paragraphs of descriptive prose about the new Germany, padded out by two large photographs which, she guessed, had been dug out of the *Mercury*'s library or purchased from one of the agencies.

She challenged Henry about it but he merely shook his head,

295

shrugged, and told her that it was the best he could do in the circumstances.

His second piece, which appeared on Monday, was even more wispy, a handful of impressions of 'Berlin by Night', printed without comment or analysis. After that no more was heard from Henry Burnside on foreign affairs and he returned to covering local politics under his familiar by-line as if the trip to Europe had never taken place at all.

March went out in a flurry of heavy rain. Bruised clouds rolled day after day across moorland and fells. The valley of Ottershaw was ribboned with standing water and on the last day of the month the river burst its banks, flooding low-lying pastures and driving ewes and young lambs on to the crowns of grassland which lay behind the hospital morgue.

The event coincided with the death of a young male patient, barely sixteen years old, which provided Alison with an opportunity to attend her first comprehensive pathological post-mortem.

Certificates of consent had already been obtained from the young man's parents on Leyman's assurance that the result would in some measure benefit other sufferers from tubercular diseases. Pathological examinations, Alison knew, were not to determine the cause of death but were focused on the body's reaction to disease. Their purpose was to analyse changes in individual organs and to deduce, where possible, why these processes had become active and at what stage they had been interrupted.

She travelled to Ottershaw on the milk train, very early. She ate a light breakfast in Leyman's office with Leyman and a young doctor, Rathbone, from Wellmeadow Hospital, who had come over to observe the procedure.

At a little after eight o'clock, she entered the post-mortem room.

First Phillip Leyman made a systematic examination of the body.

It had not yet turned completely cold. The muscles were flaccid, however, and a slight degree of rigor mortis was already apparent. Next, to provide maximum access to the interior organs, he cut a wide vee from the tip of the mastoid process to the middle line of the chest and, with the cadaver now open, began work in earnest.

In gown and gloves, Alison stood by the table and watched Phillip Leyman carefully examine the organs *in situ* and inspect the pleural, pericardial and peritoneal cavities before removing the specimens he required for laboratory analyses. He worked with a delicacy and patience that seemed foreign to his nature and Rathbone had little to do but mop up and, latterly, stitch.

Leyman talked while he laboured. He addressed the discoloured organs with peculiar familiarity as if he had a relationship with them which went beyond science.

Alison listened and watched intently, saying nothing.

Outside, rain clattered on the roof.

Shades of daylight from the skylights flitted from sunlight to gloom and back again. She could hear the wind lashing the pine trees and, riding incongruously above that ocean of sound, the blethering of lambs and the deep, maternal bleat of ewes.

The boy stretched out before her was unaware of weather or animals. It struck Alison just how complete the process of dying really was. Not a simple closing down of consciousness, the loss of cognition like sleep or trance but something too complete to register with anyone who still had their senses and the sensations that fed their senses.

The unimaginable nothingness fascinated and frightened her.

The proximity of the boy's mask-like profile, straight slender legs and small, passive penis in its grove of fine, brown hair distressed her deeply. She peeped into the wide wounds and saw the dark red stems of veins and arteries, the muted pink of flesh gone bad, soft, nutmeg brown cavities, the sagging heart pushed passive and unresisting to one side.

It was all Alison could do not to recoil for suddenly she saw there on the slab, dead and perfect, not Jim, not Henry, not anyone she loved, but herself, Alison Burnside gone on beyond the rain and the sunlight's swift progressions to a place of no feeling and no future.

She swayed slightly and took a pace backward.

Leyman glanced at her. 'Now do you understand, Alison?'

And Alison, empty and afraid, answered, 'Yes. Oh, yes.'

Jim was waiting for her when she came up through the grove and around the corner from Leyman's office.

He wore a heavy cardigan, baggy corduroys and soft-soled shoes. He had changed so much from the teacher she had known, from the neat, dapper man who had commanded a classroom in Flannery Park school. He seemed to have lost his authority and with the sleeve folded over his missing arm and his hair tousled he had a pathetic look, not mournful or self-pitying, but somehow defeated.

The mood of the morning lingered.

It would, in fact, stay with Alison for ever, an indelible and ineradicable part of her from now on, a deep stillness beneath all the turbulent emotions, all the happiness that she would experience in the years to come. No other thing in medicine, not the death of infants or the suffering of young children, would affect her so much again. She realised now what made her father's eyes turn vague, why his expression would cloud in the midst of laughter, as if that pool of recognition was in him too and had, for an instant, been feathered by doubt, if not by blank despair.

She saw it in Jim, often in Jim, and wondered at what point in his life he had looked into the nothingness and had known that it was his legacy too.

She went to him, climbing the rain-wet steps.

'How was it?' he said. 'Did you learn much?'

She nodded and put her arms about him.

For a moment he looked surprised then he drew her to him and hugged her tightly with his one good arm.

'Bad?' he asked.

'Bad,' Alison agreed and, for no explicable reason except that she needed him more than ever, wept softly against Jim's chest.

'How do you like that then, Mr Jack Burnside?' Brenda hoisted her blouse and vest up with one hand, shoved down the waistband of her skirt and, without a trace of modesty, displayed the swell of her stomach. 'All, you know, your fault. I hope you're proud of yourself.'

Jack laughed, then dabbed up a spoonful of creamed rice, added a touch of bramble jelly from the pot on the table and offered it to Lexi who, with a delicate protrusion of the lips, like a little goldfish, sooked the teaspoon clean.

'Me, me, me,' Bee yelled, sticking her arms back and extending her neck. 'Me want some tae.'

'Okay, okay, honey. Hold your horses.'

Jack was flanked by his daughters at the table in the living-room. He had bought each of them a wooden chair, low not high, perfect replicas of Grandpa Burnside's big kitchen chair, for Jack liked to have the girls close to him at suppertime so that he could feed them, and himself, simultaneously.

Money for the chairs, like the money for most of the small luxuries that now adorned the council house, had come from Jack's earnings as a bandsman. The trumpet had called the tune and Brenda, much more settled than she had been a year ago, was willing to forgo the pleasure of his company for the sake of the extra cash. Jack was happy making music. It seemed to satisfy a need in him that Brenda could not for the life of her understand. But she had no worries about letting him loose with fat Kenny Cooper to play at weddings and dances or even down at the Cally Halls in Partick once or twice a month.

If girls made eyes at him – and they'd be daft if they didn't – Jack would just smile and wink and go on with the number, for playing the trumpet, Brenda realised, meant more to him than playing the field.

'What d'you think, Ally?' Brenda swung her stomach around for her sister-in-law's inspection.

'How far into the pregnancy are you?' Alison tried to keep a straight face. 'Three months?'

'Nearly four.'

'You look fine to me,' Alison said, 'But I don't have my instruments with me, sorry.'

'Instruments?' Brenda said. 'What, you know, instruments?'

'You could borrow my trumpet, Ally,' Jack suggested, feeding Bee from the teaspoon. 'Or maybe you'd need a souzaphone, the size she is.'

'None o' your lip,' Brenda warned.

'Mammy's gotta bare bottom.' Lexi pouted primly. 'Not very nice.'

Brenda shoved her chair back from the table and contemplated her prominent navel. 'I think I'm bigger than I was when I had the pair o' them. Is that all right?'

'The muscles lose tone as you get older,' Alison said. 'You're probably not any heavier, Brenda, just – well, slacker.'

Jack cleared his throat while Lexi went on repeating, 'Not nice, not nice, not nice,' in a tutting little tone and Bee, leaning at a dangerous angle from her chair, scowled at the offending object as if she couldn't quite make up her mind if it was, or was not, threatening.

Alison cut the burned crust of her mince round and ate the soft, hot meat centre hungrily.

She had arrived in Shackleton Avenue just after the meal had started but her brother had generously shared his portion with her and had even heated up a second tin of garden peas to make the mince go further.

'What,' Alison asked, 'did Dr Lawrence say about you?'

'How did you know I'd been to see Dr Lawrence?' Brenda said.

'Guesswork,' Alison answered. 'What did he tell you?'

'He says he's sure it's only one this time.'

'One's enough,' Jack put in. 'Too many mouths to feed as it is.'

Alison glanced at her brother, fork poised.

'Hey, naw,' Jack said, 'I don't mean you. You're a visitor.'

'In that case,' Alison said, 'yes, please, I will have some of that rice.'

'Bare bottom,' Lexi tutted and shook her head.

'Aye, Brenda, for God's sake put it away.' Jack spooned warm rice into a pudding plate. He licked his fingers. 'The way you're carryin' on you'd think it was your first.'

'I just feel, you know, different about this one.'

'Why?' said Alison. 'What do you mean by "different"?'

'I was hopin' you'd be able to tell me.'

'I haven't done my midwifery courses yet,' Alison said.

'Huh!' said Brenda. 'Fat lot of use you are. I mean, are you still just cuttin' people up?'

'Brenda!' Jack said.

'I did today,' Alison heard herself say.

She had no idea why she should submit to Brenda's curiosity, why she felt the need to share her experience with her brother and his wife. They could not possibly understand. To them life was food, warmth, cigarettes, music, babies; yet it was to share just those experiences that she'd come to Jack's house tonight instead of going home to Wingfield Drive. She needed the children, her nieces, her big, fair-haired brother, the comfort they unwittingly offered.

She said, 'A boy, a young boy.'

Brenda made to speak but Jack touched her sleeve, stilling her.

'What did he die of?' Jack asked.

'TB.'

'Where?'

'At Ottershaw.'

'What age was he?'

'Sixteen.'

'Did you know him?'

'Yes, a little.'

'What did you have to cut him up for?' Brenda asked.

'To find out things,' Alison said. 'Things about the disease.'

She did not feel tearful now. She was wary in case they mocked her for her sentiments. She felt isolated by their incomprehension. Then she noticed how they were looking at her. Even her nieces were staring at her as if they understood, or could at least sense how she felt.

'I don't know how you do it,' Jack said quietly.

'Me neither,' Brenda agreed.

Glancing at the curve of her belly, Brenda was suddenly self-conscious. She jerked down her vest and blouse and, with a wriggle, hoisted up her skirt, as if birth and mortality lay too far apart to be encompassed in the same span.

Jack remained motionless for three or four seconds, an arm about

300

each of the twins, then he let out a little whistle, raised his eyebrows, and got to his feet.

'You'll stay for a while?' he said.

'If you don't mind,' said Alison.

'You can help me bath them, if you like,' said Brenda.

'Yes, I'd like that.'

'Tea then,' Jack said. 'I'll put the kettle on.'

He gathered plates, carried them out of the living-room.

Lexi slipped from her chair and toddled after her Daddy, Bee following like a little sheep. A moment later squeals of laughter came from the kitchenette.

And the mood was broken.

Brenda lit a cigarette, blew smoke.

'He's all right, my Jack,' she said, apropos of nothing, then leaning towards Alison, asked, 'Hey, whatever happened to *your* fancy-man?'

'He's getting married,' Alison said. 'Next week, in fact.'

'Who got *him* to the altar?' Brenda said. 'Some big blonde, I'll bet.'

'Some big blonde it was,' said Alison.

'Missed your chance again, eh?'

Alison looked at her sister-in-law not with rancour but with affection. They were very different in temperament but they had been girls together and were bound by the memory of those days gone by.

Alison said, 'You mean Walter?'

'He was mad about you, Wattie was.'

'Then you stole him away.'

'Nah!' Brenda said. 'Anyway, I done you a favour.'

'I didn't think that at the time,' Alison admitted.

'Did you hate me?'

'Oh, aye,' said Alison. 'Like poison.'

Plump, tousled, wreathed in cigarette smoke, Brenda grinned then, for no particular reason, laughed. And when Jack returned, bearing the teapot before him, he found his wife and sister collapsed upon the couch, giggling like schoolgirls over some secret from their not-so-murky past.

'I hope you're not talkin' about me?' he said.

'Don't flatter yourself, big boy,' Brenda retorted and, engulfed by laughter, fell helplessly against Alison once more as if he, a mere male, was the biggest joke of all.

Fine April weather made no impression on Henry Burnside. He was aware that clouds had gone from the sky over Magdalen Lane, that the old sandstone façades and tiled chimneypots which he could see from his desk in the *Mercury*'s newsroom had turned russet in the sunlight. He was aware too that the city pavements were dry and that the fierce wet winds which had lashed him as he'd tramped out his March appointments had dwindled to soft breezes. But the breath of spring in the air didn't perk him up and he went about his business, as he had done for weeks, in a kind of impenetrable trance.

He let nothing of his torment show.

He'd brooked no nonsense from his fellow journalists, had refused to discuss his early return from Berlin and the big purple-yellow bruises he'd carted back with him. He'd fed them the lie about a brawl in a bar, too much schnapps to drink, his passport held then returned with a request to leave the country. The reporters had more or less swallowed his story.

Marcus Harrison, however, had not been taken in.

The editor had lounged behind his desk. He had studied Henry attentively while Henry, making light of it, had offered invention and apologies and had suggested that part of the cost of the trip be deducted from his wages in lieu of holiday pay. Harrison had said that it would not be necessary and hadn't reprimanded Henry for wasting the company's time and money. The editor, of course, was on the spot. He didn't know what the bruises signified or if Henry had found out about the illicit cash payments to a nation which had been forbidden by international law to rearm itself from foreign investments.

Henry had been tempted to drop a hint that he'd discovered what was going on but he wasn't ready to renege on his promise to Trudi – not yet.

Meanwhile, he passed his days in a waking trance. Professional enough to produce feature copy on demand, to analyse new budget proposals and increases in unemployment benefits, to hack out articles required to satisfy his contract. He continued to spend his evenings at home in brooding silence, his nights fighting off the nightmares that the fine spring weather did nothing to diminish. He could not bring himself to make love to Trudi.

She, sensibly, made no attempt to persuade him.

Late at night, however, he would sit on the chair by the bed-end and interrogate her about her past. Insist that she told him everything, revealed every detail. The tales she'd told him before, she told again. This time Henry listened without heat for he knew that they were facts not fictions. She sat up in bed, bed-jacket fastened at her throat, silk shawl about her shoulders, her hair still neatly ribboned. She looked thinner than ever, though, as if each revelation, each confession that Henry whittled from her left her depleted so that before he was finished with her there might be nothing left at all.

He asked about her father, about Coventry, about Dante and Harrison. She admitted that she had slept with them all. Henry passed no judgements. Pressed on relentlessly. What did she know of the currency transactions? Had the Dahrendorfs been party to the frauds and extortions? How long had Coventry been involved and was Dante acting on behalf of Marcus Harrison and, through him, Lord Blackstock? What did she know of the International Fund which offered shares in ludicrous companies?

He spoke to her quietly, never raising his voice.

Trudi answered in a hesitant monotone but denied Henry no crumb of information. When she could come up with no more, when memory failed her, she told Henry so. And he believed her.

And moved on.

Trudi did not enquire what use Henry would make of the information. Did not mention his promise. She cooked, sewed, cleaned, ironed, chatted to Ruby, to Alison, even to Brenda as if all was right with the world, though she sensed that Henry had taken her back only under sufferance and because he had use for her. Where love had gone, and if it would ever return, Trudi couldn't say.

She wept miserably only when the house was empty.

And on those nights, one or two each week, when Henry did not return home until very late she would wait for him upstairs in bed.

But she did not ask where he had been. Who he had been with.

Did not dare utter the name Margaret Chancellor.

In case he told her the truth.

'Henry!' Margaret Chancellor said. 'Well, this is a surprise! Where have you been hiding yourself?'

'I've been – round and about.'

'I thought you'd stayed in Berlin. Joined the Nazis or something daft.'

'No,' he said. 'No. I came back early, in fact.'

'Didn't you care for the scenery?' she said. 'I can't believe you didn't care for the regime? I thought it would have been right up your street.'

'Listen,' he said, 'I know it's a cheek but may I come in?'

'What for?' Margaret said, spreading a hand across her bosom.

'I need to talk to you.'

'What about?'

'I need your advice.'

'How flattering.' She removed her hand from her breast, made a fist and cocked her thumb. 'Come on then. Just don't run away with the idea that I take in every handsome young man who turns up on my doorstep after dark.'

Henry managed a tight little grimace. 'Only half of them, Maggie?'

'Aye,' she said. 'I must be getting old.'

She did not look old, not to Henry. Although it was only half past eight o'clock she wore a dressing-gown and had let her hair down. The dressing-gown was not particularly feminine, a heavy garment, like a bathrobe, in brushed wool. It had a deep vee collar which Margaret had turned up. Beneath it, as far as Henry could make out, she wore nothing. She was certainly bare-legged and barefoot and he couldn't take his eyes from those smooth, sturdy calves.

It was the first time Henry had ever visited Margaret Chancellor's home. Their relationship had not always been friendly, nor had it ever quite emerged from the pretence of a mutual, and professional, interest in politics. He knew that she had not been long resident in the three-apartment flat in Menzies Gardens, in a sandstone tenement with a half-tiled close tucked into the hinterland of middle-class respectability which lay west of Byres Road, not far from the university.

It was a fairly 'posh' address for the widow of a railwayman and, Henry guessed, triumphantly signified her rise in the world.

She ushered Henry into a large living-room furnished with a squashy-looking sofa and four big, mismatched armchairs. Two of the long walls had been fitted with shelves which housed a vast, untidy collection of books. There was also a small upright piano and, on a stand by the fireplace, a wireless set in a mahogany cabinet. On a side-table, bottles and glasses.

He watched Maggie draw the curtains across a view of streetlamp-lit gardens. The room was lit by firelight and two tall lamps in parchment shades. It was a soft, lived-in room, not genteel or austere. Books, typewriter on the table, a litter of papers, a cigarette smoking in a shellcase ashtray made Henry a little more relaxed.

When Margaret moved back from the window bay, he could see the flicker of the dressing-gown, how it clung to her knees and formed soft coils about her stomach and thighs. And when she lifted her cigarette from the ashtray and drew on it greedily, lifted the whisky tumbler and drank from it, watching him, Henry, in spite of his melancholy, felt a little chug of desire for the big, soft-bodied woman.

Without asking, she poured him a stiff whisky and handed it to him, gestured to the sofa while she sank down into one of the armchairs, leaning back, legs and feet extended, the dressing-gown casually drawn over her plump knees.

She said, 'Actually, I knew you were back from Berlin. Jimmy Brewster told me. He told me about the bruises too. He said you'd got into a fight in a bar or something equally stupid. That's not like you, Henry.' She paused. 'Did something nasty happen in Germany? Is that what you need to talk about?'

Henry sipped whisky. 'That, and other things.'

'What other things?'

'I saw Kurtz. Vladimir Kurtz.'

'Good God! In Berlin?'

'Aye.'

'He was running a fair old risk, wasn't he?'

'He was in prison,' Henry said. 'In the cells at Gestapo headquarters. You know, I assume, what the Gestapo is?'

'Of course,' said Margaret Chancellor, with some impatience. 'Did you manage to talk to Kurtz?'

'Yes.'

'Officially?'

'Are you kidding?' said Henry. 'He was . . .'

'Is this painful?'

'Of course it's painful.'

'Take your time.'

'Kurtz was – he was dying.'

'Dying? Of what?'

'They were beating him to death, Margaret. Systematically beating him to death. I didn't – I didn't realise it at first. He stood at the little window of the cell and talked to me, told me things, and all the time he was just hanging on, hanging on, knowing that they would come for him again and what they would do to him and that he wasn't going to get out of there alive.'

'What did they want from him? Names?'

'Yes.'

'Which he wouldn't give them?'

'No,' Henry said. 'I thought – you know, in Glasgow – I thought Kurtz was pretty much a joke. I didn't realise . . .'

'Take your time, Henry, just take your time.' She sat forward. He could see her breasts, heavy and soft, the soft flesh of her knees. It didn't matter now. She said, 'Have you told anyone else about this?'

Henry shook his head.

She said, 'Marcus?'

'No.'

'Your wife. Surely you told your wife?'

305

'No one,' Henry said.

'What were you doing in Gestapo headquarters in the first place?'

'I was a prisoner too.'

'Did they beat you?'

'No, only once. Not the Gestapo. My – someone else.'

'What did Kurtz tell you, Henry?'

'A lot of things, things I didn't know.' He put the whisky glass upon the carpet, stuck his hands in his trouser pockets and craned backwards. He stared at the ceiling's plaster cornices for a moment then said, 'It wasn't just Kurtz.'

'What do you mean?' Margaret Chancellor asked.

'I mean, Kurtz knew what he was doing. He knew why he was there and what they wanted from him. He had no illusions, Maggie. He was – he was . . .'

She moved swiftly from the armchair to the sofa, seated herself by him. Did not touch him, though, did not yet offer the comfort of a hand or an arm.

She leaned over him and asked, 'Henry, what happened?'

'It was – it was the boy.'

'Boy?'

'The boy didn't know anything. He couldn't tell them anything. Oh, for Christ's sake, why did they have to do that to the boy?'

Henry doubled over, fingers fanned over his cheeks for he couldn't bear to let her see him weep, as if he hoped he might still preserve the images, keep them to himself and bear the burden alone.

Margaret touched his shoulder, saying nothing.

He rocked forth and back, weeping drily.

At length, he said, 'I can't stop thinking about the boy.' He darted a glance at her, his eyes red. 'He'd been screaming, screaming all morning. I didn't know who it was. When they brought him back, they had to drag him between them. Two of them. Policemen. Black uniforms. At first I couldn't tell what he was, girl or boy, though he had nothing on from the waist down. He was all over blood, all white and bloody. He wore a shirt on top and a pullover like my brother Bert's. It was pushed up all the way to his shoulders. He couldn't walk. He couldn't walk, Margaret. And he wore this silly pullover just like Bert's.'

She spoke sternly. 'Henry, was he not a communist?'

'What does it matter what the hell he was?'

'It matters,' Margaret Chancellor said, 'because of the struggle.'

He looked up at her suddenly, his eyes filled with loathing.

'To hell with the struggle. It's Kurtz's struggle. Your struggle. Adolf Hitler's struggle. Not *his* struggle.'

'He had to have done something, Henry?'

'Christ! He was ten years old, Margaret, only ten years old.'

'What happened to him?'

'I don't know. I'll *never* know. They threw him into a cell and he lay bleeding on the floor, crumpled up like a bit of old paper.'

'What about Kurtz?'

'Kurtz is probably a goner.'

She got up and found her whisky glass, freshened it from the bottle on the polished side-table. She stood very still, looking not at Henry but into the fire.

'There's nothing you can do about it, Henry.'

'Isn't there? No, you're right. Nothing I can do about Kurtz.'

He stooped, lifted the glass from the carpet and swallowed whisky. Anger had stripped him of the diffidence which had been his hallmark for far too long.

'There's more, Margaret, a lot more,' he said, and proceeded to tell her everything that had happened to him in Berlin.

She listened without interrupting him.

Only when he had completed his account and had fallen silent did she speak again. 'Why did you come to me, Henry?'

'I had to tell someone. Someone who might understand.'

'I can't tell you what to do.'

'I should write about it. I should tell what I know, shouldn't I?'

'Yes,' Margaret Chancellor said.

'But if I do,' Henry said, 'I'll lose my job.'

'Some job,' Margaret said, 'working for a fascist.' She paused. 'I know it won't make you feel any better but your wife isn't the only woman Harrison's had a fling with.'

'I can well believe it,' Henry said then, scowling, took the point. 'What? You too?'

'I'm afraid so,' Margaret said. 'Oh, don't worry, I'm no longer one of Harrison's pets. I'm not going to trot off and tell him what you've just told me. He's Blackstock's jackanapes now. He might behave like a perfect gentleman but behind his smile lurks an unscrupulous, hypocritical pig. He doesn't care about you, or me for that matter. Or anyone. The only thing that Harrison's afraid of is being exposed, of being found out.'

'You think I should name names?'

'That's up to you.'

'How can I?' Henry said. 'I gave Trudi my promise.'

'Are you still in love with her?'

'I don't know.'

'That means you are,' Margaret said. 'Otherwise you'd have thrown her out by now.'

307

'Look,' Henry said, 'I've gathered material, a lot of material, about Harrison and Blackstock and others too. What Trudi told me would fill a book.'

'There you are then,' Margaret said.

'But how can I write a book like that? I mean, who'd publish it?'

'Charlie Blackstock doesn't control all Britain's presses,' Margaret Chancellor said. 'Blackstock's kind have enemies too. I know half a dozen publishers who'd be only too delighted to print the truth about what's really happening in Germany and who really voted for Hitler.'

'If I attack Blackstock in print, though, my father will lose his job,' Henry said. 'And I've my sister to think about. It's my salary that keeps a roof over her head. I mean, Maggie, I've other people to consider. It's all very well for you, I've got responsibilities.'

'Yes, you have.'

'Oh, hell! I can't just ignore my obligations.'

'And the boy? Can you ignore what happened to the boy?'

And Henry, head in hands again, said, 'No.'

TEN

The Marrying Kind

For Alison, Easter vacation was all too short. No time to enjoy the mild spring weather. No time to lift her attention from the work in hand. Quite suddenly the fifth year of medical training and final exams loomed over all.

Summer term was itself no picnic. Lectures on public health and medical jurisprudence had to be fitted in to practical surgery at the Royal Infirmary. Saturday attendance at Gartnavel for the study of mental diseases competed, in one's head if not on the timetable, with introductory lectures on midwifery. But all of this load, as learned gentlemen like T.K. Thomas were prone to point out, would seem light by comparison with the demands of hospital practice, practical midwifery and senior medical clerking, delights which awaited all final-year students before winter came around again.

Alison's taste of 'real' medicine stood her in good stead. From Dr Leyman's example she learned the fine art of 'switching', of focusing her concentration precisely on to the job at hand, so that she seemed – and indeed was – totally engaged with each aspect of medicine in turn. For all that, she realised for the first time the alarming scale of medicine, the inexhaustible range of possibilities the profession offered and just how accommodating it could be to dedicated healers and dedicated materialists alike.

Into which category Declan Slater fell was a matter of conjecture.

Marriage, a return to favour with his family, an ascent from a basement flat in Greenfield to the lofty heights of Dowanhill had naturally altered Declan's outlook on life and his disposition. After a Saturday's instruction among the poor demented souls who inhabited the wards of Gartnavel mental hospital some students put Declan down as little more than a catalogue of neuroses. Others regarded him as incipiently schizophrenic. He certainly provided a talking point among his peers and even Howard and Alison found themselves discussing him at greater length than he deserved. Gone were the shabby jackets, shiny flannels and down-at-heel shoes.

Gone the shaggy hair and pinched features. Declan had returned from Wicklow all sleek and glossy and appeared in class in an array of three-piece suits that put the teachers to shame for smartness.

It was as if the responsibility of being titular head of the Logie household - at least until Veitch's sons reached their majority – had projected Declan into an entirely new dimension. He even spoke in soft, defensive platitudes by which means, Howard reckoned, he managed to keep everyone at a distance. He was more popular with teaching staff than ever before. Even T.K. Thomas, though he waxed caustic towards the infant prodigy, could find no fault with Declan's clinical work. And, all in all, old Declan seemed to have slipped on his dear, dead father-in-law's mantle as if it had been made for him.

'How's Roberta?' Alison asked.

'Wonderfully well. Blooming, one might say.'

'The wedding?'

'Went off without a hitch.'

'Mrs Logie?'

'Recovering from her grief, I do believe. She certainly gave every appearance of enjoying her visit to Kerridge. My parents made her very welcome, of course. But then, as you know, we are a hospitable race. Thank you so much for asking, Alison. Shall I pass on your regards?'

'Please do.'

Alison could hardly believe that less than a year ago she had shared a bed with Declan Slater and thanked her stars that she'd been sensible enough to remain in control of her emotions.

Meanwhile she clung to Howard, the last of the team, for companionship and to her wounded hero, James Abbott, as a promise for the future. She did her rounds, studied her lecture notes and tried to decide what to do about Phillip Leyman's offer of a post at Ottershaw.

Jim said, 'Haven't you given Leyman an answer yet?'

Alison, surprised, said, 'No, not yet. I thought I'd hang off a while. There's no particular urgency, is there?'

'You should accept his offer,' Jim said. 'Snap it up.'

'Why do you say that? We haven't even discussed it properly,' Alison said. 'Suddenly you decide I should "snap it up". I'm not sure you realise just what's involved.'

'Residency,' Jim said. 'You'll have to lodge on the premises, I expect.'

He looked well. His skin was tanned by spring sunshine and his eyes had something of their old sparkle. He addressed her now, though, with the air of a schoolmaster who does not quite approve of his pupil's behaviour and Alison felt as if she were being dictated to, put into a situation which made her bridle.

She had spent an hour in the lab examining tissue and blood samples with McNair before coming to call upon Jim. It was late afternoon and shadows were lengthening. Tea urns and trolleys which had been cheerfully wheeled about the terraces had been taken indoors and nurses were closing the glass doors against a cool unsummery breeze which brought dampness down from the moorland. She resented the fact that Jim hadn't asked her about her day, hadn't soothed her, didn't seem to appreciate how hard she worked.

She sat with him on one of the high-backed benches at the end of the terrace, her legs tense, as if she was possessed of the need to be up and doing something else, something more urgent and important.

'Residency,' she said, 'means I'll have to spend all of my time inside a hospital. Nights too. I'll have my first taste of it in October when I go on call as a midwife. I've a certain number of deliveries to make . . .'

'Like a postman.'

'I don't find that terribly amusing, Jim.'

'I know how tough it's going to be for you next year, Alison,' he said, still – she thought – humouring her. 'We both knew it wouldn't be easy, even before I came down with bloody consumption.'

'That isn't your fault.'

'Oh, I know that,' he said. 'Leyman explained it to me. It's a pathological disorder, not a pathognomical one. We had a nice wee discussion on the subject and set my mind at rest. I don't feel so guilty any more.'

'Well,' Alison said, nonplussed, 'I'm glad about that.' She paused. 'Do you feel that you owe Dr Leyman something in exchange? Me, for instance?'

She could hardly control her legs now. The muscles seemed to twitch of their own accord and her palms pressed down upon the bench as if to thrust her away from him by involuntary spasm.

'I wouldn't put it quite like that, no.'

'How *would* you put it?'

'The fact that I think you should take the job with Leyman has nothing to do with how I've been treated here or what I personally think of the man. He's offering you a chance to specialise, to extend yourself. He's impressed with you. He sees in you what I once saw—'

'Oh, for God's sake,' Alison snapped. 'Just tell me why.'

311

'With any luck at at all,' Jim said, 'I'll be out of here by June.'

'That's – that's good news. Great news.'

'I question if the education authorities will be keen to take me on again. You know how touchy they are about TB.'

'If it's money that worries you, my savings will see me through to my finals, after which I'll be earning enough to take care of us both,' Alison said. 'Is that why you want me to accept the post here, for the money?'

'I can't let you support me, Alison.'

'You supported me long enough.'

Jim said, 'I'm going to stay with my sister in Perthshire. Winnie will look after me until I'm well enough to work again.'

'Then you'll come back?'

'No, I'll look out for a teaching post in Perthshire.'

'Leave Flannery Park for good?'

Jim nodded.

'And our engagement?' Alison asked.

'I'm afraid,' Jim said, 'that's off.'

She lay on her back on the bed, bolster behind her head, arms by her side. She had shed no tears so far and doubted if she would now. She felt dry within herself, withered almost.

In a single stroke, Jim had excised himself from her future.

There had been times recently when she'd toyed with the idea of release from her promise to marry Jim but now it had come to pass she was filled with dismay. For much of her adult life she had been guided by him. Now he was no longer there, no longer had a hold over her. Without Jim's encouragement she might be clerking in Singer's factory, might be married to Walter Giffard, rearing children of her own. Jim and Jim alone had believed in her at a time when she did not believe in herself, had seen qualities in her which she hadn't known existed. Now he had released her, cut her adrift, given her freedom.

She lay on her back on the bed and stared at the ceiling.

'You don't need me any more, Alison,' he'd said. 'You really don't need me any more.'

It was true. Absolutely true.

She did not need him now.

She had too much to contend with to be saddled with a lame duck, a martyr to whom duty had finally proved more attractive than marriage. He had chosen his mother, his sister, his family instead of her. She had become so used to doing what Jim wanted her to do that she couldn't help but buckle to his will, let him have his way and do

312

what he thought best for both of them. She'd be damned if she'd try to talk him out of it.

She'd said nothing to Phillip Leyman about her broken engagement. Nothing to Trudi. She might have confided in Henry but Henry wasn't at home.

Besides, she knew just how the family would react. They would have opinions, pro and con, and would express them forcefully. But when it came down to it they no longer had the temerity to tell her what to do. They might turn to Henry when things went wrong but she was the one they respected, the girl who had left them behind. She suspected that there was one like her in every family, one child favoured over all the rest. They expected a great deal from her and she did not dare let them down. Yet, in the end, she was free to choose, to go her own way, to follow her instincts and pursue her own ambitions. She had escaped them, she had slipped the net.

She had finally attained her independence.

And she hated it.

From outside came the familiar sounds of night in the suburbs, a far-off clanking of tramcar wheels on the points on the Kingsway, the inevitable barking of a dog, the faint, faint wailing of a child and, just below the window, the chatter of young girls, their carefree laughter receding as they wandered home to bed. Across the park, in Foxhill Crescent, Dad and Ruby would be drinking tea and listening to the wireless. Below, Bertie would be reading a Western novel and scowling, Pete, old now and stiff, curled up on the carpet at his feet. Davy was already snoring through the wall. And Trudi? Trudi was across the landing, waiting for Henry to come home.

In due course she would have to tell them what had happened.

It would be a bit more than a nine-day wonder this time. Henry would go out to Ottershaw and talk 'seriously' to Jim. Dad would rage. Davy and Jack would fail to understand. Bertie would crow. Ruby and Brenda would fish to discover if she'd done something to offend Jim, if, for instance, she'd found herself another man. Trudi would comfort her.

She would be spoiled and defended, protected not condemned.

But after all the hubbub had died down she would be on her own.

The price she had to pay for being the favoured child.

She lay on her back on the bed and stared at the ceiling.

By her side were two thick, well-thumbed medical textbooks and a notebook stuffed with information she had gleaned from Phillip Leyman. Curled in her right hand was the little brooch that Howard had given her at Christmas. And on the wall, in lamplight above the desk, a framed photograph of Jim and herself taken on the day of Dad's wedding to Ruby McColl.

'Oh, hell!' Alison suddenly exclaimed and, reaching behind her, yanked the bolster over her face so that for several blessed seconds she could see absolutely nothing at all.

When she heard him coming upstairs Trudi glanced at her wristwatch then quickly switched out the bedside lamp and pretended to be asleep.

He went first of all to the lavatory then, washed by the sounds of a flushing cistern, stealthily entered the bedroom. He undressed in the dark, not clumsily. Eyes wide open, Trudi listened to the familiar sounds, heart beating hard against her ribs, her breath cloudy in her throat.

He slid in beside her and lay on his back, not touching her.

She heard him breathe.

He said, 'I know you're not sleeping, Trudi.'

She said, 'What time is it?'

'Half one.'

'You have not been with her so late before.'

He said, 'That's true.'

She was rigid with fear, sinews stiff, lips drawn back from her teeth not in anger but in fear. 'Have you been with her?'

'With Maggie? Yep.'

'I can smell her from your body,' Trudi said.

'That's whisky,' Henry said. 'What you smell is whisky.'

Trudi turned on to her elbow. He was there, somewhere, in the darkness.

'How can you tell such lies to me?' she hissed.

'Huh!' he said, uttering the sound so softly, so sadly that she rolled back into a foetal position and buried her face in the pillow.

Henry touched her shoulder. 'You'd better sit up. I've something to say.'

'No.'

'Come on, sit up. Will I put the light on?'

'No.'

'All right. Have it your way,' Henry said. 'I'm going to London with Maggie Chancellor. Sleeper down on Saturday night. Sleeper back on Sunday.'

'You tell me this to make me suffer, to teach me a lesson?'

'I tell you because I don't want you to think I'm having an affair,' Henry said. 'This is business, purely and strictly business.'

'I do not believe you.'

'Well, believe what you like,' Henry said. 'I can't tell you what to believe, about anything.'

'It is business for the *Mercury*?'

'It is business for us, Trudi. I can't tell you what's involved, not until I know more about it. I'm only telling you at all because I don't want you jumping to the wrong conclusions.'

'It is business about Germany?'

Henry grunted. 'You're too clever for your own good sometimes.'

She said, 'All night you have been with her?'

'We had a lot to discuss.'

'You do not discuss with me?'

'All in good time, Trudi.'

'I am still wife to you, Henry.'

'Don't I know it,' Henry said with a trace of irony in his tone which hinted that something had happened, something else had changed. 'I'm going to London overnight. On business. That's all you or anyone else has to know right now. And if you happen to be in touch with Marcus Harrison I'd be very obliged if you'd say nothing to him about what I've just told you.'

'I am not in touch with Harrison.'

'Okay.'

'He knows what it is that happened to you in Berlin?'

'Probably.'

'I did not tell him of it. Did you not tell him?'

'Not me,' said Henry. 'Though somebody would, I reckon, since cash was involved. Anyhow, I don't want Harrison to know where I've gone or who I've gone with. Right?'

'I understand.'

'Can I trust you on this one, Trudi?'

'Yes, I am to be trusted,' she said. 'Are you?'

Again Henry uttered that soft, sad little 'Huh!' and, without giving her an answer, turned on his side to sleep.

It was tempting to tell Howard what had happened. She needed a confidant. Jim had been her confidant for so many years that she felt lost without him. Howard, though, was too busy to give her his full attention and Saturday morning in the barred-window dormitories of Gartnavel mental hospital was no time to raise the topic of a mere broken engagement.

Besides, nippy little Dr Swanston wouldn't stand for casual conversation. He was the sort of teacher who believed in harnessing students to the grindstone. He had them whipping round the beds and into the consulting-rooms with a fervour that appeared to outstrip that of his more manic patients. He was not a gifted orator, far from it, but his knowledge of neurotic disorders was exhaustive and Howard, who had developed a deep interest in the subject, hung on the little man's every word and scribbled away in his notebook as if his life depended upon it. The uninhibited atmosphere of the mental hospital discouraged confidential exchanges and it was with a feeling of relief that Alison hurried out of the castellated building and headed for the bus stop on Great Western Road.

'Howard . . .'

'Listen, I really do have to run, Alison.'

'Howard, Jim has . . .'

'Jim? He's all right, isn't he?'

'Yes, he's fine, but . . .'

'Good, good! Look, I must dash. I've a ticket for the rugby international and I don't want to miss the kick-off. See you on Monday, all right?'

'All right.'

She watched him trot off towards Anniesland, gathering, as he went, two or three other rugby football fans and, alone by the side of the broad, open road, realised that she hadn't wanted to tell Howard at all.

She had invented a need to share her secret, to seek advice. She was perfectly able to keep the news of her broken engagement to herself. Perhaps she was embarrassed, more embarrassed than she had any right to be. But nobody would blame her for not wanting to marry a man who was so much older than she was and who, by the lights of the day, had nothing material to offer.

For that reason Alison decided to keep Jim's announcement to herself, at least until she'd had words with Winnie Craddock and found out how the land lay in that unfriendly quarter.

It might not, after all, be too late to get Jim back.

If, that is, she wanted him.

'I hope,' Phillip Leyman said, 'that you're not going to do anything foolish.'

'Like what?' Jim said.

'Like hurling yourself back into a full and active life.'

'Any sort of a life would do me right now,' Jim said. 'Why don't you come to the point, Doctor. What's Alison been telling you?'

'I haven't seen her for a day or two. I thought you might know the reason for her absence.'

'She's busy with other things, I expect.'

'Of course she is,' Phil Leyman said. 'That, however, hasn't stopped her visiting you before.'

'I've broken off our engagement.'

'Ah!'

'If and when I ever get out of here, I'm going back to Perthshire, not Glasgow,' Jim said. 'Healthier environment for an invalid, don't you agree?'

'You won't be an invalid. You certainly won't be bedridden.'

'What about my job?'

'I doubt if you'll be accepted by the Scottish Board of Education until you've sustained a period of good health for at least twelve months.'

'Probably longer?'

'Yes, probably longer. Do you have financial worries?'

'Who doesn't these days?' Jim said. 'I've a couple of small pensions plus some insurance. I won't be living like Lord Rothschild but I will be able to keep soul and body together.'

'Two can live as cheaply as one.'

'Dear God! Is that a medical cliché, or something you read in *My Weekly*?' Jim said. 'Look, I appreciate all you've done for me. I also appreciate the fact that you've offered Alison security after her graduation. Ottershaw would suit her temperament.'

'Which is why I'd like to have her on my staff,' Phil Leyman said. 'Salary will be commensurate with her experience, however, and our ability to pay. She's not going to be drawing down two or three thousand pounds a year.'

'The wage is immaterial,' Jim said. 'I just want to see her started on her career, that's all.'

'So that you can leave with a clear conscience.'

'Nothing cloudy about my conscience, I assure you,' Jim said. 'Anyway, consumptives shouldn't marry.'

'Ah! So that's your excuse, is it?'

'My excuse for what?'

'Ruining your life . . .'

'Don't say it,' Jim warned, threateningly. 'Don't say "And Alison's." '

'Consumptives certainly shouldn't marry while they have an active tuberculous disease,' Leyman said. 'Even I wouldn't advocate that. But look at it this way – consumptives who *are* married aren't required or even expected to divorce, are they?'

'I can't – I mean, Alison wouldn't be able to have children.'

'Of course she would.'

'And risk perpetuating . . .'

'Now *that* argument I just *will not* accept.' It was Dr Leyman's turn to speak heatedly. 'If we tried to improve the human race by refusing

317

to allow everyone who's had an illness to father a child – Good God, where would that kind of thinking end? First it would be pulmonary disorders, then rheumatic, then we'd be destroying the infants of heart patients at birth. And soon after that, it would be mulattos, or gypsies or even Jews.'

'That's ridiculous!' Jim said.

'Not so ridiculous,' Phil Leyman said. 'Who among us has the authority to deny a man the right to father or a woman to bear children? Who would make the rules? Who would pass the laws? And what abuses might those laws lead to? Many otherwise decent, respectable people believe that blood can even be tainted by intermarriage between men and women of different races.'

'Even I know that's wrong. Blood's blood, isn't it?'

'Familial disorders cannot be wiped out by eugenics,' Leyman continued. 'For anyone – doctor, scientist, lawyer or politician – to declare that selective mating is the answer to our social ills is to spit in the eye of God.'

'Meaning?'

'Meaning that you can't make TB an excuse for not marrying the young woman you love, and who loves you.'

'Even without a history of tuberculosis I'm no bargain.'

'Tell me about the arm,' Phil Leyman said suddenly.

'What?'

'When you wakened up in that field hospital in Flanders and realised that you were missing a fin, what did you think then?'

'I wanted to die.'

'But you hadn't died, had you?'

'No,' Jim said, 'it didn't take me long to realise that I was, indeed, one of the lucky ones. At least I was alive, not lying rotting in the mud.'

'And now?'

'It's different.'

'Is it? Are you rotting in the mud now?'

'Hmmm!' Jim grunted. 'I take it you think I am?'

'What do you want most?' Phil Leyman said. 'The truth now, Abbott, the whole truth. No prevaricating.'

'I want Alison to be happy.'

'Impossible!' Phil Leyman said. 'Not only impossible but incredibly egotistical.'

'Egotistical? Why?'

'To think that you can make Alison, or anyone, happy. That's not in your power, Jim, or mine, for that matter. Yes, I can help nature heal. I can restore a person who's been weak and sick to health and strength. But I cannot make them happy. No one can.'

'Why are you nagging me then?' Jim said.

Phil Leyman blinked, then chuckled. He held up both hands in a position of surrender, palms out. 'You've got me there.'

'Let Alison make the decision,' Jim asked, 'is that what you're saying?'

'Broadly, yes, that is what I'm saying.'

'And me?' Jim Abbott said. 'What do you think will make *me* happy?'

'Getting out of here.'

'Glib, too glib.'

'You're right,' Phil Leyman conceded.

'What then?'

'Let Alison decide.'

'Because I can't or because I won't?' Jim asked.

Phil Leyman shrugged and answered, 'Dead in the mud, old man. Either way you're dead in the mud.'

Henry's experience of London had been limited to taxi rides between railway stations. He was surprised how green and pretty the capital appeared that Sunday morning. Bridal-cake architecture, domed, tiled and curlicued, glittered in the sunshine and the streets, at that hour, were quiet. Margaret and he breakfasted in a friendly little café near Euston. Then, at the woman's instigation, set out to see the sights.

Henry was glad to be away from Glasgow for a spell but he was also relieved that London displayed no trace of Berlin's aggressive modernism. For the first time in weeks he felt confident, almost optimistic.

Maggie knew the capital well. She led him by broadways and by leafy back streets to the Thames, to Westminster of which Henry had often written but had never seen before. Next she took him to Downing Street, the Mall and Buckingham Palace then, just as Henry was becoming leg-weary, hailed a taxi to carry them back to Holborn for their meeting with Victor Gerber, owner of the Pembroke Press.

Maggie had already briefed Henry on what to expect. Gerber was a Hungarian Jew, rich, shrewd and as socialist in his leanings as it was possible to be without becoming a servant of communism. He published five or six limited-circulation weeklies in several languages and had part-time correspondents planted in many European capitals.

Pembroke Press was, however, Gerber's flagship and his main source of income. He had built the fortunes of the house on cheap 'railway' editions of sentimental romances and racy detective novels long before he'd floated the series of political tracts and exposés which had brought him notoriety. It was Gerber who had published English translations of Vlad Kurtz's best-known works, first in plain brown cloth and later in the trim little pocket-sized editions which had rattled through umpteen reprintings.

The publishing offices lay next to a large public house named the Hand-in-Glove. The red brick building was entered from a lane at the side. Henry and Margaret were met in the lane by a silent, very beautiful young woman who escorted them to a courtyard at the rear where four men, young too, were gathered round a table in the open air.

Behind the enclosure, trailing ivy and topped with broken glass, rose a high wall, the rear of the pub and a couple of office tenements with ranks of unwashed windows. The courtyard was dressed with trellises, painted garden furniture and tubs gay with early flowering shrubs.

In spite of the pervasive odour of beer it was, Henry thought, a pleasant and private place to hold a meeting.

The beautiful dark-haired woman acted as hostess. Margaret and he were served with food and wine while introductions were still being made. Gerber and Henry sized each other up. Henry had expected Gerber to be older, more obviously sophisticated and, reflecting his own unfortunate prejudices, perhaps, more obviously Jewish. Instead he found himself shaking hands with a lean, youthful-looking man clad in an old blue sports jacket and open-necked shirt. The others were no older, no more formal but there was in them, as there was not in Gerber, a guardedness which Henry found just a little less than friendly.

Margaret seemed completely at her ease.

For a moment Henry found it difficult to relate to his old sparring partner from the *Banner* as she traded international gossip with the gentlemen and ate heartily of the strong-smelling dishes which were put down before her. Henry ate too, but without much consideration for what he was putting in his mouth.

He was watchful, alert for the casual remark which would bring him into the conversation and test his mettle. He knew he was being evaluated by men who, in Scotland, would have been classed as milksops. Unusual names, unconventional appearances would draw scorn from Jack and Davy, Bertie and Dad, whose proprietorial identity and interpretation of the world had become so much a part of them that they believed it to be none other than reality itself.

Here in London, or in Paris or Berlin, they would be lost.

Henry, however, was not lost. He ate salt beef, drank Hungarian wine, watched and listened. When Gerber finally turned to him and casually canvassed his opinion, Henry was ready with an answer. His reading had given him a sound grasp of the issues at stake. He answered Gerber briefly, then, with Maggie nodding encouragement, cited the reason for his view at greater length. The young men glanced uncertainly at Henry and Maggie touched Victor Gerber's hand as if to say 'I told you so.'

Ten minutes later Gerber was ready to put his cards on the table. He said, 'I am told that you saw Vladimir while you were in Berlin?'

'In prison,' Henry answered. 'In so-called "protective custody", in the big new building in Prinz-Albrecht Strasse.'

'Gestapo,' said one of the other men, tight-lipped.

'Do you speak German, Henry?' Gerber asked.

'No.'

'French?'

'Not well, no.'

'Vlad spoke to you in English?'

'Yes, he spoke to me in English. There was another guy there too, another Russian, I think. He spoke English much less well.'

'His name?'

'Karl.'

'Who else did you see in Gestapo custody?'

'No one. Only a boy.'

'The boy is of no importance,' one of the young men said. 'Tell us what you can about Vladimir.'

'No,' Henry heard himself say. 'First I'll tell you about the boy, this boy who has no importance. Then, if you wipe that smirk off your face, I might consider telling you what I can about Kurtz.'

The young man's mouth opened. His cheeks flushed as if he had been slapped. He seemed more alarmed than offended. He rose from his chair and gave Henry an unGermanic bow. 'You have my apology, Mr Burnside. I should not have spoken as I did.'

'You must excuse Stefan, he is from Paris, much too used to Frenchmen to think before he speaks,' Gerber said. 'Sit down, Stefan. I am sure you are forgiven. By all means tell us about the boy, Henry.'

'No,' Henry said. 'I can see you really want to find out about Kurtz. What do you know already, Mr Gerber?'

'Very little. Nobody has seen Kurtz or heard from him in five weeks. We believe Kurtz and another of our writers, Karl Krieger, may have been taken to Berlin, interrogated and possibly murdered.'

Gerber said. 'Do you think that we are being too hasty in our judgement?'

'No, I think you're correct.'

'What did Vlad imagine might happen to him? Do you know?'

Henry said, 'Kurtz was convinced he'd never see the light of day again.'

'Did he tell you so?'

'He implied it,' Henry said. 'He also gave me a message which sounded to me like a last message.'

'What was it Vlad said?' one of the young men asked.

'He said that I was to tell Anna that he loved her and that he was thinking of her always.' Henry paused. 'Who's Anna? Does anyone know who Anna is?'

'Vlad's daughter,' Gerber answered.

And Henry turned abruptly in his chair as behind him, framed by a wall of ivy topped by broken glass, the beautiful young woman began quite audibly to weep.

It seemed strange to Alison to have to ring the doorbell of the council house in Macarthur Drive and wait for admission. The key which Jim had given her was no longer in her possession. Winnie Craddock had demanded its return and Alison, to avoid argument, had handed it back immediately.

It had been weeks since last she'd visited Jim's house. Hedge and lawn were untidy. The earth strips that bordered the garden path had not been turned over. The place was rapidly running to seed and, come summer, would surely turn into a jungle. She felt a prickle of petty satisfaction: Winnie obviously couldn't cope as well as she – with her brothers' help – had done.

Winnie opened the door.

She had grown even more baggy and unravelled, so changed from the polished person that Alison recalled from the good old days when she'd come here as a schoolgirl for extra tutoring that she, Winnie, was hardly recognisable. In her innocence, she'd assumed that Winnie Craddock was a model of middle-class respectability in total control of her circumstances. How wrong she'd been. Jim's sister had no more control over her destiny than anyone else.

Alison said, 'I want a word with you, Mrs Craddock, please.'

'I've nothing to say.'

'I want to know what you've got against me and why you've turned Jim against me. In case you didn't know, he's broken off our engagement.'

'I had nothing to do with that.'

'Nonsense! You had everything to do with it,' Alison said. 'Now, are you going to let me in, or are you not?'

The woman shuffled back into the hall and admitted Alison to the living-room. The house had an air not so much of gloom as of poverty. It had never been much of a room anyway, Alison realised, not as grand as she'd once imagined it to be. It didn't even have the benefit of a roaring fire to add cheer, only a meagre pile of coal nuts smoking in the grate. Teacups and stained saucers ringed once-gleaming surfaces. A bowl of porridge had been slopped on the hearth. Jim's bookcase, his pride and joy, had been emptied. The door hung half open on a loose hinge that Davy could have repaired in seconds.

Alison said, 'What happened to the books?'

'I – I removed them.'

'Sold them?'

'Jim has more books at home.'

'This is his home.'

'Not for much longer,' Winnie Craddock said.

Her apron needed washing, her hair too. If she had been less dictatorial in manner Alison might even have felt sympathy for her plight.

Alison said, 'So it *was* you who persuaded Jim to break our engagement?'

'He didn't need much persuasion.'

'Where's your mother?'

'She's – she's being taken care of.'

'Where?'

'You've no right to ask me personal questions.'

'Oh, haven't I?' Alison said. 'Jim broke his promise to me and I've every right to find out the reason why.'

'He doesn't love you,' Winnie said. 'He's come to realise that you're in no position to take care of him. Jim's always been delicate.'

'Delicate? What does that mean?' Alison said. 'Jim's no weakling. He's a nice, ordinary man who happened to fall ill, that's all.' Before Winnie could think how to answer, Alison asked again, 'Where is your mother?'

'My sister's looking after her.'

'Which sister?'

'Connie.'

'In that case, why do you need Jim to—'

'It's a temporary arrangement,' Winnie Craddock interrupted.

'I see. Your mother needs permanent nursing. So Jim's going to be saddled with the pair of you for the rest of his days?'

Alison had not intended to be so acerbic but she saw very clearly what was in store for Jim in the stuffy little Perthshire township, how in time he would become his sister's shadow, unable to exist without her. Winnie, Alison realised, was the pathetic relic of an age that had passed, a time of mourning, a time of fear. She, Alison, would have none of it. She couldn't live in the shadow of a tragedy which had touched her generation hardly at all.

She said, 'Well, I'm not going to let that happen.'

'You're too young to understand people like us.'

'People like you?' Alison said.

'Older people, people with experience of things you know nothing about,' Winnie Craddock said. 'What do you know about duty and family respon—'

'What a selfish prig you are, Mrs Craddock,' Alison said, coldly. 'How dare you assume that just because you suffered through a war you've got the copyright on moral virtue. It was a fairly stupid war, anyway. In fact, if your generation hadn't been blinded by a distorted sense of "duty" then it might never have happened. It gave you importance, didn't it? It gave you energy, shook you awake. King and country, the great British nation, Scotland the Brave. I'll bet you even waved the flag when Jim – and your husband too, probably – went marching off down Main Street.'

'How dare—'

'But you didn't have to fight, did you? All you had to do was stay at home, knit socks, and *suffer*. Well, if there is another war – and my brother says there might be – you won't catch me hiding behind Jim's back, or any man's back. If there is another war then I'll be fighting in it too.'

'You don't know what you're talking about.'

'No, I don't,' Alison said. 'I just pray to God I never have to find out. But if I do, Mrs Craddock, I won't be cheering and urging my brothers to go and make me proud of them. I'll be with them. I'll be one of them.'

'This has – this has nothing to do with . . .'

'With Jim?' Alison said. 'Yes, it has. It has *everything* to do with Jim. Don't you understand what Jim has understood all along. I don't *need* him. Jim made quite sure of that. He made me what I am, or soon will be. He gave me a chance to be *free* to choose. I may love him but I do not need him.'

'I need him,' Winnie said. 'We all need him.'

'For what?'

'To . . .'

'To take care of you? But surely you can take care of yourselves?' Alison could not resist the jibe. 'I thought you'd have learned how to do that, since you're so much older and wiser than I am.'

'He needs to take care of his mother.'

'No, you need him to take care of your mother,' Alison said. 'And Jim will do that. Once he's well again, which won't be too long now, thank God, then he'll do everything he can to see you settled. If it's a scarcity of money, then I'm sure we'll be able to help out.'

'We don't want *your* money. We don't want *your* help.'

'No,' said Alison again. 'You want to be both proud *and* dependent. And you want Jim back where you think he belongs – under your thumb.'

'How can you say these cruel things to me?' Winnie whimpered.

'Because I'm selfish too,' Alison answered. 'And because I love your brother as much, if not more, than you do.'

'You *don't* love him. You *can't* love him,' Winnie said.

'How can you be so sure?'

'*Because if you loved him you wouldn't let him go*,' Winnie cried.

She stopped speaking suddenly. Her eyes widened. She placed the palm of her hand against her flabby cheek as if she had scalded herself.

And Alison said, 'Precisely,' with a small, triumphant smile.

It was one of those strange phenomenon that no architect could ever account for but the heat generated by an average family in a council house in the first half-hour of a morning was enough to send a thermal regulator soaring straight off the wall. From shivering in bedrooms and bathrooms, housewives, schoolchildren and working men alike swiftly graduated to boiling in kitchenettes and living-rooms. Most of the rise in temperature was, of course, occasioned by a selfish scramble to be first into the lavatory, first into the kitchenette, first at the table with the tea and toast and first to growl 'Cheerio,' and gallop off, late, to work.

No matter how skilfully she negotiated the schedule even Trudi Burnside couldn't make mornings cool, calm and tolerable. Bertie would yelp at Davy. Davy would shout at Henry. Henry would snap at Alison and Alison, who also had an early start, would grizzle and complain to Trudi as if she, Trudi, was the great arbiter or, worse, was somehow to blame for mornings existing at all.

Monday was little different from any other weekday, except that Henry was missing from the scene and Trudi, because of it, was more tense and indrawn than ever.

Henry had given no indication when he would return from London. Hadn't even had the courtesy to inform her if he intended to go directly to the *Mercury* office or if he would manage home for breakfast first; or if, perhaps, he would repair to the Chancellor woman's apartment for one last hour of love-making if, that is, he had not done enough to satisfy her in the sleeping-compartment during the night.

Davy said, 'When's Henry comin' back then?'

'I do not know,' Trudi answered.

'Maybe he's no' comin' back at all,' Bertie chipped in.

'Aye, found himself some big English doll,' Davy suggested.

'Cut it out, you two,' said Alison.

'I tell you if I got the chance—' Davy said.

'You'd what?' Bertie interrupted. 'You wouldn't know what to do.'

'I'd learn fast enough,' said Davy, 'if she was big enough.'

Alison said, 'For heaven's sake, cut it out.'.

Then, still arguing, they were gone, scattering off in different directions to shop, building-site and classroom and leaving Trudi alone to brood on the fact that her seduction of Henry Burnside had taken place in a railway train too.

Twenty-five minutes to nine o'clock. Trudi seated disconsolately at the table, drinking tea amid breakfast debris. Pete, forepaws on the window ledge, looking out at the grey, indeterminate weather. Pete *wuffing*. Tail wagging. Pete rolling down, waddling, claws scratching, into the hall. The sound of a key in the Yale. Trudi forced herself to remain seated, to remain calm.

She gripped the cup tightly in cupped hands.

Henry came into the living-room, the dog at his heels.

He put down the overnight bag, took off his hat.

Trudi said, 'I thought it would be that you had gone to work.'

Henry removed his overcoat and tossed it on to a chair. 'Telephoned from the corner box. Said I was sick, that I'd be in at lunchtime.'

He patted Pete's head, played with the dog's ears, went into the kitchen.

Trudi called out, 'You have eaten breakfast?'

'Yes.'

'In the sleeping compartment?'

Henry reappeared, a cup of Camp coffee steaming in his hands. 'On the train, in the diner.'

'With her?'

Henry seated himself at the head of the table, penning her in with his long legs. He looked tired, very tired, yet also relaxed.

Henry said, 'How would you like to live in Paris?'

Trudi did not answer.

Henry said, 'I don't mean just you. I mean both of us.'

'Paris? What is there in Paris?'

'A lot of political activity,' Henry said.

'Is this a job of work for you?'

'Yep.'

'I like to stay here, with the family.'

'I know you do,' said Henry. 'Paris wouldn't necessarily be for ever. Six months or a year abroad. What do you say, Trudi?'

'You will give up your position on the *Mercury*?'

'Of course.'

'Because of what has happened?'

'Yes,' Henry answered, 'because of what has happened.'

'Why do you not take her to Paris?'

'Firstly, she wouldn't go. She's too involved in local politics. Secondly, I'm not married to her. I'm married to you.'

'You do not speak French.'

'I can learn. I'll have to, won't I?'

'I will teach it to you.'

He nodded. He looked at her as he had not looked at her in weeks, not since Berlin. She still did not know whether she was being forgiven or used.

Henry said, 'I'll have to ask Alison, before I do anything.'

'Alison?'

'I promised Alison I'd see her through university.' He shrugged. 'You know me, Trudi, or you should by this time. I'm a sucker for keeping promises.'

'How soon will we have to leave?'

'Not until August or September.'

'What will the boys do if we are gone?'

'Ruby'll take care of them.'

'There will be not enough money.'

'There might be,' Henry said. 'There will be.'

'This money, where will it come from?'

'From the book I'm going to write.'

'You? A book?'

'Why not?'

'Is it that you know how to write a book?'

'Writing it isn't going to be the problem,' Henry said. 'The problem is what I'm going to put in it. And that's where you come in.'

'Me?'

'There's a man in London, a publisher, name of Gerber. He's Hungarian.'

'And Jewish?'

'Jewish or not,' said Henry, 'I like him.'

'Because he has given a job to you?'

'Harrison gave me a job too, didn't he? You weren't so scathing about that at the time, as I recall?'

Trudi didn't have to enquire why he no longer wanted to work for Marcus Harrison, for Lord Blackstock. She had drawn him into that circle. She saw now that she had misjudged Henry Burnside. He was not to be her refuge, her tower of strength. He intended to be her equal, whether she wished it or not. The man-woman games they had played were over, the eternal courtship concluded. They had other, more important things to do now.

Henry said, 'I'm going to write about Germany, Trudi. Gerber's definitely interested. If it's good enough, he'll publish it. The big problem is that he wants me to name names.'

'What does this have to do with Paris?'

'Once I deliver the book then Gerber will send me to Paris to report on the situation there.'

'This is what you want, Henry?'

'No, I'd prefer to stay here, write pieces about Gaelic bards and Glasgow councillors, engine-drivers, ventriloquists and parliamentarians. I'd prefer to live in Flannery Park, watch over you and my family and die in my bed upstairs aged ninety-four. But I can't. Thanks to you, Trudi, I just can't.'

'Did you not make a promise to my Papa?'

'I didn't promise him anything. You made that promise.'

'Do you wish me to break it?'

'Yes.'

'If you reveal the truth Papa will be hanged, or shot.'

'I doubt it,' Henry said. 'Unless I'm much mistaken your old man's too slippery to be caught out twice.'

'Otto, my son, he will be destroyed.'

'And what will destroy him?'

'You, what you will say.'

'No, Trudi. Otto might be brought down but it won't be by me. It'll be by his own people, by what they are and what he is. I won't lie to you. I'm going to write about us, Trudi, about what happened in Berlin. And I am going to name names. What I need from you is evidence.'

'What if I say I have no evidence? Will you throw me out?'

'No, I won't do that.'

'But you will hate me?'

'I'll be disappointed in you, Trudi, that's all.'

'You have been disappointed in me already, no?'

'Yeah, I have.'

'Because I did not tell you about Otto?'

'Because you thought you could hide here, Trudi,' Henry said. 'You can't. There's no place for a person like you to hide. Did you think we were too stupid – no, too comfortable – to have consciences? Well, you were wrong. We're made differently, shaped differently, you and me. God knows how we ever got together or what we're doing together. All I know is that I think we're going to have to stick it out, whatever it costs us.'

Trudi got to her feet. Henry stared up at her then swung his legs away and, taking his coffee cup with him, crossed to the fireplace. He heard her go upstairs. Pete nudged a dry nose into his palm. Absently, Henry stroked the dog's muzzle. He did not have to wait long.

Within minutes Trudi returned to the living-room.

She carried a thick leather wallet, like a large handbag, that Henry could not recall ever having seen before. She held it to her breast for a moment then thrust it out in both hands.

'It is this that you want,' Trudi said.

He didn't snatch at the wallet, didn't even ask what it contained.

Trudi said, 'There is also more. I have papers keeping safe for me in Gerald Dante's office.'

'Huh!' Henry said. 'I wouldn't be surprised if they've been conveniently and permanently "mislaid". Dante's involved in this too, you know.'

'Gerald would not dare to deceive me,' Trudi said. 'He knows what I can tell about him even without documents. He would be struck down, no?'

'Struck off,' said Henry. 'Yes, I suppose he would.'

He took the wallet and opened the flap. Letters, some on headed paper, an account book, yellowing clippings; the collection did not seem at all interesting and certainly not dangerous.

Henry said, 'Where did you hide this stuff, Trudi?'

She laughed, the familiar tinkling sound, still little-girlish.

'In the back of the cupboard,' she said. 'Behind Freud.'

Henry nodded. 'Naturally!'

'You will make use of them, Henry?'

'Oh, yes,' he said. 'Unless – last chance – you want to take them back?'

'I have given you what I have. I will not take back.'

'Do you really understand what I'm going to do?'

'Tell everyone about me, and about them.'

'Yep.'

'First,' Trudi said, 'you will need this.'

She reached across her husband's forearms and extracted from the wallet three sheets of quarto paper fastened together with a brass paperclip. In smart black print the sheets bore the address of an office in Berlin, an address that Henry recognised immediately.

'What are they?' he said.

'Receipts,' Trudi told him.

'What!'

'Papa gave me receipts,' she said. 'One for each of them.'

'Dear God!' said Henry. 'I can't believe it. They go to all that bother to smuggle hard currency into the country then your Papa hands out signed *receipts*. Dear God!'

'He is a very methodical man, my Papa,' Trudi said.

'Or very, very crafty.'

'What is it you mean?' Trudi said innocently.

'He's given you protection,' Henry said. 'It seems your dear old Papa didn't *quite* let you down after all. Hmmm?'

'To commit everything into the writing it is an old Germanic custom. Papa is the victim of a habit, nothing more,' Trudi said.

Henry held up the printed documents and scanned the title blocks. He whistled. 'Dante, Clive Coventry *and* Blackstock.'

'Also Herr Marcus Harrison,' Trudi said. 'You can use, no?'

'Oh, yes, sweetheart, I can use,' said Henry.

Once, years ago, Henry had given her a copy of Thomas Carlyle's *Heroes and Hero Worship* to read. Alison had ploughed dutifully through it but, at the time, she hadn't understood the half of it. Later, just before his illness, she had debated Carlyle's thesis with Jim who, like Carlyle, firmly believed that the history of a nation was no more than the sum of the lives of great men. This, Alison was convinced, was a fallacy.

To her way of thinking every great man was ringed about with lesser men and most of the decisions which affected the fate of nations were rooted not in greatness but in trivial events. Odd that old Tom Carlyle should spring to mind while Henry was telling her about his experiences in Berlin and how his plans had changed because of them.

'Who else have you told about this?' Alison asked.

'Only Trudi.'

'What does she have to say about it?'

'Trudi is being very co-operative.'

'That's an odd way of putting it, Henry.'

'Very encouraging: is that better?'

'Dad will go up in a blue light. You know how conservative he can be.'

'His job will be safe enough. I'll make absolutely sure of that,' Henry said.

'Will you really go off to work in Paris?'

'Sure. But not until the autumn. I've a book to write first.'

'What will you live on meanwhile?' Alison asked.

'Well, we've a wee bit put away. Not much, but it'll pay the rent. Bert and Davy are in steady employment. Their wages will cover the small bills.'

'You're worried about me, aren't you? My education?'

'I made you a promise once, Ally, and I don't want to go back on it.'

'In eighteen months,' Alison said, 'I'll be on the medical register and more than able to take care of myself. Until then – well, I do have something of my own. Money left to me by Gran Gilfillan. I've used some of it but there's enough left to see me through. In fact, Henry, I'm the least of your worries.'

'Somehow I thought you'd say that,' Henry told her.

'Besides, I'll have Jim to look after me.'

'Will you? Are you sure?'

'Positive.'

'Jim won't be earning again for quite some time.'

'I'm marrying a man, not a meal ticket,' Alison said.

'Why are you marrying him at all?' Henry said.

'Because I don't love anyone else,' Alison said. 'You, of all people, Henry, should know what I mean by that.'

'Oh, I do,' said Henry. 'Unfortunately, I do.'

'Trudi will stand by you, won't she?'

'Yes. Probably.'

'And I'll stand by Jim. Same thing.'

'What about those other guys? Howard McGrath, for instance, or this Dr Leyman?'

'Friends, colleagues,' Alison said. 'Phillip Leyman wants me to work for him. And Howard – well, Howard will always be there if I need him. If I'd met Howard first . . .' Alison hesitated, shook her head. 'No, things are as they are, Henry. You do what you have to do to feel right.'

'Head not heart, kiddo, hmmm?'

'If that's a clinical diagnosis, Henry, then there's something seriously wrong with your knowledge of anatomy.'

'Oh, I wouldn't say that.'

'Stick to politics. It's safer.'

'Thank you, my child. I will.'

'When will you tell them you're giving up the *Mercury*?' Alison asked.

'Tomorrow or the next day.'

'All right,' said Alison. 'Just make sure I'm around when you do.'

'How come?'

'Because, old son, you're going to need all the help you can get.'

'The man's mad,' said Alex. 'Barmy. Nuts . . .'

'Bonkers?' Brenda suggested.

'Round the bloody bend,' Alex went on, ignoring his daughter-in-law. 'Who the hell does Henry think he is, throwin' up his job in the middle of a slump just because some Jew-boy promises him a better one in Paris? Paris! Pie in the bloody sky, if you ask me.'

'Aye, but nobody, you know, did,' said Brenda.

'Supposin' Harrison takes offence an' I get slung out too?' said Alex.

'That won't happen,' Ruby said.

'How d'you know?'

'Because Henry said it wouldn't.'

'How can we take his word for anythin', selfish bugger?'

'Will she, you know, go with him?' Brenda asked.

'Of course Trudi'll go with him,' said Ruby. 'She's the reason he's goin'.'

'Eh?' Alex stopped pacing the carpet of the living-room in Shackleton Avenue. 'You mean she's drivin' him out, drivin' him away from his loved ones?'

'I mean, she's as ambitious as he is,' Ruby said. 'Can't blame her.'

'Don't tell me you want to go to Paris an' all?'

'Not me,' Ruby told her husband. 'I'm quite happy where I am. But then I'm not Trudi. And you're not Henry.'

'Whose side are you on?' Brenda said.

'I'm not on anybody's side,' Ruby said. 'For God's sake, the way you pair are carryin' on, you'd think Henry'd committed a terrible crime, just because he wants to better himself.'

'You don't better yourself by fleein' off to bloody Paris.'

'Oh, I dunno,' said Jack, casually. 'I wouldn't mind seein' Paris.'

'Don't you go gettin' ideas,' Brenda told him. 'You're goin' nowhere.'

'You better yourself,' Alex went on, 'by stayin' right where you are an' gettin' on with what you're paid for.'

'And what's that?' said Ruby.

'Workin'.'

'Right.' Brenda glowered threateningly at Jack. 'Workin'.'

'Could you do what Henry does?' Ruby asked her husband.

'Well, naw, but . . .'

'So how do you know he can't do it better in Paris?'

Alex and Brenda glanced at each other, while Jack, whistling silently, lay back on the sofa and put his hands behind his head.

'Anyway,' said Alex, 'what's all this about him writin' a book?'

'What's he, you know, gonna write about?'

'Us,' said Jack. 'Maybe he's goin' to put us all in a book.'

'Aye, well,' said Alex, 'there's worse things he could write about. I've seen things goin' on in the shipyards that'd fill ten books. If he wants to write a book he doesn't have to go Paris to do it.'

'After,' Ruby said.

'After what?' said Jack.

'First he writes his book, then he goes to Paris.'

'You are on his bloody side.'

'Alex, it's not a war, nor a football match.'

'What,' Brenda said, 'is he gonna do for money?'

'According to Trudi,' Ruby said, 'Henry's got it all worked out. When they do go abroad then I'll take care o' the boys.'

'And who'll take care of me?' Alex demanded.

'Dear God!' exclaimed Ruby in despair.

'We could take Ally in here,' Jack said. 'She could sleep in the twins' room. The twins would love it.'

Brenda opened her mouth, changed her mind.

'What need is there to take her in anywhere?' Alex asked.

'If you're givin' up the occupancy of 162,' said Jack.

'Givin' up . . . What would we do that for?'

Jack shrugged. 'Ally'll be out of there too in eighteen months. Davy an' Bert on their own will rattle around in a five-apartment.'

'What if Davy decides, you know, to get married?'

'Aye, or Bert?' said Alex.

There was a vague, uncomfortable silence while all four paused to consider Bert's matrimonial prospects and contemplate what sort of woman would take him on. No satisfactory conclusion having been reached, Alex cleared his throat and said, 'I'm not givin' up my house.'

'*Your* house?' said Ruby.

'I mean, the family home.'

'Who the hell do you think we are?' Ruby demanded. 'Landed gentry? Are you for handin' on the Burnside estates to the twins or the son-and-heir, if it is a son-and-heir. It's a *council* house, Alex. It belongs to Glasgow Corporation not to flamin' posterity.'

Alex slumped down on the couch beside his son.

He scowled, looked towards Brenda for support but she seemed suddenly disinterested, wrapped into herself.

'What's wrong, honey?' Jack asked. 'Is it kickin' again?'

'Yeah.'

'It's not arrivin' early, is it?' Alex asked in alarm.

'At five months? Don't be ridiculous,' Ruby told him.

'Do you want a wee drink, darlin'?' Jack asked.

'Nope, I want a wee, you know, pee.' Brenda hoisted herself to her feet. 'God, I'm tired of spendin' half my life in the toilet.'

Jack got to his feet too and, a hand on her arm, asked solicitiously, 'Can you manage, Bren?'

'Course I can manage. I've done it often enough.' She did not resist his attentions, however, and permitted him to accompany her into the hallway.

As soon as they were gone, Ruby hissed, 'Now see what you've done, you an' your silly nonsense.'

'Me?' said Alex. 'What've I done?'

'You've upset her.'

Alex, abashed, said, 'Shouldn't you go an' see if she's okay?'

'Jack'll look after her.' Ruby smoothed her skirt over her expanding hips. 'Let them get on with it. Henry'll look after Trudi and, if we have to, we'll look after the boys.'

'What about Alison, but?'

'Alison,' Ruby told him, without rancour, 'can look after herself.'

'Naw, naw. She still needs her Daddy,' said Alex.

'Not any more,' said Ruby.

She looked down on him, saw how much he had been hurt by the pace of events, the disintegration of the family, the dispersal of his sons and daughter into lives of their own. She felt irritation dwindle into sympathy and sympathy, as it usually did, meld instantly into affection. She slid on to the couch beside him and put an arm about his shoulders.

She blew into his ear, then said, 'But I do. Need you, I mean.'

'Really?' said Alex.

'Really,' said Ruby and, a little to her husband's embarrassment, proved it by giving him a kiss.

Trudi had gone shopping in the middle of the afternoon and, for a couple of hours, the house at Number 162 had been deserted.

The matchbox-size packet had obviously been pushed through the letterbox during that period and had been lying on the hall carpet when Trudi had returned. She'd lifted it, had read the name printed upon the stiff brown paper – *Miss Alison Burnside* – had given it a tentative little shake and had heard something rattle inside it. She'd had an unjustified impression that it might contain a bone or kidney stone or some such grisly artifact and, holding it between finger and thumb, had carried it straight upstairs and had placed it carefully on Alison's desk where it remained until Alison came home that evening at around half past six o'clock.

On being informed by Trudi that there was a parcel for her, Alison had gone upstairs immediately and had opened the package carefully.

Inside the wrapping paper was indeed a matchbox of the flat, pasteboard variety. Alison pushed open the box with her thumb and tipped out the object which the box contained.

Still wearing her hat and overcoat she went downstairs again and sought out Trudi in the steam of the kitchen.

'Who delivered this?' Alison asked.

'It was not the postman. It came when I was at the shopping,' Trudi said. 'What is it that is inside, please?'

'This,' Alison said quietly and held up a key.

'How mysterious,' said Trudi. 'There is no letter?'

'No,' Alison said, 'just the key.'

'It is Jim's key, is it not?'

'Yes,' Alison answered.

'Who would send it to you?'

'Oh, I know who sent it,' Alison said, frowning slightly. 'Winnie Craddock sent it. What I just can't understand is why.'

Even in the pretty light of a showery April evening Jim's house had a sad and disappointed air. The lime trees and old oaks that backed the villas on the upper end of Macarthur Drive had put out new leaves and the afternoon's soft little squalls of rain had washed and refreshed them so that the quiet wet nuances of sunset were reflected upon their upper tiers while pavements, hedges and housefronts were already gathered into dusk.

Lace-edged brown paper blinds had been lowered to half-mast on the living-room windows but the curtains had not been drawn and darkness, dense as oil, filled the interior of Jim's house. Alison had no need to ring the doorbell but she did so in any case. She listened to the tinny sound echo within as it might have in a dungeon or a keep. Then she fitted the key into the lock, turned it, pushed open the front door and stepped over the threshhold.

Winnie Craddock was not there.

Winnie Craddock had gone.

The house smelled once more of pine polish and lavender but

335

lacked the warmth that Alison remembered from her visits here as a girl. No tobacco smoke, no aroma of baking, no faint wisp of coffee brewing in the pot in the kitchen. The house was spotless, each article of furniture polished to a high gloss. Winnie Craddock had worked hard, Alison thought, to leave things right. Cleanliness did not equate with homeliness, however, and the empty bookcase with its broken latch, the bare table, the grate without a fire, all seemed so sad that Alison experienced Jim's absence more than she had ever done before.

The letter had been placed on the mantelpiece.

Alison opened the envelope, unfolded the single sheet of paper and read what Winnie had written: *I have gone home to be with Mother. I will not come back to Glasgow. Concerning the house, do what you think is best for Jim. Winifred Craddock (Mrs).* And that was all, that was it.

The simplicity with which Winnie Craddock had turned her life over on itself had about it a faint air of spite, as if that dour, embittered woman had finally achieved a kind of elegance. But Winnie Craddock lacked that degree of subtlety and had bowed out selfishly. Without grace, without acknowledging defeat, she had handed responsibility back to Alison.

Do what you think is best for Jim.

Whatever that might be, it was Alison's problem now, a problem to which there was no simple solution.

Holding the letter in one hand and the key in the other, Alison slumped on to a chair by the hearth and, in that cold, hostile room, did something she hadn't done since Jim had been taken away.

She wept.

Henry arranged his departure skilfully. He used the *Mercury*'s formal channels of communication to request an appointment with the managing editor.

Of course, he might have dialled Harrison's secretary's number on an internal wire and have toddled upstairs without any fuss at all. He chose, however, to send a memo to the features editor and, at the same time, arrange an interview with the NUJ's Father of Chapel. From the union representative he ascertained the precise procedure for transferring pension fund payments and enquired in a general way about requirements for affiliation to the Foreign Press Association. Naturally the interview was conducted in strict confidence – so that by lunchtime word was all over the office that Henry Burnside was on the move.

Some reporters expressed surprise that Burnside had a big

enough reputation to command a better job elsewhere. Others argued that young Henry had too much talent and tenacity to be accommodated in a provincial rag like the *Glasgow Mercury*. Dark hints and direct questions failed to wring answers out of Henry Burnside and when he left the reporters' room at half past four o'clock to ascend the narrow back stairs to the top floor no cries of 'Good Luck' or 'Give 'em big licks,' cheered him on his way.

Harrison was waiting for him.

Old Marcus, smooth, soft and seemingly casual, was tucked behind his littered desk, a small cigar in his fingers and a small, cautious smile on his lips. Henry was not deceived. Old Marcus was as alert and dangerous as a honey badger and his affable manner hid sharp teeth and raking claws.

'What is all this, Henry? There's a wild rumour circulating that you intend to leave us. True?'

'Quite true, Mr Harrison.'

'You do have a contract of employment, you know.'

'Two weeks notice, either side,' Henry said. 'I've eleven days holiday to come. If you take the holidays into account and I leave on Friday then . . .'

'All right, Henry. What's really on your mind? More money?'

'No,' said Henry. 'This.'

He extracted Papa Keller's signed receipts from the pocket of his jacket, unfolded them carefully and, equally carefully, laid them on Marcus Harrison's desk. The editor flicked over the sheets, glanced at them and then looked up at Henry without apparent surprise and certainly no sign of panic.

'So?' he said.

'Currency deals with Germany are not kosher, Mr Harrison.'

'Nonsense! Who told you that? Keller?'

'You're funding a fascist organisation.'

'Buying shares in a registered company is not, repeat not, illegal.'

'For cold cash, it is,' said Henry.

'At worst, a minor infringement of the law. I doubt if I'll be sent to the Tower or have my head chopped off for it. Lord, Henry, half the businessmen in Britain are ploughing capital into Germany.'

'Into rearming the enemy?'

'Oh, come now!' Harrison said.

'If it's just a little bit of capitalist sleight-of-hand,' said Henry, 'then you won't mind if I write about it, will you?'

'Not in this newspaper,' Harrison snapped.

'I do intend to write about it,' Henry said, 'which is the reason I'm quitting my post with the *Mercury*.' He placed another typed sheet on the desk. 'My letter of resignation, Mr Harrison.'

'Henry, I know what happened to you in Berlin. It was all rather unfortunate and I understand why you're upset, but there's absolutely no need to resign.'

'I suppose now you'll offer to promote me?'

'Is that what this is about?'

'No, that's not what this is about,' said Henry.

'I know you're ambitious and, I might add, an exceptionally good journalist. I can't make any promises, Henry, but I imagine Lord Blackstock might be able to find an opening for you as a foreign correspondent or, if you prefer it, as an on-the-spot parliamentary reporter in Westminster. How would that suit you? Trudi would like a change of scene, I'm sure.'

'Trudi has no say in it,' Henry told the editor.

'Did Trudi put you up to this?'

'What makes you think she would?'

Harrison shrugged. 'It just seems to be her – her style.'

'You mean blackmail?' said Henry. 'Well, it isn't. Not exactly. By the way, Mr Harrison, I know you slept with her.'

'She wasn't married then.'

'No, but you were.'

'Does that matter. To you, I mean?' Harrison said. 'You can't be that much of a prude, Henry, that much of a moralist. It was a passing affair, anyway. I was – we were both – carried away.'

'Were you also carried away by Margaret Chancellor?'

'I'm not on trial for my . . . damn it, Burnside, I don't have to answer to you.'

'Of course you don't, Mr Harrison,' Henry said. 'Oh, we could argue about the fine line between personal morality and public responsibility but that wouldn't get us anywhere, would it? The notion that you and Blackstock are actively supporting a Nazi rearmament programme wouldn't raise any eyebrows either. The slant of every paper Blackstock publishes is geared that way. But you know how exposé journalism works, how by matching one trivial piece of evidence with another you can *imply* anything. And get away with it.'

'And these receipts are your idea of damning proof?'

'I have other material,' Henry said. 'Quite a lot of it, in fact.'

'What . . .' Harrison cleared his throat. 'What sort of material?'

'Letters, documents; that sort of thing.'

'Going back how far?'

'Ten years, more.'

'Trudi!' Harrison said, thinly.

'And others.'

'Others? What others?'

'All those you got into bed with,' Henry said. 'Metaphorically speaking.'

'This is *so* petty, so makeweight, so far into the past that it's hardly worth giving up a job for, Henry. If you'll listen to me . . .'

'I have listened to you, Mr Harrison. I've listened to you for far too long. I've been hearing your voice ever since I was born. Now, at long last, I'm learning *exactly* what message you're delivering. And I don't like it.'

'Only words, Henry. We're really all much the same, you know, under the skin. Whether you work for Blackstock or Beaverbrook, *The Times,* the *Mercury* or the *Star,* in the end it all boils down to the same thing. The public are gullible and forgetful. Give them free coupons, racing tips, football results, a whisper of glamour, and the rest is just bread and circuses are far as they're concerned. You don't really think that John Bull cares tuppence what goes on behind the scenes, do you?'

'Good God!' said Henry. 'And I thought *I* was cynical.'

'Keep your job, Henry. Stay with Blackstock Press in some position or another. You're one of us, you know. We really do need smart young men in our ranks. Withdraw your resignation. Put it down to experience. We won't hold it against you. In fact, we'll forget that this unfortunate incident ever happened.'

'And the receipts?'

'They stay here with me.'

'And Vladimir Kurtz?'

'What does Kurtz have to do with it?'

'Free coupons, racing tips, bread and circuses? And Vladimir Kurtz, a free-speaking journalist, beaten to death in a Gestapo cell? How about that for a whisper of glamour?'

'Kurtz is an active communist, Henry.'

'Oh, I know what he was all right,' Henry said, 'and what he stood for.'

'Don't tell me you've gone red?'

'Certainly not,' said Henry.

'Why concern yourself with Kurtz then?'

'Why concern yourself with anything, is that what you're saying?' Henry answered. 'I'm just a shipyard worker with a talent for writing and a notion to get ahead. Nothing wrong with that – provided I don't get ideas. I don't mean just ideas above my station – you're good at squashing those – I mean *ideas* of any kind.'

'You can be stopped, Henry.'

'From doing what?'

'Publishing these half-baked lies.'

'I thought you believed in press freedom, Mr Harrison.'

'Not when it involves – not when it's wilfully malicious and destructive.'

'Like putting an innocent man out of work,' said Henry.

'I'm not putting you out of work. You're putting yourself—'

'I mean my father,' Henry interrupted.

'Your father?'

'He works downstairs in the mechanics' shop.'

'Of course he does.' Harrison smiled.

'Now you wouldn't go and sack my old man just because I went to work for another publisher, would you?' Henry said.

'What if we do?'

'Margaret Chancellor will take up his case.'

'Maggie? What can she do?'

'What can't she do,' said Henry, 'when she sets her mind to it? Besides, she has friends in mighty high places too. And not all bedfellows.'

'I see,' said Harrison. 'All this fuss is simply to protect your father's job.'

'Yep.'

'And the rest of it?'

'My resignation? That stands.'

'So you *are* going to work elsewhere, are you?'

'I am,' said Henry.

'Where, may I ask?'

'Paris – for Victor Gerber.'

'Gerber!' Marcus Harrison spat out the word. 'That damned Jewboy!'

Henry leaned suddenly across the desk. Harrison flinched. But Henry did nothing, offered no violence. He drew Papa Keller's receipts away and held them firmly in his fist.

Outside, the sun shone passively on Glasgow rooftops and from the streets below rose the guttural cries of news vendors marketing the evening editions, touting their latest small sensations. Henry felt a pang of regret at what he was leaving behind, not least his innocence and naïvety. How easy it would be to accept Harrison's offer, to pretend that he did not care, that he too was dedicated only to preserving the status quo, to selfishness, and had no talent at all for telling the truth.

He hesitated for only a moment then said, 'I hope you heard what I said about my dad, Mr Harrison. Remember, he's only a wee guy.'

'So's Hitler,' the editor retorted then, with an angry gesture, dismissed Henry from his office so that he, John Marcus Harrison, might get on with the business of covering up his tracks.

'Come now, Alison,' said Dr Phillip Leyman. 'We've known each other too long to beat about the bush. You're not taking the job, are you?'

'No.' Alison shifted uncomfortably in the office chair. 'I've decided against it. It's not that I don't appreciate your offer and the opportunity for serious post-graduate work but . . .' She shrugged, embarrassed.

Phil Leyman placed his heels on the edge of his desk, his hands behind his head. Brilliant Sunday-afternoon sunlight glinted on his spectacle lenses and hid his expression. He was restless, though, rocking the castored chair back and forth while he contemplated her.

At length, he said, 'It's Jim, isn't it?'

'Yes.'

'I could put up sound medical arguments for *not* marrying James Abbott, you know,' Phil Leyman said. 'Peddle the party line about consumptives and heredity and all that stuff, including the possibility that Jim might not live out his full term of three score years and ten.'

'But you won't, will you?'

'Be a waste of breath,' Phil Leyman said. 'If you fell in love with a man who had only one arm to begin with then adding a few dormant tubercles to the equation isn't going to deter you.' He brought his heels from the desk, clacked the chair's castors to the floor, and got up. 'What you could do, of course, is accept the post here on Ottershaw and find a little house in one of the nearby villages. Marriage *and* a career.'

'And a compromise,' said Alison.

Phil Leyman stroked his chin and considered her remark.

Alison went on, 'It wouldn't work, Dr Leyman. What you require from an assistant is a dedication to match your own, complete commitment to the speciality and to Ottershaw Hospital.'

'Pretty much, yes.'

'I can't make that commitment,' Alison said. 'If things had been other than they are I'd have leapt at the chance to do post-graduate work under your tutelage. But if I marry Jim then I'll have to find work that will allow me to be with him. If children come along then I'll want time off to be with them, at least while they're babies.'

'Don't tell me you're giving up medicine before you even graduate?'

'Of course not,' Alison said.

'What then? General practice?'

'Probably.'

'That's hardly a compromise,' Phil Leyman pointed out. 'It's also a waste of your talents. Do you intend to spend your life in some shabby consulting-room in – where is it – Flannery Park, doling out cough mixture and laxatives?'

'Aren't you being just a wee bit snobbish?' Alison said.

'Yes, you're right. I am. There are many excellent, dedicated GPs tucked away in urban and rural practices. The backbone of medicine. It's just that I had you marked as a high-flyer. Do you know what that means?'

Alison nodded.

'Look,' Phil Leyman went on, 'you don't have to make up your mind for another few months. I'm willing to hold the post open.'

'No,' Alison said. 'I have to make up my mind now.'

'Why, for heaven's sake?'

'Because if I don't then I might lose Jim.'

'He isn't going to die, you know.'

'Oh, he is,' said Alison. 'Perhaps not tomorrow or even the next day, but he is going to die. And you, not even you, can predict when it will happen or how or if, perhaps, I'll be the one to go first.'

'That's a very pessimistic outlook for a young woman.'

'I don't think it's at all pessimistic. On the contrary. What I've realised,' Alison said, 'is that I can't have everything I want laid out all ordered and neat. Life isn't like that. I don't want to waken up one morning to discover I'm forty-five years old and have nothing and nobody except my career, my "position". I have to make sure that I make the right choices now so that my decisions won't come back to haunt me in ten or fifteen years' time.'

'I suppose it's different for women,' Phil Leyman conceded.

'Very different,' Alison said.

She thought of Roberta, how Bobs had been caught by Declan Slater and, in a manner more random than ordained, had been sucked into a future that was no longer her own. Thought of Brenda, happily married, fulfilled in motherhood, compromising not with a career but only with vague, whimsical dreams of a grand and glamorous romance and a future that had never stood a chance. Thought too of Trudi, of the dark, abrasive burdens Trudi carried with her, how a past made up of compromises, wilfulness and strange, unlovely secrets had rendered all Trudi's relationships precarious, not least her present marriage.

'Perhaps I expected too much of you,' Phil Leyman said. 'Perhaps I should look for a smart young man instead of a girl to fill the bill of assistant. I just thought – Well, we all live and learn, don't we?'

'Not all women are like me,' said Alison.

'That's for certain.' Phil Leyman smiled and leaned his shoulders against the big plate glass window. 'I'll hold the post, won't advertise it, until September, just in case you decide to exercise the other privilege women have over men.'

'And change my mind?' Alison said. 'I won't.'

'Have you told Jim Abbott yet?'

'Not yet.'

'Better tell him soon.'

'Why?'

'To put him out of his misery.'

'Is he miserable?'

'Of course he is,' Phil Leyman said. 'I would be too if I'd lost my guiding light. But then I've never been fortunate enough to have a guiding light.'

'Medicine?'Alison suggested. 'Ottershaw?'

'That's not quite what I meant,' said Dr Leyman and hurried brusquely from the office before he said something that both he and Alison Burnside might later rather regret.

Gardening was one of many subjects about which Alison knew nothing. She could not separate pansies from nasturtiums, dahlias from chrysanthemums. She had no idea what genus of plant Jim was bedding out in the dark earth of the Ottershaw borders.

She watched him, unnoticed, from the tail of the gravel pathway. Once, not so very long ago, she had watched him attend his garden in Macarthur Drive, had been amazed at how ingeniously he had devised ways to work one-handed and how much he seemed to know about the art and science of growing things.

The little velvet-leaved plants in the strawberry basket on the gravel by his side seemed ideally suited to a man of Jim's temperament. Tender herbs fine-rooted in pouches of sandy soil needed sure and gentle treatment.

Kneeling on a fibre mat Jim worked swiftly and delicately, lifting in turn the little fork, the trowel, the plant. Without an arm to lean on, he held his body poised by the strength of his muscles, his skin browned by contact with the earth and the early summer sun. Three other men, and one woman, worked along the length of the border, weeding and planting, raking the soil lightly to aerate it. Now and then Jim would turn his head and call out to them and they would answer and they would laugh and, it seemed to Alison, that was not only the best manner but the best mood in which to make things grow.

She was almost by his side before he noticed her.

He looked up, unsurprised.

'Oh, it's you again, is it?'

'Yes, it's me.'

She put a hand on his shoulder and knelt by him. She could feel gravel prickle her knees, afternoon sunlight warm through her dress. She leaned towards him and, not caring who saw, kissed him on the mouth.

He sighed and asked, 'Won't I ever be able to shake you off?'

And Alison, firmly, answered, 'No.'

May had taken its toll of Roberta Slater. A spell of sullen city heat had sapped her strength and she'd been snappish and fretful and at her poor husband's throat every hour of the day and half the night.

Declan – wisely – had shipped her off with Daphne to rest in the cool of the Wicklow hills for three weeks. There, mercifully, it had rained. And with the rain, and much pampering, Bobs had discovered stoicism, a virtue which she ascribed to the example of her new-found Catholic kin.

She returned to Glasgow larger but calmer, conditioned to accept the inconveniences of pregnancy and to wait patiently for her term to be fulfilled.

In fact, she was rather proud of herself. She took to preening before the bathroom mirror, admiring the image of motherhood and, as if years of medical training had made no impression at all, wondered at the resilience of bone and muscle which had grown to accommodate the new life within her. She did not even object when Declan clipped on his stethoscope and listened solemnly to the corporeal orchestra that squeaked and chirped and thudded within her, as if she was merely his patient and not his wife at all.

To alleviate Roberta's boredom and avoid the risk of some obstetric mishap upsetting things Declan planned a celebration in advance of having anything to celebrate. Howard had not yet left for the Borders. Alison seemed to have settled her differences with her fiancé. And, because there was a feeling of endings as well as new beginnings in the air, Declan decided to pull a last eccentric stroke and arrange a supper party for what remained of the team.

'Damned cheek, really,' Howard said. 'Three days before exams.'

'An evening off will do us good,' said Alison.

'You and Declan, perhaps, with your natural ability to cram facts into your heads can afford to waste an evening. Mere humble grafters like myself – that's an entirely different story.'

'Stop grumbling. We haven't seen Bobs in ages.'

'No,' Howard said, 'I must admit I'm curious as to how *La Belle Dame sans Merci* is putting up with Declan, not to mention impending motherhood.'

'She was in Ireland, you know. I had a postcard.'

'I didn't have a postcard,' Howard said. 'But Declan told me he'd sent them away – mater too – so he could have the house to himself for a while.'

'Except for the servants,' Alison reminded him.

'Yes, of course – except for the servants.'

'You sound rather bitter, Howard,' Alison said. 'You're not jealous of our Decker by any chance, are you?

'Certainly not. Why should I be jealous of that little Irish upstart?'

'I thought you rather fancied Roberta, once.'

'Never,' Howard said. 'Fancied you once, though. Still do, matter of fact.'

'Well, it's too late now, Howard. You had your chance.'

'That's the trouble, I didn't have my chance. Didn't *stand* a chance.'

'I know,' Alison said, sympathetically touching his arm. 'I'm sorry.'

'When does he get out?'

'Soon, I'm told.'

'How soon?'

'This week or next.'

'Really? That's fast. Is he cured?'

'Healed,' Alison said. 'He'll have to report to Ottershaw for treatment for another twelve months. He certainly won't be teaching again for some time.'

'So marriage isn't exactly on the cards?'

'Jim waited long enough for me,' Alison said. 'The least I can do is wait a year or two for him.'

'What do your family feel about all this hanging on?'

'Their attitude,' said Alison, 'is quaintly Victorian. Provided Jim "does right by me" in the end they seem perfectly happy to leave it up to us.'

'And you always bow to their wishes, do you?'

'In theory,' Alison said. 'Now, chin up and look cheerful.'

Together they climbed the steps to the front door of the Logie residence which, before they could thumb the bell, was flung wide open by Mr Declan Slater, clad like a little ring-master in full evening dress.

'Good Lord!' said Howard. 'Where did you get that rig, Decker?'

'The old boy's Sunday best. Had it cut down. Suits me, don't y'
think?'

'Very distinguished,' Alison said, while Howard just snorted.

'Come in, come in,' said Declan. 'Welcome to my humble abode.'

It was after eleven o'clock before Alison and Howard left Dowanhill.
They walked in silence through the West End's twilit streets,
heading for the tram stop on Great Western Road.

The supper party had been neither a complete success nor a total
failure. It hadn't been much of anything, in fact. Declan had
entertained them lavishly with quantities of food and drink and had
narrated tall tales about the Logies' adventures in Wicklow, told how
Bobs had ridden out in Dr Flynn's jaunting cart and how Daphne had
accompanied his Da to the races and won thirty-two shillings, how
well everyone had got on together.

Roberta seemed content to let her husband commandeer the
conversation and did not correct or contradict. There had also been a
good deal of 'shop talk', speculation about the difficulty of imminent
exams and the rigours of the winter term which lay ahead. The
gaiety had gone, however, that amicable, affectionate fizziness which
had once been the team's hallmark. Realism had replaced optimism,
opinion had taken over from gossip.

Heavy and red-cheeked as a country wife, Bobs listened in silence,
as if she'd forgotten all that she'd ever learned and had never been a
student at all.

Mrs Logie had not been present. Apparently she had gone to
Edinburgh to attend her sons' school prize-giving and would board
overnight with the solitary cousin, a spinster Stalker with whom she
was still on speaking terms. The boys would not be coming home for
the holidays. They had elected instead to visit a distant relative on
the Isle of Clova and, later, to undertake a walking excursion in the
Italian Alps.

Declan referred to the pair guardedly. He called them 'young
rascals' as if he was three times their age and could look back on his
own improvident youth now only through a dark glass. Declan, it
seemed, had already mapped out a career as a consultant surgeon.
He described his future as if it had already happened, as if he had
already passed his finals, completed his post-graduate studies, been
accepted as a member of the college and obtained a top position in a
teaching hospital.

'Where will you live, Declan, while all this is going on?' Alison had
asked.

'Here, of course,' Declan had answered. 'No reason not to.

Roberta's quite comfortable here. Aren't you, dearest? Sure an' she'll have her mother to help look after the children while I'm off doing my residences.'

'All cut and dried, I see,' Howard had said. 'How does it suit you, Bobs?'

'I'm happy for Declan,' Roberta had answered and had shaken her blonde curls in a manner which, just for a second, reminded everyone that girls like Roberta Logie always fell on their feet, no matter what.

Alison and Howard emerged from the tenements into Byres Road. The church on the corner loomed like a fortress against the sky and the last of the tramcars rattled over the junctions, bobbing like Chinese lanterns against the leaves of the plane trees and the massy shrubs of the Botanical Gardens.

Most faculty students had already gone, fled from the city, abandoning quads and courts, classrooms and lecture-halls, bedsits and boarding-houses with sighs of relief, heading for the seashore and the hills. Dipsy McDonald had graduated at long last. Peggie Lockhart and her foul-mouthed novelist-to-be had graduated too and had celebrated by announcing their engagement. Soon nothing would be left of those years but myths and memories, legends of drinking bouts, love-matches, anarchical events which would grow more robust and less credible with each telling and then, like the children who gave them birth, would pale away and fade into the speckled page of history.

Alison felt sad, not for herself but for Roberta. Sad too for Declan. Sad even for Howard. For Howard's perspectives would not be her perspectives. Howard's future would not be her future.

She looked up at him speculatively. He was casually elegant in an expensive seersucker jacket and silk cravat, taller than she was, a man on her scale, her wavelength. She did not, however, love him.

She recalled a moment from years ago when she had waited in warm autumn sunlight for her brother Davy to come out of Mrs Kissack's little wooden-walled shop by the banks of the canal. She had leaned against the planking, one leg extended, the bicycle balanced under her. She had reason to remember that afternoon. Before it was over she would be told that her mother was dead, her childhood at an end, and her life would be turned over on itself and altered for ever. It wasn't sorrow that endured, however, but the memory of the hours which preceded it. How happy she'd been, how *aware* of happiness. Vivid moments when the past was put aside and the future was yet unshaped were rare and precious. Those unremarkable moments which divided one chapter of life from the next were never really monumental but occurred unbidden for no reason at all. This, Alison realised, was another of them.

In three days the team would gather under the soaring beams of the Bute Hall to begin fourth-year exams. Then they would be separated by desks, drawn apart by the tensions, lost in the whispering crowd. She would sit calmly before the paper and prepare herself as Jim had taught her to do. She would glimpse Guy's back, stiff and upright, in one of the rows ahead of her; Declan, perhaps, to her left, wiping the gold nib of his brand-new fountain pen; Howard, hand to his brow, paper in hand, sneering fearfully at questions he could answer and those, alas, which might catch him out. They would all be alone again, individual and apart. And Bobs not there at all.

'Do you think she's happy?' Howard asked suddenly.

'I'm not sure,' Alison said. 'I think she might be.'

'How can she be happy with Declan Slater?'

'Perhaps Declan's what she wants, what she needs.'

'What'll become of them, I wonder?'

'Bobs will have several children, whom she will love. She'll raise them strictly but fairly and take them on holiday once or twice a year to visit the Irish relations whose influence will, on the whole, be beneficial. Her mother will love them uninhibitedly and will spoil them dreadfully. And Declan will work like a Trojan and will ensure that his wife, children, even his mother-in-law are well taken care of and want for nothing, ever again.'

'Can he do that, our Declan?'

'No,' Alison said, 'but he thinks he can.'

'Does he actually love her? That's the question.'

'Yes, I do believe he does,' said Alison.

'Funny kind of love, if you ask me.'

'It's always a funny kind of love,' Alison told him, then said, 'Do you remember what we did on the station platform last Christmas?'

'Of course. How could I ever forget?'

'Would you do it again now, please.'

Howard shook his head.

'No,' he said. 'It meant something then. It doesn't mean anything now.'

'To me it does,' Alison said and held up her face to his kiss.

'I didn't know you could drive,' Jim Abbott said.

'I can't,' said Henry. 'I've taken a few lessons but apparently not enough of them. I'd hold on tight, if I were you.'

'You mean we might not get home in one piece?'

348

'Oh, yes,' said Henry. 'I'll get you home safely even if I have to carry you and push this bloody vehicle with my nose.'

'Whose car is it?'

'It's hired for the afternoon.'

'I didn't know you could do that,' Jim said. 'Hire motorcars, I mean.'

'My God, you have been away a long time,' Henry said.

'I suppose I have,' Jim said. 'It certainly feels like it.'

'This, by the way,' Henry rammed the gearstick forward, 'was Ally's bright idea. She paid for the thing. She wants you to travel home in style.'

'Style's hardly the word for it,' Jim said.

'She's feeling guilty about not being here. She has . . .'

'I know. Exams.'

The car reached the bottom of the drive and Henry, biting his lip in concentration, fisted the big steering wheel and braked almost to a halt. He guided the Austin through two narrow bends and, yanking on the gearstick again, jerked the vehicle out on to the Glasgow road.

Two pheasants scuttered across his path and lifted themselves, craking, on to a wall. In the confines of the Austin's boot Jim's luggage shifted ominously.

'It's a hell of a road for a novice,' Henry said.

'I can see that,' Jim said.

Hanging on to the grab-handle that jutted from the dashboard, Jim inched round in the passenger seat and looked out of the small back window. He remained in that position while Henry encouraged the Austin to pick up speed.

Behind them the pine trees slithered away and, in hot July sunshine, the contours of the moorland ridge, sticky with heat, accompanied them for a while. Ottershaw's towers and glassy pavilions appeared briefly then vanished as the road lifted and twisted and the trees closed in once more.

Jim laughed.

'Yes,' said Henry, 'you must be glad to see the back of that place.'

'Unfortunately I haven't seen the back of it,' Jim said. 'I'm obliged to report to Leyman every month for the next year or so. On the other hand, I *will* be glad to get home. You've no idea how glad I'll be to see Flannery Park again.'

'So you aren't going to Perthshire?' Henry said.

Jim shook his head. 'Later perhaps, for a day or two. Right now I just want to sit in my own chair, sleep in my own bed, potter about in the garden.'

'Have you settled your differences with your sister?'

'I doubt if I ever will.'

'She's a . . .' Henry hesitated, 'a somewhat formidable lady.'

'All bark, no bite,' Jim said. 'Even so, I couldn't live with her again. I thought I could but, thank God, I came to my senses in time. Ten years of Winnie was enough.'

'What'll she do without you?'

'I know what I'd like her to do.'

'Bugger off,' Henry suggested.

'Not quite. Find a man,' Jim said. 'Somebody to take care of her. She won't, though. She deliberately frightens them off. I imagine she wants to remain "faithful," if that's the word, to Sergeant Craddock until the day she dies.'

'Faithful to a memory,' Henry said. 'Not much of a life, that.'

'It's her choice, Henry,' Jim Abbott said.

'Not yours, though?'

'No, certainly not mine.'

They drove in silence for several miles. Mountains soared above them, farms and hamlets rolled past. Henry and the gearstick seemed to have come to a temporary understanding. The Austin's tyres hissed on soft, warm macadam.

'How do you feel?' Henry asked, at length. 'Are you okay?'

'I'm fine.'

'Really?'

'Yes,' Jim Abbott answered. 'Really, I'm fine.'

'Just as well for you,' said Henry.

'What do you mean?'

'I mean, hang on, sport, we're about to take to the hills.'

The closer Jim came to home the more his sense of isolation increased. He had enjoyed the ride with Henry and appreciated the gesture of the hired car but he could not have predicted how much he would be affected by the sight, the sounds, the smell of suburban streets. He was, he knew, no hero, no warrior returning from the wars, no sailor home from distant shores. There would be no gaudy welcome for him, no bunting and flags.

Hidden behind the Austin's windscreen he slipped undetected into Flannery Park. Past the building site where Davy worked. Past the Co-op store, the church, the school where he had taught and, with luck, would teach again. Past little gardens brilliant with summer flowers, trim privet hedges, painted gates, saplings in the park, chimneys dabbing smoke against the evening sky, bus stops, dogs, and children everywhere.

They turned into Kingsway. Clattering trams, a flush of re-employed shipyard workers trudging up from Scotstoun. The faint odours of old Clydeside wispy in the sweet evening air. Tar, burnt kippers, stewing steak. The aroma of pubs doing a roaring summer trade along Dumbarton Road.

They turned into Macarthur Drive. Climbed the hill.

And stopped before the council house.

He felt weak now, disorientated. For a split second he longed to be back in Ottershaw, to hear the tea-bell ringing, to have nurses attend him, the long evening ahead, nothing much to do, nothing much to think about, no problems.

He hesitated, leaning against the Austin's side window.

'Where's Alison?'

'Davy licked the garden into shape at the weekend. It's not what it was, of course, but at least it's tidy.'

'I thought Alison would be here.'

'Trudi and Ruby have cleaned the house. Everything's ready for you. Tea's on the table. All you have to do is boil a kettle. If you feel like having a lie down first, the bed's . . .'

'I don't feel like having a lie down,' Jim said.

'She'll be here,' Henry said. 'I'll bring the bags in for you then I'll have to shoot off and get this vehicle back before they charge me for an extra day.'

'Yes. I understand,' Jim said.

He opened the gate and walked, steady enough now, down the path to the green-painted door. He had a half-notion that it was all a trick. That he would open the door and be greeted by cheers, shouts of welcome, handshakes and laughter. By Alison. Surprises were typical of the Burnsides.

But the house was deserted. It smelled of polish and emptiness.

Henry put the bags down in the hallway.

'Can you manage?'

Jim nodded. 'Thanks.'

'Are you all right?'

'Yes. Fine.'

'Good to have you back,' Henry said. 'Now, I must gallop.'

'Of course. I'll be fine.'

He stood by the door and watched Henry hurry to the Austin, clumsily reverse it and nose off down the hill towards the thoroughfare.

The bags rested against his calf. He should unpack them. He guessed that the clothing inside would smell of Ottershaw, however, and he did not want to be reminded of those lost months, of sickness, of lassitude, of vacillation, of the stigma – with him still – that

351

consumption imposed. For weeks now he'd protected himself by
thinking only of Alison, had imagined the moment when he would
stand in his own house, free again, home again, with Alison waiting.
He had no right to complain, however. He had brought this upon
himself. She would come when *she* was ready, when *she* was free,
when *her* programme allowed.

In the meantime, he was home again, alone again.

And all he could do was wait.

'Well,' Alex shouted, 'where is he then? Where's the teacher?'

'Not here,' said Bertie, daintily pouring cream on to a slice of apple
tart. 'Didn't the doctors let him out?' said Alex, deflated.

'I took him home,' said Henry.

'An' left him there?' said Alex. 'Poor bugger, on his own.'

'He won't be on his own for long,' said Bertie.

'Eh?'

'He needs to be with Alison,' Trudi explained. 'It is right that they
should be together.'

'What's that supposed to mean?' said Alex.

'It means keep your neb out of it,' said Ruby.

'She's not – not stayin' there with him, is she?' Alex demanded.

'That's up to her,' said Ruby.

Davy, seated at the table too, sipped tea, lit a cigarette and looked
out into the little park across the drive. He could see a ball, a scarred
leather bladder which appeared now and then over the hedge and
hear the cries of a horde of young boys as they pursued it over
the grass in defiance of the bye-laws. He envied the youngsters the
simplicity of their pleasure, their manic energy. He had to train
for football now, to take it seriously, and something had gone from
the game because of it. He tried not to hear, not to understand what
they were saying about Alison for that too made him feel achey and
old.

Bertie said, 'It shouldn't be left up to her.'

'What do you know about it?' Ruby snapped.

Bertie dabbed his lips with the napkin that Trudi had put by his
plate. He said, 'At least I know the difference between what's right
and what's wrong.'

He glanced slyly at his father, his brothers and finally at his sister-
in-law seeking approval, an ally. He was never sure where he stood
with Trudi. He felt he could comprehend the others, even Henry, and
knew how to barter with them for his place in the household. But
Trudi made him uncomfortable. Because she was deep and secretive
Bertie fancied that she mirrored him in so many ways that she might

have been a sister under the skin. For this reason he both hated and loved her at one and the same time.

'Ally's a doctor,' Davy said, vaguely. 'She knows what she'd doin'.'

'What is she doin'?' said Bertie. 'Nothin' to be proud of, I'll bet.'

Henry stirred on the chair by the fire. He had that indrawn look to him, a somnolent heaviness, brooding and watchful. He crossed one leg over the other and his brothers, his father, his stepmother all stared at him as if they expected some pronouncement, something profound and unequivocal.

Trudi did not look towards Henry, though. She knew that he was consumed by other things, that Alison and Jim, Jack and Brenda, all the Burnsides, kith and kin, had begun to spin away from him.

It was not that he did not love them, not that he would not always love them as a son and a brother but that he had glimpsed realities that lay beyond the rim of Flannery Park and, knowing that they were safe, had taken himself elsewhere, to the house within his head. She could not be sure if she had courage to follow him or if, as she had once believed, her history ended here, just as Alison's was about to begin.

'Nothing to be ashamed of either,' Henry said.

'A sick man, a cripple . . .' Bertie began then, with Trudi's eye upon him, reddened and shrugged. 'None of my business. Ally can do what she likes.'

'What about you, Bert?' Henry said. 'Can you do what you like?'

'He would not dare,' said Trudi.

The sun had slid down towards the west and slanting shadow filled the depth of the living-room. He had put a lump of coal on the fire and had eaten the cold meat and salad that the women had left out for him. He wanted a cigarette but had given up the habit, less easily than he had given up many another, for the longing had not yet left him and perhaps never would. He seated himself in the chair by the side of the hearth and, weary now, had gradually fallen asleep.

He did not hear her come into the house. The sound of the key in the door had been almost inaudible, footsteps in the hall as light as thistledown.

When she kissed him on the brow he opened his eyes.

Light lay in bands across the garden, painted the façade of the house across the drive, sharpened the black slate roof that stood against the sky and caught the corner of the oriel like live flame.

She seemed mysterious in the soft half-light. He was afraid to touch her in case she was not there at all, was only something he'd dreamed of, something he had imagined while he lay, far back and

353

long ago, in Flanders mud when he was young and whole in body and spirit. He didn't dare stir, didn't dare rise.

'How was it?' he said. 'The exam, I mean.'

'Not as bad as I'd expected,' Alison said.

She wore a summer dress, a cardigan. Her hair hung softly about her oval face and brushed against his mouth when she kissed him again.

'Did you have a nice sleep?' she asked.

'Yes.'

'Are you awake now?'

'Yes.'

'Take me upstairs.'

'What time is it?'

'Nine, a little after. Take me upstairs, Jim.'

'I thought – I thought you'd be here.'

'I'm here. I am here.' She put her mouth close to his and said, 'Now.'

Henry had been hard at it for the best part of an hour. He had gone upstairs as soon as his father and Ruby had left to walk round to Jack's house.

Bertie, oddly chastened, had slipped away to catch the last picture show at the Rialto and, for once, had taken Davy with him for company. Pete lay out in the garden where he had been most of the day, drowsing among the raspberry canes. From next door came the sound of music from a wireless set, accompanied by little Juliette's singing. The Rooney boys had been out in the park bashing a ball about, but the football game had apparently lost its edge and the young lads were at rest, squatting on the grass, pow-wowing like braves too tired at the day's end to organise another war path.

Trudi brewed a pot of coffee, set it on a tray with cups and sugar bowl, and carried it upstairs.

She was pleased to hear the chatter of the typewriter, sustained bursts punctuated only by the *ting* of the line-end bell and the harsh grating of the old Underwood's carriage as Henry automatically flung it back. She heard too the soft shriek of the platen as he ripped a sheet of finished work from the machine, the click of the rollers as he fed in another blank. There was something satisfying about listening to her husband caught up in the process of creation, something so physical about it, not weak or soft or contemplative.

Over the weeks she had watched Henry's files of notes and clippings fatten, books and journals accumulate beneath the rigid old card-table which he had erected in the space beneath the window.

Had seen a snaking black cable appear to feed light to a shaded bulb that hung above the table, a tin ashtray, a cut-glass vase bristling with pencils, a dusty horse-hair cushion tied to the back of a dining chair to protect the long muscles of his spine while he typed. He had taken over the bedroom, had built a nest for himself, made visible somehow the furnishings of the house within his head.

What Trudi still did not know was whether or not he had built it large enough to accommodate her too, or if this place was his and his alone.

Balancing the tray, she knocked upon the door.

'Yep.'

'Coffee?'

'Yep.'

The tempo of the machine did not falter. The room was hazed with smoke. It was as if the process of creation involved combustion and, like many a more respectable industry, burned off its waste in clouds.

Henry was crouched over the Underwood, fingers flying. Loosened collar, rolled-up sleeves, hair plastered to his brow in dark, sweaty curls. The cigarette bobbed in his mouth, spilling ash like snow upon the keys. He did not turn round. She heard the *ting* of the bell, the grate of the carriage, a last little *pizzicato*, a conclusive peck with the forefinger on the full stop, and he ceased.

He sat back. Light from the half-open window, light from the electric bulb sharpened his features and made him look almost vulpine. He scanned what he had written and then, carefully this time, removed the sheet from the typewriter and floated it into a wire basket in which, Trudi noticed, five or six other pages already reposed.

She placed the tray on the counterpane, poured coffee and, as soon as he glanced at her, gave him the cup.

'It seems to me that it is going well,' she said cautiously.

He stubbed out his cigarette, sat back, cup in both hands, and sipped.

'It's a start,' he said. 'A real start, though.'

Afraid of a rebuff, she had asked nothing about his work, his plan, until now. She said, 'Do you wish for me to go?'

'Nah,' Henry said. 'I see you brought two cups. Who's downstairs?'

'No one. They have all gone out.'

'Join me,' Henry said.

Trudi sat on the side of the bed, knees primly together.

She said, 'Alison will not come back tonight?'

'I dunno,' said Henry. 'Probably not. It's up to her.'

'She does not rush into things.'

'Who am I to tell Alison what to do?' Henry said. 'Oh, I suppose Dad will mutter and Bert will grouse about moral degradation and the shame of it all but what the hell do they know about girls like Alison?'

'Or men like you,' said Trudi.

He touched his brow with a bowed wrist and grinned.

He said, 'If I didn't know you as well as I do, Trude, I might take that as sarcasm not flattery.'

'It is the truth, Henry. I do not think there are many like you.'

'Sure there are. Lots. One in every family.'

She had her shoulder to him, facing away from him. She too held the cup in both hands but she did not drink from it. Cigarette smoke had drifted away through the window and the air in the room seemed clear and pure now.

She said, 'What is it that you write about?'

'So that's what's bothering you, is it?' Henry said. 'You want me to tell you what I'm up to, what I'm about.' He reached into the wire basket and took out the little sheaf of typewritten paper, offered it to her. 'It's no big secret. Here, see for yourself.'

She took the sheaf but did not look at it at once, continued to stare at her husband as if she doubted his promise or feared his integrity.

He nodded. 'Go on.'

She brought the pages to her knees and, without her spectacles, peered down at them, at the typewritten characters, the chapter heading that stood out boldly, black on white: *With Trudi in Berlin*.

'God in heaven!' she murmured softly. 'I thought you would write about politics, about Germany. Instead, you write about me.'

'It's an old trick,' Henry said. 'It's called "Hooking the Reader". We'll get on to the politics soon enough.'

Trudi felt as if the pages floated in her fingers, as if she floated on the bed.

She read: '*Mrs Trudi Coventry was the most beautiful woman I had ever met. I loved her from the first moment I saw her and, in spite of all that happened to us in Adolf Hitler's Berlin, I love her still.*'

'Got the principle?' Henry said. 'It's really a romance.'

She wept for two or three minutes, very softly, in the still, clear air of the upstairs bedroom. Henry put a hand on her shoulder, fingers firm and consoling, but he said nothing, offered no explanation or excuse.

At length Trudi could endure no more. She turned towards him, let him gather her into his arms. He rocked her gently, very gently until her sobbing ceased. Even then he did not let her go.

'What you write here,' she whispered, 'it is true?'

356

'Of course it's true.'

She pulled away just far enough to see his face. 'But you will not tell everything about me, Henry, no?'

'Hell, no,' Henry said. 'I intend to keep the best bits to myself.'

'For us to share?' she asked anxiously.

'Yeah, Trude,' Henry answered, smiling. 'For us to share.'

At last she knew what she was doing. It was as if she'd spent the last three years balanced on a tightrope and had only now stepped safely to the ground.

How easy to yield to the illusion that she had attained independence, to shake off all that she had learned, all the virtuous circumstances which had given her freedom in the first place, her love for Jim not least of all.

Fortunately she had not lost all sense of perspective in her march into womanhood. She had learned not to take kindness for granted and also when to seize the initiative. She wouldn't go to Jim out of whim or wilfulness, as a gesture of defiance or desperation, not even as a reward for his terrible patience. She would penetrate the stubborn defences of the man, make him admit that he not only loved her but wanted her, only because she sensed behind his frailty a passion to match her own.

She remembered that autumn day in Miss Osmond's when she'd told the team about her engagement to Jim Abbott. How Roberta had thought him chivalrous. How the boys, Declan among them, had mocked her commitment. If only they'd known then what they knew now. Declan had learned, Howard too perhaps. She was even generous enough to wish a blessing on priggish Guy Conroy. But the boys she had loved had become men and they, like her, now had to match themselves against a difficult and distorting world. She would never be quite free of affection, never indifferent to their fate, for she had shared knowledge with them, had learned from knowing them, and now it was time to put that knowledge to the test.

They had kissed for some time in the living-room, kissed as they had never kissed before.

It seemed to Alison that Jim too had learned how brusque and fleeting life could be. He held her close, touched her breasts without inhibition, no longer able to deny the force that moved them both. He was no longer cautious, no longer afraid of her.

'Not here,' he said. 'Not like this.'

'Upstairs,' Alison said. 'I told you.'

'You can't stay, Alison.'

'Yes. Yes, I can. As long as you want me to.'

'I want you to,' Jim said. 'God, how I want you to.'

'Go first,' Alison told him. 'Be quick.'

She felt very calm and composed. She took the briefcase from the hallstand where she'd left it and unpacked her nightdress, fanned it over her forearm. She could hear Jim moving about upstairs as, there in the hall, she undressed.

The air was warm, the house dark, the staircase mysterious.

She knew what the bedroom would be like, the brown counterpane, books on the side-table, the little walnut-wood wardrobe with its vertical mirror, the narrow bed pushed hard against the wall.

When they were married they would need a bigger bed, she thought, and suddenly her mind was crowded with urgent practicalities, silly, trivial details that seemed ridiculous in the circumstances, the future, not the present.

She hugged her arms about her, and waited.

'Alison?' His voice sounded distant, strained and strange.

At the last moment, one foot on the stairs, she hesitated.

What if someone came? What if Henry came round, or Ruby, some teacher from the school? She took a deep breath. Then they would lie together in the darkened bedroom, holding each other tightly. Pretend they were not there.

'Alison?'

She ran upstairs.

He had drawn the curtains and was already in bed. There was light, though, a soft infiltration of the afterglow that filled the sky above the river to the west. She could see herself, slender, long-bodied and very solemn-looking in the upright mirror, the nightdress clinging to her breasts and thighs. Jim too was reflected there, watching her, his arm above his head, his head upon the white pillow. Somehow she had expected him to be wrapped in the flannel pyjamas, to put up a last unromantic line of defence, but she could see his chest and shoulders quite naked, scar tissue against pale flesh.

She came to the edge of the bed and leaned on it. She could feel the mattress firm beneath her thighs and his hand touching her. He moved suddenly and kissed her stomach and her breasts through the sleek layer of silk, wetting the fabric with his tongue.

'You look beautiful, Alison,' he told her, thickly. 'So beautiful.'

She leaned into him and kissed his mouth.

'What are you wearing under there?' she asked him.

'Nothing,' he said. 'Not a stitch, I'm afraid.'

'So that's the way of it, is it?' Alison said.

She stepped back and taking the nightdress by its hem, tugged it upward and stripped it over her head.

She shook out her hair.

Curious and amused, Jim said, 'Alison, what is this?'

'The happy ending,' Alison told him and, peeling back the bedclothes, slid in beside her teacher before he could change his mind.

Exclusive CDs to enhance your reading pleasure

There is nothing better than a relaxing read and nothing quite like your favourite music to compliment your mood.

Each of the CD compilations are performed by the world's top artists. The choice is yours, all you need to do is send £1.98*per CD to cover postage and handling and indicate which CDs you would like. Please allow up to 28 days for delivery.

HOW TO GET YOUR CDS:
Simply complete the coupon below with the quantity of each CD you wish to purchase and send with your cheque to Hodder Headline CD offer, P.O. Box 2000, Romford, RM3 8GP.

Hodder Headline CD offer
Please send me:
Qty........HH01 Essential Opera @ £1.98 p&h each
Qty........HH02 Classical Masterpieces @ £1.98 p&h each
Qty........HH03 Rockin' n' Reading' Hits of the 60's @ £1.98 p&h each
Qty........HH04 Unmistakably Jazz @ £1.98 p&h each
Qty........HH05 Movie Sensations @ £1.98 p&h each
Qty........HH06 Gregorian Chants @ £1.98 p&h each
*Please note these prices apply to the UK addresses only. Please see below for other areas.

Enclose a cheque/postal order payable to FM LTD. Please write your name and address on the back of your cheque/postal order.

Name & Address...

....

....Postcode ☐ ☐ ☐ ☐ ☐ ☐ ☐ ☐

POSTAGE AND HANDLING PAYMENT METHOD
UK & Ireland – Cheques or Postal Orders ONLY £1.98 per CD
Europe including Eire – Eurocheque in £Sterling ONLY or Visa/Mastercard Credit Cards £3.25 per CD
Rest of the World including USA and Canada – Eurocheque in £Sterling ONLY or Visa/Mastercard Credit Cards £4.25 per CD

Please debit £................ from my ☐ Visa ☐ Access

Card No ☐ ☐ ☐ ☐ ☐ ☐ ☐ ☐ ☐ ☐ ☐ ☐ ☐ ☐ ☐ ☐

Expiry Date ☐ ☐ Signature...

ENQUIRY HOTLINE: 01708 336888
If you do not wish to receive further mailings for products within the Hodder Headline Group or carefully selected companies please tick here. ☐ Offer subject to availability. Please allow up to 28 days for delivery.

Offer closes 31st December 1996   *you may photocopy this form*